Praise for the novels of Mike Chen

"Sweeping, heartfelt, and harrowing. As always, Chen enthralls by combining pulse-racing stakes with charming characters. Carter and Mariana are partners in a time loop conundrum, colliding in a multitude of meet-cutes."
—Noelle Salazar, *USA TODAY* bestselling author of *The Flight Girls*

"Mike Chen strikes an effortless balance between science fiction, action, and heart. This book kept me turning pages late into the night with its propulsive plot and irresistible characters. *A Quantum Love Story* is a love letter to second chances and beyond."
—Natalka Burian, author of *The Night Shift*

"Time isn't a flat circle; it's a donut. Love isn't mystery; it's a miracle. This book beats like a patient heart that can't stop reliving the moments when it last loved you."
—Meg Elison, author of *Number One Fan*

"A delight of a novel. Mariana and Carter join Chen's pantheon of richly drawn characters in a story that offers freshness and surprises throughout a time loop. Also, there's a really good dog. I enjoyed it immensely."
—Kat Howard, author of the Unseen World duology

"I'm a sucker for a time loop, so my expectations were high and *A Quantum Love Story* did not disappoint. A delightful twist on the time loop story—warm, fun, pacy, unexpected, and satisfying."
—Catriona Silvey, author of *Meet Me in Another Life*

Also by Mike Chen

HERE AND NOW AND THEN
A BEGINNING AT THE END
WE COULD BE HEROES
LIGHT YEARS FROM HOME
VAMPIRE WEEKEND

For additional books by Mike Chen, visit his website, mikechenbooks.com.

A QUANTUM LOVE STORY

{ a novel }

MIKE CHEN

mira

mira™

Recycling programs
for this product may
not exist in your area.

ISBN-13: 978-0-7783-6950-9

A Quantum Love Story

For questions and comments about the quality of this book, please contact us at
CustomerService@Harlequin.com.

TM is a trademark of Harlequin Enterprises ULC.

Mira
22 Adelaide St. West, 41st Floor
Toronto, Ontario M5H 4E3, Canada
BookClubbish.com

Printed in U.S.A.

For those who made it through.

1

Carter Cho wasn't really into science experiments.

Otherwise, he might have completed his degree in quantum mechanics. Cooking experiments, though? Totally different, because there was a real joy to that process. But setting a hypothesis, identifying controls, and looking for...stuff?

Seriously, that seemed like such a slog.

Except for this particular Thursday morning, on the corner of a crosswalk and standing across from the world's biggest, most advanced particle accelerator, a science experiment felt necessary.

He didn't really have a choice. It seemed to be the only way to possibly understand or even escape his very strange predicament.

Carter checked the time on his phone, waiting for it to tick specifically to twenty-three seconds past 8:22 a.m.

At that moment, the crosswalk light would switch, signaling for pedestrians to go.

Then everything would cascade, a waterfall of specific actions by the world around him:

The person on Carter's right would step out first.

The person behind him would wait an extra four seconds, eyes stuck on his phone.

Annoyed, the woman next to that person would let out an exaggerated sigh, move around, then rush forward six steps into the street before catching her shoe.

Then she would stumble, her coffee spilling. The first time he went through this, he'd noticed the spill just in time to side-step it before continuing on.

All of these actions sat line by line on the old-fashioned paper notebook in his hands, a checklist of what was to come with the precision delivered by his photographic memory.

Science experiments all led to a result. As for this, he wasn't quite sure what the result, or even the purpose, might be. He already knew he was in a loop of some sort, something that started the instant he woke up on Monday mornings.

And it always ended up with the huge facility across the street exploding.

The Hawke Accelerator, both a modern marvel of technology circa 2094 and also some sort of weird top-secret project that no one really understood—now also the place that would simply go boom.

Carter should know. The first time he experienced this, he was in the accelerator chamber's observation room, right in the heart of where the *go boom* happened at precisely 12:42 p.m. on Thursday. Which was today, again. Just a few hours from now.

He'd been through this six times before, each time expanding his acute understanding of the details surrounding him. Usually he wrote things down at the end of the day, a memory trick he'd learned about himself very early on that helped cement the details into place, so even when he started the loop over without any scribbled notes to organize his thoughts, his photographic memory recalled it.

But this morning, he went in reverse, writing out the exact steps as they were meant to be.

And then he'd make sure it played out that way, bit by bit.

After that, he wasn't sure. Carter thought of his parents, their usual voices chastising him for his lack of planning and fore-thought, how his teenage foray into coding and hacking was more about fun than applying himself, and now look at him, simply a technician running tests and tightening screws. Even now that he'd been through this loop several times, he hadn't bothered to call them back from their birthday messages. Part of him used the excuse that he should stay as close to the original path as possible, but he knew better.

Even if this weird loop existence meant a complete lack of consequences, calling his parents was the last thing he wanted to do.

Carter checked his phone one more time, five seconds remaining until the crosswalk kicked off the sequence. He gripped the notebook, staring at the list of things to come.

A chime came from the crosswalk. And Carter began to move.

The person on the right moved.

The man behind Carter stayed.

An exasperated sigh came from behind him. Carter kept his eyes on his notebook, counting steps in his head. "Ack," the woman said, right when Carter sidestepped. His focus moved down to the next item on the list, then the next, then the next, not once looking up. Instead, he executed movements through a combination of memory and instinct, sliding sideways when a cyclist rolled by on the sidewalk and slowing down just enough to follow in a group waiting at the front entrance of Hawke.

Someone coughed, his signal to pause and wait thirteen seconds, enough time to review the next items on the notebook still in front of him:

Front desk hands out mobile device for the David AI digital assistant.
Security guard says something about visiting group from ReLive project.
Passing scientist asks what time Dr. Beckett's flight gets in.

He moved through the security gate designated for employees, taking him past the lobby threshold and over to the main hallway that split in three directions. He stopped, leaned against the wall and waited for the final item to come to pass. Nothing special or unique, just the sound of heels walking in a hurried cadence from his right to his left. Carter checked the notebook, waiting for the visitor's David AI to speak exactly what he'd written.

"Your next meeting starts in two minutes," the AI said from the small mobile unit in his familiar London accent. "Oops! Looks like you might be late. Should I give the meeting notice of that?"

Carter mouthed the words as the visitor spoke, his voice fading down the hallway. "No, thanks. I'll just hurry."

David's simulated voice could still be heard as Carter put the notebook down, holding it at his side while considering what just happened. He wasn't particularly religious, though part of him wondered if he'd been condemned to some sort of purgatory. The predictability of it all, the strange exactness of everything he saw playing out as written in the notebook in his hands.

The first few times, he'd felt disbelief. Then curiosity. Then amusement.

This time, well, he guessed that was the purpose of this experiment: to figure out how he felt knowing he could predict every exact movement of every person he encountered.

Disbelief, curiosity, amusement, and now the whole thing was just unnerving.

Nothing out of turn. Nothing different. Nothing unexpected.

He blew out a sigh, hands pushing back his wavy black hair. Something tugged at him, a wish for things to be different. A person walking from his left instead of his right. Or the plant behind him coming to life and biting his arm. Or a piano dropping out of the sky and smashing his foot.

Anything at all to end this.

★ ★ ★

Ten minutes passed with Carter lost in his own thoughts, but that in itself turned out to be a change. Normally, he'd take a walk to clear his head, but the list's *finality* wound up freezing him. All the previous loops, he'd tried to follow his original path as closely as possible, always ending back in the observation room where the accelerator started to deteriorate and a massive blast of energy struck him. Perhaps that was the only real difference, as he'd changed spots in those final moments to see exactly where the bolt landed on the floor, even using his photographic memory to draw a precise grid of the floor panels.

What he could do with that information, he wasn't sure. But it had to mean something.

This time, though, a weight paused him, an all-encompassing blanket that left him pondering far longer than he'd ever done.

And then it hit him: he'd deviated farther from his path than before, and nothing bad had happened.

Heck, if he wanted something bad to happen simply so it could, maybe it'd be best if he pushed farther. Or even went in the complete other direction.

At this point, he'd normally turn right, check in with the technician's desk, grab his cart of tools and begin going through his assignments for the day. But a sharp, almost foreign defiance grabbed him.

He would turn left. He would *not* check in with his supervisor. Instead he'd go…

Carter's eyes scanned, looking for the most opposite thing he could possibly do.

Of course.

His steps echoed as he pressed ahead, a strange jubilance to his feet. He moved around people milling about or talking about actual work things, practically skipping with joy until he turned to the entrance of the Hawke cafeteria and straight to the bakery station and its waft of morning pastries.

"Bear claw," he said. "No, apple Danish. No, wait." The poor worker probably didn't understand the grin that nudged his cheeks or sparked his spirit. "I'll take them both. And the almond croissant, and the banana nut bread. And the cranberry scone. Oh, and a blueberry muffin."

Tongs pulled pastries out, and each slid into small paper bags before getting dropped into a larger bag. "Anything else?" the man asked after counting through the items.

"Yeah," Carter said, tapping on the glass case at the lone item, a surprisingly tasty selection for a corporate café. "That. A glazed donut. The last one."

His relaxed pace took him down the hallway, taking a bite or two out of each pastry as he went, notebook tucked under one arm. He chewed slowly, relishing the individual flavors and savoring the delicate textures. Despite his love of all things delicious, he'd always tried to pull back, one eye always on his health—one of the few disciplines he'd managed to pick up from his parents.

Here, though, he ate with glee, enjoying the pureness of experience without consequences. He closed his eyes, walking straight while considering the blend of sweet and savory in the almond croissant, when something bumped into his chest, followed by heat dripping down his shoulder.

"Oh," a woman said. "Oh, I'm so sorry." She stopped, coffee dripping out of the cup in her hand and narrowly missing the cuff of her gray jacket. Her brown eyes met his before looking him up and down. "Oh no," she said, setting her coffee down before reaching into her shoulder bag for some tissues. Her movements came frenetically enough to cause her chin-length hair to swish back and forth, her hands pressing tissues into the setting stain on his technician's uniform. She looked over her shoulder at a group that had started to head toward the main conference hall. "I'll catch up," she called out.

Guess he was meant to get spilled on after all.

"Don't worry about it. It's totally fine. I, uh," he said. She bit down on her lip, brow scrunched, though eventually they locked gazes. "I should have watched where I was going." He gestured at the growing coffee stain on his outfit.

"You sure?"

"Absolutely. It's work clothes. It gets dirty. No big deal."

The woman's expression broke, relief lifting her cheeks into a toothy grin, one of those unexpected sights that made everything a little bit better. She looked back at the group, then the coffee cup in her hands. "Damn it, I spilled a bunch. Is there a place to get a refill?"

"You're going to the main conference room?"

"Yeah. Spent all week there."

All week. All the times Carter had been through the loop before, even seen the names of various guest groups on schedules, and yet they'd never crossed paths—not until he did the exact opposite of his routine.

Funny how that worked.

"We finally get to see the observation room, though. In a little bit." She held up her coffee cup. "Just need a refill somewhere along the way."

"Café is back there," he said, thumb pointing behind him. "Way back there."

"Ah," she said with furrowed brow, a conflicted look that seemed about much more than a coffee refill. "Probably should meet with the team. Not enough time."

Not enough time. The concept almost made Carter laugh. "Well," he said, pulling out a bag, "a donut for making you late?"

She took the bag and peeked inside, cheeks rising with a sudden smile. "I don't usually like donuts. But these glazed ones. Simple, you know?" She shuffled the bottom of the bag to nudge the donut out the opening. "Are you sure? I spilled coffee on *you*."

"Yeah. I'm, uh," he started, pausing as their gazes lingered. "My fault for running into you."

The wrapper crinkled as she examined it up close before taking a small bite. "I should get back to my team. Maybe they'll hand out free coffee by the time we get to the observation room. Thanks for this."

Carter dipped his chin, a quick farewell as he considered the inevitability of the next few hours, a march toward a chaotic and violent reset. He matched her smile, though as she turned, he pondered saying something.

Normally, he wouldn't. But with the world exploding soon? He went with the opposite of normal.

"My name's Carter, by the way," he said. "Carter, the guy who gives people donuts."

Her gaze shifted, first looking at the floor, then up at the ceiling, even at the bag on her shoulder before finally locking eyes again. "Mariana," she said, holding up the donut bag, "the woman always looking for coffee." She bit down on her lip before glancing around. "I'm going to tell you something completely random."

"Okay?" Carter said slowly. "About donuts?"

She laughed, an easy, bright laugh, though her eyes carried something far heavier. "No. The group I'm with. We're touring the facility. But I'm quitting. They don't know yet. Today'll be my last day. Science is great until it's not." Her shoulders rose and fell with a deep breath. "I don't know why I'm telling you this. Probably because we'll never see each other again." She spun on her heel, an abrupt move followed by determined steps forward.

"Not unless you need another glazed donut."

She turned, slowing as she walked away backward, this mystery scientist who spilled coffee on him and then caught his attention. Because the idea that someone didn't like most donuts, well, that was as opposite as anything he'd ever encountered in his life. "Maybe that," she said with a small grin.

"I'll remember your name in case we do," he said. "Mariana."

Her fingers fluttered in a quick wave, then she turned, and

Carter leaned against the wall, ignoring the people who came and went.

Mariana. Maybe he should write that down, just in case she became important. He pulled the notebook out from under his arm, only to find the pages soaked with coffee.

A pen would rip through those pages. He'd have to trust his memory to recall her name, her voice, her face. On the off chance that they ever met again.

None of it mattered anyway, but as experiments went, this morning did at least prove helpful.

Now Carter knew that he could do anything, even the opposite of normal. And that might just lead to him escaping this thing. Or, at the very least, a lot more pastries.

Mariana disappeared into the sea of people, and as she did, her words echoed in his mind. First her group went to the conference room, then the observation room above the accelerator core. He knew that space well; after all, he'd been in that same room when everything began to explode and—

Wait.

That was it. A possible connection that he'd somehow missed before. He'd been *there*, of all places, summoned to check some of the power conduits lining the walls as the whole thing fell apart. Could that exact space be important?

Carter's head tilted up. Maybe the observation room held the key to everything.

And if it did, what would happen if others were caught in it too?

2

Mariana Pineda's eyes snapped open.

Today was the day, this particular Monday of all Mondays. She *knew* that, and as if her whole body and mind had calibrated to that single thought, she woke up early. An intent carried with her since last night, culminating in waking at 6:14 a.m., six minutes before her usual morning alarm rang.

Someone else noticed too. Several seconds after she came to, a new noise arrived. It pierced loud and direct, an announcement about the morning's *real* priorities.

A meow, straight in Mariana's ear. Then the shift in blankets as a fuzzy critter jumped next to her, followed by a paw tapping her forehead.

"Maggie," Mariana said, turning over and blowing strands of her brown hair out of her eyes. Maggie meowed again, the cat's long black-and-gray fur making her seem bigger than she was. With one hand, Mariana reached over and picked up the dwarf-sized cat and set her as far away as she could manage. "You're early. But you remembered, huh? Guess this is it."

Maggie didn't seem in the mood to listen, instead coming right back with another loud meow that said that the cat wasn't *too* early. Mariana wondered if Maggie did this to her previous owner as well or if this was merely her way of saying she missed Shay.

The thought caused Mariana to huff, then slump. Because it was reasonable. Because Mariana missed Shay too. But nothing was going to bring her college teammate/best friend/eventual stepsister back. "Breakfast first," Mariana said, and Maggie rubbed her face against Mariana's cheek, so much so that the tips of fur tickled her nose.

A chime rang through the room, the usual morning alarm now going off, and Maggie meowed again, the cat version of *I told you so.*

"All right, all right. Point to Maggie," Mariana said, rolling out of bed. Maggie jumped down with a trill. "System, open windows and start one cup of coffee, black. And turn on the US Open." The apartment's dark-tinted panes faded to transparent, letting the full morning light in, and the bubbling on the counter gave way to the perfect aroma of brewing coffee. Mariana looked out the window, the familiar sounds of a tennis match starting behind her. Normally, the simple din of tennis worked like comfort food: it was Mariana's happy place.

This time, though, something grabbed her attention.

Not Maggie or the view of San Francisco or anything visible. But a gnawing at her gut, like her annual ritual of watching the US Open's first day over morning coffee suddenly pulled her into a different dimension.

In a way, it did. Because one vital piece was missing.

Ever since they'd met as freshmen on the UC Davis tennis team seventeen years ago, Mariana shared this ritual with Shay Freeman. When they lived together, it was how they started the day. And when their lives split into different paths, it evolved, technology connecting them despite miles of distance.

And now? Nothing.

Though Mariana heard the sounds of the first-round match, she focused on the object in her hand, a blank tablet coming to life. The display showed paragraphs composed last night, every single word chosen with a precision that probably was unnecessary.

She could have written *I'm quitting my job and leaving science* to the same effect.

Still gripping the tablet, Mariana sipped the coffee, the almost-too-hot liquid bringing a welcome burn to her lips and tongue. She moved to the small kitchen table and settled in, her finger hovering over the display's Send button.

Shay gave so much grief over the years for the way Mariana framed her life in scientific method, all observations and experiments. But, as Mariana would often protest, there was a reason she always turned to this way of thinking, combined with an intent to focus and plan her way out of anything—what Shay dubbed Mariana Mode.

Because it *worked*, in any issue, any circumstance. Even now.

Fact: Something was very, very wrong with her mind and life.

Hypothesis: Shay's death three months ago pulled like a thread, breaking Mariana's foundation and casting a thick fog over everything else. It had to be that.

Experiment: Life without science? Perhaps. *Something* had to change. And the only thing she could think of was work. Because really, that was where her life existed. And it couldn't possibly fix the chasm created by Shay's loss.

Somehow her life continued without Shay. Not well, of course. But it ambled forward, a gradual progression marked by the simple, steady march of time.

Leaving science, stepping away from the thing that she'd shared with Shay as much as tennis, might make it easier to escape. Because despite the success of the ReLive project, the lack of closure gnawed at her, a sliver of hope all because Shay was still technically a missing person. They searched Joshua Tree National Park for weeks, using drones and scanners and dogs, and even then a body hadn't been recovered. All the logic in the world pointed to death.

Even Shay would have admitted that. Probably more like *Fuck it, I'm dead. Move on.* That's what she'd say.

Shay studied quantum mechanics. Mariana studied neuroscience. Shay led the team as a scholarship player. Mariana pushed her way into recruitment, at least until her ACL injury. Shay had her dad. Mariana had her mom.

And then their parents married.

Always joined, always in mostly friendly competition with each other, even when they became adult stepsisters. And now, nothing except grief colored by uncertainty.

Do it, Mariana thought, and her finger nearly tapped the button to fire the letter off to her ReLive colleagues. Her other hand moved instinctively behind her back, fingers crossed. But a notification popped up with a new message from her boss, Curtis, the subject line reading Urgent! We're going to the Hawke Accelerator!

The words snapped Mariana back into the present, and she opened the message rather than send off her resignation.

Hi, everyone! Exciting news today. As many of you know, the team at the Hawke Accelerator led by Dr. Albert Beckett has been working with ReLive on an aspect of their classified project for several months now. This morning, Hawke invited our lead scientists to a four-day tour of the facility and discussion of the science behind our product, culminating with a viewing of the accelerator's test run. Dr. Beckett is flying back from a conference and will guide us on the final day.

I apologize for the short notice, but please arrive at our office per usual this morning, and we'll air-bus over to Hawke together. Our hard work is being recognized!

If you are interested in going, please reply to this message ASAP and we will send the guest list over to Hawke.

Mariana sat looking stone-faced at the message in front of her, not even moving when Maggie jumped on her lap to announce that she'd finished her breakfast. The Hawke Accelerator. Shay's dream job. She had joked about how she felt destined to work there while finishing her doctorate, though when Mariana poked her about what the place actually did, she laughed it off with "I dunno, it accelerates particles. The brightest minds work there. What else do you need to know?"

Funny, then, that a literal inch from ending her career, science tempted her to hang on for a few days longer.

Mariana's laugh startled Maggie enough that the cat jumped down before returning to do figure eights between her feet. She leaned back in her chair, taking the last sips of her coffee before letting her mind wander over to the least complicated thing in her life: the tennis match on the wall screen. Her eyes tracked the ball back and forth, a hypnotic pace between the world's top player and an up-and-comer she'd never heard of.

Yet, she hadn't noticed the score until now. She blinked, making sure she'd read it correctly: 15–30.

But more importantly, down 1–5 in the third set.

Was the top-seeded player about to be upset in the first round by some teenage upstart?

The world, it seemed, was full of surprises today.

Mariana turned back to the tablet, and as she did, a glint of morning light reflected off the mineral countertop. She blinked the blind spot away, then read the last paragraph of her resignation message again.

It's been wonderful to work with you all. My heart's just not in it anymore, but I know you'll go on to do great, groundbreaking things. As for me, I just need to step away. Maybe I'll teach tennis on a cruise ship or something.

Four days. A delay of four days.

Mariana walked across the small apartment's floor to the far bookshelf. Most of the trinkets offered the sheen of modern technology, from brilliant screens that took up half the wall to the glittering hologram projector on her shelf displaying a nearly-lifelike 3D hummingbird. But next to that virtual bird sat something out of time, a purposeful anachronism born of impulse.

Her fingers traced over the edges of the metallic photo frame, the shiny material reflecting both the thin beams of morning sun and the bright display of the US Open. She took the photo, its weight different from the thin digital frames found everywhere, and stared at it.

On the left stood Mariana, her dark hair a little longer than its current bob, her sharp chin pointed down as her mouth caught open in a candid laugh, the slight gap in her front teeth barely visible. Despite being a photo print, its color hadn't faded with the years, and the way the sunlight hit them brought a richness to Mariana's tanned face, hours of tennis giving a deep hue over her skin's olive undertone.

On the right stood Shay, one eye closed and her tongue sticking out, her mane of curly black hair framing her dark cheeks, accentuated with a bright red streak colored through it.

Seven years had passed since that moment. Mariana only just starting a career that would ultimately become the ReLive project. And Shay, captured between grad school and starting her doctorate. When did printed photos phase out? Fifty years ago? Seventy-five? And this one was a real printed photo with ink on specialized paper, not the digital light-up ink commonly found these days.

No, they'd decided to make this image a relic.

Mariana closed her eyes, the moment coming back to life thanks to the secret and somewhat unauthorized dose of ReLive she'd taken weeks ago.

"They're going to take fancy pictures of us at the wedding. But let's print this," Shay had suggested with a laugh. "It's who we are right now." Mariana pictured it as clearly as this morning's memories of Maggie at her feet: a cold, drizzling San Francisco Saturday spent looking for a shop that could actually produce such an authentic print, something flimsy, easily torn, and capable of fading. Some paper products still existed: notebooks for the office, print books for collectors and young children, and the practical nature of recyclable paper bags and shipping boxes kept them commonplace.

But photos when there were pixel sheets?

The place they found sat nestled in the Richmond District, tucked away between a pair of bars. Even the smell of the dingy, one-person operation came alive in her senses. They'd haggled over the shockingly high price of a single print, the owner arguing that it was dated technology that required care while Shay pointed out, "You're literally just pushing a button."

The result was a twenty-percent discount and a little embarrassment on Mariana's part. No brightness-adapting ink or natural-color resistance against UV exposure, but a real anachronism of dated technology, a gift few people in their society bothered with or even remembered. "Just because our parents are into each other, we suddenly get new titles. Stepsisters. What the hell, right?"

In that moment, Mariana and Shay decided that they'd—

The sound of applause burst from the tennis broadcast, shaking her out of her ReLive-induced memory and back to her apartment. She turned and her head tilted as the display showed a slow-motion replay of the most improbable point: top-ranked Thomas Song, known for his devastating spin on his serve, double-faulting to put himself down for match point.

He bounced the ball several times, sweat rolling down his grim face, and rather than waiting for the crowd to settle, he tossed the ball and swung, launching a perfectly placed serve that landed on the corner of the court's painted lines. He charged forward, his typical strategy as his teen opponent stretched for a desperation return. The ball floated over the net, and Song hit his trademark slice volley. Except instead of his usual precision, the ball nicked the top of the net, its trajectory deviated just enough to drop an inch out-of-bounds.

"Out!" called the umpire as the crowd erupted. On one side, teenage newcomer Onyebuchi Hudson shook his fist in disbelieving victory. On the other, Song fell to knees, mouth agape and head in hands.

A slow-motion replay showed the final hit, each rotation of the ball's spinning with clarity. The image faded to a live moment, both men frozen in shock but for completely opposite reasons. Mariana took in their reactions, then looked again at her messages on her data tablet.

It seemed that on a day like today, anything was possible.

Including delaying the inevitable. Mariana brought the photo frame with her as she sat back down at the table. She pulled the tablet over, now defaulting back to her unsent resignation message. Rather than hit Send, she tapped Save with a sudden sense of authority. It faded away, leaving only Curtis's message about the Hawke Accelerator.

Mariana hit the Reply button. Sounds good, she typed. I'm in. See you at the office.

Four days. Mariana told herself she'd send in her resignation in four days. And in the meantime, she'd go to the Hawke Accelerator.

And she'd bring Shay, the only way she could right now.

Her fingers gripped the photo frame.

Maggie came over and plopped in front of her, arms stretched wide and belly accepting rubs. Her purr grew louder, even over the broadcast of the US Open. But Mariana ignored it all and instead stared at the photo in her hands, as if all of the unfairness of the world existed in a thin piece of glossy paper.

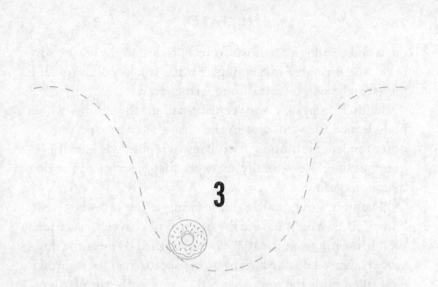

3

Every Monday, Mariana stuck with her routine. Even today, when giant life choices hung in the balance, she still moved to the instinctive rhythm of her day. She'd stepped swiftly through things, from resetting Maggie's self-cleaning litter box to getting dressed, the only difference being that she'd put Shay's photo next to her bag by the front door.

Her cadence continued, including her usual walk from the building's elevator to the coffee kiosk. Across the way, bright eyes of a yellow pit-bull mix awaited her, shifting her gait into an easier step. Buddy Ed sat patiently at the security station, the building's unofficial mascot and somewhat protector, though Mariana always assumed the security team enjoyed his gentle company more than finding him useful.

And Monday for Buddy Ed meant an extra treat from the coffee kiosk, the only day they offered canine baked goods. Ahead of her, the barista handed a guard three cups in a tray, a dog biscuit and a pastry precariously balanced on top. "Last one of the day for doggos," the barista said, gesturing to the kiosk's empty tray. The guard took it and walked, carefully stepping with the hot drinks until the building's front door whooshed open and a sudden car horn from outside caught her by surprise. She stumbled just enough for the baked goods to fling forward, the dog biscuit sliding farther away.

Buddy Ed stayed at the security station, though his whole body leaned forward, and in the chaos, Mariana spotted another resident rushing by, two bags swinging while half jogging out the door—totally unaware that he crushed the dog biscuit underfoot.

"Damn it," the guard said, looking at the crumbly mess. "Sorry, B.E. You'll have to wait until next week." Mariana took her drink from the barista, then turned to meet the dog's gaze. He stared up at Mariana as she approached, large brown eyes filled with the look that only came with canine disappointment over food.

She knelt down, giving Buddy Ed ear rubs. "Maybe I'll get you an extra treat next week too. Your reward for guarding our home. B.E., our mighty protector." The dog's head tilted, either in appreciation for the ear rubs or because he understood English a lot better than suspected. Her phone buzzed, a reminder that she had a train to catch to the ReLive office before taking the air-bus flight to Hawke. She gave the dog one final pat, turning to the building's entrance.

Mariana sighed as she stepped onto the sidewalk and headed toward the transit station. Between the surprise invitation to the Hawke Accelerator, the upset at the US Open, and Buddy Ed's breakfast, it certainly seemed like the world was tilting just enough to throw routine out the door.

Despite the strange start, everything else went exactly per schedule throughout the rest of the day, in the most mundane way. The Hawke Accelerator facility welcomed them in, each member of the ReLive staff getting a visitor ID badge and a digital assistant named David to guide them. David took them from meeting to meeting, office to office, his digitized British voice coming out of small thumb-size devices hanging around their necks. In many ways, it was the same experience as working at her usual office, as they spent most of the time discussing ReLive: its protocols, mechanism, parameters for usage, safety trials, and so on.

In front of the Hawke team, Mariana led an explanation about how memory was a construct, how ReLive encoded those thoughts and feelings like fresh memories but boosted with a stability enzyme coupled with specific guided visualizations and recall practices. Audio frequencies, light patterns, ultrasound waves—words and descriptions tumbled out of her.

How *clinical* it all felt. Despite being in the world's most advanced facility.

"Limitless potential," she said. "Helping senior citizens retain precious childhood memories. Permanently encoding life milestones freshly after they happen. ReLive creates stability in cognitive health, and the potential to extrapolate it into further physiological areas is untapped." That last part was more for impressing investors. But the bit about memory retention?

It absolutely worked. She *knew* it, inside and out, and not just because she'd helped put together the presentation or handled the underlying research.

No, she knew because she'd defied the ethics paperwork she'd signed and lied her way into a ReLive trial group six weeks ago. Well, not really *lied*—she'd used her middle name and her dad's last name, which really was the only thing he was good for in the twenty years since he'd left the country. The dishonest part probably lay more in how she'd used her authorization to approve the application, and that part no one could ever know about. It was the type of thing that *maybe* she would have revealed to Shay and only Shay under a combination of a few drinks and Shay's relentless pursuit of gossip.

Shay often made fun of how Mariana was always really good at following the rules. So she would have really gotten a kick out of Mariana bending the rules to preserve her memory.

The first day at Hawke concluded with one final meeting in the main conference room, a discussion with Hawke's planning team led by Chief Science Officer Samantha Pratt, a gregarious older woman who finished with "Come say hello before you all leave on Thursday. My door is always open. I love talking science." Mild applause and smiles came, and they stepped out in single file, though Mariana lingered.

She opened her bag and looked down at the photo frame stashed among her things. "Sorry it wasn't that exciting today. Hopefully the next few days will be better," she said quietly to the picture of Shay before taking in the view from the large window. The Hawke facility sprawled out, a small village of concrete and metal surrounded by cafés and other small shops supporting the massive workforce. But beyond it sat the Gardner Nature Preserve, a stretch of Californian trees up and around a large hill, the complete opposite of the power-consuming hardware and teams of international scientists at Hawke. "It should be you here. Not me."

Chatter from the outer lobby picked up, bringing Mariana back to the moment. And as she scanned the view in front of her, she saw her party steps ahead, though something else caught her eye.

A man. An Asian man in technician coveralls, his long hair hanging over his eyes with flirty waves, and though he stood next to a cart of tools and hardware, he leaned against the wall, eyes tracking the ReLive team. As he watched, he scribbled furiously in a red-covered notebook, pausing only to nibble on a pastry he picked up from a napkin on the cart.

Mariana observed him for a second, watching as the side of his mouth curled up into a half smirk the instant he bit into the pastry, then shook her head before rushing out to catch up with her group. It's not like she knew what was on the technician's to-do list for the day.

4

For all of Mariana's good intentions, Tuesday and Wednesday meant more meetings and presentations, and the symbolism of bringing Shay's photo to Hawke didn't actually amount to much. The ReLive team spent more time discussing technical aspects of the treatment than actually touring the facility. They took turns leading the discussion, though it all felt like rehashed and repackaged versions of the same answers, a constant stream of questions from the Hawke staff focused on physiological safety under extreme conditions.

Yet once a day, something caught her eye.

There he was again.

Crossing paths? That might have been putting it a little too formally. But floating within her orbit, that same technician. Always writing. Always eating pastries, which seemed extra weird considering he was working. But he wasn't making repairs or taking system scans, just jotting notes with pen and paper, his pensive look only breaking when he took a bite.

However, Thursday presented the team with an immediately different situation. Rather than turning to the business and operational wing of the facility, a security guard took them straight down a second hallway, then another and another. More importantly, their walk came with the announcement that Mariana had been waiting for:

They were *finally* going to tour the accelerator itself. And better yet, Hawke founder Dr. Albert Beckett would be arriving at the facility soon to lead them through the various sections of the accelerator, culminating in a view from the observation room as the current test cycle completed.

After days of meetings, Mariana finally took Shay's photo out of her bag.

First came a presentation from the power staff, who detailed how the overall requirement was supported in conjunction by several nearby counties. Then came the civil engineering team, who went into the history of the facility's construction, from its immense structural needs, including precise alignment with the earth's magnetic fields, to the way it withstood the massive 8.1 earthquake that had hit the Bay Area eleven years ago.

Next came the test group, who demonstrated the different milestones for speed, particle collisions, safety thresholds, radiation emission, and more, along with the fact that standard test cycles required a four-day cycle from initial power-up to completion and reset.

"It's a milestone, really. The first time we've actually run this particular version of the process cycle," one of the scientists said. What that actually meant, Mariana missed. Because in the back of the conference room came that same technician, still scribbling away. He'd snuck in, though the sound of the sliding back door hadn't grabbed her attention. Instead, it was the fact that he'd caught a toe or elbow or something on the doorframe, muttering *dang it* loud enough for her to catch. She turned to see him, his black locks framing a focused stare, though she caught something else under that, a glint of...

Curiosity? Was he investigating something?

As she pondered that, he looked up—and when his eyes caught hers, a flush rushed to her cheeks.

Especially when his mouth curled up in a smirk.

His eyes broke away, though she swore she saw him shake his head, taking notes for several more seconds before dashing back out.

"Did you see that guy back there?" Mariana whispered, nudging her coworker, Dean.

"What guy?"

"He came in and left. It was weird."

"No, I missed him," Dean said. "What was he—"

The door opened again and footsteps approached, interrupting the presentation and stealing everyone's attention in a way the anonymous technician had not. Mariana turned and recognized Dr. Albert Beckett—and considering he was the world's foremost leader in theoretical physics, he looked more like a tired older man, with messy graying hair framing thick eyebrows and strong chin, a sheepish grin in full display while he waved.

"Hello, everyone," he said. "Oh, don't bother about me. I'm going to take you to the final presentation before we go see the observation room. But finish your discussion here first, please."

While the test team reviewed the last steps of the cycle, Mariana's mind drifted—not to Shay, not to the US Open, not to ReLive, or life without ReLive, but to that technician. Even from across the room, he'd carried an air of tension, and while Shay used to joke about Mariana's lack of intuition with people, something about this guy felt out of step, like he was visiting from another dimension.

Her thoughts lingered enough that she missed the rest of the testing presentation and only stood when everyone else did, Beckett apparently motioning them to follow him. As they shuffled out, Beckett offered a handshake and greeting to each person, only pausing at Mariana.

"Most people don't usually have that on their tours," he said with a soft smile.

"What?" It took several seconds for Mariana to put together his comment with the weight in her hands. Shay. Of course, she still held the photo frame. "Oh. I'm sorry, I just—this is my best friend. She, uh—" Mariana glanced around at her teammates "—she passed away a few months ago," she said, surprised at how easily the statement came out. "She studied quantum mechanics. Hawke was her dream." Saying this produced the strangest reaction: rather than feeling crushed by emptiness, something released, and the air around her suddenly seemed lighter. "I wanted to bring her here."

Beckett's brown eyes softened as he looked at Shay's image. "Welcome," he said to the photo before meeting Mariana's gaze again. "Welcome to you, too. We're glad to have you both aboard." He turned back to the group. "Now, let's go chat with Hawke's theoretical physicists."

Everyone else shifted except for Mariana, the ghost of Shay still pulling at her enough to linger. Beckett didn't seem to notice; he returned to the front of the line, waving them along. Mariana eventually followed, listening to Beckett's speech that felt halfway between scientific vision and sales pitch, phrases like *truly groundbreaking* and *unseen possibilities* mixed in with other technical phrases that sounded like when Shay would practice her doctorate presentations in front of Mariana. "What we're hoping to ultimately achieve, though, is something that will impact humanity," Beckett said as they turned the corner, "and that's where a partnership with ReLive comes in. We work in a high-radiation environment and—"

Beckett paused in his steps, causing a ripple effect in the group. Next to him, a panel beside an elevator door showed large red letters stating *Inactive-Diagnostic Mode*. "Well, you can't always trust technology, can you?" he said with a contagious laugh.

At least, the first time.

Because the next four elevators along their walking path were also malfunctioning. Beckett's frustrations grew with each attempt, a self-mocking chuckle giving way to pursed lips that eventually led to a confused call with security. If Mariana decoded his end of the conversation correctly, it sounded like the elevators were caught in some sort of feedback loop, locking the facility crew out of the control system.

Of all the days for the elevators to go awry, it had to be this one, enough time passing that they now fell behind schedule to get to the observation room and watch…whatever it was they were going to watch. "Sorry about this," Mariana whispered to Shay, as they went through hallway after hallway, turn after turn, even a back entrance with a one-by-one processing through a decontamination chamber. Though it took probably an extra thirty minutes of searching for an elevator that worked, they finally found their way to the basement level of the actual accelerator.

"Change of plan," Beckett said at the end of his final presentation. "Sorry about the delay. We've made good time, but we really should get to the control room for the end of the cycle. Sorry you didn't get to see more." He cupped his mouth and spoke in a mock whisper. "Honestly, the observation room is more of a nice view than anything else, but don't tell the monitoring team that I said that." His voice returned to normal as he tapped the far window. "You can see down there, beneath the dome is the base of the accelerator loop. But that's really bells and whistles. The interesting part is what's in the control room down the hall. Any questions before we move on?"

Shay's voice rang out in Mariana's mind, the vibrance perhaps an echo of what ReLive could do: *All that money just to move a particle really fast. You think they're actually doing something with it, or is it just a cool toy?* "Something that I don't quite get," Mariana started as she looked out the window at a small semicircular chamber, latticed beams creating a dome over what looked like several consoles and stands, entrances at either end leading to the massive looping track of the particle accelerator. She chose her words carefully, taking Shay's intention without her bubbly abrasiveness, and she angled the photo frame, as if it were a portal in her hands and Shay might hear the entire answer. "I'm still not quite sure what the accelerator *does*."

"Does?" Beckett repeated with a blink. He opened his mouth, though it took longer than expected for an answer to finally emerge. "We're running many experiments across the hardware's three stages. But I can't say too much more about the nature of them. They're classified. I suppose I *can* say that we have invited the world's brightest minds. Not much else without getting in trouble, but," he said as he tapped the display on the wall and the door slid open, a new hallway awaiting them, "I can show you the end of this cycle. Shall we?" Beckett started explaining the mechanics of the accelerator hardware, but the words drifted past Mariana's ears, her focus turning to the movement out in the hallway.

Because that technician was there *again*.

As if on cue, the man shook his head, closing his notebook before stepping out of view.

"We should head to the control room before the final sequence kicks in. If you'll follow me," Beckett said. The rest of the group turned and walked in step with him, though a loud, muffled pop came from somewhere beyond the wall, causing the window to rattle for a moment.

Mariana took a step forward, eyes drawn to the view out the observation-room window, technicians and scientists far below suddenly moving like worker ants scurrying from a rainstorm.

"Guess this is it," she whispered to Shay. "As close as I can bring you."

"Excuse me," a voice said, and only when Mariana looked up did she realize who spoke these words: the technician.

Mariana watched as he sidestepped the exiting group. Notebook still in hand, he breached the threshold of the observation room, then tapped the control panel. The room's door slid shut behind her team, though unlike before, the clicks and thunks of a locking clamp came through.

They looked at each other, locking eyes like before, but no smirk lay on his lips. Instead, it shifted, lines of concern on his face. And right as she was going to say something to break the stalemate, he pointed at the window, his finger precisely angled at a bright display on the back wall.

A second later, sparks shot out from where he pointed, like he'd had superpowers or at least incredible timing. Except he certainly wasn't gloating or showing off, not from the grim expression on his face.

"I need to go," Mariana said, composing herself to get words out. "I'm with that tour group."

"I know. Your name is Mariana," he said. "And it doesn't matter. At 12:42 p.m., this whole place is going to blow up."

5

Mariana wasn't sure which part stunned her more, the fact that he knew her name or that he claimed the Hawke Accelerator would blow up soon. She eyed him, enough desperation lining his face for her to consider that he might be a terrorist.

And she was trapped with him.

"Do you remember our last conversation?" the man asked.

That wasn't the follow-up question Mariana expected. Logical questions would have been something involving reasons for taking her hostage, like environmental issues with the accelerator itself or moral quandaries about ReLive—the usual protests that became the unwritten part of a scientist's job. He didn't ask that or even the more obvious question *Why are you holding a photo?*

But...what conversation did he mean?

"I..." Mariana weighed the different options in her mind, though the man's frantic air probably meant that this wasn't going to be a rational discussion. One look at the side exit showed that it had locked into place, a complete seal between this room and the hallway to the control room. Beckett and the others may not have even noticed that she lagged behind in the first place, let alone failed to follow. "I don't. I'm sorry," she said, choosing her words carefully. "I don't remember talking. When was it?"

"The last time we were here."

This conversation failed any logic test. "You must have me confused with someone else. I've never been to Hawke before this week." What could cause Hawke to blow up? A bomb. Or sabotage. "Look," she said, taking a chance, "I'm sure you have your reasons, but there's no need to harm anyone."

"You don't remember. I'm not trying to harm anyone. I'm trying to save all of us."

Above her, yellow warning lights started rotating, and the various displays flashed their system status, bright red letters stating *Structural stability issue detected on strut QL89*. The mobile AI unit hanging on her neck chimed, David's playful voice coming through. "An emergency has been detected in your sector. Would you kindly walk to your nearest evacuation area? I'll lead the way. First, turn to the door on your right…"

David continued, urging her to leave. She would, of course, if that was at all possible. But between David's calls, the flashing on the monitors, and this *guy* here, nothing felt like a routine test run.

Under her feet, the floor rattled, a rhythmic bumping that jabbed her heels hard enough that she reached over to the panel to steady herself.

"No, no, no." The technician shook his head, biting down on his lip as frustrated lines creased his forehead. "This conversation. Do you remember any of it?"

"*This conversation*. We've never talked before."

"No, not before. *This* conversation. Right now. Do you remember it?"

How was she supposed to answer that? This man failed to operate in reality, and Mariana's concerns suddenly went far beyond the rumbles and shakes rippling through the Hawke Accelerator.

"Like," Mariana said and took in a breath, "what we're discussing right now? Are you talking about a bomb?"

"No. Jeez. You've never asked about a bomb before." That statement caused all sorts of other questions, but he kept going. "Carter. My name is Carter." He held up the paper notebook in his hand, fingers pressing against the red cover. "When we talked, this was blue. Do you remember it?"

Part of her neuroscience degree involved a few electives in psychology, and Mariana tapped into what little she could of that here. Had they done any de-escalation exercises in undergrad? She couldn't remember and instead went with a calm, neutral tone. "I'm sorry. I don't think I understand the question."

"Oh, freaking crap," the man said. Sweat now dotted his forehead, and though he turned skyward, his shoulders slumped. "Okay. It didn't work."

"What didn't work?" The flashing yellow lights now came with a steady beeping, and above them the display indicated that system temperatures were rising. David continued talking, though any personality he'd exhibited before was gone, simply repeating evacuation instructions. "I'm afraid you'll have to explain—"

"It's okay," Carter said, blowing out a breath. "You don't have to talk me down. I'm not unstable."

"I don't think you're unstable, I just don't under—"

"I thought it was going to work last time, but it clearly didn't." He tossed the notebook aside; it landed open, pages coming to a rest. Mariana squinted at the neatly written tables on there, numbers and details captured in some sort of flow chart.

"Why not?"

Any agitation left his tone, and instead a resignation took over, one that matched his slumped shoulders. "It doesn't matter. We'll try again next time. I should have brought donuts for us," he said, a sudden grin on his lips.

"Next time?"

"Yeah. We got about two minutes left." The man sighed, then started looking around. "You drink protein shakes for breakfast," he said, without turning to her.

Mariana turned to the photo still gripped in her hands. "What?"

"See, that's my proof. I know these things because you told me. But we didn't have enough time to discuss what it all means. Guess it doesn't really help now, does it? The notebook," he said, pointing to the floor, "it's red this time. Last time I grabbed a blue one. That was our experiment. That was," he said laughing, "your suggestion. You wanted to see if you'd recognize it. You're the scientist."

"I'm a scientist. Yes."

"We've had this talk a few times. Last time, it didn't take this much convincing, though. I stopped for one extra bear claw today and it threw our whole rhythm off. Guess you can't account for all the variables. Before that, you once spilled coffee on me." Carter looked at the rolling clock above the screens. "Three, two, one," he said, and he snapped his fingers.

Somewhere by them, a massive boom rattled the room.

"That's still on time."

Beyond the walls, the sound of bending metal tore through the space.

Sparks sprayed from one of the screens, a brilliant sprinkling of yellow-white as the panel disappeared. Somewhere, voices cried out, and Mariana tried to steady herself.

"Fifty-two seconds," he said. "What can we do different this time? Hey, maybe the key is you having something better than a shake for breakfast. Have you ever had a pastry from Bellisario's?"

"I don't know what you're talking about, but we need to get out of here."

Carter's face tilted, a grin beneath his hanging locks. "You didn't suggest that last time."

"What does that even mean?" Mariana yelled before shaking her head and moving to the door. But Carter stepped in front of it, arms and legs extended to form an X. Seconds ago, he'd been the bigger issue, but now the situation had changed, an emerging rumbling and sudden bangs from all around.

"Listen," Carter yelled back, and the facility's shaking reminded her of the occasional California earthquake, though this came with rattling booms like fireworks and a cacophony of shouting voices outside of the room. "It won't matter. We've got like, thirty seconds. Try..." His eyes darted around the room. "Dang it, why didn't I think this through? What's new, what's new?"

Mariana may have had her tennis ambitions cut short by a knee injury, but she remained in good-enough shape that she could easily knock this lanky guy off balance and take the door. She primed her body, hands still holding the photo frame, and told herself to sprint and go for the exit. Her back leg coiled up, ready to release when Carter spoke with urgency in his voice.

"Just wait. Um, listen to what's going on."

Carter glanced up at the clock, panic returning to his face. He mumbled something to himself as he looked her over, his eyes tracking the path between him and her, though the chaos around them blocked out anything he might have said.

Shay used to give Mariana so much grief about how she overanalyzed stuff, the way she *abided*. And here, her stepsister was right. Mariana needed to stop thinking and move *now*, and this guy stood in her way. Her back foot pushed off, and while running through someone wasn't exactly part of tennis training, she didn't have much of a choice here. Carter met her eyes, but he didn't turn or even brace to try to stop her. One step passed, then a second, and a third, though just when she'd made it halfway across the room, his mouth opened.

"You're doing this for Shay," he yelled, his voice louder than any other moment in the room.

Just hearing that stopped her momentum, an invisible wall in five short words. Suddenly the cacophony of the Hawke facility didn't matter more than what he said.

"You're doing this for her. In the photo," he said, this time quieter. He looked at her, then at the floor before glancing up to the corner. "Tell me about her," he said, a sudden slow drawl to his words. "You said you're here for her. That's what you told me before, but what does that mean?"

Words suddenly failed Mariana. The floor rattled beneath her, the door remained locked, and displays flashed all sorts of warnings, but here she stood petrified by a question. Carter glanced back at the top corner, worry lines returning to his brow, and he shook his head. "Time. Never mind. Look, just one question. Tell me something that happened to you Monday morning."

"What?"

"Anything. Anything that happened. You mentioned a dog in your building lobby before," he said, his arms moving with emphasis. "Something unexpected."

"B.E.? His biscuit dropped."

"Okay, okay. B.E.'s biscuit dropped. That's it. That's all you have to remember."

"This is ridiculous."

"You need something to hook onto." Carter's fingers went up one by one with each sentence. "B.E.'s biscuit dropped. If you don't remember anything else, put that into your brain. For Monday. If you remember, that's your proof." He glanced again at *that corner*, and Mariana considered returning to her original plan of rushing him. "And if *that* sticks, then remember that this is a loop. It's all looping. I'll be waiting in the lobby first thing when you arrive on Monday. Right past the security check-in."

She would have, in fact, if she'd had the chance. But in that moment, metal sprayed out in all directions from the ceiling. She turned, lost in the chaos, and as she did, he lunged forward, grabbed her leg and planted a foot down one tile over. In the corner above, an exposed cable dangled, green sparks firing off every which way. They showered her, singeing her shoulders and burning through her coat. Carter covered himself, though she heard him yell, "I'm sorry."

Carter looked at her again—specifically, where she stood. His eyes tracked, from the place she stood to a spot on the wall adjacent to them, right in a corner where a burst of sparks erupted and a severed cord swung down, electricity dancing off its end. "Stay right there," Carter yelled, his voice now barely audible over the pops and crackles. "Four. Three. Two."

The final second played out in slow motion for Mariana. First, the exposed cable on the ceiling danced, driven by a whipping pulse of violent green. The surge of energy sent a zap outward, landing several inches from her left foot. All around her, different things snapped and shattered: display glass, metal grates, console switches, like a domino run of bursts, the final one bright enough to cause a blind spot in her iris. The lashing beam of greenish energy flailed again, recoiling upon contact with the floor, leaving a charred scar on the metal grating at her feet.

"One," she heard Carter say. But what happened next, she wasn't sure.

Because the beam of energy came alive again, striking her foot and spidering up her leg, her torso, her neck, a feeling of simultaneous burning and freezing across her senses before everything disappeared.

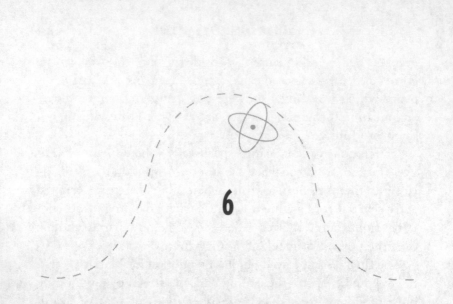

6

Carter exhaled, a weighty sigh with his eyes still closed. His fingers dug into the familiar bedspread, clutching them as he remained prone, his face pressed against his pillow. Eleven times he'd faced the day *after* his thirty-third birthday, which did earn the universe some gratitude.

He really didn't need to deal with his family over and over again.

Instead, he waited, having spent eleven loops with the day starting off exactly the same way.

The twelfth, though, remained to be seen.

He stayed still and listened, counting breaths as he waited for the now-familiar sequence of events. One breath passed, then another, then another, then enough that an inner giddiness suddenly tickled his imagination.

Nothing came.

Was that a *difference* in the world?

He had, after all, convinced Mariana to stand in the right spot, an idea that had just come to him when he saw how and where she stood. That shouldn't have changed anything about the first few seconds of the day, though. His simple hope was that it triggered a loop-to-loop recall in her so he'd finally have a partner in all of this, a real, live person capable of thinking and remembering instead of this strange passive existence.

That was all he'd wanted. Getting something different, though, that hadn't occurred to him. Perhaps the universe smiled on him for the first time in who knew how long.

He kept breathing, the count going up. Eight now passed, and he hadn't heard a single morning bird yet and suddenly his mind started sparking in so many different directions...

Then the first chirp came. Along with a pause, and then a trill of three. Then a passing car, followed by the wind causing a tree branch to tap against his apartment window.

An entire list passed, and of course it was the same as usual. It's all right, you expected this, he told himself, though the pounding in his heart and the lump in his gut showed him that even a few seconds of hope was too much. Carter rolled over to do his usual scribble in the notepad on the bedside table, something he'd tape into whatever notebook he chose to use for the loop. Then he loaded his phone, turning off the high-security mode that filtered out any messages or calls from unknown contacts.

Carter knew that his instinct prior to this whole looping business had him wait two days before resetting the device's security and adding his family members back in, the minefield of his birthday come and gone. At this point and after so many loops, his defenses lowered a little bit, a certainty of the repetition of knowing that they wouldn't reach out again. The usual screen refreshed with notifications that the number belonging to his dad had an associated voice mail.

He'd ignored it the last few loops. But out of curiosity, he played it again, just to see if it repeated. Which, of course, it did.

"Carter, happy birthday," his dad's voice said over the speaker. "Hope you had a good day. Your brother is flying out to see us in two weeks. You could join us, if you could afford a flight.

Too bad Hawke didn't give you a raise this year. Government projects, all bureaucracy and no—"

Carter clicked the phone off, then spoke the final part aloud to himself. *"All bureaucracy and no money. Call us when you get a chance."*

That remained the same. The rest of this twelfth loop? Things played out like muscle memory now, though this loop started off with one key difference.

Does M remember? He wrote the short question at the top of the notepad, then underlined it for good measure, before considering the noises around him.

Every loop started exactly the same, down to the timing. So why would this one happen to be different? The question echoed, relentlessly repeating as he considered all the possibilities. Problem was, he wasn't a scientist. He did the things the scientists told him to do at Hawke, but coming up with insight and experiments remained well out of his grasp.

Carter took another breath to try to get his body and mind to settle, then another and another, and the very act of doing so brought the answer to the surface. His chest gradually settled, and he put his hand over his heart, palm flat to feel the rapid thrum.

He wasn't quite sure at exactly what moment the loop started, just that it was always this Monday morning while he slept. At 5:49 a.m., he woke up. This time, his brain must have carried those final moments in the observation room, enough that it snapped him awake a few seconds earlier. And the very novelty of that different experience led to an accelerated heart rate, quicker breaths, things like that.

At least until it all crashed back to reality.

A car rolled by, then more birds chirped, though Carter tuned the rest out. Instead, he rolled out of bed and walked over to his desk, a stack of blank paper notebooks of different colors waiting, his easiest and favorite tool to work with his photographic memory. Next to them sat a small gray rectangle, a mobile AI unit similar to the ones handed out to visitors at Hawke, but this one programmed for employees.

He tapped the top of the device, something he hadn't bothered with for the last few loops. "Hello, Carter. It's dark and early," David said, his cheeky accent coming through. "How are things?"

The funny thing about David was that his greetings must have worked on a random generator. Even though Carter was stuck in a loop, the voice sounded just a little bit different every time. Perhaps if he activated the unit at the exact same millisecond, he'd finally get the same response a second time.

"Oh, same old. Hey, David?"

"Yes, Carter?"

"Do you remember the fact that I'm in a time loop?"

"You'll have to repeat the question. I didn't quite understand it." The AI let out a polite chuckle. "These old ears don't catch everything."

"Forget it. It's time for breakfast. I'll talk to you later when I have some data to process."

"Data to process? You can take the credit for my hard work—"

David was in the middle of his response when Carter shut him off. Sometimes the AI's sass proved an amusing foil even though no data from the previous loop ever carried over. It was nice to have *someone* to talk to, and David's AI capabilities certainly elevated Carter's own rudimentary hacking and coding skills.

This time, though, Carter just didn't want to hear it. Too many other things might or might not have been playing out. Because everything here was the same.

But somewhere else, wherever Mariana woke up, things might be different.

As Carter got dressed, he considered stopping along the way, a short break to grab something super indulgent for breakfast, like ordering the most expensive steak-and-eggs within walking distance. After all, his bank account reset to the same small amount every time—last time, he'd actually checked. He caught himself, though, a rare discipline that would have made his parents proud. Though, really, they'd also probably be irritated. If he could stem his impulses on day one of the twelfth time loop, why not every other time it interfered with his upbringing?

Such a thought prompted a grimace, and he shook it off as he considered the bigger picture: he had to get to Hawke as soon as possible to intercept Mariana's tour group.

Because this time might be different. And that thought made his heart race again.

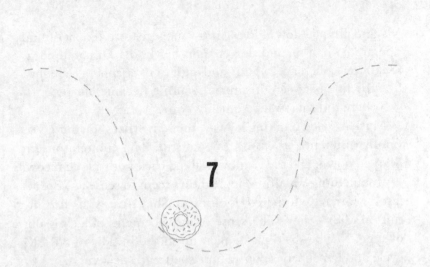

7

Mariana Pineda's eyes snapped open.

Today was the day, this particular Monday of all Mondays. She *knew* that, and as if her whole body and mind calibrated into that single thought, she woke up early. An intent carried with her since last night, culminating in waking at 6:14 a.m., six minutes before her usual morning alarm rang.

Someone else noticed too. Several seconds after she came to, a new noise arrived. It pierced loud and direct, an announcement about the morning's *real* priorities.

A meow, straight in Mariana's ear. Then the shift in blankets as a fuzzy critter jumped next to her, followed by a paw tapping her forehead.

Maggie was early.

No. That wasn't true.

Maggie *wasn't* early.

Maggie was right on time. Because this day was *supposed* to start a few minutes earlier than normal, and it had nothing to do with the resignation letter she'd worked on last night. This was a *pattern*, now with some variables changed.

A jolt rippled through Mariana, enough tension that the cat must have noticed. Rather than meowing and fluffing her tail,

Maggie jumped down. Every movement felt off, like her mind operated a half second slower than her body. Disparate ideas fought for coherence, a push-and-pull of overlapping thoughts, like the line between dream and waking became blurred.

Where did this strange instinct come from?

Mariana tried blinking it away, the sense that something was simply different and wrong. She sat still, long enough to calm Maggie down, and the cat now walked back with a loud meow.

If something was off, Maggie didn't seem to sense it. "Breakfast," Mariana whispered, looking at Shay's cat. Cats had intuition, didn't they? This sense of displacement, of feeling out of sync. Maybe she'd just woken up in the middle of a REM cycle and her subconscious whiplashed with déjà vu.

That had to be it. She knew déjà vu was nothing more than the temporal lobe of the brain trying to reconcile similar situations. Nothing else made sense, and besides, a cup of coffee would set things right. "System, open windows and start one cup of coffee, black. And turn on the US Open." The dim room gave way to morning light, soon followed by bubbling on the counter, a sequence of events that felt routine, yet something remained out of reach. Mariana walked barefoot over to the small kitchen with the full intention of getting a can of Maggie's food as well as her own scalding-hot coffee, when the sounds of a tennis match came into the room.

A hit. And a grunt. And another, back and forth until applause. Even though today was the first day of the US Open, something in Mariana *knew* what was unfolding at a stadium across the country in Flushing Meadows, New York. She stopped, fingers wrapped around mug's handle, and before she turned, the thought popped in her head, a hunch that she felt deep in her gut, something as certain as she knew her own name.

Thomas Song was going to lose.

Not just lose. He was going to be completely blitzed in straight sets by a teenage upstart, the final set being a 1–6 disaster.

Details colored in without her needing to see the broadcast, a complete record captured in her mind's eye. More certain than a dream, less certain than reality.

What did that make it? The question slashed at her thoughts, a cognitive dissonance that generated way too much anxiety for something as benign as a pro tennis match, as if something really bad might happen if she saw for herself either way.

But when she finally allowed herself to turn and look, the angle of the sun created a sharp glare that pierced through the window. It caught her eye, and as a blind spot came and went in her vision, something else fluttered through as well.

A dream.

Or a memory.

Or a vision.

Something like that. Something about a brilliant green beam that whipped and lashed, sparks dancing around it until it finally struck...

Her.

Mariana blinked. Then blinked again, a flood of images and sounds appearing from the void, so much that she jolted in her stead, coffee spilling out over the edge of her mug. "Shit," Mariana said under her breath as she set the drink down. She grabbed a hand towel from the counter, then dropped to her knees to start dabbing up the drops of coffee. Maggie took that as an invitation to say hello, rubbing her small fluffy body back and forth. "Not now, Mag," she said with a laugh. The cat turned to her, with her eyes wide and a single, loud meow, equal parts greeting and demand.

And in that moment, Mariana *knew* that this was different. It *wasn't* supposed to be this way. She gave in to the insistent cat, scooping her up for morning-hello snuggles, but her concentration went elsewhere, *something* on the cusp of becoming clear, like if she just thought hard enough everything would snap into place.

Maggie still in her arms, Mariana activated her tablet, not even bothering with the resignation email drafted and ready to send. Instead, she knew what she'd see: an invitation from Curtis regarding her ReLive colleagues and the Hawke Accelerator.

But Hawke Accelerator...wasn't there some kind of disaster there?

"System, display the morning news," she said slowly. The broadcast switched from the US Open, but instead of any news about a catastrophic accident at Hawke, news anchors talked about the weather. Mariana adjusted, straightening her posture and closing her eyes to think, just *think*.

About the worst, most vivid, most terrible dream. About a series of meetings and tours within Hawke, about a low-lying rumble that turned into a wall-shattering blast, about cracked screens and flying sparks and *that* green energy beam.

About a man named Carter. Who'd talked about how they'd had their conversation before, but not necessarily in the same way. His notebook, it was red, and he'd said that was different as well.

"System, display the morning headlines as text," Mariana said, and lines began scrolling by, each without any mention of an accident or catastrophe at Hawke. "No, switch back to the US Open." The screen flipped, going from talking heads to a wide view of the tournament's first round. Mariana focused on the display in front of her: it *was* tennis, the US Open, a sunny day in New York. Yet her eyes drew immediately to the score written across the top corner, *Song* and *Hudson* by the numbers.

And Song was about to lose in one of the biggest early-round upsets in years.

Just like her hunch.

"Double fault," Mariana whispered, as the defending champion tossed the ball to serve. It smacked with the same power that had won him championships around the globe. And even before he finished his swing, she knew that it would land about a foot wide of the line, the ensuing events playing out like a script. First, the umpire yelled "Fault!" Then the crowd let out a collective "Ooh." Then Song paced back and forth, yelling at himself before stopping to stare skyward, the match now one point from slipping away.

Mariana watched the final point unfold, every action playing out in a way that processed through her mind in slow motion. Song would serve, then Hudson would return, then Song would charge the net for a slice that would nick the top of the net before spiraling just out of the line. The crowd would erupt at the mighty upset, Hudson shaking his fist in to celebrate the impossible while Song knelt, stunned.

"System, screen off," Mariana said.

This couldn't be one singularly incredible coincidence. Not moment after moment, a clear checklist of things lighting up her mind. Not the mental trickery of déjà vu either. No, this felt stronger than that, like vague blurs snapping into fully fledged details with color and sound and feeling.

That man—*Carter*—he'd asked her to remember something. Something about…

If you remember, that's your proof.

B.E.

Lines crinkled across her brow as she dug deep, trying to unearth the details.

Buddy Ed, at the security desk. Events replayed in her mind as she got dressed, both the way the dog lost his usual Monday snack *and* the rapid-fire explanation she'd given Carter playing out in parallel. An autopilot took over, mind too caught up in the strange possibilities suddenly emerging. It took a passing glance at the bathroom mirror for her to hesitate while different pieces slowly came together into the most impossible epiphany.

"This is a loop," he'd said. "It's all looping."

What could that possibly mean?

Only one way to find out. Maggie chirped while Mariana

dashed around the apartment, recalling that, despite the morning being extremely weird, a cat's food bowl still didn't fill itself. Mariana started with that, then responded to Curtis's message confirming a trip to Hawke, though as she passed by the hallway bookshelf, another image struck her.

Her eyes locked with Shay's image, a sliver in time captured in print on her shelf.

Her thoughts rippled, an absolute certainty came when she saw the photo. She'd brought Shay with her to Hawke for the tour, the whole visit as much for Shay as it was for her. Perhaps even more.

Her finger traced the edge of the photo frame, the same object staring back at her with a suddenly different context, everything both impossible and very, very real.

Not too long ago, Mariana had considered stepping away from science, moving to a simpler life where things didn't seem so consequential and detailed. But for now, she needed that part of her mind.

And one thing would be different this time. Shay would have to stay here. As much as her sister would have appreciated an adventure into the unknown, Mariana's instinct to limit variables in a completely out-of-control situation won out.

Halfway to the exit, Mariana glanced at her kitchen, and though it was, as usual, in need of restocking, she grabbed a piece of sourdough bread off the counter.

If B.E.'s Monday treat would be ruined as expected, he still deserved a treat.

And then, she would find this Carter person, whoever he was.

8

If you remember, that's your proof.

Mariana did, in fact, remember.

Just like with her hunch about the US Open, B.E. lost his Monday snack, the events replaying the way she'd seen in her mind's eye. But unlike before, the slice of sourdough seemed to make the dog's day, earning her a few grateful licks in return.

What to do about the situation, though, she wasn't sure. Instead of bringing clarity, such a concrete validation made disbelief creep into curiosity and panic. For now, she forced herself to clamp down and give herself any bit of stability possible.

For about two hours after, Mariana went through the exact motions that sprinkled her memory. She took the train to the ReLive office and met up with her colleagues. They rode the air-bus through the skylanes together on the way to Hawke. She acted like she should, a mixture of excitement and curiosity about pending scientific discovery coupled with jokes about boring meetings and what to get for lunch near the Hawke facility.

But when they arrived, none of the awe from her previous visit carried over. Even though this technically marked her first trip to the Hawke Accelerator, a greater understanding resonated within her, the clear knowledge that she'd done this before.

Was this only the second time? Or were there more? Those were questions for Carter, so many questions, all of them seeming like the most pressing issue. She stepped through the doors in line with the rest of the ReLive team, keeping pace while recalling all of the wonder and grief such a moment delivered before. Those feelings came as a secondary echo, arriving from another world, another lifetime where things worked in a simpler, more straightforward way. The scientific possibilities of the accelerator's wonders, the deep grief from carrying Shay's photograph, the awe at the facility's size and scope—all of that evaporated, leaving only the details of her final moments in the observation room.

They checked in, registering with security and getting mobile AI units for their stay. As she waited her turn, she questioned her sanity again, whether the morning itself was the anomaly, the result of perhaps a minor gas leak or something in her home. But then she saw Carter.

He stood dressed in fresh dark blue technician's coveralls, elbow propped against the wall. At the top of his cart sat a pastry of some kind, and Mariana realized that of all the things he'd said to her in the observation room, he had included a random comment about donuts.

As he waited, he wrote in a notebook, but a different one than last time. In the observation room, it had been red. Today, the cover was black. And though his eyes darted around to take in details, he kept looking past the flow of people and in her direction, a searching hidden among his casual glances.

She walked methodically, her eyes locked onto him, waiting. He broke from his notebook as someone approached him, prompting him to take a meter from the cart and activate it. A small holographic display came to life, and across the entry space she heard its activation beeps and boops. Carter squinted at it, while still checking around him, probably a routine he'd kept up for appearances as he continued to sneak looks toward the entrance.

Mariana's heels clicked on the tiled floor, keeping pace with her team, and while everyone else took in the sights of the facility, she scanned the constant flow of people moving in all directions.

Then they saw each other.

She caught it, the subtle shifts in his expression when she nodded. The way his shoulders relaxed, the way his lips curled in exhale, the way his eyes widened but the lines on his brow disappeared.

They were both there, at Hawke. And whatever had happened with the last disaster, the how and why of a shattering room and an uncontrollable green spark of energy from a particle accelerator, well...

If nothing else, they had been, in common, the victims of an unexplained massive energy explosion.

"Hey," she said to the group, "I gotta use the bathroom. I'll catch up at the first meeting."

Before her colleagues even acknowledged her words, she broke away toward Carter.

"Four days," Carter said, pushing his technician cart. The wheels squeaked as they moved at a slow pace. With all the people passing by, it didn't seem like anyone noticed that they walked a simple circle, stopping every twenty steps or so to give the appearance of busywork. "Each loop lasts four days."

Mariana glanced at the people passing them: some in lab coats, most in street clothes. They moved to the west wing of the front building, circling around a closed auditorium before coming back around. "It's always the same?"

"Yes. I wake up at the same time, at 5:49 a.m. on Monday," Carter said. He paused, pulling out his notebook from the cart and flipping it to the first page. "I always check the clock. You should note the time when you wake up, every loop." Mariana took the notebook, her finger tracing over the time stamp written at the very top of the sheet. "Today was a little weird at first. Might just have been a little spark because you're here," he said with a quiet laugh, and she couldn't tell if he was joking or serious. "Otherwise, it's never changed. Nothing does." Their eyes met, a sudden weariness to his pupils. "Except me."

"And now me."

"Yeah. It's…" he bit his lip "…nice to not be alone. Everyone's living their lives, and I'm just here." He turned, the light catching his eyes enough to show a glisten. "It's almost like playing a video game. You can do a few things differently, but everyone just returns back to start. You can scream and yell at the world, but everything snaps back. No one is aware. They just resume their lives. And then it repeats." He bit his lip again, eyes scrunched as he shook his head. "It just repeats. Nothing matters. Nothing changes."

Nothing matters. Nothing changes.

Mariana fought the idea that time loops weren't the only reason things felt that way.

"What have you tried?" Mariana asked. He responded with a full list, something much longer and more thorough than she expected, from running through the exact same path multiple times to doing the complete opposite to trying—and failing—to get her attention, all captured by what he called a photographic memory.

Mariana's scientific mind processed everything he said, slotting the information into appropriate categories and data as she considered their options on how to proceed. But one thing remained unanswered, one nagging mystery to it all. "Why me?" Mariana finally asked as he handed her a screwdriver for no reason other than appearances. "All this trouble to get me here with you? Is there something you learned about me that makes you think I can fix this?"

Since they had come together, Carter's expression had cycled through a number of emotions. It defaulted to a certain tension, squinted eyes and carved lines on his face. But it also moved to worry, relief, and fatigue, as they discussed the ins and outs of the strangest of temporal situations.

This question, though, seemed to catch him off guard. His head tilted, and his lips pursed as he took in a breath. "Well," he said, scratching his head, "you were the last in the room."

"And?"

"You were the last in the room," he repeated, this time with a shrug.

Mariana blinked at his explanation. "That's it?"

"Yeah. I mean," he said as he shrugged, "seemed like the best shot. But we did meet before that." He turned, and Mariana had to look to see if…

Was that a flush coming to his ears?

"We met? How?"

"Sort of. I mean, I promise, I haven't been stalking you," he said with a sheepish grin. "It was the time I tried doing the opposite of things, and we bumped into each other. That's how I found out ReLive was in the observation room before the explosion. Originally, I'm called to check something there as it's falling apart. That's how I got zapped. But I thought if I could use the maintenance grid to close off elevators and delay your group. You all might be there at the same time, and *someone* might get in the loop too." He shrugged again. "That's what I mean, you were the last in the room. It took a few tries to get it right, though."

"What did we talk about that first time?"

"Honestly?" Carter laughed, then looked down at his shoulder. "You spilled coffee on me."

"You're joking."

"Nope. Right here," he said, tapping the spot where the stain used to be. "I was eating pastries with my eyes closed. Which sounds weird. But, like, if you're really going to enjoy the flavor of something, you should shut out other sensory input. So kind of my fault. Oh, but—" his voice brightened, his whole mood shifting "—I gave you a donut," he said with the wag of a finger. "Which you said you liked."

"You gave me a donut. And you brought me into a time loop." Mariana said the words lightly, but something about it caused Carter's demeanor to shift.

"Yeah. You know, I just realized, I don't know if this is better or worse for you. I'm sorry," he said, eyes looking past her. "I was just so focused on breaking through to someone, I didn't think about it."

What *had* he gotten her into? That seemed like a worthwhile question, though his explanation broke all of the logic her brain typically relied on. "I was hoping it would have been some kind of cool savior-of-the-world stuff. So if I forget this, just lie to me next time, okay?"

Carter returned to the wry grin she'd seen him flash from time to time. "Well, you tell me. Maybe ReLive *can* turn you into the person that saves us all. What do they even do?"

All sorts of nondisclosure agreements and legalese protected ReLive's details. And even though they faced an exploding particle accelerator and a time loop, Mariana stuck with those restrictions. Because if this, whatever *this* was, actually worked, she'd still have to abide by those.

"I can't tell you," she said.

"We're, uh," Carter said, gesturing around them, "in a time loop?"

Mariana's lips pressed, and her toes curled within her shoes. He was right. However they got here, they *were* in a time loop, and they needed to work together. At the same time, breaking legal agreements worked against her thought process. Actions like that needed complete moral justifications, like finding a way into the ReLive trial. *That* was worth it given the context of everything.

This? She wasn't certain about this. At least not yet.

Shay, though, would have totally told him.

Despite not having the photo frame there, Mariana still felt her stepsister's presence. And it wasn't just because the ReLive dose helped preserve her memory.

"If we're still doing this in a few days, maybe I'll tell you. But rules are rules."

"Will it help get us out of this mess?" Carter's eyes filled with hope.

That was why he pushed. His question had less to do with career curiosity and more with desperation for any solution. "If it prevented explosions, you probably wouldn't have needed to convince me. I remember my favorite memories of my best friend. They're even more vivid now than before. It's ironic, really. I can remember her better now that she's gone," Mariana said, her voice low. "That's what ReLive does."

Carter's face fell before he took a step back. Swatches of oblivious people strode by them, too caught up in their own conversations to understand what was happening between the two static people in the hallway. "Oh," he said. "Her. You mentioned Shay in the observation room two loops ago. The photo. You've never said why you brought that, though. Or even why ReLive is here."

"Yeah," she said, her face naturally scrunching. "Honestly, I still don't know why they wanted us here. Last time, Beckett said something about examining the effects of radiation exposure on memory. But then he left the room with the group and…" Her fingers fluttered as she blew out a poof, and Carter nodded in return. "I'm a neuroscientist. Quantum mechanics was Shay's thing, not mine."

"Wait a minute." Carter's eyes lit up, a spark that hadn't been there earlier, not even when they first connected. "That's it." Something she said had caused Carter to leap from disappointment to confirmation, but it certainly wasn't intentional on her part.

"If I wasn't clear, when I said my friend is gone, I meant that she's dead." She had said that once before, to Beckett in the last loop. But the definitive way she declared it this time, the actual word *dead* coming from the air in her lungs...

That was a new level of definitive statement.

Without a body, without a death certificate, she let herself dream that maybe Shay freaked out about finishing her doctorate and simply ran off. Being Shay's friend meant rolling with her impulsive decisions on a semiregular basis, so why wouldn't she simply *vanish* for that long in the middle of the California desert to who knows where?

But Mariana knew those were simply ways to avoid speaking, even thinking the cold, hard truth.

Shay was dead.

"Beckett," Carter said quickly, like the ideas outran his thoughts. "What if we can get through to Beckett? He's in charge of this whole thing." That proved unexpected, a curious-enough proposition that Mariana's thoughts sparked back into the comfortable groove of hypotheses and processes. "I am sorry, though."

"About what?"

"Your friend. I'm sorry she's gone."

Outside of family, that may have been the first time someone had said that. Mariana tried so hard to avoid the topic with everyone, it took a disaster and a time loop for it to slip through. "Yeah. I am too." She shut her eyes for a moment, and on cue ReLive-powered memories vibrantly arrived.

No. Not now.

"But I suppose it doesn't matter if we don't figure this out," he said. "Beckett arrives on Thursday. How do we get him on our side?" Carter took out his notebook, flipping through several pages filled with notes until he got to the next blank one, then he pulled a pen out of the spiral binding.

"David?" Mariana said, tapping the mobile AI device hanging around her neck. "What time is the ReLive meeting with Dr. Beckett on Thursday morning?"

"Eleven o'clock."

"We're going to need to coordinate," he said, pulling out his phone. "What's your number?"

She paused, considering the possibility that this was all some elaborate hoax or accidental psychedelic trip. Should she give this guy who crashed into her life a way into her private life?

Yet given the clear evidence that *something* weird was unfolding, it seemed logical. "Yeah," she said. "Good idea."

9

The next two days moved quickly, the constraints of the impending reset building a suffocating pressure with each passing hour. By day, Mariana followed the ReLive itinerary while using *an unfortunate bout of food poisoning* as an easy excuse to disappear for research opportunities. And while her colleagues went through the questions and discussions like they'd never done it before, Mariana pushed herself to capture any possible detail from passing scientists and monitors for clues. At night, she and Carter formed an investigative team, their phone numbers swapped and texts now flying between them as he sent over new findings about the Hawke facility: public records, history, design specifications. For her, the hours flew by with Maggie on her lap and the US Open on in the background, all while learning everything she possibly could about Dr. Albert Beckett.

Beckett's education, his career history, even his affection for musical theater and late twentieth-century rock music, Mariana studied all of it, trying to think of the best formula that might break the scientist's understanding of what was possible and get him to accept the impossibility of a time loop.

On Wednesday night, though, Carter reached out with an unexpected message.

I have something to show you. Can I come to your place?

Her home. The place where she grounded herself from the chaos of the world. In many ways, the place she *hid* from the world. No one had been over for months, not since Shay had dropped by with the sudden announcement that she was going off on her own.

In true Shay fashion, on that Monday evening some four months ago, that life-changing decision was something she simply threw in as Mariana was about to leave. In fact, knowing her, she might have made the decision in that very moment.

"Oh, I'm gonna disappear for two weeks," Shay had proclaimed, like that was something totally normal people do.

"Like, literally or emotionally or metaphorically?"

"All of the above!" Shay said with a laugh, though Mariana couldn't tell if she was laughing at the situation or her own joke.

"You just got back from a week in Toronto. That's why I have a supply of cat food now." Maggie jumped in between them on the couch, walking back and forth to emphasize the point. "No, Maggie, you're just visiting tonight, you're not staying."

"Right, and Toronto was loud and busy. So I decided, I got some time before the semester. Fuck it, I'm gonna go to Joshua Tree. By myself."

"Shay," Mariana said, her voice turning stern, "that's a terrible idea."

"No, it's a great idea. Have you seen the state of the world? The bullshit is endless. But I had an epiphany." Her eyes brightened, her black eyebrows rising like she'd discovered the secret to everything. "The world is terrible. So you go away. By the time you get back, it doesn't seem so bad. Oh, do you remember that place Ben recommended on Highway 5 with the good tacos?"

"Taco...Place?" Mariana replied, shaking her head. She'd never retain that level of detail about some random taco restaurant. "Taco Plaza? I can't remember. It was Taco Something."

"Can you ask Ben?"

"Oh, I decided to stop seeing him," Mariana said, the words coming out as if a magnet pulled them out. Silence grew between them, though Maggie audibly purred.

They'd had this talk before, multiple times. It wasn't like Mariana had dated too many men over the years, and she'd certainly enjoyed their company—she wouldn't have bothered spending time with them if she didn't. But she knew Shay would react. *How* she reacted, that remained to be seen. There were multiple paths to this. Shay might give the speech about how she was too nitpicky, or how she needed to trust people more, that sort of thing.

Shay inhaled to say something, and Mariana braced herself. "When did this happen?"

Asking *when* wasn't on the list. But, Mariana supposed, getting further information at least made a little bit of sense from a clarification perspective. "While you were in Toronto," she said. "I mean, we only went out a few times—"

"I thought you actually liked Ben."

"I did."

"So why'd you break up with him?"

"*Break up* implies some sort of exclusivity. We just went out a few times. Besides, work's busy."

"You hear that, Mag?" Shay asked. Under her voice came the distinctive whiny meow of her cat. "Maggie says she's disappointed in you."

"Why have I disappointed your cat? He was nice, we had fun, the end. I have things to do."

"Maggie, what do you think?" Shay's voice shifted into a higher pitch as she scooped the cat up. "Fact, meow-meow, Mariana is afraid of human contact." Mocking Mariana's life-long approach to problem-solving was nothing new for Shay, but this was the first time she waved cat paws to accentuate each methodical step of it. "Hypothesis, meow-meow, Ben was a good guy. Experiment, meow-meow, Mariana might need to show actual commitment for once." On cue, Maggie let out an actual meow. "Huh. Seems like reasonable insight for a cat. And you don't even have a degree in neuroscience like Mariana."

"Ha ha, Shay," she said, giving her stepsister a fake scowl. "Ha ha, Maggie."

"Engaging with other humans is a good way to live a fuller life, Mariana."

"I work with other humans every day."

"See, you keep giving yourself away. *Work.* Ever since I've known you, it's been some form of work. Replace *work* with *classes* or *tennis* or *physical therapy from tennis.*"

"You spend all your time on your PhD."

"You say that, but I actually went out to karaoke last night. And I have a cat."

Maggie meowed again as Shay set her back down, and Mariana wondered if Shay had a button or something to activate cat noises. "I should get to bed. I have to get up early…" Mariana grimaced as she formed the words "…for work."

"At least you're consistent. Okay, so I guess there's no pinging Ben to find out that taco place?"

"I forget his number," Mariana said, though she didn't. Numbers stuck in her mind, probably thanks to years of scientific training.

"Bullshit. You *love* numbers. You remember all of them. I've seen you spout off pi to, like, forty digits for no reason. His is still probably lurking around in there."

"Okay, okay. His number is three point one four one five nine two six."

"Ha freaking ha," Shay said, punching Mariana in the shoulder.

"Then, here's the truth. It would be weird. Okay?" Mariana

gave Shay a smug lip, and the honesty seemed to win over the conversation.

"Right, right. No weirdo shit. Okay. Guess I'll try—" her voice changed to overenunciate every word "—something on my own. So I'm leaving in four days to escape the world. Can you take care of this cat again?"

"After her flawed hypothesis? I guess so. She's lucky she's cute."

"She's looking at me, Mariana. This cat is looking at me and throwing shade. I'll tell her you didn't mean that." Maggie's fluffy face turned upward, like she actually understood what they said. "I don't think anyone gets phone signal at Joshua Tree, but I'll check in whenever possible. I'll get her on my way back. I can't be late picking her up, otherwise she's gonna love you more than me. Seriously, though. We are going to have a talk about your neuroscience education and your complete avoidance of human commitment."

Four days later, Mariana drove seventy minutes to Shay's place in the college town of Davis. She packed Maggie up in a carrier, along with a bag full of extra cat food and other supplies.

And Maggie had been with her ever since.

Perhaps subconsciously Mariana was waiting to have one final conversation with Shay before she let anyone else back in. Her specialty was in the neurons and impulses of the brain, not the mysteries of emotions.

She snapped out of her ReLive-enhanced memory, her phone buzzing again. A new message displayed:

I'll bring something good to eat too.

As if Maggie could read, she meowed an enthusiastic reply. "Are you giving me attitude?" The cat looked her way before rubbing her fluffy forehead into Mariana's open palm. "I never claimed to be a chef. It takes too much time," she said, replying to the message with her address.

The knock came as Mariana read over a ten-year-old report Beckett had written called "Temporal Observations in Accelerated Particles as a Cluster," though she might as well have paid attention to the background US Open, given how little she actually understood it. If Carter brought his David AI it might help, especially since her visitor version was returned at the end of each day at Hawke. "Come in," she yelled. From behind her came the sounds that followed her most of her life: the distinctive *pop* of a racket hitting a ball, the squeaking of shoes over hard court, the grunt of a player's exertion.

The applause when the point came to an end.

"Hello?" Carter called out as the door slid open. She heard him shuffle in, though the aroma of mixed spices arrived first. If she cared more, she'd try to decipher the individual smells, but for her purposes it all lumped into *pretty good*.

"I brought brain fuel."

"Over here," Mariana said, trying one more time with the report.

"I'll trade you good food for good news," he said. She finally turned to see him carrying a large, sealed bag, and from that he pulled out individual cartons. He popped them open one by one, the intensity of the spices escaping, and the weariness that Mariana had seen on Carter over the last few days disappeared, replaced with the flash of curled lips. She caught him leaning over, a quick inhale as he inspected the food cartons, though he straightened up when their eyes met.

"I don't know if it's good news," she said, stacking data tablets on top of each other, "but it's something. *'Once an accelerated particle reaches the target speed, the directional velocity can be controlled if proper compensation of the Gushman Function has been applied to minimize—'"*

"Mariana."

"I don't really understand this, and I might be reading too much into this but—"

"Mariana," Carter said again.

"What?" she asked, meeting his eyes.

"Have you had anything to eat today?"

Maggie had run to her usual hiding spot behind the couch, and though she usually took several hours to warm up to people, she at least poked her head out for Carter. "I had a breakfast shake. And, um, something for lunch. Something from the Hawke café. I can't remember what."

"Okay. So you had sustenance today. That's not eating. Every single meal is a chance for a new experience." He took a carton in each hand and waved them in front of her. "Smell this. This is eating. It's different from sustenance."

Such a thought seemed like a declaration in a foreign language. Of course she enjoyed a good restaurant, but when every second counted, taking the time to savor a single meal seemed, well, a little counterproductive. "Fine. Give me a few of those. Vegetarian, please."

"No, no, no. Let's stop everything for—" Carter looked at the clock on the wall "—twenty minutes. We can still talk but put all the reports and research away and just try this. Look at this. Veggie *gyoza*." He held up another carton of steaming dumplings. "Mushroom. Leeks. Ginger. Onions. Rice vinegar. Sriracha, oh sriracha. It's the best. And not just those ingredients, but the way they come together to form something. It's science *and* magic combined. You need to eat." He started setting the cartons on the table, then lined up chopsticks and napkins strategically around Mariana's notes. "But more importantly, you need to enjoy. Look," he said, one finger up before he knelt down and inhaled deeply, "take it all in. Because you may never smell this exact combination again. Here," he said, pulling out two fortune cookies. "Start with dessert."

"Is this some sort of time-loop joke?"

"Some cultures use sweets to cleanse the palate. They're smarter than us," he said, cracking open a fortune cookie before the meal started. "Hey, look. *You will get out of a rut.* Bodes well, right?"

"Point to the fortune cookie," she said as he grinned, a wide smile colored with...optimism? No, not quite that. And she'd seen him enough to know that he wasn't always exactly a sunny person. But his emotions presented without filter, and in this moment he let himself simply be with his dumplings.

The tablets clattered as Mariana moved them aside, then she gestured at the open space on the table. More cartons soon landed, steam bursting out as Carter opened each one. "I just keep coming back to one idea," she said. "We shut down the accelerator."

"Is there a big Off switch we flip somewhere?" he asked, arranging the table.

"Not from what I can see. Unless there's a power plug in the back we missed."

"I can look tomorrow," he said, breaking apart a pair of chopsticks and handing them over, square-side toward her. "I do have access." He tapped the table, a mock activation of his AI. "David, where's the On/Off switch on the Hawke Accelerator?"

She laughed, but mostly to cover up the fact that she was terrible with chopsticks.

"You could," she said, taking the thin wooden sticks, fingers pressed tightly. "Though I think Beckett's still the priority. Unless David's got something we've missed, it seems better to convince Beckett we're in a time loop. I've been reading his old academic papers."

"You mind?" Carter asked, raising his own pair of chopsticks, then reached into one of the cartons before she answered. "So let's say we win him over," he said, mouth half-full. She shook her head, prompting a grin as he took another dumpling before finishing.

"We've got a short window tomorrow." Mariana nodded, then looked at the various tablets and papers in front of them. "I don't know how long it takes to power down. But hopefully he can do it."

Carter tapped the top tablet, an active display of power schematics that she still didn't fully understand. "It shuts down," he said between bites. "Nothing explodes. We move on."

"Yeah," Mariana said. Behind them, the broadcast of the tennis continued with a loud burst of sudden applause. "And I'll get to see who wins the US Open this year."

Carter's eyes trailed to the match as well. "I've never watched tennis. But now I really want to see who wins. You know," he started, pointing at the boxes of takeout around them, "one thing kind of sucks."

"What's that?"

"Every time a loop resets, my bank account does too. I splurged tonight. This place has three Michelin stars." Carter said that like she would understand, and instead she simply smiled and nodded. "It's not like I can normally afford these dishes." His chopsticks tapped against the side of the nearest carton. "So if we actually succeed, that means that I'm kind of screwed."

"It's a reverse jinx," Mariana said.

"Yeah, exactly. Either we continue to be stuck in purgatory, or I spent a bunch of money I don't have." Carter popped the lid off two bottles, then slid one over before holding his up. "Take what you can get." Their bottles clinked, the contact hard enough that several drops spilled over the edge of hers, rolling between her fingertips. "I suppose it's a worthy trade-off."

"How about this?" Mariana said, taking a sip. "If this doesn't work—"

"Don't say that. I've been stuck for weeks." With that lone

statement, his entire demeanor shifted, a sudden change as if a table of expensive dumplings no longer existed. "You know what this is like? It's like being in a train going toward a giant brick wall. And you keep going, you're speeding up. And once you realize that *oh no, this is actually happening*, you try to poke and nudge everyone to do *something* to avoid it. But they just don't hear you. You're invisible, silent, and the few people who see you think you're out of your mind." Any humor in his tone disappeared, a weight that pulled Mariana down until the emptiness of his situation grounded her. "The first few times are interesting. Then it just gets worse and worse."

She'd only been through this once. The repetition still tapped into extreme reactions for her: shock, surprise, amusement, even curiosity. How many times did it take for the experience to numb into something worse for Carter? At least when he *wasn't* eating expensive dumplings.

"Hey," Mariana said softly. "We've got a plan."

"Yeah." He huffed out a sigh, then glanced down at the open carton between them. "Well, we're here now. Someone's gotta eat these dumplings. Less loop, more food. And," he said, pointing at the US Open playing out across the room, "tennis. I don't know any of the rules."

10

Mariana had always been the type of person that could snap out of bed and jump into her tasks for the day. So it caught her by surprise when a torn notebook sheet sat on her counter right next to the stack of cat-food cans.

Slow down. Eat some breakfast. Coffee doesn't count. Check your front door. —C

Carter must have snuck that before he left last night, the thought making a smile creep onto her face. She shook off the urge to do her daily morning checklist. That pattern had worked for her dating back to college when she had to juggle classes, tennis practice, and a part-time job. Doing anything else felt foreign enough that Shay would joke she needed to go into Mariana Mode when the combination of tennis and coursework proved overwhelming.

Here, Mariana took the hint. She needed to review the day's plan anyway. Maggie seemed to agree, walking in a circle with persistent meows until her own canned breakfast landed on her plate. After that, Mariana opened her front door and grabbed a small carton, the name Bellisario's Bakery on it. She set it on the table, the cardboard lid catching as she popped it open. And though her instinct was to finish it quick and get on with things, Carter's voice echoed in her mind.

Smell this. This is eating. It's different from sustenance.

The last time she thought of something Carter said, it stemmed from frantic actions as Hawke exploded around them. This time? It came in the form of a scone with some berries in it. She laughed to herself, and though she had a tablet in her hand, she forced herself to sniff the scone's distinct aroma before loading up notes to review.

"Did you eat?" Carter asked when he saw her, his priorities clearly out of step. She nodded, and it was true, she had told herself to slow down, enjoy her scone rather than thinking ten steps ahead. But once that passed, she'd snapped back into executing with precision. Perhaps not the time, but the methodical nature of her goals: those were still executed step-by-step. First, she got Maggie set up for the day. Then she called the ReLive team to let them know she'd meet them directly at the Hawke facility.

Next she reviewed her notes, memorizing every detail she could about Dr. Beckett's schedule, about how she might explain the situation and produce a shred of evidence that validated things instead of making her sound completely out of touch with reality.

Fact: Carter and Mariana were stuck in a time loop.

Hypothesis: This happened because a strange green bolt exploded out of the wall of the control room and zapped them.

Experiment: If they shut down the test sequence, would it prevent whatever caused the explosion that led to the time loop?

Part of her still wondered if this was an enormous practical joke, something constructed through bribed coworkers and holographic technology. But every time that doubt arrived, she pictured B.E. in the lobby and the dropped biscuit. That wasn't exactly something that could be staged over and over.

She hoped Carter had done similar prep work, though she wasn't sure based on his casual stance and wry smile. "It's Bellisario's. Best bakery in, like, a ten-mile radius. Not an exact number. But everyone should try it at least once." Mariana nodded, but her acting skills clearly weren't convincing enough. Carter laughed with a head shake. "My ex once told me that ninety percent of food falls into the category of *good enough*. I just thought that was such a sad way to live. We've only got so much time but you can't take joy in something you do three times a day?" His lips pursed, head angled as he reached into his technician bag. "I got you something."

"Another scone?"

"Not quite as good." His eyes darted around, checking the area twice before pulling something out of the bag. "It's a security-qualified badge. Doesn't actually do anything. We wear them when we go into restricted areas so it's easy to identify. Doors and sensors still depend on identifying signals from your phone." Mariana took the badge, a simple piece of composite material with the words *Restricted Access* printed on it, then put it in her coat pocket. "You ready?"

"Not really. But it's either do this or we start over."

"Right. Let's hope I have no money when tomorrow happens."

Familiar voices carried through the lobby area, and Mariana craned her neck to see the ReLive team arriving. "There's my group," she said with a nod.

Carter reached in his bag again, this time pulling out two clear earpieces, each the size of a fingernail. "More technician tools. We use these when coordinating fixes with test engineers. They've got movement trackers, so I can see where you're at. I'll head to the restricted area."

"This is part of your job?" she asked.

"Not really. But when you're in a time loop, you can experiment. I've figured out how to get access to all sorts of places. No consequences, right?" His chin rumpled and he looked up thoughtfully. "Except now, maybe. Let's get some consequences."

Mariana slid the comm device in her ear before standing up and waving at the approaching ReLive group. "Right. Let's get some consequences."

An hour passed before Carter's voice broke through the earpiece with Beckett's itinerary. More importantly, the list of elevators and paths he'd blocked off—a means to funnel Beckett's possible movement between meetings.

"Just like old times," Mariana whispered, the noise mostly ignored by her coworkers as they sat together. She cleared her throat and offered a weak smile for anyone who glanced her way.

"Hey, if it works. He got in an hour ago. He's almost done with his meeting. I'm not sure how he'll react, but," he said and chuckled through the tiny speaker, "you can't argue with last time's results. You should get here as soon as possible."

"Mmm-hmm," she said as inconspicuously as possible. It didn't work, though, as the entire group in the conference room turned to her. They leaned in, the main presenter pausing as well, and Mariana showed a quick smile before clearing her throat. "I'm sorry," she started before another idea sparked. "I'm not feeling well right now. Food poisoning. Please excuse me."

Sympathetic nods and murmurs came her way, and she walked with a slow, hunched gait until she stepped out of the room. Its sliding door closed behind her; Mariana waited until the hydraulic pressure gave a short hiss to announce the door was shut. "Carter?" she asked, her steps now swift and purposeful. "I'm on my way."

For the next ten minutes, Mariana hustled through the operational side of the facility. With Carter chatting in her ear about Beckett's current status and where to go, she wove through passing people, taking stairs and marching down hallways, pausing or speeding up when he said so, her mobile AI device ditched into a garbage can halfway through.

Not once did she ask how he managed to do this. Though, it certainly crossed her mind. But heading into the restricted wing of the Hawke Accelerator didn't seem like the ideal time to have any deeper conversation.

Besides, the tunnel ahead with two guards and a massive security scanner proved enough of a challenge.

"Beckett just got out of his meeting. I can't track him, but I've blocked his path, so I think if you hurry forward now you can find him ahead."

"There's a big security station here," she said under her breath. "Is this badge enough?"

"It's not. Hold on." On the other end, some muffled noises passed by, along with a short grunt. "It's the scanner you have to worry about."

"I don't think I can lie my way through this."

"You won't have to," Carter said, his words picking up into a frantic pace. "Just hold on."

"Can I help you?" a man asked. He wore the same technician overalls as Carter, and around his neck hung the same red badge that Mariana wore.

"I'm fine, I'm just waiting for someone," she said, though their discussion was enough to draw the guards' attention.

"Okay," Carter said through the earpiece. "I'm almost done. Get to the scanner. Show your badge like it's no big deal. Pause at the scanner, and when I tell you to go, step through. Confidently."

Mariana flashed a smile at the technician, then walked in a slow, controlled pace to the scanner. "Confidently?"

"Fake it till you make it, you know?"

"This is not a sound strategy," she whispered upon her approach. "Ready."

"Go, show your badge." Mariana moved, making brief eye contact with both guards before pausing at the scanner. She raised the badge, though only one of them nodded in acknowledgment, the other distracted by a screen. *Confidently*, she told herself, like talking her way into a job interview. "Go, go," Carter said, and she moved as directed.

She crossed the threshold. One foot landed, then the other, and it repeated until she was clear, the scanner a good ten feet behind her.

No alarms rang. No sensors beeped.

If she had the time and space, she would have exhaled, smiled, possibly even laughed. But here, a simple breath was all she gave herself before moving on. "I'm through, Carter." At the very end of the hall stood a man, and as her eyes adjusted to the light, details filled in to reveal that maybe they finally had a little luck on their side. "And I think I see Beckett down—"

"Ma'am?" a voice called out from behind.

Mariana knew the question was for her but kept moving regardless. "Ma'am? We need to run you past the scanner again."

"Carter?" Her voice carried a sudden, tight urgency. "They're calling me back."

"The freaking reset window is closed," he said quickly. "Hold on. This worked last time."

"What's that mean?"

"Ma'am?" the guard repeated, more force in her voice. "You need to step through the scanner again. The record didn't log."

"Sorry," she called out before turning on her heel. "Running out of time here."

"Never mind. I'll force the reset."

If they had to do this again, she'd grill Carter about *what* he was actually doing. And if they didn't, well, pretty sure he'd get fired if the Hawke security team discovered all of the ways he'd tried to push his illicit access. The badge caught against her shirt's fabric as she pulled it up, and she held it, raising an eyebrow. She forced a sullen squint and crooked mouth, telling herself to try her best to look really, really annoyed. She moved past the threshold back to the other side, fingers balled into fists. "All right, I'll step through again," she said forcefully enough for both the guards *and* Carter to catch it.

"Still glitching," one of them said, shaking his head.

"I've shunted power to the scanner so it can't fully operate," Carter said in quick cadence. "Can you make a scene and see if they'll just let you go?"

Making a scene wasn't exactly the way a noted rule-follower worked, but at this point, it was either try that or turn around. Mariana thought back to that morning with Shay at the shop with the photo printer, how her friend managed to huff and groan her way into a better price. Mariana walked louder, big gestures and annoyed grimace on full display. "Can I go? I have a meeting," she asked, putting as much bile in her voice as possible. "With Dr. Beckett. I'm with the ReLive project, and I'm already late. You can look me up on the visitor registry." All of this was true, with some context twisted and turned. But it provided enough of a corporate threat to turn security guards who probably weren't paid enough to care. "Mariana Pineda. P-I-N-E-D-A. All right? I have to go."

The guards looked at her before turning to each other, and she stood, unblinking, hoping that her panicked expression looked sour enough to work.

"It's fine, we'll log it manually," one guard finally said to the other. His partner nodded, and Mariana turned, this time not even pausing to relish the moment. Instead, she kept her head up and eyes peeled for Beckett.

Every turn pulled her deeper into the developmental wing of the Hawke Accelerator, the surroundings transitioning from technology office to industrial facility. Smooth corporate walls with bland decor gave way to monitors and displays with various data and schedules, along with the occasional locked set of doors beneath flashing lights, some actively rotating and some static.

She moved quickly, speeding up every time she found herself free from passersby and observers. And despite several dead ends and wrong turns slowing her down, some luck must have been on her side.

Well, luck and whatever Carter did to close off sections and elevators.

Because with a little guidance and speed, Mariana caught up to Beckett. She did a double take to be sure, but given the *last* loop, she knew what he'd be wearing, his gait, and the salt-and-pepper hair.

And better yet, she caught him alone, arms folded as he stared at a glowing display showing a multicolored table of data. Behind him stood a massive sliding door, a sign above it stating *Decontamination Chamber.*

"Carter. I've found him. Right outside—"

"The decontamination chamber. Got it. I'm on the opposite side. I'll head over. See if you can keep him alone."

Mariana hung back, gauging Beckett from afar. Did that secure door only let one person in at a time? Or would it linger long enough for her to squeeze in? She was about to ask Carter if he knew, when Beckett made an unexpected move.

He turned around. And though his voice remained soft-spoken, the acoustics of the hallway carried his words well enough to tell Mariana that their plan needed to pivot yet again. "Yeah, I'm at DeCon. You're running late? Okay. See you here in five. I've got an eleven o'clock with ReLive."

"Carter," she said, a new urgency coloring her words. "He's meeting someone here."

"Oh. Hmm. Maybe that person will know what to do?"

"No, convincing one person is going to be hard enough. Two may be impossible." Mariana eyed Beckett as he waited, and she heard him singing softly under his breath. "I'm going in. I'm gonna try to talk to him."

"Wait, what are you going to say?"

Normally, Mariana had plans layered upon plans. But that was for mundane things, like squeezing in time to take Maggie to the vet. This particular task came with a much loftier goal. And, given the security of the restricted area, also a lot more risk than simply missing an appointment.

"I had a big explanation planned. But I don't have a lot of time." Carter audibly sighed in her ear, but she shook it off, instead scanning the space around them. No one else lingered or even passed. If there was a time to do this, it would be now, even if she wasn't fully ready and her prepared speech had suddenly disappeared from her mind. "Dr. Beckett?" she finally said. He turned, and Mariana offered the most casual wave that she could muster.

"Oh," he said, looking up from his tablet. "Hello."

"Hi, I'm Mariana Pineda. With ReLive." Now what? Options raced by, from technical disclosures to simple questions meant to stall. But talking about ReLive here wouldn't explain why she happened to be in a highly secured area with a staff badge. "I got lost, and I think I'm taking all the wrong turns. Is that—" she pointed to the protected corridor ahead "—how to get back to the conference rooms?"

Beckett shook his head and ran a hand through his hair. "Yeah," he said with a laugh, "this place is confusing. No, that's a decontamination chamber. It's—" he pulled out his phone "—I'm sorry, one second." His stance shifted, and it became clear that his comms were active. "This is Albert," he started before his voice dropped. Mariana looked at the various charts on the wall, though her ears tuned into his muted words.

Most of it got lost among the hum of the facility and din of people in the distance. But she caught one word clearly.

Security.

"Carter," she whispered.

"I was just about to say," he replied, his voice with a strange huff. "We got a problem."

"Security?"

"I might have triggered it with the scanner resets. Make note of that for next time. No, wait, we are *not* having a next time. Heading your way," he said, his breath getting heavy. "Try to get him in the chamber. I'm gonna open the door. It's all electronically controlled." At the same time, Beckett finished his call, looking her way.

"You mean, like…" What obtuse thing could she say that Carter would understand? "Put the dough in the oven?"

"What?"

"I can't be any more clear about the recipe we planned last night. Take the dough and put it in the oven?"

"Oven. Oh. *Oh.* Yes. Do that." Over the earpiece, Carter's huffed breaths mixed with beeps and boops from whatever he was trying to do. "There," he said, and at the same time, several loud clicks caught Beckett's attention. "Security's on alert. We need a place where no one's going to bug us. There's a side panel. Put in override code seven five six six three eight once you get him in, and that'll shut the door."

"Got it. Put the dough in the oven," Mariana said with a shrug at Beckett. "Domestic bliss."

"No problem. Don't want dinner to be ruined," he said with a laugh, one which Mariana quickly matched. "So to get back to the conference rooms, turn around, then make your first left—"

Before Beckett could finish, Mariana took large strides into the now-open decontamination chamber. "Can I see this first?" she called from the inside. In front of her sat various control panels, a mix of screens and physical switches and buttons. What *wouldn't* be catastrophic to flip? With Beckett not quite in the room, she tapped her fingernails against the panel, miming interaction without actually changing anything. "I'm curious to see how it'll react to a ReLive treatment."

"Wait, what are you doing? You can't be in there without authorization." Beckett's shoes clanged on the metal grating as he stepped in, and Mariana moved from panel to panel, tapping close to—but not quite on—digital buttons on various panels. Beckett followed her path, checking each display she touched, and as he did, she dashed to the entrance and its adjacent panel. "Seven five six six three eight," she said to herself before entering what Carter had suggested.

A series of mechanical whirrs and clicks pulsed by before the sliding door slammed shut. Mariana threw her back against it, arms and legs out wide.

"What's going on?" Beckett asked, his voice a blend of ire and confusion.

"Okay, I know this looks strange. But something really bad is about to happen, and I need you to—"

From across the way, more mechanical grinding came, and the far door slid open. Carter ran in, then turned and tapped away at the access panel. The door slammed shut with a low thud that echoed through their metallic surroundings, and behind Mariana, she heard an additional series of locks click into place.

"That should hold," Carter said, "but we have to hurry."

"You're a technician?" Beckett asked.

"And I'm a scientist. A neuroscientist with ReLive. All of that's true," Mariana said. "But what we're going to tell you next is a little harder to believe."

Beckett lunged forward, with surprising agility given his age, and instinct drove Mariana to grab the first thing within reach: a foot-long scanner with composite casing and buttons across the top.

She held it up, arm instinctively poised like a tennis racket, and the makeshift weapon probably looking much more strange than intimidating. But in a situation where Beckett's presence might be the difference between forever and normal, her stance provided enough surprise, if not exactly fear or caution, that Beckett stopped.

And for now, that was all they needed.

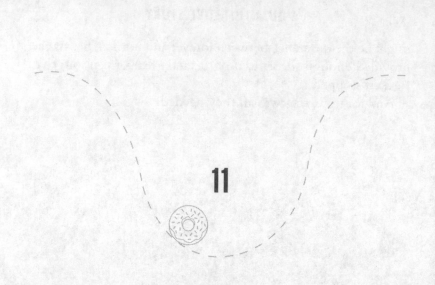

11

Beckett stared back at them, and as he did, Mariana considered the absurdity of what was unfolding.

Here she was, in the place that Shay described as housing *the brightest minds*, and yet rather than taking in the scientific wonders around her, she held some scanner in her hands while the project lead, the *founder* of the Hawke Accelerator, stood slack-jawed and wide-eyed, deep lines framing his open mouth.

"We just," Mariana said, adrenaline causing a tremble in her hand, "need you to stay here for a moment."

"You said you were from the ReLive team," Beckett said.

"I am. My name is Mariana. And this is Carter—he really is a technician here."

"We've met," Carter said. "In passing."

Beckett rubbed his strong chin, lines forming around his eyes.

"Just..." Mariana searched for words that might make sense out of this. All of this planning to get Beckett into a room with them, and now they had to wing it? "Listen for a minute." She shook her head as she held up the scanner. "No need for this, right?" she asked, moving slowly to a shelf of supplies jutting out next to the main console. "I'll put this down now that we've got your attention."

"Next time I'll try bringing dumplings instead," Carter said. "That might come off better."

Carter. Always with the food stuff. Maybe he'd spent the last hour bribing the Hawke systems with recipes. "How do we explain this without sounding like we've lost our minds?"

"In a few hours," Carter said, "the Hawke Accelerator will blow up, creating a time loop that only me and Mariana experience."

Mariana shot Carter a sharp look, to which he replied with a shrug. She returned to Beckett, who surprisingly didn't ask if this was a practical joke or even show any signs of skepticism. Instead his head cocked at an angle, as if mathematical equations sprinted through his mind.

"A time loop?" he asked.

"Is that the technical term?" Carter asked. "I never finished my degree."

"I don't think this is something you learn even with a master's," Mariana said.

"That's good. Now my parents can stop being disappointed," Carter said with a chuckle, his eyes still on Beckett. "We think you're the key to breaking this loop. We need to prove it to you." He turned to Mariana with a shrug. "I'm just not sure how."

"Science has taught me to keep an open mind," Beckett said, his voice steady and calm. "Let's say I believe you. Describe what you've seen when the facility explodes."

"We're in the observation room. The far-left corner breaks apart. The displays shows *Structural stability issue detected on strut QL89*. Thick cables snap in half, and from them," Carter said, his hands miming the situation, "an energy whips out. Like a lightning bolt, but green. The first time, it struck me. Last time, I got it to hit her."

"And after that," Mariana said, "I remembered."

From outside, footsteps and voices arrived before fading away
again. Beckett's phone buzzed, ringing until it finally timed
out. Mariana maintained a careful watch on Beckett, and next
to her, Carter tapped his foot to an anxious rhythm as they
awaited a response.

"Green energy?" Beckett finally asked.

"Yeah. Like a lime peel." Carter adjusted his posture, then
looked straight ahead. "I can see it now. It starts off zigging and
zagging, then it hangs to one side before it hits out and strikes
the floor about five feet from the console." He turned to Beckett, then tapped the side of his head. "Photographic memory.
Convenient for this sort of thing."

"You see? We need to shut it down," Mariana said. "Something is very wrong, and we're telling you how to find it."

"If you power down," Carter said, "you'll lose, what, a single test run?"

"Green energy," Beckett said again, though this time his posture shifted. Such a detail nudged him off his axis, defensive-
ness and disbelief evolving toward a clear curiosity.

What might get him to the finish line?

"You can call security to escort us," Mariana blurted out
as a new idea sparked. Carter turned with a sudden glare, but
she put her hand up. "I know that you'll never really be sure if
we're telling the truth. But if we surrender to security, I hope
this shows that we mean it."

"If tomorrow gets here, please don't fire me," Carter said.
"I spent all my money this time loop on gourmet takeout."

"Maybe give him at least a decent severance?" she asked.
Beckett laughed at Mariana's joke, and though their quips
weren't designed to be strategic, they seemed to dissolve the
tension. "Sorry about the scanner thingy earlier. I'm sure Re-
Live will fire me too."

As she spoke, she considered the last big stressor of her life
before time loops. She had, after all, written a resignation letter,

even talked about it with her mom. So if this worked, if they escaped this supposed time loop, would anything really change?

She'd still leave ReLive. She'd still move on to something else with her life.

Shay would still be dead.

Other than a very odd few days, nothing else would change. Her life would pop back in line, like a rubber band that snagged before snapping back. She'd probably never even bump into Carter again.

"I am," Beckett said slowly, "going to take you at your word." He moved methodically, first taking his phone from his pocket before holding it up to show them. "However, I'm going to call security now."

"What did you eat this morning?" Carter asked Beckett as they walked. Would he ever stop with the food questions? The founder raised an eyebrow as well, though Carter put up a hand. "In case we have to do this again, maybe those details can convince you. That's why I know her building has a dog at the lobby's front desk."

Mariana thought they'd jet off in a frantic sprint, throwing switches and turning dials until the accelerator's test cycle shut off section by section. But it turned out to be much easier. A pair of security guards did escort them, and Beckett did have to be involved, but only to authorize various shutdowns and power-offs across five different stations. And in doing so, Mariana wished she *had* brought Shay's photo after all. The things she'd seen before, even the tour that ReLive received during the loop, those were nothing compared to the guts of the Hawke Accelerator. The world's most advanced scientific investment lurched and moaned, its many moving parts and flowing electrons grinding to a halt.

"Reverse jinx?" Mariana asked, only half joking.

"Oh, good point. Okay, um, I was just curious about your breakfast."

"To be fair, he probably was really curious about your breakfast," Mariana said. "But also probably a good idea to prove ourselves. If—" she turned to Carter with a finger up "—if we need it."

"Eggs over easy. Home fries. Pork sausage." Beckett counted each item off with his fingers. "Oh, and a side of toast."

"Any details about it? Was the toast underdone?"

"Wheat toast, buttered. And the coffee was weak," Beckett said with a laugh.

"See, that part I care about. Weak coffee is the worst," Mariana said. Her voice shifted into a brightness that belied the fluttering within her gut. "Well, we *won't* need to use that. I'm sure of it. This is totally going to work." She nodded, first to herself, then at Carter and Beckett, even the security guards who trailed behind them. "It's gonna work. We'll be fine."

They walked, the facility's low-lying hum gradually fading, and by the time they got to the observation deck, it had all but gone quiet, the remaining noise a familiar din of any professional facility. Footsteps echoed against tile, notifications chimed, and the voice of the David AI gave different directions and suggestions across passing users, though none of that carried the emerging panic Mariana experienced the last time.

The relative peace seemed to unsettle Carter, who kept looking from side to side, the same sort of constant checking that turned their stroll into an observational anxiety. Beckett strode forward as well, his body language inscrutable.

Mariana considered the possibilities of the next few minutes. With things shutting down, they'd go into the next day, but what happened then? She supposed Beckett would want a detailed explanation of what went wrong, what led to the catastrophic failure—what even *was* the catastrophic failure?

Something had shaken the facility enough to cause wall panels to fall and power conduits to explode.

But at the same time, what if it all created another loop the next time the accelerator ran? Mariana's mind raced through possibilities, a list of what few variables she knew of. It all came down to the improbability of Carter getting struck with that specific cable at that specific charge in that specific spot.

How might they even replicate that?

An inner panic set in, a fluttering as Mariana's mind wandered from best-case scenario to worst.

"Two minutes," Carter said as they walked into the same observation room they'd visited before. Except nothing rattled. Screens remained intact, displays held yellow and green status data instead of bright red warnings.

No cables shot off sparks. And no beams of green energy whipped out.

"That corner," Mariana said, "that's where the cable broke out. The green electrical charge."

"That corner." Beckett rubbed his chin as he looked. "That makes sense."

The clock above the observation window continued, each second passing by. They watched in silence, the digits flipping as time slipped away.

Next to her, Beckett flexed his fingers, then tapped on his tablet. Carter's head swiveled, taking in the scene across the still room. Beneath them, the view from the observation room showed workers simply doing their jobs, no back-and-forth scurrying driven by panic.

Behind her back, Mariana crossed her fingers.

"Ten seconds," Carter whispered.

They waited, seemingly linked in attention. The slightest movement, the smallest breath, the quickest blink—it all came down to the idea that ten seconds might snap the world back into a normal timeline, one where Mariana might spend her time going back to mourning Shay and thinking of all the things she should have said in their last few conversations.

The remaining seconds passed by. Three, then two, then one. The threshold came and went.

Air left Mariana's lungs, an exhale so deep that she leaned forward, and next to her, Carter began laughing. They turned, and as if by instinct, they wrapped arms around each other, a spontaneous joy at their invisible escape. "It's over." Carter laughed, his head tilted up, his hair dangling past his cheeks. "Get the champagne. Real champagne, not sparkling wine."

Mariana had no idea what he meant but didn't bother asking. "I'm sorry I only had to do this twice," she said as they swayed back and forth, and when they looked at each other, for the first time she noticed Carter had deep brown eyes.

So much easier when world-ending panic didn't live in them.

"While you had to go through it over and—"

12

Carter opened his eyes. He was back in his bed. In his apartment. A little bit of a headache.

That was new.

And new was good.

He closed his eyes before opening them again and repeated several times. The last thing he remembered was joking about champagne. But now a headache stung, and he woke up somehow at home.

Maybe he wound up here the old-fashioned way. A celebratory drink turning into a celebratory bottle, which could have led to this moment, right here: in bed, with a headache, the morning sun shining. He thought back, searching for the last thing in his photographic memory and—

Mariana. How she'd looked at him. Joy and relief in her face, mouth open in a wide smile, and her eyes…they lingered.

His thoughts interrupted, a single noise triggering a full-body pause.

A bird chirp.

Then a pause.

Then a trill of three. Followed by a passing car. And a gust of wind, causing a tree branch to tap against his apartment window.

Carter didn't even wait for confirmation from other noises. He didn't check the news or look at messages or anything else that might have provided proof.

He just *knew*.

And that was enough to cause him to turn over in bed, face buried in his pillow. "No, no, no," he growled as the list of noises and events progressively checked off.

His eyes squeezed shut, forcing a recall via his photographic memory now that the morning haze had shaken off. They had stopped it. Hawke was shut down. Beckett had been *right there*.

They'd even had a celebratory hug.

If that didn't work, what possibly could? He groaned, a low, extended moan straight into his pillow before rolling over.

Screw it, he thought.

Carter made a decision right then and there that he'd do the *opposite* of the responsible, constructive thing. Screw this time loop. Screw solutions, screw time itself.

He was going to blow his life savings on the best restaurants in the world over the next four days. Then he'd consider disappearing into the woods on the longest hike ever, or maybe a trail run, or both, like he did as a teen. His two paths of solitude— gourmet food and movement in the isolation of nature—offered a respite worth taking.

Because really, did anything even matter?

13

Mariana's eyes snapped open, and she blinked quickly, senses sharpening into the moment before she rolled over. The movement seemed to throw off Maggie, who trilled from the floor before standing up on her hind legs, her long fur and longer whiskers poking up over the edge of the bed. Mariana lay still, gauging everything with her senses.

Around her, darkness covered the room, the artificial tinting of the windows only allowing a fraction of the natural light through. She stretched in bed, limbs reaching while she craned her neck to look at the clock.

Still minutes before she usually woke up.

What happened yesterday? She remembered Beckett and the power-down. The deadline had passed.

She had hugged Carter.

No. They had held each other.

And he had suggested champagne.

After that, it was a blur. Or maybe a blank space. Did they have too much champagne? It'd been a long time since she'd drunk to the point of turning hazy, probably not since an ill-advised college excursion with Shay and some of her tennis teammates.

But still, escaping a world-ending time loop felt like a reason to celebrate.

"Well," she said to Maggie, patting the lumped blankets next to her. "What day is it?" Maggie responded by jumping into the spot, her purring immediately kicking in.

Mariana weighed her options, her day—really, her whole life—in a strange limbo, the dim morning filled with both possibilities and dread. Dare she shake it off, find out the truth? There was the morning news, the US Open, even just looking at her daily calendar.

She supposed it didn't matter which one she picked. Only one way to find out.

She didn't roll out of bed, instead turning to take in the low light of her studio apartment. "System, open windows and start one cup of coffee, black," she said, fingers scratching Maggie's little white chin. In turn, the cat closed her eyes, pulling in the black stripes across her face. From across the studio, natural light began to brighten the ceiling, the tinted windows gradually returning to their normal daytime clarity. On the counter, water began to steam, the churning and bubbling of in-process coffee.

Though still in bed, Mariana's mind felt fully activated, synapses firing like she'd already had her morning cup of coffee. Her pulse quickened as words formed, ready to enter the world and determine the reality in which she existed.

"And turn on the US Open."

She continued staring at her ceiling when the glow from the wall display blended with the natural daylight. The volume gradually came to life, silence fading to the expected scuffs and thumps of a Grand Slam tennis match. Her eyes stayed locked on the blank space above, and though she could turn her head and look to see who was playing, she waited.

"Out!" yelled the umpire, soon followed by crowd applause.

"The unthinkable has happened," the commentator said

above the crowd's roar. "And with that, Onyebuchi Hudson is on the verge of one of the biggest upsets in Open history."

Onyebuchi Hudson.

It didn't work.

Nothing worked.

And Maggie probably didn't even remember that they'd done this dance not that long ago.

A rolling nausea arrived, wave after wave of an uncertainty that eclipsed *everything*. She moved in autopilot, instinctive motions to feed Maggie and take sips of coffee. She looked around her space: at Maggie quietly eating cat food, at the tennis tournament broadcast on her wall, at the tablets on her table. A few days ago, the idea of a time loop created a curiosity, a puzzle to be solved, a task too surreal and too strange to grasp the scope of what was happening.

Today, though, reality sank in. Did it really only take Carter a few loops of awareness to have despair creep through?

Mariana's palms planted on the counter, the cold stone gradually warming from her touch. She took in a breath, then two, then held it, as if pausing the act of respiration might claw back some control over the world. Her thoughts turned, an instinct activating in the face of catastrophe. What was happening, what were the options, what could she *do* about it? She'd first recognized this in herself around seven, when a noise down the hall interrupted her reading by flashlight. Quiet, controlled sobs came through when she silently opened her door, and a day later, she discovered the reason: her mom had lost her job, and the impending pressure of being an unemployed single mom with little support, well, it needed to vent somehow.

That morning during breakfast, she'd asked her mom, "Can I help?"

And the question stuck, evolving once she learned more about scientific method and analytical problem-solving. It was intrinsic to who she was, no matter how many times Shay joked about it.

Fact: She was still in the time loop.

Hypothesis: Since powering down the accelerator hadn't worked, they'd have to discover the root-cause variable.

Experiment: Well...

For that part, nothing came to mind. Or everything, depending on the framing. The last time loop represented a call to adventure, like a peek into a surprise life where the crushing weight of her recent life got put on hold. Now? Quitting ReLive didn't matter. Teaching tennis on a cruise ship didn't matter.

What happened to Shay, even that didn't matter. Nothing did, unless they escaped this.

An experiment to do that, though? She tried considering the variables: her, Carter, Beckett. But the biggest was the most guarded, most secret, most advanced technology on the planet, and understanding just how to affect that in a meaningful way...

Her neuroscience background wouldn't exactly help that.

Mariana squinted at the purring fluff ball lying in a small patch of sun. Maggie noticed her and reached one paw up in a stretch before closing her eyes, the quiet simplicity of the morning enough to satisfy the little creature.

Maybe Maggie had it right: keep it simple. But not by lying in a patch of sun. No, Mariana needed to get back to the only person that understood this circumstance.

She needed to find Carter.

Thoughts formulated in her mind, options and plans falling into place while she had her usual morning breakfast shake. If shutting down the accelerator didn't work, then what might? And would they need Beckett? Or someone else? Was there a chance that Beckett had retained any memory of the last loop?

The only certainty was Carter. But how to find him? He'd come over to her place, but she didn't have his address.

At least she could call him, though. Because Shay was right, she *did* remember details like that. Her brain loved numbers, after all.

Mariana picked up her phone, then typed in Carter's contact details. It pinged, a pensive beeping trying to locate him, but he wasn't answering.

Had he given up? Or maybe he was already on his way to Hawke? Either way, he knew how to get in touch with her, but she needed to know where to start, *how* to start.

And that meant she needed his eidetic memory. There was work to do, and if he wasn't picking up calls, then she'd just have to find him other ways.

As she went through her morning routine, she cross-referenced records and data, digging up what appeared to be Carter's address. A double, then triple check confirmed her hunch, and determination fueled her steps as she got dressed and ready to dig her—no, them—out of this hole. Just to be sure, a quick look at her messages showed her drafted resignation letter and the excited invitation to Hawke, to which she jotted a short reply about not feeling well today.

In a way, that was true.

Mariana set out, except halfway to the door, she stopped and turned. If this Monday was going to repeat indefinitely, then Buddy Ed's treat would get dropped whenever things restarted.

And until she figured out the cause and effect of her actions, she was going to get B.E. his piece of bread.

Every time.

14

Scalding cups of coffee seared Mariana's palms, and as they did, she wondered how science could create the Hawke Accelerator yet no disposable heat-safe coffee cups existed. "Carter?" she asked through the door, though no response came on this Monday morning. Coffees still in hand, she kicked the door several times, light enough to sound close to knocking but rough enough that the motion still flung drips of too-hot coffee over the spout of each cup. "Damn it," she said to herself before calling out again. "Carter? It's Mariana. Come on, you can't just disappear on me after—"

The door slid open, revealing someone who looked close to the Carter she'd known for a few days. Considering everything had reset, appearing hungover, disheveled, or with a sudden five-o'clock shadow seemed way out of character, at least until Mariana reminded herself that she'd only known him as a semi-coworker. Here, everything from his expression to his posture withdrew, like the events of the last loop had broken something inside of him and the rest struggled to stay upright.

Good thing she'd brought coffee.

"How'd you find me?" he said, looking behind her. "What time is it?"

"Weren't you the one asking Beckett questions about his breakfast just in case? So much for reverse-jinxing it. I called you."

"Oh. I was busy eating," he said, stepping back and motioning her in. "I'm tired of this. So I thought, screw it." She walked into the dimly lit apartment, a space slightly bigger than her own studio but with partitioned rooms and aged cabinets. "Close your eyes," he said before drawing back a curtain, the lack of AI system interface to adjust dimming on smart-glass windows showing the different economic worlds between a lead scientist and a technician.

Light flooded the space, and only then did Mariana see what Carter had truly done this morning. On the small square folding table sat four—no, five—food containers, one empty one with the lid peeled back and the others cracked open. Mariana took in a breath and the mix of smells proved more confusing than anything else. Perhaps if she cared on Carter's level, she'd be able to differentiate the different aromas, but she had more important things to do.

"Did you order five breakfasts?" she asked, pointing at the different containers.

"It's my new thing. Screw this time loop, I'm eating expensive takeout. It's four breakfasts, actually. And a lunch sandwich. Which I ate first," Carter said, sitting down in front of his food. "Want something? I got enough to share."

"Yeah. I'd like a way to get out of this time loop so I can see who wins the US Open."

"I don't know about you, but I'm out of ideas on that." He flipped the lid of the nearest container open, revealing what looked like biscuits with gravy poured all over, enough that some spilled over to the hash browns and sausages lying next to it.

"Carter, this stuff will kill you."

"Hey," he said, stabbing at the biscuit with a fork, "maybe that's the way out."

This sudden apathy felt so out of place compared to the determination and desperation from the last loop. Here, all he wanted to do was eat until his stomach exploded. The hope that lurked beneath the quips and smirks disappeared, leaving only a very raw and very burdensome wound.

"You know," he said through a bite, "if my bank account resets each time, then maybe my cholesterol does too. I could spend an entire loop eating steaks for every meal and never have to worry about heart disease."

"You're really bright-siding this, aren't you?"

"Why not?" Carter laughed, though his expression suddenly fell. "I mean, if shutting it down doesn't work, what else could possibly undo this? Nothing exploded. Nothing zapped us again. Nothing went boom. We're stuck, done deal. Eat all the food you like."

Shay was supposed to be gone for two weeks in the desert, and in the days following her missed return, Mariana's own frenetic pragmatism mirrored the Carter she'd first met. And after days turned to weeks with no word and no evidence, it gave way to an unsettling acceptance, a silent understanding that something very bad had happened.

Perhaps that was what Carter felt in his own way.

"Okay, look," she said, her mind churning with ways to answer him. Shutting off the power had been the most logical choice, a way to control the root cause. Without that? "Damn it," she let out, more questions coming to mind, but none of them felt like the right ones. "I study the brain. I have no idea how any of this accelerator stuff works."

"You see?" Carter asked. He gestured to a chair, then pointed to the mountain of gravy over biscuits and sausage. "We're screwed. Have a bite."

"I'm a vegetarian."

"I have options," he said with a grin, snapping open a different container. "Spinach and mushroom quiche. Delicious."

"I have coffee. I'm good." Mariana raised her cup, then took a sip of the now-bearable liquid. "And one is for you."

"Ah." He took the cup and drank, though his mouth pursed unexpectedly. "Thank you."

"What?"

"I'm actually more of a tea drinker. Less intense than coffee." He shrugged, though he still took another sip. "But hey, I prefer tea, and you're a vegetarian. See? Food brings us all together. Try it."

"I'm not hungry. I had my shake."

"Am I going to have to explain *sustenance versus eating* again?" Carter looked up, one eyebrow raised and his mouth curled upward.

"Okay. I'll eat," she said, finally sitting down. "But we're gonna brainstorm and put that eidetic memory to use. Let's start from the beginning. Again."

Ten minutes passed, and surprisingly, Carter *wasn't* eating the whole time. Instead, he answered each of her questions with detailed explanations courtesy of his brain's unique retention. "That spot in the observation room. The first time, I was there, and the green energy hit me. So I went back for several loops just to make sure it hit the same spot every time. Didn't let it hit me, but I observed from different angles." He pointed to his stack of notebooks on his corner desk. "Wrote it down in one of those. Writing didn't carry over, of course. But I can see the spot."

"Okay. That energy is clearly something. Why else would Beckett note it? It somehow causes structural damage, right? The warning message said a strut had failed. Maybe we can get access to schematics?"

"Oh!" he said, springing up. Carter dashed over to the other side of the room, then returned a thin device in his hand. "David, you awake?"

"Hello, Carter. Are you skipping work today?" David asked, a slight irritation in his synthetic voice.

"You could say I'm working from home."

"Is he always this way?" Mariana whispered. "I shut mine off on the tour."

"Employees get a different version than visitors. You get a tour guide. He acts like an assistant for us. The attitude emerges the longer you work with him. I think he's programmed that way. David," he said, "do you have facility schematics available?"

"Not here. I'd have to download them directly first."

"But you can help with that?" he asked, finally taking a bite of something Mariana didn't recognize.

"I'm always helpful," the AI said. Carter nodded, then clicked the device off.

"He's right," Carter said after swallowing a bite, "he is helpful. I hacked stuff as a kid when my parents forced me into coding class. My form of tween rebellion when they wouldn't let me try out for junior cooking challenges. But with David, I was able to put some of that to use at Hawke. Like closing off the elevators from public access. I did the illegal part. Not sure if David goes for that. But who knows, maybe he's got a rebellious streak."

"We can work with that." Mariana took a smaller, more polite bite of her vegetable quiche. "So, get schematics. What else could we use? Test data? Power levels? There was an alert about structural integrity. That might be a variable too, and—"

"Whoa, whoa, whoa." Carter put his hands up, palms out to stop her. "I've got a photographic memory and an AI I can convince to crunch some numbers for us. What I *can't* do is actually bring the things through from loop to loop. That's why I write things down, it sticks in my brain better. We gotta slow down, focus on one thing at a time. I'm a college dropout with two years of quantum theory. It's not like I have Beckett's insight."

"If only we could pick his brain," Mariana said. "How do we do that?"

Carter's fork dropped against his table as his hands clapped. "Oh my god. It's so obvious." He raised a hand, then did a quick gesture, like a lightning strike to his temple. "Push him into the green beam."

Mariana silently kicked herself for not thinking this up. Point to Carter.

"If we can get Beckett into the loop with us, we'd stand a much better chance, right?"

"He's gotta know more than you or me," Mariana said.

"And he can probably afford the best restaurants around," Carter said. "He doesn't get to Hawke for a few days. What do we do until then?"

Three days to go. And no rules.

How would they even fill the time?

Mariana considered the different options as she looked at Carter. When she first met him, he'd been determined, desperate. As the accelerator shut down in the last loop, relief colored his face, shifted his posture. And when she'd arrived here, he'd been on the verge of giving up.

It'd been a while since she'd taken basic psychology, but she recognized the various stages of grief when she saw them.

"Here's an idea. I'll go to Hawke, tell them I'm feeling better and didn't want to miss anything." She took her final bite of quiche—which, to Carter's credit, was better than a basic breakfast shake. "Try to do some digging. But you," she said, with a soft smile, "you should relax for a few days. I think you've earned a break."

15

A break for Carter, apparently, didn't involve taking naps or going to the beach. Instead, Mariana arrived back at Carter's following a full Monday at Hawke to find him in front of the kitchen stove, the counters lined with chopped vegetables, jars of spices, and a bunch of cooking tools that did...something. She wasn't sure. But Carter's clear exuberance felt infectious, despite Mariana not understanding quite what was going on.

"Can you help me for a sec?" he asked after catching her gawk. "Just keep an eye on that pot. Let me know when the water boils. I'm multitasking."

Multitasking in the kitchen was a bit more than she'd ever cared to do. She knew enough of the basics, of course. Surviving to adulthood kind of required that, though she was much more of a whatever-was-easiest person. *Sustenance*, as Carter might say, and she definitely was the type of person who could eat the same thing for days at a time if needed.

But watching a pot boil? That was within her scope. She nodded, Carter whirling around her grabbing produce and grinding herbs, but her eyes focused on the stovetop, a ReLive-fueled early memory of Shay triggering in absolute clarity.

Still watching a pot boil. But unlike the present with Carter, this moment was outside.

That night, most of the UC Davis tennis team opted to stay inside the bus, a standard ground coach for the long highway journey instead of the air-buses that started to be used around then. Richer schools with bigger sports programs might have invested in that, but they stuck with a five-hour drive capable of stranding them in the middle of nowhere. The blown battery meant a complete loss of power—no broadcasts or data on window screens, no lights, no satellite data signal, but at least it was warm. And it was one way to make the team's first road trip of Mariana's first year memorable.

No position felt comfortable, no matter how she twisted her legs or neck on the seat, and she stepped outside for fresh desert air, the near-black of Highway 5's long, empty stretches around her while stars poked through above. Behind her, clicks and beeps came from the open engine compartment at the base of the bus, the coach driver talking with someone on the emergency support line about getting some assistance.

And though she didn't see it at first, her eyes adjusted to the form of a teammate kneeling down, tinny metallic sounds coming her way. The sight became clear, and Mariana recognized the long braids of a fellow first-year, someone she'd barely spoken to in their initial few weeks with the team.

"Hey," Mariana said, tracking Shay as she crouched down. "You all right?"

"Not really," she said, tiny clinks and clanks coming through. "But I will be."

"Do you need help with something?"

"The driver said I could use the emergency supplies in the back." She stood up, then pointed to a square-shaped silhouette at her feet. "There's a propane camping stove. We might be here a few hours. I don't know about you, but I'm hungry and snack bars are not going to cut it." She pulled something out of her bag, a cup-shaped shadow that rattled as she shook it. "I was saving this for the hotel, but why not here?"

It took several seconds for Mariana to recognize what she held. "Is that ramen noodles?"

"Sure. You can make them anywhere," Shay gestured to the desert-night horizon around them. "Including the middle of nowhere. Just gotta boil some water. I always took ramen when my dad took me camping." She gestured around them. "Life experiences, am I right?"

Mariana knew enough about cooking by that point in her life to do some basics, though she'd grown to rely on anything that hit the overlap between cheap, healthy, and quick. But actually setting up a makeshift stove?

"You hungry? Wanna share?" Shay asked, metal clicking as she snapped things into place. She filled up a small metal kettle from her water bottle and brought the stove to life, a flame flickering out of nowhere. "Time's gonna pass anyway, right? Might as well enjoy it."

And Shay had been right. Time did march along as the team awaited the repair truck. They sat on two adjacent rocks, placed perfectly like jagged and very uncomfortable stools, passing the instant ramen bowl back and forth for an hour while discovering that between tennis, scientific pursuits, and single parents, they had much more in common than they thought.

Except for the fact that Shay adored cats.

Mariana blinked, returning to Carter's small kitchen, bubbles starting to form and elevate within the heating water. She saw it as water vapor forming due to extreme heat, the air rising and escaping—chemistry and physics, all in one metal pot. But here, Carter seemed more like he was celebrating as he whirled around, the tension of their strange existence simply evaporated, his soft voice singing under his breath. The slow melody came, enough bits about motion sickness and rolling windows down that Mariana recognized the words as one of those ever-present songs that came out in the decades before she was born and simply *existed* now. She waited a minute for any sort of pause in the song to say something, but Carter kept repeating it. Even when she dumped information about her day's research on him and all the data she downloaded into his employee David unit, he simply said, "Mmm-hmm," and kept going. His eidetic memory didn't help when all of his focus was on sautéing vegetables and checking simmer levels and some other…cooking stuff.

"It's boiling," she said, her mind returning to one of Beckett's research papers on temporal causality.

"Awesome. Great timing," he said, grabbing something off a cutting board and tossing it in the pot.

"I've heard I excel at following directions," Mariana said, a joke that only she and Shay would get. "You need anything else?"

"Yes. I absolutely need you here. It's super important. Like, life-changing," he said, sliding past her with a tray of something in his hand before glancing at the oven.

Mariana sighed as she glanced back at the stacked tablets in the other room. "I don't think *life-changing* applies in our circumstances."

"Nah. See, science is science, but cooking," he said, turning back to his jars of herbs, "cooking is magic." He moved quickly, measuring out various things before checking a pan and flipping salmon fillets in it and unleashing a range of aromas. "Don't worry, I know you're vegetarian." He tapped the handle of a large covered pot. "That's lentil soup for you. If you like it, I'll show you the recipe."

"How are you doing this?" she asked as he continued to multitask between chopping vegetables and dropping herbs over the pot.

"Photographic memory. I just see something and in my head—it's different from *you just thought of something.* I see images, all of the details. Recipes are like loading a list in my head. You can practice it, you know," he said, checking the time. "You don't need the brain for it. I've heard of people just learning to memorize images of, like, an individual message or number." He took a sliver of raw carrot and popped it into his mouth, then dumped the cutting board's veggies into the pot and poured a cup of broth over it. "Best thing about this time loop is I've cooked so much since I realized everything just resets. The best ingredients, new recipes. It's like a free culinary academy with just myself. One of these loops, I'm going to nail this vegetable Wellington recipe I found. Three types of mushrooms. I mean, come on. But it keeps coming out soggy."

"I thought you said this was life-changing. This—" she pointed at the pan "—just looks like an exothermic reaction. That happens to smell good."

"Well, there's that part of it." He clapped the tongs in front of her, then opened the oven to reach in. "Baked falafels. Try it. Blow on it first. I added some extra spice to it."

Steam escaped as Mariana took a small bite into the ball, the crispy exterior giving way to a softer filling. "It's tasty."

"Just tasty? Like, what about the combination of textures?"

"It's..." Mariana slowed down the pace of her chewing, letting the individual flavors sit. But nothing distinguished itself other than the simple fact that it was enjoyable. "It's just...good?"

"Good?"

"Good. Not *life-changing*, but *good*."

Carter took one off the tray and bit half of it apart, chewing with a thoughtful look on his face until he held it up. "At the end. You get a slow burn?"

Which, now that she thought of it, she did. "Yeah. Surprising."

"A hint of cayenne. Slow down enough, and you might discover something in each bite. See," he said, setting the tongs down and wiping his hands on the hanging towel, "you put down your work for five minutes. I haven't seen you do that since we met. You even work while watching tennis. Or drink-ing coffee. So that—" he flashed all five fingers on one hand "—is life-changing. Time's gonna pass, but if you slow down a little, you might enjoy it. That's what eating is all about."

Did being in a time loop somehow grant Carter the ability to peer into her memory, to steal that line from Shay? Mari-ana really, really wanted to roll her eyes at the sight in front of her, from Carter's dopey grin to the too-expensive grocer-ies sitting on the counter to the ridiculous amount of pots and pans on the stove.

Their definition of *life-changing* definitely differed. A single burst of flavor was nothing more than a moment of enjoyable taste, a flutter in her busy day. He clearly saw it as something monumental and experiential, and though she didn't think she'd ever quite get that, she supposed that in this sliver of time, he got her to understand differently.

That, in itself, was sometimes remarkable enough.

"Hey." He pointed. "I see it. You're smiling. It worked."

It took Carter pointing it out for Mariana to realize that she had a dopey grin as well. In fact, the more she watched Carter, the wider it pushed, and an even stranger thing happened: *weirdo shit*, as Shay would say.

Her entire posture relaxed. And with that epiphany, she wondered if she'd judged everything about Carter completely wrong.

"Yeah," she finally said. "Five minutes changed my life."

16

Mariana approached the front doors of the Hawke facility, the third successive Thursday that she arrived with a plan of some sort. The first time, her plan was to simply bring a photo of her best friend on the tour. Last time, she and Carter had dabbled in espionage, moving swiftly in forms of disguise to locate Beckett and shut down the accelerator.

This time around landed halfway between those ideas. No spylike hijinks would be needed, at least they hoped. Instead, she set her sights on a simple conversation that hinged on the merits of science and logic in the face of the illogical.

The first steps into the facility remained similar, walking in stride with her crew from the ReLive project. Once they passed the main lobby, she spotted Carter and turned to her colleagues. "I gotta use the bathroom. I'll catch up," she said, stepping off with a polite acknowledgment from the others, the large glass clock on the wall displaying 9:42 a.m.

They walked with purpose, Carter in his technician overalls and Mariana dressed for a corporate presentation in her gray coat and matching slacks. Carter had a notebook in his hand while his mobile David interface offered a surprising amount of help accessing Hawke's facility-management system. Status displays and mechanism controls glowed, David offering comments like "I don't believe this elevator needs a diagnostic right now. Are you sure?" and "Locking these doors might annoy the janitorial staff," but processing the requests anyway.

Mariana's phone buzzed, the ReLive team trying to pull her back to her normal schedule. But she ignored it, focusing on the singular act of funneling Beckett's path. Carter's tricks worked before, both times. This time, however, they moved to get to Beckett right when he arrived at the facility.

"He's going to come in through the back, the executive entrance," Carter said, pointing at the glowing map. "Last time, he went this way," he said as his finger traced along the image, "and there's a security checkpoint here. So we'll block him here, then get him right when he comes by." He turned to face her. "You have your speech ready?"

Mariana sucked in a breath, bullet points and outlines running through her mind. In theory, this was fine. In practice, though...

This would be a little different from giving a planned presentation with visual aids to a group of distracted investors.

"You remember what he had for breakfast?" she asked. "That might be a good icebreaker."

"Of course," Carter said, lips turned in a smirk that was becoming all too familiar. "It's like, the one thing I'm really good at talking about."

They waited, standing next to a large mural of the Bay Area as it had looked a century earlier while Hawke employees passed by, oblivious to the situation at hand. Mariana studied the painting, the way the city looked the same but devolved by several stages. Buildings stood shorter, pathways lacked density, and the whole thing seemed simpler, a world built for individual vehicles rather than public transport up and down the peninsula. She traced the different regions, squinting at the area north of the Golden Gate where she grew up, at least until Carter nudged her.

There he was.

"Dr. Beckett?" Mariana called out. He stopped, looking at them, and though they recognized him, his face remained blank. She scanned for security, anyone that might be concerned at their sudden interest but *looked* like they belonged at Hawke.

Maybe that was enough.

Behind her back, her fingers crossed right before she spoke up in a firm, professional, and very nonthreatening tone. "I know you're busy this morning, but can we get five minutes of your time? I'm with the ReLive team."

"I'm on a tight schedule, but I'll be talking with you later—"

"Not five minutes," Carter said, shaking his head. "One minute. Thirty seconds?"

Carter's abruptness prompted a sideways glance, and though Mariana recognized his urgency, she cursed Carter's lack of tact.

"It's really important. We just need you to listen to something," she said.

"We're going to tell you something that seems really weird at first," Carter started back up, this time at a smoother, calmer pace.

"But trust us," Mariana said with a nod. "We can prove it. It will change everything if we can just get a moment."

Beckett's brow furrowed, lips forming a thin line as he paused. Then a single eyebrow rose. "Cryptic," Beckett said after a breath, "but I'm listening."

Mariana and Carter turned to each other, and she saw it: his face carried the same mix of anxiety and hope bubbling in her. "We," she started, trying to take the best of what had worked last time, "are in a time loop. Associated with the test cycle at Hawke. It repeats every four days, and today, at…"

"At 12:42 p.m.," Carter said, holding up the page in his notebook.

"At 12:42 p.m., it all ends. This place," she said gesturing around them, "explodes. And we'll prove it. Last time, we asked you what you'd had for breakfast. You had..." Mariana looked at Carter.

"Eggs over easy. Home fries. Pork sausage," he said. "And toast."

"You said the coffee was weak," she said with a laugh. "That part I can appreciate."

The older man darted his eyes between the two, a pause long enough to show that something had cranked in his mind, though Mariana failed to read if that was progress or panic. "You're hitting me with a lot of information right now," Beckett said.

"Oh," Carter said, "and an electrical beam of green energy. In the observation room. That convinced you last time."

"That's right. And you shut everything down. We counted down the seconds together, and it just...passed. And then it started back up." Mariana decided *not* to include the part about Carter melting down and buying five breakfasts upon restarting the loop.

"So that didn't work. We're—" Carter shrugged as he inhaled "—trying something different this time."

Mariana tensed as Beckett turned halfway, seemingly prepared to leave or at least call for security. His feet scuffed the floor, teeth digging into his bottom lip, then his eyes scanned all around, and a wry grin broke on his face. "Either this is a practical joke, or you're really stuck. But either way, I love a good challenge." He pointed down the hall before stepping out. "Let's go to a conference room."

Over the next hour, Mariana and Carter went over the events of the loop in detail, Beckett interrupting only to either ask questions or cancel upcoming meetings. "So," Carter finally asked, "do you think you know what's happening?"

"Well, from a science perspective?" Beckett laughed, running a hand through his hair. "Not really. But my intuition says there's a logic to it. We just need to figure it out. If shutting it down didn't work, then the trick might be to make sure the test cycle completes."

Mariana considered her next words carefully. It wasn't every day that you asked someone to willingly electrocute themselves. "We had an idea."

"Everything starts with an idea," Beckett said.

"Look, we're not smart enough to tackle this," Carter said. "I mean, maybe she is. But I'm not. I failed out of my degree. So if you're around to brainstorm with us through the loops, I think we stand a much better chance."

"And to get you into the loop, we'll need you to get struck by that green energy." Mariana studied Beckett's face, though it remained frozen. Which hopefully meant he was considering the proposal instead of figuring out a polite way to exit the conference room. "We think."

"If it makes you feel any better," Carter said with a shrug, "I don't remember it hurting that much."

Beckett's face finally broke, turning to deep creases and squinting eyes. "*Green energy*," he said slowly. "CTD wave."

So that's what it was. At least they had a name for it, though *green energy* was certainly easier.

"Think of it this way," Mariana said. "If there's any doubt in your mind, the fact that we're asking you to stand in a very specific spot at a very specific time has to mean something, right?"

"And look at us—" Carter gestured to the two of them "—do we look like the kind of people who could sabotage this place on our own?"

"To be fair, I thought he was an ecoterrorist when I first met him," Mariana said.

"Wait, you did?" Carter asked, eyes wide.

The question prompted a laugh from Beckett, a chuckle that became infectious to both Mariana and Carter, perhaps the sheer ridiculousness of the situation sinking in. "All right. Let's say I do that. Then what? On Monday, I was in DC for a conference. I didn't get here until this morning."

"You have to start thinking differently," Mariana said. "Nothing you do will have any consequences until this breaks."

"This is why I ordered five breakfasts this morning," Carter said with a grin. Mariana sent over a shocked look, which he shrugged off. "I know I did it on Monday, but it's the end of the loop."

"I still wouldn't recommend that. If this works, then you'll suddenly need to see a cardiologist," Mariana reminded him, shaking her head. "But for now, it means you can leave your conference."

"Then, meet up with us. You won't need to check out or pack. Just get on the first flight out and go."

Beckett pulled out a tablet, then tapped the screen. "Looks like most early flights get to San Francisco by ten. This is what I'm thinking." Mariana and Carter leaned in, the momentum of ideas pulling at both of them. "You're asking me to stand in a precise location in a highly secured room at a very specific moment. And you claim that things will be falling apart around us. If all of this happens like you say it will, it's pretty hard to refute. So if things track like you claim, well—" he shook his head, with a cheeky smile that projected that his curiosity carried a certain giddiness to it "—I'll see you Monday morning when I get into town."

For the past hour, Beckett toured the facility with Mariana and Carter, checking safety and stability data at various stations and junctions. And on cue, things started going wrong—what specifically, Mariana wasn't sure, but Carter wrote in his note-book about things Beckett listed regarding power fluctuations and hardware failures. All that led to the observation room, a checklist of happenings on the road to cumulative disaster.

Carter knelt down to inspect before looking up at the cor-ner where green lightning would eventually emerge and lash out. "Yeah." Another rumble struck, this time enough to rattle the space around them. From across the room, maintenance monitors changed their indicators from standard-status screens into first-tier warnings, and yellow lights above them started to flash.

"You've certainly provided evidence to back up your claims," Beckett said, curiosity lingering in his eyes as he looked around. "Good science. A time loop. Fascinating. Not what I expected out of this."

"What were you expect—" Mariana started before sparks flew from a corner display. The flash caused Beckett to jolt back, though Carter didn't even move. How many times had he seen that by now?

"Monday morning," Beckett said. "My favorite local restau-rant is the Blue Light, in the Financial District. A rooftop café. We'll meet there."

"As long as they serve good coffee." Though Mariana knew the next burst was coming, the violence of the shattered metal paneling and the sudden blast of green energy still startled her. She inhaled quickly, this whole experience so different stand-ing several feet away. A weight landed on her shoulder, and she turned to see Carter's hand there.

"I'd say it gets easier but—" one side of his mouth turned up "—not really. It's pretty hard-core every time."

Beckett exhaled, and at his sides, his fingers flexed. Though he remained planted in the exact spot determined by Carter, he angled his neck upward, now drawn by the visible whip of green energy. His eyes widened, and his posture shifted. Seconds ago, he'd said that the shattering room was evidence. But now, his mouth opened and his eyes focused with a belief that hadn't existed earlier. "If this doesn't work—" he started.

"Don't say that," Mariana interjected, mind suddenly filled with questions about jinxes and reverse-jinxes.

"No, this is important. If this doesn't work, you'll need data." Beckett held a hand out. "Give me your notebook."

A large boom rattled the room, kicking off the sequence of shattered glass and flying sparks within and around the space. Carter steadied himself despite the burst of debris and handed his notebook over to Beckett. The old scientist looked down at his feet, then flipped to a blank page. "Remember this," he said, writing furiously while keeping his feet planted in the proper spot. "Access codes to my data archive. Just in case." He thrust it back at Carter, who took it and stared at the drying ink. "Your photographic memory. You'll need this. If this doesn't work."

"And if this does work?" Carter asked. "And we see you at the café?"

"Well, there's classified material there, so I'll make sure to change my password before I book my—"

Before he could finish, the green-energy beam burst out. The last time Mariana had witnessed this, the whole thing played out in slow motion, like her mind tried to catch up to the unfolding chaos. But here, everything seemed to go in double time, the beam connecting first with Beckett's feet before pulling back and zapping him in the chest. His arms stretched out in reflex, a burst of steam billowing up to encompass him while the energy danced all around him.

Mariana gasped at the sight of green and white snaking all over a human form. Without thinking, her hand reached out. She grabbed Carter's, the heat of his palm pressing against hers. Their fingers intertwined, and their eyes met, a short smile on his lips before he spoke. "See you on the other side," he said, squeezing her hand.

And just before everything went white, she nodded and squeezed back.

17

Mariana's eyes opened, a determination to her focus that didn't exist before. She flexed her fingers, the invisible weight of Carter's hand still touching her senses. Moments before, they'd stood in the Hawke observation room on the cusp of...

Well, something. Something new and different, possibly a way out. Or at least the start of it.

Her mind moved with a clarity despite the early morning. Was this her brain adapting to the nature of time loops? She angled to see the clock, and as expected, it showed six minutes before her normal wake-up time.

Of course, Maggie had her part to play, and the little cat jumped up on the bed, completely unaware that they'd done this dance before. "Morning," she said to the cat. "Let me guess. You're hungry."

Maggie meowed an affirmative, and Mariana got on her feet. "System, open windows and start one cup of coffee, black. And turn on the US Open." The coffee was necessary, but the US Open? Even though she knew how the story ended for Song and Hudson, seeing the end of the match provided a strange comfort, a foundation to a world that offered equal parts drone and surprise.

Her alarm chimed to start the day, and instead of dealing with the usual logistics of messages and resignation letters, Mariana moved like only minutes had passed since the observation room.

Which, she supposed, was true. Her body reacted with the vigor of a somewhat-restful sleep, but how she got from that point A to this point B, well, a giant claw might as well have picked her up and dropped her here.

Her phone buzzed, and though she hadn't added Carter as a contact yet, she recognized the number. "Good morning," she said, answering the line.

"Are you having one of those terrible breakfast shakes yet?"

"Not yet. Coffee first. Have you ordered something you can't afford yet?"

"Just about to. Apparently my loop starts about thirty minutes before yours. We should experiment with a wake-up call to get you up earlier sometime," he said with a laugh.

Mariana matched it, though a second later, the axis of her world tilted. Not enough to push her off balance, but Carter's use of the word *sometime* triggered a different path for them, and he might not have even noticed it.

Because *sometime* meant that he assumed they'd be here again. And again. And again.

Reverse jinx indeed.

Mariana took a sip of her newly brewed coffee, then looked at the cat rubbing against her ankles. "Maybe. Sometime," she said, the words soft before she returned to normal volume. "But I gotta feed this cat first. See you at the Blue Light at ten? Maybe it's actually good."

"Ha," Carter said with an audible scoff. "I've already looked up the menu."

She made a mental checklist of the morning ahead, starting off with bringing a treat to Buddy Ed before hopefully rendezvousing with the one mind capable of solving the time loop.

★ ★ ★

Of course, Carter was already at the rooftop café by the time Mariana arrived, though it took a moment to recognize him. Rather than his usual technician's outfit, Carter dressed like a normal person, dark pants and a loose-fitting shirt with big sunglasses reflecting the morning light. "Pacing myself," he said, holding up a small plate with half a slice of pie on it. "I really should get my cholesterol tested to see if it resets. Bank accounts do, why not our bodies?"

Carter's logic made sense, though it wasn't like randomized controlled studies on time loops existed, nor did it really matter since cholesterol and other health checks wouldn't get them out of this mess. She supposed, though, they should take whatever got them through the repetition. For Carter, that meant pie for breakfast. Cherry, from the looks of it.

For Mariana? She hadn't quite figured that out yet, though she did dash in and let herself enjoy the smell of the café's ground coffee beans while she ordered. By the time she came back to the table, he'd moved on from his pastry and instead was looking at a tablet. "I've been checking flights," he said. "Every morning flight out of Dulles is on time."

"So what do we do until then? Have you logged into his data archive yet?"

"What?"

Mariana blinked, a sudden fear that Carter's eidetic memory failed him in the mayhem of the observation room. "Beckett's data archive. You remember that, right?"

"Oh, this?" Carter pulled his notebook out from a backpack at his feet before flipping it to the first page. Right below notes he'd scribbled from their tour with Beckett was an exact copy of the data archive's log-in credentials. "Haven't tried it yet." He set it down and leaned back, tilting his back to take in the sun. "This is pretty amazing, isn't it?"

"Pie for breakfast?"

"No, this." His arms spread out, gesturing around them. The altitude wind picked up, nearly tipping over the vase holding a single flower; Carter steadied it and then pointed beyond the cityscape to the glimpse of the Pacific Ocean. "I love the water. You can just lose yourself in it. Out there, none of this stuff matters. Bills, work," he said as his eyes fell with a laugh, "time loops."

I'm gonna disappear for two weeks, Shay had said. *Fuck it, I'm gonna go to Joshua Tree. By myself.* The water, the desert, there was *something* about isolation that Mariana clearly did not understand. "I've actually never been to the ocean."

"You've lived here for how long and you've never been to the ocean?"

"Well, I mean, the beach, sure. But far out there?" She pointed the same direction he just had. "Nope. Never had time. That's why when I said I would teach tennis on a cruise ship, I was only half-joking. Something different."

"I've been through so many loops now. Every day is just about getting through it, finding a way out. Put on the overalls and go to work." He picked up the tablet and chuckled. "That's what happens when a time loop starts on a Monday, huh? It's work." His head lifted, looking back out at the sea before returning to the work. "I like this. I'm glad we're just *existing* for a morning. Pie for breakfast is pretty amazing too, though."

The only pie Mariana considered amazing had 3.141592653 as its first ten digits, though a small slice of pumpkin pie was always nice at Thanksgiving. But not for breakfast. She almost asked Carter for Beckett's archive information, for *her* to get a head start while he enjoyed *existing for a morning.* The tablet lay there, secrets of the Hawke Accelerator ready for them to go, and the clock was ticking.

Or was it?

Beckett was surely on his way by now, and there seemed to be little chance that they actually solved this mystery in the next few days. So maybe Carter, with his head back and lips in a wry grin, San Francisco breeze tossing his hair into a mess of black crisscross, maybe he was right.

Mariana took a sip of her coffee, telling herself to shut off Mariana Mode for now. Instead, she let the deliciously hot bitterness of the drink linger a second longer than she normally would.

Beckett never made it to the Blue Light.

Nor did he reach out on Tuesday or Wednesday. Which meant Thursday brought Mariana and Carter back to the Hawke Accelerator just as they'd been before. In many ways, it played out as a repeat of the previous loop, Carter checking itineraries to see if Beckett had changed anything until eventually the two of them waited for his arrival. The entire time, questions peppered Mariana's thoughts. What if Beckett had some trouble getting back? What if he found a reason to replicate the loop as closely as possible? What if he'd gone off and done his own research while waiting for this moment?

It *had* to be something like that. It simply couldn't *not work*.

Just like last time, Carter hacked into the facility admin with a little help from David, the AI spouting similar-but-not-the-same cheeky comments while they funneled Beckett's movement to the same spot from the last loop. They waited in silence, Mariana taking watch over the ticking clock on the wall while Carter waited for Beckett, complete with fidgeting fingers.

As Beckett approached, Carter stepped forward, a newfound confidence in this loop. Or maybe it was panic. "Dr. Beckett. How was your breakfast this morning?" Carter blurted the question out. "The toast?"

Mariana searched Beckett's eyes as he processed the moment, a blank stare of confusion rather than any sharp turn of recognition. "Fine. It was fine," he said before stepping back.

"And your coffee?" Mariana asked, matching Carter's sudden intensity.

Beckett let out a nervous laugh and eyed both of them. "Are you two with the facilities department?"

"What?" Carter said, looking at Mariana. He swung his bag off his shoulder, then unzipped it. "No, we're—"

Mariana stepped in front of him. "We're just surveying for the campus café. That's all. Have a good day, Doctor. You should try the donuts."

Beckett gave them a sideways look, which prompted a larger-than-necessary smile from Mariana. She turned to find Carter frozen, his notebook halfway pulled out. "That," she said, guiding his hand to put the notebook back, "isn't going to help us now."

They stood, watching Beckett disappear toward his morning meetings. The current of passersby resumed, scientists and businesspeople coming and going, even another person with the same technician overalls as Carter. Mariana blew out a sigh, then looked at Carter, their eyes connecting as if they had the exact same terrible thought at the exact same time.

It didn't work.

And no one was going to save Mariana and Carter from this time loop but themselves.

18

They didn't stay at Hawke.

Instead, Mariana and Carter walked straight out the front exit and set out eastward, or at least she thought so. Her loose understanding of the sun's position and time of day put it roughly in that direction. Though lines of barbed wire separated the boundary of Hawke from the neighboring Gardner Nature Preserve, they stepped through it. Carter went first, having clearly done this before and cleanly ducking in between the lines. Mariana took a little more effort, and despite Carter holding down a line to give her more room, a barb still caught the back of her shirt, tearing a thread loose.

Not like it mattered.

They moved among the landscape, one hill of overgrown weeds and vines gradually giving way to redwood trees. Shay would have laughed at this, Mariana walking very carefully through the middle of nature in uncomfortable work shoes, especially given the history of her injured left knee.

"Sometimes I'd come here on my lunch break. Hop the fence and take a walk to clear my head," Carter said. "You just gotta watch out for stuff. Poison oak over there. Foxtails here.

Ticks are nasty—they get everywhere. But honestly, it doesn't matter." He pulled out his phone. "It won't be that long before any bug bites go away."

"Are we just wandering?"

"No, uphill." He pointed to the distance. "There's a path to the right. You can see the tallest tree in between things. Just keep track of that, and that's the waypoint I use."

"I'm still trying to figure out why Beckett didn't remember. It was the exact same spot. The exact same beam," Mariana said as she followed his lead. She'd dressed in business wear to get into Hawke with the ReLive team, which meant clothing unsuited for tromping around nature. Burrs and other prickly things stuck through her pants, but Carter was right: it didn't matter other than a momentary annoyance. She turned from their spot, and even though they'd trekked thirty minutes into the wilderness, the sheer size of the Hawke facility meant that it was still visible. "I don't like hiking, by the way."

"You don't like food, you don't like hiking," Carter said with a laugh. "Do you not like cute animals either?"

Mariana, in fact, didn't. Not for the longest time. Not until one night when Shay had forced one into her life.

Forced might have been a strong word. More like *sprung* a cute animal into her life.

That night, Mariana had gone to Shay's. Usually, when the door slid open, Shay's bear-hug greetings bowled her over. Instead, her stepsister had walked with a tentative step. Shay kept looking over her shoulder and at the floor, long dark braids swinging with each movement.

"Are you playing hide-and-seek?" Mariana asked as she stepped in.

"Sort of," Shay said, straightening up after a quick leaning hug. "You know how I said I have a surprise?"

"Your surprise is hide-and-seek?"

"Better." Shay showed a toothy, can-you-believe-this grin. "I got a cat."

Mariana fought back the surprised expression on her face—not surprise that Shay would make an impulsive move like bringing a living creature into her life, more surprise that she picked such a *normal* pet rather than a ferret or a Komodo dragon. "I don't see a cat."

"That's what I mean." She stood up, then looked around. "Maggie?" she called out, voice in a singsong pitch that Mariana had never, ever heard in the years they'd known each other. "Mag-gie?" she called again, each syllable drawn out, followed by kissy noises. No cat appeared, and Shay's pursed lips twisted into a scowl as her brow furrowed, eyes in a squint.

"When did you get a cat? I was just here, like, last week."

"Well, this adorable little fluff ball showed up in the courtyard yesterday, and it kept following me around. She purred when I pet her, so I thought that was a sign." Mariana wondered just how Shay managed to get her bachelor's, master's, and halfway through her doctorate while still making decisions like *I'll take in the cat I found outside*. They walked together into the apartment, stepping softly until settling in on the couch. "Just stay really still," Shay whispered. "I think she's scared. I took her to the vet a few hours ago for a checkup."

"Look at you, caring for another living creature and bringing it to the doctor."

"I even bought food and a litter box. So I'm already more successful than I've been with any plant I ever got," she said, her voice still quiet.

And then Mariana heard it: a low rustle from behind where they were sitting. Which didn't make sense, given the couch was against the wall. She started to lean over for a look when Shay held up a hand. "Wait," Shay whispered before raising her voice. "Maggie? Come here, little baby." More noises came, moving from behind the couch to under them, then a little dark-gray ball of fur revealed itself, black lines dashed across its body. The cat turned and looked upward, locking eyes with Mariana, and the simple gesture threw off her rhythm. Maggie rolled on her back, her back legs still partially obscured under the couch's bottom flaps, and the cat stretched one paw into the air, floofs of fur sticking out between dark pads.

"Oh my god," Shay whispered, the last syllable elongating, "she totally likes you." She reached down and picked Maggie up, the furry mess reverting to a curled cat shape between them, purrs already audible. Every time Mariana shifted, Maggie moved with her, refusing to leave her newfound sleeping spot. "See how tiny she is? I thought she was a kitten, but the vet said she's a dwarf cat, she'll always be this size. Fucking adorable, right?"

"Can't she tell I'm not an animal person?"

"You like dogs," Shay said.

"I like nice dogs that I don't have to take care of. Like the security dog in my building. But cats?" Mariana said, tilting in her spot. "Cats are strange. They're so hard to understand."

"They *are* strange. That's why they're great. Stop always looking for patterns, embrace the weirdo shit. Look, Maggie, it's Auntie Mariana." The cat stood and arched its back in a stretch before peering at Mariana again; she offered a wave in return, unsure of what worked best for feline interaction, though Maggie seemed to choose for them.

The little cat leaped, flying from lap to lap with a trill before settling on Mariana, paws tucked in and purr at full volume.

"She likes you," Shay said. "Damn, she didn't even do that for me, and I bought her food. I think you'll be good buddies. Hey, maybe you can cat sit her when I'm traveling? Cats are easy, and you totally excel at following directions."

Good buddies, Shay had called it back then, and now, Carter's question echoed in her mind, and she considered it in the context of their strange time-loop existence. "I didn't like cats. Until

I got one. My cat." *Her* cat. She'd called Maggie that before —at the vet's office, to her landlord, when someone came in to make a repair. That all stemmed from simplicity, a shorthand to get things in and out. In her mind, though, Maggie had always been Shay's cat. Several trips through a time loop with no end in sight, though, turned that idea on its head. "She hides when you are over." Her voice took on a sullen tone, and Carter's look softened at the shift. "She's not actually my cat. She's Shay's. She *was* Shay's."

"Ah," Carter said, his voice dry. "Your friend who died."

"Technically still missing. She would have loved this place." Mariana waved at the expanse of nature around them. "I mean, who plans on going to Joshua Tree by themselves for two weeks? That doesn't sound fun for anyone."

Carter nodded. "I like hiking, but that goes beyond clearing your head."

"You know how the ReLive project is all about memory? When the last round of trials happened, I found a way to get myself into it. It was after Shay was supposed to come home, when we were starting to lose hope of finding her. And I wanted to preserve this person as who she was. Not the pain I felt at her disappearance. But this radiance of who she was. She was a beacon. Funny. Brilliant. Bit of an asshole. Sometimes stupid in the best way. And to possibly have all of that get sucked away, like she fell into a black hole. What she was." Mariana kept pace, though her eyes fell to the leaves and dirt crunching under her conference-ready shoes. "That's what I focused on during the treatment. The trials showed that memory-engram stability was boosted as a whole, but the network built for specific memories was particularly strengthened." She paused, wondering if any of that technical detail actually got through. "I wanted those memories forever. I guess people like you don't have to worry about that, huh?"

"People like me?" Carter asked.

"Your memory. A mutation of the DLG4 gene. That gene was the foundation of the ReLive project." They moved through the preserve in a quick, silent march, eventually breaking through the thickness of weeds to lighter groves of massive redwood trunks. "Hold on a minute. I just realized something about the loop." Mariana stopped in her tracks, on the outskirts of a density of trees. She looked up at the tallest one, a wonder of nature that reached impossibly high into the sky. About twenty feet off the ground, a small box was nailed into the tree, along with a sign that read *Smile, you're on our bird nest camera.* She offered a wave as wind blew hair in her face, and still looking at the camera, she did a very un-Mariana thing.

She stuck her tongue out. Then waved again.

"They'll never know," she said.

"I will," Carter said, tracking her look. "Photographic memory."

"It's actually called *eidetic.* It's a spectrum of enhanced-detail recall." She turned to face him. "How much time do we have?"

"A few minutes before things go—" he said, finishing the sentence with his hands mimicking an explosion.

"I think the reason we're here, remembering all this stuff, is that you've got the gene. I've had ReLive. And we've both been struck by that green beam." She shook her head, picturing Beckett standing in such a precise spot, and yet nothing. "Beckett doesn't. He's missing those."

"What if we break into ReLive, get a dose, and treat him?"

"It won't work. It's a multidose treatment over four weeks. We've only got four days to work with. I don't see a way around that."

Mariana turned to the trees, then glanced over at Hawke, its dome-shaped exterior and handful of short office towers poking up over treetops. "Come on," she said, reaching up to the lowest tree branch. Her fingers gripped it, bark and splinters digging into the meat of her palms, and she pulled herself up as best she could. "Race you."

"I'm not coordinated enough to do that," Carter said, trying to follow her path upward.

"It's a view, huh?" Mariana said. Not much of one—they were only an extra seven or eight feet off the ground. But it provided a better angle of Hawke and whatever was to come.

"I ran cross-country and hiked to get away from my family. I guess I should have climbed trees instead," Carter said between breaths.

"Time loops mean we don't have to worry about poison oak."

"See, you worry about poison oak. I worry about my bank account," he said, his familiar smirk emerging. "What a team." He pulled out his phone. "About a minute."

Mariana turned to the camera on the opposite tree and waved again, and as she did, another idea hit her. "What if we escape the blast radius?"

"We'd better start running for that."

"No, not this time. Next time. Get in a car and just drive. Get away." She looked up, gazing past the tall trees at the scattered clouds above. "Maybe this has some spatial limitations."

From afar, the first crackling noise came from Hawke, followed by a succession of quick pops. The noises echoed through the distance, rolling toward them in waves, and though Hawke appeared a large, stable facility, she knew the insides of it were buckling.

"Anywhere far away you want to go?" Carter asked.

Further pops and booms carried through the wind, soon followed by a visible burst on a side structure. Two more bursts pierced the structure's ceiling, followed by a plume of black smoke.

"London. That's far enough away. I've always wanted to go to Wimbledon. Centre Court, the Grounds, all of it."

A low, consistent rumble started, like an engine coming to

life deep beneath the earth. From Hawke's massive dome, an explosion ripped upward, orange-yellow fire soaring skyward before peeling away to reveal dancing green lightning striking out in all directions. The dome itself began to crack, pieces around the explosion giving way to the inevitable pull of gravity.

"Okay. Let's go to London," Carter said, turning to her. She matched him exactly, now looking into his eyes, and their gazes held, even though the Hawke Accelerator exploded with a blinding white to end this loop.

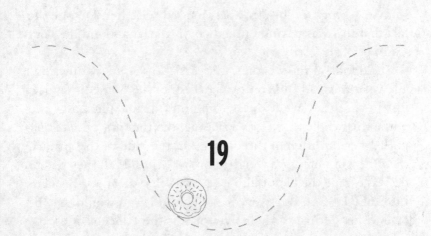

19

This marked the first time Mariana would be away from Maggie. Would she really, though? She wondered that Monday morning as she considered all of the things the little cat might need during Mariana's impromptu trip to London. After a few days, everything would theoretically reset. But even with that, Maggie's safety and comfort was a top priority, so in between packing, she messaged her neighbors just to make sure someone might come in once a day to top up the food dish.

And of course, she made sure to get Buddy Ed a morning treat. Some things didn't change.

That part was straightforward. And booking a flight to London was straightforward as well. Carter insisted on finding the hotel based on proximity to various restaurants he'd read about. She'd tuned out when he started to explain further, though she *had* enjoyed the things he'd had her sample. That part was one surprising element of the time loop. But while Carter thought about restaurants and bakeries, Mariana's thoughts lingered only on visiting the All England Club on the final day.

The rest of it? The idea of a *vacation* of all things during the middle of all this, when there was so much left to discover and so many things to do—that part messed with her. Despite the fact that this was testing out a theory, Mariana found the very act of packing a struggle.

She'd look at the weather, of course, so she knew function-ally what to wear. But comfort? Access? Style? Something nice, just in case they went out? Going out meant splurging, and while this whole thing was a splurge, the thought of *succeeding* pulled her in different directions. On the ride to the airport, the different outcomes weighed on her mind. If all they had to do was escape the blast radius, what did that mean for Beckett, the ReLive team, and everyone at Hawke? And would they be able to just return to their lives or was the concept of escape a relative expectation? Carter didn't seem lost in any of these philosophical questions, instead focusing on what a reviewer had said about one of the places he'd picked.

Yet on the plane, their approaches seemed to swap. The early Tuesday low-orbital flight from San Francisco to London took only three hours. During that time, Mariana found herself look-ing outward for nearly all of it, the view of the land below dig-ging into her thoughts. All those people, all that space, from the adults going about their day to the children chasing each other to the animals taking a nap, then insects buzzing, then microscopic creatures simply existing. And the sea life, all the wonders of the ocean.

Did they all get in this loop?

Or the alternative—what if everyone else on the planet es-caped it, and only Mariana and Carter were stuck in it? In some timeline, the Hawke Accelerator exploded, taking away what-ever scientific marvels came with it, but allowing the world to move on.

Here, they simply ran. Flew, technically, traveling at about 1,700 miles per hour with the blue horizon line barely break-ing into the blackness of space. Where did it lead?

Such questions peppered her mind, a serial daydream where

ideas became concerns became something else while she stared outward, so much so it took the attendant checking in to snap her out of it.

"Oh," she said, looking up at the politely smiling man clad in a burgundy uniform. "Coffee, please. Black. That's all." An hour had passed, and her eyes turned to Carter, half expecting to see him with a loop-exploiting tray of cookies and muffins. Instead he stared intently at a tablet, not a single pastry in sight, though the mobile David unit sat by his side. "Carter?"

"Huh?" He jolted up, then pulled tiny earbuds out of his ears before looking at the attendant. "Oh. Nothing for me."

"Are you all right?" she asked as the attendant moved on.

"No. Not really," he said.

"Did David find something concerning in Beckett's data?"

"Yeah. Well, maybe. I'd thought about if this didn't work, what if we met Beckett out in DC and tried to convince him there. You know, more time to pick his brain. But," he said and tapped the screen, then held it up, "his archives don't have access to any of his DC schedule. Guess there are people even more important than him."

Classified: Requires Clearance Level 7.

"What does that mean?" Mariana asked.

"That he's doing something important, I guess. I knew Hawke had some government funding, and it hosted international scientists all the time. The café would sometimes update their menu for them." Mariana knew Carter well enough by now to know he was totally serious about that point. "No way I can hack that. But David has flagged some weird patterns in a few of the data sets. I have to dig a little more." As Carter laughed, he shook his head before his face fell to neutral again. His fingertips tapped the chair handles as he bit down on his lip. "You asked if I'm all right. I don't know if I can get used to traveling like this. I've never done a sub-orbital flight before. It *feels* different. It's like the air is pressing against my skin. I can't even eat." His smirk returned for a flash. "That's saying something."

The fact that Carter lost his legendary appetite over a sub-orbital flight amused Mariana to no end, though she sympathized enough with travel anxiety to change the topic. "How is David working with Beckett's data?"

"David's not the problem. He does what I ask him to do. Sometimes with attitude. But it's the same problem with everything else. Thousands, maybe millions of records?" Carter shook his head. "That's even more daunting than this flight. Thing is, even with my memory, it's not like I can recreate data sets each time. And David resets too. So even if we find something, I don't know how much good it will do."

Mariana nodded, considering the impossible situation in front of them.

Fact: They couldn't bring any data forward except in their own memories.

Hypothesis: But carrying forward the knowledge of *how* that data was achieved, that might be feasible.

Experiment: Perhaps they could find something to help them quickly replicate the results of the previous loop.

"What if you don't need to remember the numbers but the paths themselves?" she said, her voice picking up pace. "In neuroscience, the hippocampus uses a different circuit for retrieving memories versus forming them. That way the brain's not lugging around absolutely everything ever in your history. It activates the path to the memory when you need it. So how do we put Beckett's data archive to the test?"

"*The paths themselves,*" Carter said, tapping on the tablet. The screen changed, moving from Beckett's repository to something else, a basic-looking table with the title Programmer's Hub at the top. "I can't customize everything. But this is an open-source archive of tools and algorithms for data science. I can load these into David."

"The path to the memory."

"It's not going to be the same as building it from scratch. But it's something I can bring from loop to loop. All I have to do is remember which ones to use, in what order, then run them through David." Carter reached down under his seat into his bag, only to emerge with this loop's notebook—a yellow one. He flipped it open, then took notes, circled and underlined words to capture his epiphany.

"Hey," Mariana said, taking a glance at the afternoon horizon over the Midwest before turning back to him. "We got this. We can make actual progress."

"Actual progress. And I thought I was trying out different restaurants."

The ship rumbled, a bump that didn't feel too different from the observation room at Hawke. Carter didn't quite seem to take it that way, the motion causing his eyes to grow wide and his fingers to grip the armrest.

Except unlike at Hawke, the bump was simply a bump. It didn't escalate into something catastrophic, and it didn't involve fireworks and shattering.

It simply came and went.

Mariana reached over, resting her palm over his. As she did, she felt the tension beneath her hand relax, a release that eventually worked through his whole body.

"Okay," he said, turning to her.

"It's just a flight. We'll be there soon."

"You're right." He nodded, his voice soft. "I'm gonna focus, try to work with this." The attendant came by, taking a cup of coffee from his tray and handing it to Mariana. "You know what?" He looked up, and still carrying an air of queasiness, one side of his mouth turned up. "Maybe a muffin will do me good."

★ ★ ★

"It's safe to say I'll never live quite like this again," Carter said, arms outstretched as he flopped onto the couch. As he sank in, Mariana crossed the room and tugged the curtain open. Early dusk had fallen over London, and she took in the sight from twenty floors up: the same combination of twinkling city lights below and stars above that she saw in San Francisco, but all arranged in different patterns, highlighted by Tower Bridge, St. Paul's Cathedral, and a spire with a golden statue up top.

She cracked the sliding door on the tiny balcony, and the altitude wind hit differently than the last loop at Gardner Preserve. Something about the air felt different here, and it wasn't the humidity or the air pressure. From behind her, Carter laughed, shaking her out of her stare.

She turned to find the obvious, of course. He was thinking with his stomach.

"Look at this," he said, continuing to chuckle. "People live like this? I mean, I know they inflate prices for hotels, but this doesn't even make sense." He pointed at the room-service menu broadcast on the wall display. "Thank you, time loop. I appreciate living like a king for a few days. I'm going to try all the desserts. My cholesterol does reset, I got it tested."

He actually did it, she thought, and she considered the paradox that was before her. Here was someone who clearly knew what he wanted out of life, yet it seemed like he lacked the bridge to get there.

"This is strange," he said, checking off boxes on the tablet interface.

"British food?"

"No, just this," he said, pointing to the menu. "I feel like my brain can't understand this. Life without pressure. What is that even like? Do people exist, like, happy?"

"That part, I don't know."

"I bet if this loop was seven days instead of four, some people wouldn't have even noticed for a bit." He tapped the tablet several more times before the larger screen projected a floating green checkmark. "Maybe they wouldn't want to. I mean, if you're just here enjoying everything, it's not the worst deal."

She looked at the man sitting on the couch across from her: failing his parents' expectations, apathetic to his studies, stuck fixing things in a machine he didn't care to understand, and only seeming happy when he was around food.

Had he been in a loop his whole life?

No, not quite that. Had he been *forced* into a loop his whole life, pushed there by so many things outside of his control? Yet somehow, she'd seen the real Carter underneath, the one who found joy in something as simple as a pan on a stove.

Part of her was envious. And part of her was grateful that, despite the circumstances that brought them together, this particular moment belonged to them.

Though the suite's lounge offered stylishly inoffensive artwork and decor, they tried something different when the food finally arrived, moving the small dining table within view of the open sliding-glass door. "Look at that view," Mariana said. Some ninety minutes had passed since they'd settled in, and now they sat quietly with neatly sectioned samplings on their plates. Carter ultimately decided that the hotel restaurant wouldn't cut it for him and instead ordered four dishes from four local restaurants. He claimed it would be a surprise when he finalized his selections, though looking at it now…well, she wasn't sure how this was supposed to go, since the only thing that seemed to make sense here was that they looked vegetarian.

"*Conchita pibil*, traditionally a Mexican meat dish with pork shoulder, but this substitutes with eggplant," he said, excitedly pointing from left to right on his plate. "Then a bowl of French ratatouille with eggplant, tomatoes, bell peppers, the works. Then from the Mediterranean region, roasted eggplant falafel bites. And from Asia, Chinese eggplant with garlic sauce. See? A West to East culinary adventure." Carter chuckled again, his face practically glowing at this. "I could rearrange this by appetizer, soup, entrées. But geography seemed more fun. 'Cause, you know, we're traveling."

Mariana took him at his word on that. She preferred the view of the city; he preferred the view of the food.

"I get it," Mariana said. "They all have eggplant."

"Yes! So, different flavors, different techniques. But see how they transform eggplant in so many different ways?" he said. "You know what I said before. Slow down and experience it. It's not just sustenance. It's life-changing stuff. Especially at this price."

Mariana obliged, trying to take it in with as much precision as Carter prescribed, starting with the French rat-a-something. "How'd you wind up as a technician at a particle accelerator when your brain is ninety-nine percent food and cooking?"

"How else do we wind up doing what we do? You played tennis. You got into science. I bet your parents brought you up to be disciplined, right?"

"Single mom. I had to help out. My work was our work."

"See, I had it different. Stable parents with expectations. Brother who did more. And believe me, I heard about it. Know what the difference was?" he asked, dipping his falafel in some type of creamy sauce.

"Is it one of the things on this plate?"

"Better. I didn't care. And that set the bar for everything. All we ever do are things others plan for us. Either we go with what our parents taught us, or we fight against it."

"Not here," Mariana said. She tried one more time with the French stew thing, taking the bite slowly, and to her surprise it worked, distinct bits of texture and flavor registering in ways that she'd simply never noticed before. "This is a time loop. We do whatever we want."

"Fair enough. To flavors," he said, holding up a drink, "instead of sustenance."

Other than Carter explaining flavors and cooking techniques, they largely ate in silence, Mariana doing her best to clear her plate in the proper order Carter suggested. All the while, the lights of London stared back at them, a constellation of one of the world's biggest and oldest cities, and here they sat as just another light in the darkness.

"I think I'm going to turn in," she said, putting the plate down on the table.

"No dessert? I ordered three of them."

"I'm not a dessert kind of person." She offered a shrug, and he held his hands up in mock horror. "You should get some rest too."

"I'm going to look at Beckett's archives again." He reached over to grab the David device. "Something caught my eye right when we landed."

"Sounds like an excuse to stay up and eat all the desserts."

"That too. David will keep me company," he said with a laugh, and he looked up as she moved.

Mariana took a step toward her bedroom on the left side of the suite, then paused to soak in the skyline in front of them. But her eyes were drawn to the man who had dinner with her, someone that she would have never possibly encountered had it not been for this mess they'd gotten themselves into. And though they remained completely different people with completely different life experiences and journeys—and traumas— here they experienced life with a hard reset every four days.

And they were going to figure it out.

Together.

She turned again and rested her hand on Carter's shoulder. "Thank you for a lovely evening."

"You paid," he said with a grin, though a different lightness laced his voice.

She matched his smile, then paused for a breath. "I couldn't spend this much on food if I tried." Her laugh sparked his laugh, their amusement framing the absurd fact that there were just *so* many desserts on their way. Mariana breathed, a rare instance of letting herself simply enjoy the moment, and her eyes somehow found his. They locked, and though 12:42 p.m. on Thursday would roll around again soon, this particular sliver of time carried a certainty to it that felt impossible anywhere else.

They stared at each other just long enough for her to feel the weight of his look, a smolder that felt both unlike him yet made complete sense in the moment. His lips parted as he held her gaze.

Before the moment might turn into anything else, Mariana caught herself and blurted out, "Good night." She didn't gauge his reaction, instead marching to her bedroom and closing the door.

And though fatigue tugged at her to simply collapse on the bed, she took a minute to close her eyes and just be.

20

Mariana was in the ocean.

Surfing? When did she learn how to surf?

No, not really surfing—instead, her body simply rolled along the waves, the gravitational pull of *water* of all things causing her to stick like a magnet to the surface of the wave. Until she looked down and suddenly glided through the wave's curl, and it turned into a dark blue tube, and now she slid, like a slide at a park except the slide *moved*, a rotation that started slowly but began to pull her into dizzying speeds, all while accelerating on her way down. All around her, metal clanged and... Was she in a dryer?

But the metal clang soon turned to car horns and shouts, noises that didn't come with drying clothes. It twirled her over and around one more time before a light popped in at the end and another car horn blared.

When Mariana opened her eyes, that dizziness continued. Not a real spinning-till-you-fall-over type of reeling, but the confusion of a state where sights, sounds, and logic didn't quite line up. The familiar walls of her studio apartment didn't greet her, replaced by bland darkened walls and no cat wandering around begging for food. "System, open windows," she said out of instinct, though nothing happened. She blinked the drowsiness away, each breath pushing her deeper into grounding her reality.

This wasn't a strange departure from the loop they'd been in. No, this was part of it, and she awoke with the sounds of London's business district on a busy morning—the whirrs and hisses of modern transportation, the occasional dog bark that carried through, the low buzz of countless people walking and talking on the sidewalk below, the symphony of angry car horns, all building to a vibrant din in one of the busiest cities in the world.

Of course the system didn't respond. It was for upscale homes, not hotels. Her mind recalibrated to her surroundings, then she looked at the time.

Ten o'clock? On Wednesday morning?

There was jet lag and time zones, but still, this was way off the plan. Mariana changed her clothes as swiftly as possible, an internal pressure considering all the things they were meant to see and do today. The clock was ticking, after all, and she stepped forward with an intensity that suddenly paused as she got to the bedroom door.

A switch flipped for her, the realization that their destination *was* the experiment, an overwhelming distance from Hawke proving to be the only variable. The rest of what got her up and moving, that was all her and her instinct.

Her fingertips tensed against the wall, the texture of paint and plaster pressing against skin. From the other side, she heard shuffling, and she told herself that this day, of all days, she didn't need to hit any objectives or goals.

If she was going somewhere to test that limit, Wimbledon sounded like an excellent idea.

And with that, the door slid open, morning light from the window flooding her vision. She blinked, needing a second to adjust to the light until the silhouette of Carter staring at the large wall display came into focus. Unlike her, he didn't watch tennis or morning headlines or anything along those lines.

Instead, he watched nature. Sort of. Greens and blacks stared back at him, the inverted colors of night vision playing out in front of them. And from there, her brain gradually understood the different visual language, identifying trees and shrubs, various insects and animals, including a family of jackrabbits stopping to show off their glowing eyes.

It took several seconds for her to recognize that beyond those trees sat the now-familiar silhouette of the Hawke Accelerator. A bird fluttered in front of the view, head moving in sharp distinct moments and trilling a few times before taking off again.

"A little better than the view we had, huh?" Carter said.

"You found the Gardner stream?"

"Yeah. You can see more here. Not much is happening though. Even the wildlife is taking it easy. I did see some raccoons run across, though," he said, holding his hands up like raccoon mitts. "It's odd, watching from here. This whole thing's just going to light up and evaporate. It's too bad we can't take the footage to the next loop."

"When you say *next loop*, you make it sound like we've already lost." Mariana stepped out, then assessed the options at the table. "I thought you'd have four breakfast plates already."

"Nah. I kept it simple today." He gestured at the pastries and carafe of juice. "Sometimes, simple is better."

"Simple?" Mariana held up a glazed donut.

"Compare that one to the Hawke bakery. It takes a lot of effort to perfect something simple. Locals rave about this place. You can judge the quality of a restaurant by its snacks. It's not quite Bellisario's, but it's close. And more expensive. Juice?" he said, pouring her a glass before she could answer.

"I thought you were studying Beckett's data this whole time."

Carter tapped the side of his temple after a bite of pastry. "Photographic memory," he said through chewing.

"Eidetic."

"You know what I mean. I got a whole list of places to try around the globe."

Mariana couldn't fight the oncoming grin as she wondered what might be in that mind of his. If she had eidetic abilities, how would she take advantage of it? Surely something besides memorizing menus. "You know—" she started, though an epiphany halted her in midsentence.

Of course. Just like the things in his notebook. Just like the restaurant menus in his head.

"We don't need to carry the video of the explosion over." She pointed at the breakfast spread before them. "The same way you knew where to get this. We just have to load the stream when it happens. Watch it closely. Let your brain process it frame by frame. And when you wake up next, you can write it down and then…" She exhaled, finally allowing herself to enjoy a simple glazed donut. "We'll find a way."

Carter held up his glass of orange juice. "Until then?" Mariana picked up her glass and tapped it against his. "We've got some time to be tourists before the train to Wimbledon tomorrow."

They took pictures on that Wednesday. They took *so* many pictures, selfies in front of places like Big Ben and Underground stations, wearing silly hats and posing with the guards at Buckingham Palace. To anyone else, they might have looked like a couple on vacation, but Mariana and Carter carried a different vibe to them, a strange weightlessness that came with the epiphany that things were going to go one of two ways.

Either the trick of flying half a world away would work, and they'd wake up in two days in a mountain of debt, the Hawke Accelerator destroyed, and a changed world to consider.

Or they'd start the loop over, all options of getting away seemingly exhausted, but between Carter's eidetic memory, the access to Beckett's data archives, and Mariana's sheer will, it felt like a solution would be within their grasp.

One or the other. One would be sudden and kind of shocking. The other would be gradual, a push toward the finish line that went as simple as taking one step at a time, even when the calendar reset. Either way, they'd break free, a certainty that Mariana hadn't felt…well, certainly not during this experience of time loops, and perhaps even not before.

It just was, built from a growing trust between the two of them. Except, it was more than trust. Mariana knew that as Carter ordered from a tiny fish-and-chips shop shoved between other stores, buildings well over a century old. Carter took the paper-wrapped cone of greasy food and stepped away from the order window before taking in a deep breath and grinning.

What actually went deeper than trust?

Faith? In each other, in the balance they struck, in what they were capable of, even if it took beyond this London excursion?

And believing that a way out existed, that was enough to create a sense of liftoff, enough that they could simply enjoy being in London as Wednesday night turned into Thursday morning, their bodies still out of sorts with time zones. They set out early Thursday for a final vacation day, hitting as many tourist locations as possible. A walk through Hyde Park. A ride on a traditional double-decker bus. And finally, an Underground train to the Wimbledon stop, followed by a fifteen-minute walk just on the cusp of 6:00 p.m. until the All England Club came into view.

Except, the lights were off. "Oh no," she said, checking the time. "Did we get our booking mixed up? It looks closed."

"Well," Carter said, an impish smirk on his face. He raised a single eyebrow and nodded ahead. "If you look closer, I think you'll find someone waiting for us." Her brow crinkled in confusion while Carter held a finger out, and she turned to where he now pointed. It took a squint, but then she saw it: a man standing there in a simple gray suit.

"What's going on here?"

"I told you. I booked a tour," he said, gesturing her forward. "Just not the usual kind. Hey, if you're going to use up all your money in a time loop, make it count, right?"

"We came here to get *out* of the time loop. Remember?"

"All this time together, and I picked up something from you." He leaned over, then cupped his hand to his mouth as his voice dropped. "Reverse jinx," he said in a low whisper, the two words causing a flutter through her body that stole her breath and made her pause, stuck in the moment.

Before she could respond, he jogged ahead, then turned to face her. "Come on. First serve awaits." He kept walking backward as he spoke. "I just learned that term today."

First, they were surrounded by darkness.

Then, a row of lights popped on overhead. Followed by a second, then third row, then another pop around them, illumination materializing seemingly out of nothingness. The medium brightness quickly amplified, soon an artificial lighting that turned the surrounding black into a fully lit center of Mariana's dreams.

Centre Court.

Shay had talked about the US Open, about someday playing Arthur Ashe Stadium in front of a raucous crowd. But for Mariana, Wimbledon's tradition and legacy always held a greater appeal, the mix of discipline, athleticism, and sportsmanship that reflected the annual early summer tournament's vibe. The silly dreams of college first-years talking on a long coach ride for weekend tournaments, their discussions imagining those dreams were closer than the advanced degrees they'd eventually get.

And then on one afternoon practice during their junior year, that dream ended for Mariana, a searing pain through her knee following a hard charge to the net for a volley shot that didn't even go in. Two days later, she'd headed into surgery to repair a torn ACL, and that was the end of her tennis ambitions, of Wimbledon.

The afternoon following the surgery, Mariana had opened her eyes to a bright white room. Several seconds passed before her vision adjusted, bringing the post-op curtains into focus. She flexed her fingers, the fog of anesthetic starting to wear off, and several tubes remained stuck in her arms. "Got any coffee?" she said to no one in particular, but the noise was enough to trigger movement beyond the curtain. It slid back, only for Shay's face to poke through.

"You made it. No torn ACL is gonna get my girl down," she said, a rare softness to temper Shay's usual fiery brand of talking.

Rather than hitting as the intended encouragement, her words seemed to trigger a return to reality for Mariana's body, postoperative pain spidering outward from her left knee. "Oh my god, this hurts," she said, twisting in her bed.

"Yeah, but think of the badass incision scars. You're going to intimidate all of your opponents as soon as you walk on the court." Shay stepped fully inside, and Mariana saw now she carried a small bag. "Are you awake enough to take gifts?"

"Is it a knee that works?"

"Close." Shay reached in and pulled out a large lump wrapped in tissue paper. One by one, the layers fell away to reveal a stuffed bear in Wimbledon whites with the familiar purple-and-green logo embroidered on its little sweater, a plush racket in its right paw. Mariana took the bear as Shay held up a card signed by the entire team. "I may have rallied the troops. Get it? *Rallied* the troops?"

We hope you ace *your recovery.*

Back-to-back tennis puns caused her to smile, though as she adjusted, a sharp pain stabbed at her knee, then radiated outward. "Puns are very unbecoming of you," she said through a wince.

"Ha. But it got your mind off the pain for a second."

"I think I need more than puns to get through this," she said. "How is modern medicine not better at painkillers?"

"Got it. More puns, more healing." Shay propped her chin with a hand in mock-thinking pose. "These meds will give you a *leg up* at recovery."

Mariana groaned, equal parts from the joke and from her throbbing knee. "No more leg jokes. My career is done."

"Nonsense. Nothing means nothing until something happens. You're gonna destroy rehab. Like a tennis cyborg."

Shay's unrelenting Shay-ness sometimes tipped into levels of irritating, but here, her unique blend of optimism and obnoxiousness gave more comfort than any medicine in the catheter. "Shouldn't you be in Santa Barbara with the team?"

"What are you talking about? My girl needs me."

"You'll never go pro with that attitude," Mariana said, only half joking. Shay stood a better chance at turning pro than she did, even before her surgery, qualifying for a few weeks at the very bottom of the WTA rankings, thanks to some summer tournaments.

"Ridiculous. You, my friend, are being ridiculous. I can nurse you back to health *and* go pro. And get my master's in theoretical physics. And take over the world." She tented her fingers like a villain, then tossed her hair back, cackling loud enough to probably disturb the patients recovering on the other side of the room. "I've never met a rule I couldn't smash. You'll see, this time next year I'll be at Wimbledon. Centre Court. Like this bear."

Neither of them went pro, of course. Neither of them ever made it to Centre Court, not even on vacation, at least not until now. And though Mariana had brought her photo of Shay to Hawke all those loops ago, she kicked herself for not taking her along here. She gazed upward, eyes looking somewhere past the retractable ceiling.

"Excuse me," a voice said, and the very polite, very efficient gentleman who'd given them the tour now reappeared with a cart of rackets and a basket of tennis balls.

"How did you do this?" Mariana asked. "This had to be way more than ordering extra desserts."

"I've always had a savings fund. Some inheritance from my grandparents. I promised them I'd never touch it until I found something to invest in. That's how they rolled. Capitalism and all that." Carter walked over to the cart, picking up a bright green ball, and even from a few feet away, Mariana could smell the fresh rubber of newly opened tennis balls. "I used my own bank account for all of the other loops. Partially out of respect for them. Partially worried that I'd lose it. Partially because I knew that if we *did* get out of those, my parents would shake their heads and think about how Carter had just had another moment of being irresponsible. But this?" He waved around them, a complete silence surrounding the most hallowed space in tennis. "This seemed worth the money."

Carter turned before she could respond, though her body froze, like it purposely paused and forced her mind and heart to process what was happening and why. She watched as Carter held up a bright green tennis ball for close inspection. What was he thinking? Clearly it didn't mean anything to him, but on so many days of her life, that mix of rubber and felt had meant *everything* to her.

And of all the days in the time loop, a significance like that might have applied to this very moment as well. Not just being here, but for Carter to have created this, like a recipe made out of emails, scheduling, travel, and bank accounts.

Mariana picked up a racket, and though it'd probably been six months since she'd played, her fingers eased into the grip formation, and she selected a ball, instinctively bouncing it several times. Each bounce echoed across the massive, empty space, and she paused to take in the sights around her: the empty bleachers, the ads on the surrounding boards, the finely trimmed blades of grass. "You don't know the rules, right?"

"Nope. Never played once."

"Before all this time-loop stuff, I thought about getting out of science. Teaching tennis on a cruise ship." Mariana took in a deep breath, letting the Wimbledon air become a part of her. "This is a little different from a cruise ship, but you can be my first student. I'll go easy on you."

21

Mariana thought back to historical footage from Wimbledon, when competitors were forced to wear all-white clothing, before modern sensibility finally won over to allow some variation to the base color. She'd chosen her day's attire for walking, which was more about comfort than competition, but their tour guide had brought some tournament merchandise that helped them get into the mood of things: two white vests and caps ready to help them look the part.

Style, though, didn't help Carter at all. "Sorry," he called out, another of his hits launching far too high. They watched it sail into the first row of seats, Mariana stifling her cringe reaction. "One more," he called out before the ball flubbed off the racket frame, spinning out at weird angles.

At least he connected, though. There were, of course, plenty of outright misses too. No matter how much Mariana tried to set him up, tennis seemed to be something that just didn't work with the mechanics of Carter's body. He'd said that he'd been a runner and hiker for most of his life, but that didn't quite help him with swinging a racket.

"Ahhh," he said before shaking his hands in mock grunt. The

next ball bounced behind him, and as he trotted off to get it, Mariana stopped, picturing the stadium full of fans—not quite the rowdy crowds at the US Open, but their own type of intensity. Carter moved to the baseline and stood in a ready position, something he probably learned from background broadcasts at Mariana's apartment more than anything else. "You know what?" he called from across the court. "I'm gonna try something different. Serve it to me for real." The racket twirled in his hands as he nodded. "Like, your best shot."

"Are you sure?" she shouted in return.

"Yeah. Nothing else is working."

"All right." She walked to her baseline, eyes closed, absorbing the unique stillness of the venue, from the fresh-cut lawn to the captured atmosphere of the closed roof. Not quite the same as morning daylight, but this would have to do, probably the only time a massive private rental would be found even remotely acceptable. This whole time, though, she'd stood halfway up the court, lobbing soft shots to help Carter get used to hitting a return.

This was Wimbledon. Centre Court. Perhaps not a true moment at the Championships, and no Grand Slam title or ceremonial dish were on the line, but she bounced the ball like she would before any serve. Her eyes gauged Carter's position between the lines, and she went through a split-second decision of the type of spin she might put on her hit.

The ball flew upward.

Her racket swung with all of her shoulder's strength, a slight twist of her wrist to apply topspin.

She followed through, her natural grunt came as the ball contacted. She landed, both feet planted in the grass, and she tracked the ball's flight, perfectly clipping the corner lines as it bounced. The spin pushed its trajectory even farther out, a subtle nudge on its path.

And Carter. Well, he didn't know what he was in for: he

reached out, a last-chance lunge with his racket swinging more out of reflex than anything else.

It hit right in the center of his racket, the sweet spot of the strings. The ball sailed, hugging the inside line, barely making it over the net before bouncing right at the baseline, a perfect winner shot worthy of the sport's greatest returners.

Point to Carter. Literally.

Carter dropped to his knees, arms raised in mock victory, and Mariana couldn't hold back her laughter. What was this moment they shared, standing in Centre Court? She trotted to the net, hand outstretched as if she'd just lost and had to congratulate her rival. He met her, sweat trickling down the side of his face as she took his hand, though they held on long enough to meet each other's gazes.

They stood still, seconds ticking by until she broke with another laugh. This one was softer, shorter, an insertion simply because she wasn't sure what else to do. He quickly followed suit.

"Carter, if you're still listening to me," David's disembodied voice said, "your countdown is coming to an end."

"Oh," Carter said, suddenly releasing her hand. He set the racket down, then rushed to his bag to grab his tablet. "Hawke."

She followed him, and they crouched down side by side to watch the livestream of the Gardner preserve, a squirrel sprinting across the nearest branch. "About two minutes," he said. "Look at the wildlife. They don't even know what's going to happen." The squirrel turned to the camera, its head tilted, before jumping off, kicking up dirt as it scampered out of view.

Seconds ticked by, and though no audio came from their view, the rest of it played out as expected, from the small bursts of destruction to the larger central explosion and ensuing plume of smoke. Carter zoomed in, counting down seconds under his breath.

"Here it comes," she said.

Last time, they watched the explosion from the preserve, a

wave of destruction overwhelming that final moment. Here, it might as well have been a movie, the blast captured in pixel-perfect resolution as fire shot out of the Hawke facility, pieces of its ceiling tumbling inward.

But something completely new emerged, an impossibility had they been observing within the confines of the blast radius rather than their remote location. From the left side of the building erupted a burst of green, a beam that shot straight into the air before a lime-colored shock wave rushed outward toward the camera. The camera stabilized as Carter spoke.

"The green beam."

"Yeah," Mariana said. "That's gotta be—"

Before she could finish her sentence, Mariana's eyes snapped open and she found herself in bed, six minutes before her usual alarm would go off. Several seconds passed, then Maggie leaped up to greet her.

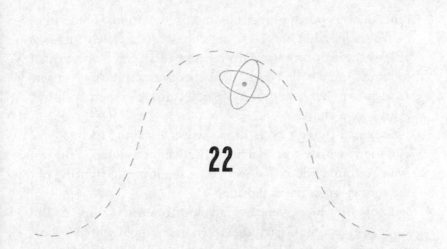

22

A green beam. Green *meant* something. What specifically, they weren't sure. Beckett had referred to it as a *CTD wave*, which Mariana soon discovered to be an acronym with about twenty different meanings. So for them, it continued to be a mystery green beam that somehow tied into time loops. And, she supposed, looked cool. But maybe the uniqueness of the color was a clue in itself.

When lightning struck the ground, photographs captured purple due to various atmospheric conditions such as humidity and air pressure, a simple chemical reaction from ionizing the air around the lightning bolt.

Natural exposure of electricity to the air created a glow on a spectrum of colors, usually some form of purple or violet, sometimes a deeper blue.

Green, though? A rich, solid green with only a thinned sliver of white in the core? Mariana and Carter spent the next entire loop focusing on this clue, the idea that such an energy didn't really seem possible in nature. And though Carter brought David into the fold, asking him to process data queries and work with downloaded tools, she spent her days at Hawke itself, prodding answers during meetings and presentations. Sometimes her colleagues shot her the strangest looks, completely unaware of how she suddenly went from being a ReLive neuroscientist to requesting detailed data about energy drain during particle acceleration, but other than the odd smirk or raised eyebrow, things went along.

Stopping the test cycle didn't work. Escaping the blast radius didn't work either. Beckett had suggested allowing the test cycle to finish, and if that were the case, it meant figuring out the root cause of the explosion.

Loop after loop went by, frivolous interests falling to the wayside except for Carter's never-ending sampling of new local restaurants. Beckett's data archive opened the door, and the combination of Carter's amateur hacking skills, David's number crunching, and the freedom of experimenting without consequences meant he bypassed security layers to pull both historical data and live-test results. His use of open-source data science tools propelled them forward, a simple shorthand that meant he only needed to remember where details came from rather than the details themselves. They moved from loop to loop, discovery happening across four-day cycles, each step a blunt but effective way of digging deeper, each restart bringing them a little closer to the secrets of the Hawke Accelerator.

Energy drain. Maximum velocity of particle acceleration. Facility stability and containment. Data flowed down to them, all of it in, of course, very illegal ways. So it surprised Mariana when she got to Carter's on a Wednesday night during an umpteenth loop that he blurted out a wholly unexpected question before she even put her bag down. "Do you trust me?"

Her head naturally tilted to a quizzical angle. Trust him? What else had they been doing this whole time? Wimbledon had provided a detour, an end to one phase and the start of another, and since then, every moment had become a step toward a greater goal, every evening offering a debriefing of new findings and new possibilities. It made things simpler, really.

Because as much as that night at Centre Court stayed ever present in Mariana's mind, part of her still wasn't sure what it all meant.

Shay gave her grief all the time about engaging with people, trusting in people, like her mission in life was to shake Mariana into a different state of existence. Carter's question would have amused her no end. The fact that Mariana took several seconds to ponder it would have amused Shay even more.

"Of course I trust you," Mariana said. She stepped forward into Carter's small living room, the place surprisingly free of his usual assortment of different take-out containers. "Did you already eat?"

"I've been too busy." He leaned back, arms stretched overhead with a groan, and he let out a laugh. "See? I'm full of surprises."

"What else is in store?"

"You know Beckett's protected test results I've been trying to download forever? Even David can't crack it."

"Yeah," Mariana said as she considered going back out to pick up dinner. Her making the choice for food? There was a first time for everything.

"I found a way to download it and—" Carter started before David interrupted.

"I tell Carter that I can process any data set, it's *his* fault for not using the right parameters." Even though David didn't have a face, Mariana practically felt a sarcastic grin to go with the AI's claim. "So *we* found a way to download it."

Carter pointedly cleared his throat. "David suggested a few variables to try. And it worked." He held up a tablet, dialogue boxes and a blinking cursor awaiting input. "Like right now. Ready to do something highly illegal?"

"I'm not allowed to do illegal processes, Carter," David said.

"Why would it be illegal if I have Dr. Beckett's log-in? It's a joke," Carter replied before mouthing *no, it's not* to Mariana.

Before their life switched to this, Mariana considered herself a very law-abiding citizen. And even in this world of no consequences, she still drew the line at hurting anyone. But logistically illegal stuff?

Whatever it took.

She flashed a thumbs-up at Carter. At this point, why not?

"All right. Here we go." Carter tapped on the screen, and even though the screen remained obscured from Mariana's angle, it changed enough to tint the light on his face.

"I'll be busy for a little bit," David said.

"Enjoy yourself, David." A status bar showed up, beginning the slow creep from left to right. "So don't tell David this, but last year I found a back-door hack to disable his process inhibitor. You can't do anything fun with it, but it lets me process any data sets I need. I did it just to make my job faster so I didn't have to work as hard. But it comes in handy these days. My parents would be so proud of my ingenuity," he said with a laugh.

Self-deprecating comments like that seemed completely unrelated to illegal activities, and yet Carter always snuck in those little jabs, a different type of verbal sparring than the kind he did with his AI companion. Most of their actions focused on the time loop, but moments like this lingered, peeling back layer upon layer while everything around them stayed the same. "Why is that?" Mariana finally asked after several moments of silence.

"What?" Carter asked without looking up.

"You're always saying stuff like that about your parents. Why is that?"

"Oh, you know how parents are." Carter shook his head. "They always give you grief about stuff."

Mariana knew some people didn't get along with their parents, but the level of resentment in Carter's voice brought a new dimension to this. "Shay has been my best friend since college. My mom met her dad through us, and then they got married. Like reverse-engineering a sister. The only way we've gotten through her disappearance is because of each other." Her eyes fell, a heavy breath grounding her in the moment. "So I don't know how parents are, not the way you're saying."

"Yours listen?"

"My mom does. My stepdad does."

"Well, there's hope for us all." Carter's normally light touch disappeared, the topic clearly striking a raw nerve. "Some people their age are just a lot more stubborn. And hold grudges. That sort of thing." The easy thing to do now would be to change the topic, go back to research, perhaps order something expensive to eat. Yet Mariana found herself pulled to his plight and the possibility of doing something about it. "I've never told you this, but the day before the loop started was my thirty-third birthday."

"Oh. Um, happy birthday?"

"Nah, it's not that. Feels like ages ago. But I'd deleted their numbers as contacts on my phone for that day. Reset the security on my phone too, so it filtered out any messages from unknown numbers. Saved me from any of their crap for a few days." He laughed, holding up his phone. "Every loop, I have to reset the security, though. It's kind of a funny ritual."

"What if you told them how you felt?"

Carter's brow rose. "You're joking, right?"

"I'm totally serious," Mariana said with a nod. "What if you told them that? That you didn't need their crap. That they were stubborn and held grudges and it clearly affected your life in ways that you're not happy about." She pointed at the tablet, at the information being compiled and processed. "Look at that. Look at all we've accomplished. I mean, you're a technician. You failed out of college. I'm in a completely different field. And yet, we're figuring out the impossible. So being difficult, *cruel* to you?" Though she could take the tact of imitating her high-school tennis coach pumping the team up for regionals, her tone shifted, connecting on a softer level. "They don't know you. Not the person I've been with for however many loops now. And they should hear that."

Carter's eyes went wide despite looking away, and Mariana wondered if anyone had ever been that frank with him during his entire existence. "What," he started before clearing his throat and trying again. "What would I even say?"

"Who knows? Who cares? It's a time loop. If your cholesterol resets every time, then so will your relationship with your parents. Yell *Fuck you* to them all you want. Or give them the biggest guilt trip." Several minutes had passed since she'd walked in, and yet only now did she finally scoot out the chair to sit next to Carter. "I know you don't swear much, so think about using it. Make that *Fuck you* count. You deserve this. And in the end, the loop finishes, and it doesn't matter. Except you'll have done it."

Carter's face went through a complete evolution, cheeks and mouth and brow all shifting as her words sunk in. Finally, he stood up, a glint in his eyes like infinite options had suddenly come to life, and not just restaurant menus. His posture tightened, then relaxed, and his eyes darted around the room, an aimless gaze as he considered his next steps. "Watch the data process, will you?" he finally asked, tapping the tablet. "David might ask you to do a second pass. Buggy algorithm. I don't think I'll be long." Without a further word, he walked in a slow, even cadence, only pausing for a low *thank you* as he passed her, then he disappeared into a room at the end of the small hall.

Ten minutes passed, and though she heard Carter's muffled voice through the walls, she told herself to focus on something else. The data process continued, numbers and acronyms flying by in an infinite scroll while the word *Compiling* flashed across it. She kept still the entire time, switching between watching the process meter inch toward completion and studying the latest notes in Carter's open notebook.

Hawke track length = 20.6 miles.
Database notes limitations in "mass transference." Ask M for ideas?
Particle velocities don't make sense, data error or algorithm error?
What is the "test object" and why is it 5.6 grams?

Finally, the sound of a sliding door broke the silence, and Carter emerged from the hall, inscrutable emotions pulling his face, the only thing discernible from his expression being that *something* had changed. "How did it go?"

"Not good," he said, though a laugh shortly followed. "For them, anyway."

"I know we've only known each other for a short time." Should she sit? Stand? Offer a hug? Their relationship blurred somewhere between coworkers, friends, prison mates, and... something else. Yet they had each other. Helped each other. Even when the world didn't. "But do you want to talk about it?"

He stepped forward, hesitating with a quick glance before his eyes dropped to the floor. "Nah," he finally said, a self-effacing grin on his face, but his tone was soft. "For what it's worth, I feel better." He picked up the tablet, and though he didn't look up, the grin remained. "I couldn't have done it without you. No, that's not right." He bit into his bottom lip, brow scrunched in thought. "I *wouldn't* have done it without you. You showed me that I had a choice."

"Having no consequences helps."

"Yeah," he said. "But not as much as having the right person by your side. I feel like I can suddenly see so many possibilities that weren't there before."

He met her gaze now with clear eyes, and suddenly Mariana was aware of everything around them *except* Carter—the hum of the ventilation, the quiet chirps of the tablet as it processed the data set, the way evening dew formed along the edges of his windowsill. "Happy belated birthday," she finally said.

She took in a breath, or at least tried to, a second passing before her lungs filled, and she needed *something* to come to mind, something brilliant to follow up with or at least—

"Carter?" David said from the tablet's speaker. "I'm done processing this. There's an error in line item nine thousand and forty-nine. I'm afraid you'll have to examine the parameters to complete the data set. It may take another day."

"Another day," Carter said with a sigh, holding the tablet up. "You mean past 12:42 p.m. on Thursday."

"It would finish about six hours after that. That is," David laughed, "if you fix the error now."

She recognized the look on Carter's face, the combination of exasperation and frustration that happened when they knew the loop's end was imminent and nothing tangible could be carried forward quite yet, at least not without further digging. He let out a sigh, shaking his head. "Back to work."

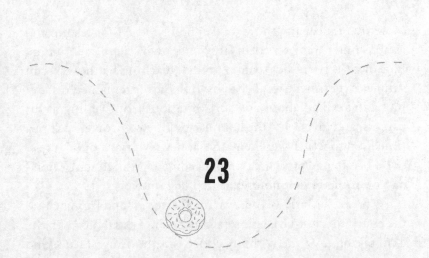

23

"We need a break," Carter said as soon as the front door slid open.

Several more loops had passed since Carter's close-but-not-quite completion of processing Beckett's protected test results. Each one dug a little deeper, David-powered algorithms crunching through the test results, millions of data points capturing everything from energy usage to particle speed to structural integrity. Some of the columns were simply strange acronyms, and the best they came up with was looking for anything inconsistent with it.

It didn't really amount to much, though, other than the fact that the data sets followed three different patterns. Patterns of what, they weren't sure, so Mariana suggested that *this* time they run the analysis strictly from the view of structural integrity.

Basically, forget accelerating particles, and see what broke to make things, as Carter would put it, *go boom*.

At least, that's what they agreed to. Carter seemed oddly distracted, and maybe he just wanted to try a new recipe or something. While he went offline for hours at a time, she marched forward, using what he'd taught her about data analysis. And in a way, the puzzle pieces started lining up for her, perhaps more due to learning how to use the David AI for testing and establishing parameters than any of her own scientific intuition. Plus, he was friendlier than expected, teaching her how to run simpler experiments on her own. But Carter remained distant: he hadn't talked about any sort of fallout from yelling at his parents, and given that the boundaries for two people stuck in a time loop together were tentative at best, Mariana didn't press.

So his strange proclamation of needing a break to start Thursday morning? It felt both expected *and* unexpected.

"A break?" Mariana said, waving Carter in, and from behind the couch she heard Maggie scratching things she shouldn't have. "I'm taking my time with my coffee this morning. That's kind of a break."

"That's because she's putting me to work," David said before Mariana muted the AI.

"You mean like a hike?" Mariana asked. "You like hiking, not me."

"No, not just a hike. A real, full break. Let's take one today." Carter stretched his arms over his head, then peeked over at the couch. "One of these days, I'm gonna see this mystery cat of yours."

"If it makes you feel any better, she still doesn't like my mom. Or Shay's dad," she said, leaning over to find a fluffy tail still sticking out from Maggie's usual hiding spot. "So what are we doing? I was thinking about the last data set, trying some of the algorithm tweaks you showed me. The energy-containment data was off by a fraction of a percent. But," she said, walking carefully over to the stack of tablets on the counter, sifting through until she found the right one, "this simulation got me thinking. Why is the mass-transference variable here five-point-six grams in the second set of tests?"

"You're using really big words here."

"Right, but that's way more than a particle. You see? And

when it ran with that mass, the energy containment dropped. And then—"

"Whoa, whoa, whoa. Is this what you were like getting your PhD?"

"Sometimes." She laughed, staring at the data table on her tablet. "My brain just gets on a roll. Shay called it Mariana Mode."

Carter put his hands up, palms out. "Let's switch to vacation mode. For a few hours. This loop's almost done anyways, right?"

They hadn't had any sort of pause since Wimbledon, and even then, that trip had offered some purposeful observation. This, whatever it entailed, sounded like shutting off. Which was not how Mariana worked.

That was the thing about four-day time loops. There was no weekend.

"Okay. Taking a break today. But," she said, "I'll have David continue the process. He'll send me results. You still need to look at it, though." She pointed to his forehead. "Eidetic memory."

"Fair enough. Until then? Dress in layers," he said. That wasn't what she'd expected, and from Carter's chuckle, he clearly didn't expect her confused look. "You said you've never been out on the ocean, right?"

The ocean, it turned out, wasn't a metaphor for something else.

An hour later, Mariana followed Carter as they stepped out onto a small pier along San Francisco's north harbor. At the end of it awaited a yacht bobbing up and down with the waves. Carter turned to her, and from his wry grin, he clearly already knew what she was thinking. "Inheritance money," he said, gesturing ahead. "Pretty sure our bank accounts reset tomorrow."

Mariana nodded, and a man greeted them as they stepped onto the vessel, the strange tilting and turning of a craft on water different from the steady floor she was so accustomed to.

"The groceries were delivered and put away an hour ago," the man said. "I'll take us out. The kitchen downstairs is all yours."

"Boats can have kitchens?" Mariana whispered.

"Propane stove, boiler, the works," Carter said, the grin on his face stretching from cheek to cheek.

"Was this break to take me out to the ocean or for you to cook in some badass kitchen?"

Carter's chin tilted up, optimism still painting his expression. "We can both want nice things, right?" he said with a laugh. "It's like I told you the other night, so many possibilities that weren't there before."

Mariana had often wondered about the stars, staring out at the blanket of black that just peeked out over horizon colors on sub-orbital flights. Such an expanse felt endless, a pathway to everything and nothing.

Strange that she felt this way in the middle of the ocean.

As far as she could tell, they'd only gone out a few miles, and after they'd gotten settled in, Carter excused himself to the kitchen with palpable exuberance: wide eyes, an ever-present grin, and an energy that made all of his movements extra visible. But for her, she quietly sat in the deck chair, feeling the waves rolling beneath as she stared out at the blanket horizon.

And though she'd brought a tablet with her, it stayed safely in her bag and totally out of her thoughts, at least until she heard its distinctive chime. She pulled it out, half expecting simply to tap a button to resume a stalled process, a hiccup of servers and algorithms. David couldn't be done *that* fast, could he?

Except she got an actual result, the processed data showing several fields of red highlights, shorthand for the fact that *something* was indeed wrong. She squinted past the late-morning sun to read through the algorithm's generated findings. Energy containment. Mass transference. And facility stability. All of these played together, and Mariana closed her eyes, trying to picture it as a series of events. The mass transference in the intended experiment, whatever the five-point-six-gram object was, came off larger than expected. Because of that, it shook the facility's stability—negligible at certain levels and conditions, but when pushed much in different ways? David's generated graph showed a line of cross-referenced structural data with one distinct spike. Mariana slid between graphs, each averaging numbers from different types of tests, then clicked on the summary David had attached to the findings.

In most test conditions, this discrepancy in energy containment produces negligible influence except on strut gyroscopes. Stability appears to be dependent on particle direction. "Pushing" the test subject creates a smaller impact. "Pulling" the test subject creates a larger one. Three sets of tests have been used on "push" tests with subjects of classified masses. Only one set of "pull" tests has been completed using an individual particle.

Even her science brain struggled with the report's vague-but-specific findings. Push versus pull. What could that possibly mean? Mariana took in the data, closing her eyes to find a logic to all those terms, repeating them to herself while thinking through methodical definitions and connections until...

Her eyes flew open, and she swiped through the various graphs again, looking for data markers at a very specific time stamp on the fourth day.

A Thursday.

Days upon days, all staring at data or asking questions or digging through reports, pushing each other to learn new skills and new ways of thinking, it all led to this. "Carter," she yelled. "I may have found it!"

"What?" he yelled from beneath the deck.

"I said I may have found it!"

"I can't hear you, I'm sautéing something. Give me ten minutes."

Every graph showed an energy spike around the same time on the fourth day. And on almost all the graphs, it corresponded to a structural issue, something that identified as a vibration in one of the accelerator's support struts—strut QL89, in fact, the one they'd seen the warning screens about. Yet in most cases, it came and went. Mariana did the math on the time stamp, the short span between when the energy spike happened and the strut encountered its problem.

Approximately seventy-nine hours.

Or, if the accelerator cycles started on Mondays at 5:00 a.m., a little after 12:00 p.m. on Thursdays.

It figured that Mariana would have finally found the root cause to all of their troubles and Carter was off cooking something. At least he wasn't eating.

But *why* would the structure break in the first place? David seemed to be thinking for her, as his next message provided a simulation of the accelerator process. Mariana loaded the video, a model of the different pieces supporting the energy-containment chamber. Now, what would happen if she simulated this *pull* process, whatever it was?

David, she typed to the AI, can you produce a same simulation with a subject mass of 5.6 grams?

Within seconds, a new video arrived. It played out, a computer simulation that seemed eerily familiar as a strut on one corner of the chamber moved.

No, not just moved. It vibrated in the simulation, the intensity of the process enough to impact it more and more until the strut eventually snapped.

That corner. *That* corner, the one nearest to where the green-energy beam exploded out of the observation chamber. It all started to lock together, Mariana's mind alive with puzzle pieces snapping into place, though one question remained.

Of all the design simulations and build checks that happened in the past twenty years, how come this specific one failed after all that testing?

And the mass? *Everything* on the planet weighed in beyond the size of a particle. Mariana's fingers flew, loading schematics before running an angle-and-dimensional analysis on the corner strut in question. She took those images, then moved them so they overlaid against the original design blueprints pulled from Beckett's archives.

There it was.

The strut didn't fail because of a faulty design. Its materials were properly selected to withstand the load and frequency of the accelerator process. All of that checked out. But it was based on one very crucial element.

It had to sit exactly per specifications.

The existing strut, something buried deep underground at the facility's foundation, was off from the original design by a fraction of a degree.

Mariana loaded up Beckett's archives, a mixture of files and messages, searching for any reason how or why such a mistake might have happened. Or perhaps it was sabotage? That many eyes couldn't have been wrong, could they? Mariana tried search after search, query after query, sifting through countless messages and design iterations until it hit her like a lightning bolt.

No. It hit her like an earthquake.

A structural analysis of the energy-containment unit following the earthquake of 2083 shows no damage in support struts and beams. Our geological consultant noted that the sediment and its level of compaction appears to have shifted incrementally with the earthquake, but it bears no impact on the integrity of the structure.

Mariana's hand went to her mouth as the information sank in: the earthquake of 2083. An 8.1 jolt that moved the ground just enough to knock the energy-containment unit's holding strut just out of alignment.

All this time, their hypothesis was that the various explosions and damage on Thursday morning caused a catastrophic break in that strut. But no, it was the other way around: the strut itself was destined to fail. Which meant unless they somehow managed to convince an excavation team to dig into concrete and metal, disassemble everything, and rebuild it, realigning the angle of a support strut by a few degrees in a four-day span, they were stuck.

The view expanded into a small hologram, the simulated wireframe of the facility's architecture and hardware lit up in a full 3D rendering that Mariana could slow down, rotate, and zoom in—cutting-edge holo tech that had just hit the market for scientific usage a few years ago. And no matter how she changed her view of the process, it all ended the same.

Mariana's breath shook with her exhale, her eyes drifting back to the endless sea. Her fingers gripped the edge of the device like it was the only thing left in the world.

24

Carter had said to give him ten minutes, but Mariana wasn't sure if that estimate held true by the time he finally emerged. His eventual arrival came unnoticed, her focus remaining on the different data screens on her tablet. Half the time, she'd sat, staring into the lineless horizon, while the rest of the time filled with checking and rechecking her calculations, the simulation, the algorithm. After all, she was *not* a data scientist; she'd only learned what Carter and David had taught her. And she was *not* a structural engineer, so she could be interpreting it wrong.

Or maybe David was just pulling a fast one on her. He was awfully opinionated for a helper AI.

But the core of any scientific education rooted itself in logic, and *that* told her that this was not good news.

"All right, who's ready for appetizers?" Carter asked, emerging from the kitchen with a tray. "Paper plates. Sorry, it's all we got."

"That's okay," Mariana said, a forced brightness to her words.

"You know, I've never worked as a waiter. You'd think I would have at some point."

"You can try getting that job for a loop?" she asked as he walked slowly around her.

"Nah. But I was thinking about other things." He brought the tray over to the small table between the chairs, though he looked over at the ocean breeze kicking his hair into his face. "Paper plates aren't working, huh? On second thought, those might just blow away. Stuffed baked mushrooms," he said, gesturing at the cheese-covered spheres. "Try them as finger foods."

Mariana obliged, picking one up and biting into it, and though Carter didn't say anything, she heard his voice telling her to slow down, savor it. "It's got a crispy exterior," she said as specifics came to mind. "Juicy. And some cheese. A little salty."

"Savory."

"Yeah. That. Oh, and a little bit of heat at the end. Like your falafel." A small smile formed across her lips, amusement at the fact that she even picked up those details. "That was surprising. Did I get that right?"

"Yes!" Carter's hand clap rang out over the noise of the boat. "You're learning! I can pass along more than cheap algorithms and poor hacking. One more thing," he said, reaching down into a cooler at his feet. "Champagne. Well, sparkling wine. The grocery service ran out of champagne, so they sent this instead."

He laughed, which prompted her to laugh too, even though she didn't quite get the joke, and he poured it into composite glasses before a blast of wind knocked both of them over. "You know what," she asked, "why don't we just share the bottle?"

"I like how you think. Classy." He held it out, and she gripped it, taking a swig. "So I was thinking. If we ever get out of this loop business, what should I do? I can't work at Hawke forever. They might even fire me. And owning a restaurant sounds terrible. All of the business stuff you'd have to deal with? Besides, restaurant menus get boring. But this," he said, gesturing around them, "this is great. People get hired as personal chefs in all sorts of ways. Rich people, who are kind of assholes but also appreciate fine taste. I could charge them more *and* cook what I want." The words rolled out, a spirit to Carter's tone that she'd rarely seen, as if gravity couldn't contain the way he'd felt. "I just gotta figure out how."

Consequences didn't carry over from loop to loop. The conversation with his parents, that would be forgotten by the world. But for him, something had changed. She saw it, from the smile lines around his eyes to the pace of his voice. "It's like what I said about quitting ReLive and teaching tennis on a cruise ship," she said.

"You see? Let's do it. Hey, cruise ships hire chefs. Look at us, throwing corporate caution to the wind. If we can break a time loop, we can get jobs on a cruise ship. Oh," he said, taking a mushroom for himself, "what was that thing you were saying earlier? Did your tests complete? I had all four burners going."

"Ah." Mariana took a bite and pretended to consider the different flavors from it, though her mind kept veering back to the findings. Should she say something to him? She'd have to run it again to be sure, and validating it with several other cross-reference checks, well, that would take much more time than a few hours out at sea, especially when they were supposed to be taking a break.

Besides, Carter seemed so *happy* right now. In his element, cooking with fancy food in a fancy kitchen on a fancy yacht. Who was she to take that all away from him? To say, "Thanks for making lunch. And the view. By the way, it might be impossible to leave the loop"?

No, that wasn't worth it. Not right now.

"I was just trying to tell you that my report froze. We'll have to run it again next loop."

"Got it. I'll blame David. Oh, hey." He reached into his bag for his notebook and pen. "What algorithms did you download for this? And the data format?"

Carter took judicious notes as Mariana explained what she

sourced from the algorithm repository and how she had David manipulate them, the details coming alive in a way that really felt closer to Carter's eidetic memory. Or the way ReLive enhanced her own memories of Shay.

Yet the way the simulation failed, the story told by the data set, it burned into her consciousness, a clarity born of stress and defeat rather than the neuroscience of memory encoding in engrams.

ReLive-boosted or not.

"Can I see the tablet?" Carter asked once he put the pen down. "Cement it into my brain. Oh, there was something else I was going to show you. Something in Beckett's archives. It came up. I just…" He paused, looking at her with a quick laugh. "I just can't remember it right now." His reaction caused her head to tilt, though he spoke before she could reply. "It's fine. I'll show you that too during the next loop."

"Eidetic memory," they both said at once, and though Mariana picked up the device, she shut it down instead of handing it over.

"Nah," she said, putting it back in her bag. "We might as well enjoy where we are now."

"Of course. It can wait. Hey, it's us." He popped another mushroom into his mouth. "We've gotten this far," he said with a smile so broad she knew he believed everything he said. "We can do anything. I even got vegetable Wellington for you to try. More mushrooms, but I promise it's worth it."

Carter explained the technicalities of the Wellington with an enthusiasm that Mariana couldn't quite grasp. Something about the way the mix of mushrooms, beans, and nuts had to sit together just right in order for their juices to not make the crust soggy. She nodded and smiled, and though she knew she didn't appreciate the difficulty of the dish, her expression remained genuine.

Because the way he talked about it, not just the dish but the process of learning to perfect such a difficult recipe, the words came with a marked shift in tone, like he *believed* things were possible instead of just knowing they existed. And that was enough to make her smile.

Even if she didn't understand half of what he said.

The clock counted down to the end of this loop, and Mariana figured that if they were pointed eastward back toward land, the Hawke explosion might be visible, even from this distance. What kind of light show might it project out from the ocean?

They both knew this was a possibility. And yet, they sat opposite of that, looking farther west out to the ocean. In the helm, the captain left them alone, probably relaxing as the yacht stayed anchored, not a single clue about the looming catastrophe on land. Carter had moved from appetizer to lunch before bringing out a simple dessert of a carton of ice cream, a circular logo with *Magic Scoop* on it, proclaiming, "It doesn't need any toppings. It's the best local creamery in the Bay Area."

She leaned back into her chair, shoes kicked off now, everything about to start again, yet another four-day cycle of research and data.

And that very thought struck her in the oddest way. All this time they'd spent pushing and digging, experiment after experiment as they broke laws and snuck through the Hawke facility.

All to have it rendered inert, useless, thanks to a natural disaster a decade ago.

Why were they even rushing to solve this? Why even bother?

She felt the water underneath them, this expensive yacht, this ridiculous food, and while it might seem like none of it mattered, it *did* matter. Because *they* experienced it. Consequences, debts, logistics, *cholesterol*, those things evaporated, but what they took with them, that mattered. Hell, their bodies might even be frozen. Were they aging? Probably not, not if Carter's blood work reset.

Literally every experience on earth was open to them.

Shay had always given her so much grief about work. *Ever since I've known you, it's been some form of work.* Mariana had wanted to ponder life without work. Perhaps that was the unintentional gift of the time loop.

It struck Mariana suddenly, there was luxury in this. A new way to live, one that gave them space to be whoever or whatever they wanted, without judgment or reservation. They could be true to themselves.

And maybe finally admit that there was more to their relationship than just science and cooking.

That singular thought caused the world to shift, a surprising revelation that painted things in new colors and new angles. She adjusted in her seat, crossing her fingers by her side quick enough that the gesture remained both a private affirmation and a wish for only herself.

"I say we don't look at Hawke," Carter said, as if he'd read her mind. "The view's too good here."

She turned, taking in his crooked smile as they looked at each other. "How much time's left?" she asked.

"Like, a minute."

"A minute," she said, softly under her breath. She reached over and took his hand, the action causing him to sharply inhale. But before he reacted further, she moved close and made a decision.

A decision that would have caused Shay to pump her fist and cheer. A decision that felt impossible for the Mariana that existed before the time loop but now seemed as real and as true as the ocean they rode on.

Fact: Carter was special. She knew that now.

Hypothesis: Though they'd both seemed to keep a cautionary distance, a respect for the fact that this loop, this *everything* was only them, denying their feelings seemed ridiculous knowing that they might be stuck here.

Experiment: Mariana was going to go for it.

She leaned in quickly, pressing her lips against his, the cold ocean air stinging her ears while a warmth rose to her chest. He pulled her in, a sudden magnetism locking them into an embrace where nothing else mattered.

The moment felt instant yet endless, and as everything ended one more time, Mariana wondered why they hadn't done this sooner.

25

Mariana's eyes opened. She woke in the same position that she always was in at the start of a loop: half-tangled in sheets, the emerging sun dimmed out by tinted windows, and a cat several seconds away from jumping onto the bed. All of that felt familiar, routine, like taking the same path every day to get to the elevator and out of her apartment building.

But inside, all of Mariana's instincts pulled in new, unexpected directions. A flutter in her chest, a tumble in her gut, and the still-there impression of Carter's lips against hers. The whole thing made her turn over on her back and stare straight up at the ceiling.

She'd done that before at the start of loops, usually out of frustration, occasionally despair, always with a desire to fast-forward time and get out of this perpetual existence that locked them into this four-day cycle. This time, however, she wanted to *rewind*, to go back and experience that single moment on the boat, a slice where nothing else mattered except the two of them.

Not even the exploding Hawke Accelerator could take away that.

Well, sort of. The explosion *did* interrupt them. Yet other than that, the world expanded in ways she'd never considered, never even thought possible. Sure, she'd had boyfriends before, but Shay would have been quick to point out that none of them ever danced close to being serious or legit, even if they lasted for a year or longer.

With Carter, the world felt clearer, brighter, a certainty in detail that previously just didn't exist. In theory, the two of them never should have worked. For one, Mariana still preferred her protein shakes for breakfast. For another, making plans would always be hardwired into her brain.

Versus his ease at just rolling with things. His ability to be in the moment. His obsession with *food*, of all things.

Their connection went beyond that, beyond needing to break out of a time loop.

Carter Cho was a good, authentic soul, in a world that didn't always want those. In fact, they tried to push people like Carter out, hampering them without the means to become who they really were.

At least until they got stuck in a time loop. Then none of that mattered.

Mariana felt the bed beneath her, the sheets over her, the shifting as Maggie walked back and forth to get her attention. Just *thinking* about the moment ignited the world, time loop or not. She rolled over and looked at her phone, mind wandering to possibilities. Should they take another break? Should they plan a full trip? Nothing would change around them, but this fundamental shift in their relationship meant so much more.

Maggie interrupted with further urgency, her tail up and eyes wide in full-on demand. The little cat clearly did not care for any epiphanies or romance in her life. "All right, I get it. System, open windows and start the coffee, black. And turn on the US Open."

The wall screen activated, the same first-round match that she'd seen countless times by now. The sounds of the match felt closer to habit than anything else these days, a comforting background noise the same way that people could hear songs so many times that they no longer registered. Comfort, in the form of sensory inputs that simply and predictably existed.

She moved through the first few minutes of the loop, doing everything with a buoyant autopilot: feeding Maggie, messaging the ReLive team, getting her coffee and protein shake. Carter always woke up earlier than her, and she had an urge to reach out and see if elation rippled through his world the same way it did for her...

It took all of her inner discipline to quell that. She wasn't exactly an expert at relationships, and giving it a little space seemed like the smarter, saner choice. Rather than call him, she pulled herself back, remembering that they still had other responsibilities, both to themselves and to each other.

Maggie meowed, finished with her breakfast, then trilled to demand some ear scratches.

And responsibilities to cats.

When enough time passed, Mariana typed out a message.

Good morning. That was wonderful.

No. No, that was too direct. She didn't want to make it weird.

Good morning. Let's push forward.

No, no, no, far too businesslike. A kiss on the ocean needed more care than that. Mariana typed out several more messages, starting and stopping, writing and then deleting. Several minutes later, she landed on something simple and appropriately vague but optimistic, complete with a stupid cooking pun just for him.

Good morning. Excited to see what this loop cooks up for us.

The smell of the morning brew wafted into her nose, Mariana inhaling deeply to appreciate the stillness of the moment. She held the mug steadily, then walked over to Shay's printed photo. "You'd like Carter," she said. "He's a bit like you. Except he wastes money on fancy food."

Mariana went back to her kitchen seat, hot coffee in hand. Maggie hopped onto her lap without invitation, and even before she stroked the cat's fluffy back, audible purrs began, accompanying the rising sun over San Francisco, like anything was possible.

Carter never showed up. Or called. Or responded to her messages.

For years, Mariana had focused on science, on the magic of what ReLive was developing. Dates and relationships came and went, usually with fond farewells at best, a little bit of wistful regret at worst. And yet, a single minute sitting out in the middle of the ocean with Carter turned a sudden lack of communication into a panic that rippled through her nerves and wrecked her focus.

Maggie kept her company, sometimes following at her feet and sometimes curled up next to her. And Mariana kept busy, running and rerunning the same data she'd explored from the last time to the best of her abilities. Without access to Carter's David AI *or* his eidetic memory, things went way slower. The silver lining to the news being so catastrophic was that at least she retained the details, probably the same mechanism that caused trauma to imprint into memory. She pulled down data sets from Beckett's archives, then used David's lessons to help her put together patchwork algorithms. The whole thing ran slower than if Carter and David were at the helm, but it seemed to work.

Or work enough that the patchwork version kept spitting out a consistent result: a simple, unpredictable, and slight shift in the way dirt and rocks packed the ground following a massive earthquake.

That confirmation should have held Mariana's focus. It wasn't every day that she'd discovered the likely cause of a time loop, and yet she kept turning to the phone strategically set out of reach. The coffee table, the couch cushion, even the windowsill, all close enough to check it but theoretically far enough to create some separation.

That didn't work, of course. She still peeked over the reports to see if it lit up with any notifications.

All those impulses were completely unbecoming of who she was. She was a professional, a scientist, an adult, someone who'd dealt with grief and loss and adversity, and here a simple *kiss* kept tugging her thoughts away from the task at hand.

Not that long ago, she would have laughed at such things. *Shay* would have laughed too, the idea that this random guy somehow changed her emotions' center of gravity. She told herself to simply do it, to pick up the phone and check it one more time.

No sense in fighting it.

The screen lit up. And no messages awaited her.

A single tap on the Call icon sent a signal all the way to his device, wherever that was.

And nothing.

Mariana turned to the window, morning having transitioned from the bright day to the midafternoon sun moving through, patchworked clouds creating puffy silhouettes dotted across the sky. A police siren interrupted, and while that type of sound happened all the time in San Francisco, it triggered a new type of panic in her head.

What if something had happened to him?

What if he'd been injured? On his way to surprise her and he'd got in an accident?

What if his absence had absolutely nothing to do with an

emotional hesitation at the moment they'd just had? Even if he felt that way, they were *stuck* together in this time loop and actively working to find a way out. Simply disappearing from the world didn't seem likely at all.

Mariana typed out one more message to send: Are you all right?

It marked as Sent, then she went back to the test data on her tablet. Or at least she tried to. Numbers and graphs scrolled by, and even though each line offered precise data, it all jumbled into a massive blur, and the very act of scrolling proved hypnotic enough that Mariana decided to try a cozier way to sit on the couch. She eventually found herself lying on her side, hair falling in her face as data passed before her eyes. Maggie took advantage of the position, leaping up and as the cat circled by her waist, her tail brushing by Mariana's nose several times. She blew a loose bit of floof away, but then the warmth of the cat's purring body rippled outward, enough that the highs and lows of the past twenty-four hours coalesced into an impossibly forceful drowsiness, a reset for her mind after the reset of a time loop.

She drifted, barely conscious as episodes of zoning in and out came in waves, usually triggered by Maggie rearranging herself on the couch.

Then a sudden bang came from…somewhere.

Startled, Maggie jumped off and disappeared to her spot behind the couch. Mariana's eyes opened, her heart rate having quickened at the violent, unexpected noise, though the disorientation of couch sleep created a veil of confusion. What happened? What time was it?

Another bang occurred, and Mariana realized that it wasn't from a neighboring apartment or outside construction or anything like that.

It came from her door.

The noise came one more time, and as she sat up, her mind

pieced back together just what she'd been waiting for, why she was there. But as she debated the safety of opening the door, there was another sound, a muffled shuffling that gave way to a voice.

"Mariana! Have you seen it? We've got a big problem."

At 2:15 p.m. on Monday afternoon, Carter had finally arrived.

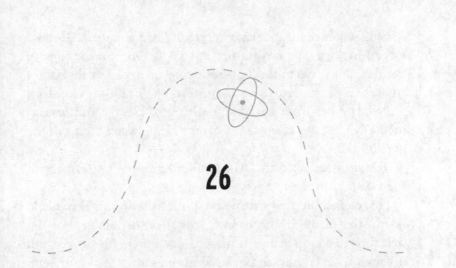

26

This loop had started differently for Carter. But he couldn't figure out why. Something needled the back of his mind, from the moment he woke up at 5:39 a.m. to the start of his usual routine. He ate first, of course, then got dressed and picked a notebook to use for this loop. Strange, though, that something kept bothering him, like forgetting the punch line to a really obvious joke.

That nagging feeling trailed him for the first hour of his day, and despite writing critical things he remembered from the last loop, a haze covered his thoughts, enough to make him consider if lack of sleep could follow him from loop to loop. But he pushed forward, and as he loaded up David to consider Beckett's data archives, his finger slipped on the tablet's home screen. Rather than pulling up the first layer of a secured sign-in process, his accidental tap loaded the morning headlines.

He squinted at the text on the screen, reading it several times over to make sure every letter formed words, every word formed a sentence, and that sentence digested properly in his brain.

Yet it made no sense.

Prehistoric Mammoth Suddenly Appears at Gardner Preserve.

One sentence meant that everything had changed. Because something had *changed*. But not just a difference in the flow of the day. This was more than someone turning left instead of right, or a pair of birds singing instead of a single set of chirps.

No, the headline stated something so clearly and fundamentally new and *wrong* that Carter's mind began racing at the possibilities.

"David," he asked the AI module, "give me a summary of the Gardner Preserve news. Please."

He tracked the news as he ate, both listening to David and skimming through photos and videos on his tablet. For the first time in a long time, his meal acted as mere fuel to get him through what lay ahead. Because this presented an anomaly to the seemingly unbreakable, and if a mammoth could show up right next to the Hawke Accelerator, then that meant...

Well, that meant *something*. What specifically, he wasn't sure. But it was enough for him to gather his things and rush out the door, propelled by a newfound sense that after all this time, a clue to the outside world might finally exist.

Carter walked for hours around the Gardner Preserve. He took the back way in, sneaking through barbed-wire fences like he was simply walking to clear his head on a lunch break. He moved swiftly, a light jog as he wove through shrubs and trees, exploring every possible angle until finally settling upon a spot up on the preserve's largest hill.

On one side sat the Hawke Accelerator.

On the other side, a crowd had gathered at the preserve entrance, like specks of dust magnetically pulled together. Ahead of them were the flashing lights of police cars, and even farther still wandered people, a mix of lab coats and athletic gear all headed towards a living, breathing impossibility. "Columbian mammoths went extinct approximately eleven thousand years ago. They existed primarily in North America, including in

California. Notable fossils were found in the Monterey region in the early 2000s," David said before rattling off factoids that confirmed the impossible out here.

Carter knelt down, weeds tickling his forearms as he leaned forward. Every Monday morning for the past however many loops, he'd come to the facility. Was there a chance that he'd simply missed this? He could have gotten so caught up in his own frenzy that this would have totally flown past him. He checked the news again and skimmed through the headlines: talk of a *prehistoric anomaly* filled Bay Area newsfeeds, but on a national level, it was buried far down underneath the usual political chatter.

But eventually, he saw the headline sitting on the sidebar:

Strange Discovery Captures San Francisco's Imagination

Carter had experienced this loop so many times, seen the news through so many different lenses. His own tablet, local broadcasts at the Hawke café, simple chatter around the city and the facility. There was no way something this strange could have slipped past him.

He stood up, watching again as scientists looked at tablets and held up various examination and scanning tools. What could it all possibly mean? Dirt and leaves crunched beneath his feet as he paced, pondering the ways that he might possibly dig deeper into this. After all, if this was new, it wouldn't necessarily be in Beckett's archive. Nothing at Hawke should have anything to do with this.

What to do, what to do, what to do...

Then, like a switch suddenly flipped in his mind, his legs stopped and his gaze turned back, far beyond the Hawke facility and to the horizon where San Francisco lay.

He should ask Mariana.

Of course.

As if by muscle memory, Carter began to move, starting the long trek back out of the Gardner Preserve and to San Francisco, to the...

House? Office?

No, apartment building. With Buddy Ed the dog. Yes, that was where he should go, the apartment building where Mariana Pineda lived with her little cat, Maggie.

Because if anyone could figure out how this creature had suddenly crash-landed into their time loop, it was Mariana.

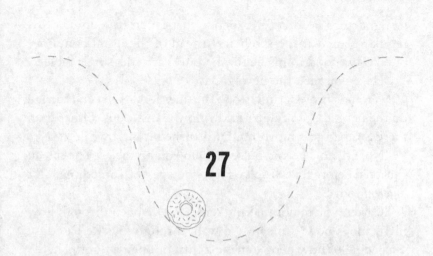

27

Mariana thought back to the first time she'd met Carter, or at least consciously remembered him. That first time loop, when he'd come at her wide-eyed, a sense of desperation and purpose driving him as he pleaded with her to just *stand* in one specific spot at one specific moment.

Since then, her experience with Carter was much more about what ridiculous amount of expensive food he'd ordered. Or him trying to teach her the chemistry behind cooking. Or his frustration at swinging a tennis racket. Or even when looking at test data in the midst of being trapped, a shared purpose often overriding any panic about their never-ending existence.

This moment etched differently in the lines across his face. Like that first time in the observation room, and yet somehow worse.

Desperation returned, shoulders sagging, voice pleading for belief. The person in front of her, though, he carried something that felt foreign, nearly unrecognizable.

Carter was scared.

"Come inside," she said, waving him in. Maggie did her usual bit, hiding behind the couch from this stranger, and normally Carter joked about it. This time, though, he moved in straight steps, a forceful cadence that failed to pause for his regular glance at the kitchen. Instead of the usual container of take-out food in his hands, he only carried a single tablet.

"Have you seen the news today?"

Mariana's brow scrunched at the question. "I haven't turned on the news in, oh, I don't know how many loops. Other than the US Open this morning, but I turned it off a while ago."

"No, no, no," he said before tapping on his tablet. The screen flickered before text dissolved into footage of…something. "It's *different* today."

"Carter, you're not making sense. We've been through how many loops now? I mean, we walk through Hawke based on a schedule of how people make a turn or open a door. There's no way we've seen everything that's happening. You're probably just—"

Before she finished, Carter put the glowing tablet up to her face.

First, she saw the image—some type of elephant standing in the field. But then the headline, "Prehistoric Mammoth Suddenly Appears at Gardner Preserve."

"What is that?"

"It's exactly what it says. It's an extinct prehistoric beast. At the Gardner Preserve. It's this, um, big patch of nature right next to Hawke." Mariana's head tilted, and she wondered if there was a different preserve and Carter got confused about the fact that they'd been there together several loops back. "It's called a Columbian mammoth, and it shouldn't exist. It shouldn't be here. Not just for, like, the time period, but for us. For the loop." His face craned upward, eyes locked onto the ceiling of Mariana's small studio apartment. "This is new."

"Are you sure…" Mariana started before pursing her lips, her mind grasping for logical possibilities—not just for the mammoth but also for, well, everything about Carter. Though, something as world-changing as this might have made him lose his cool. She told herself to focus on what *he* focused on: an anachronism could be anything—a trick, a prank, a combination of acting and robotics and holographic projection.

But one that they'd somehow missed? In all of their time here?

"I mean," she said, "it could be anything."

"It *is* anything. That's what I'm saying. I saw this in the morning, and I just took off as fast as I could. Tried to track it down," he said, his words tumbling over themselves. "On my way to the preserve, I walked through Hawke. I stopped and listened to people, not just there but also outside it, around it." His fingers tented over his nose, eyes shutting and a deep crease forming across his brow. "Everywhere I went. People were talking about this. *Everyone* was talking about this. How could you not? It was a freaking mammoth and whether people thought it was real or not, they talked about it. That didn't happen last time. I would have known."

He said *I* rather than *we*. Was that a slipup due to stress? Mariana shook it off, and she tried to stay on the bigger issue of a prehistoric beast being pulled into the time loop. Her instinct went to science, trying to find logic in the illogical. How could something so vastly different materialize out of nowhere, an anomaly that rippled into the words of every passing person Carter encountered? For endless days, the loop acted with precision, to the point that they'd been able to make a simple stroll down the street into a dance of avoiding passersby and oncoming traffic without stopping. He'd showed her how to do it, detailing all the way back to how he handled a simple crossing of the street on Thursday mornings by knowing when to speed up, slow down, avoid the woman who stumbled and spilled her coffee. But such a fundamental chasm between that repetition and whatever was happening now?

That seemed very bad. *How* bad, she wasn't sure. But certainly bad.

Her thoughts quickly turned, so much so that it surprised

her when she realized where her mind went to. Not to solving the mystery of the mammoth or the physics behind it, but a question so much more urgent, even in the context of the day.

The anomaly explained where Carter had been. Instead of answering his messages, instead of coming over. *He* had deviated from routine too, skipping over the part where they came together at the start of every loop.

"Did you," she said slowly, "see my messages?"

"Huh?" He leaned back in the couch, weight resettling as he pulled his head from his hands.

"I reached out. A bunch of times. I was worried that you were injured or something." Her breath held, a question about their kiss caught in her throat. And rather than force it out, she decided to simply let it be for now.

Carter's eyes met hers, a steadiness to them that calmed the frantic pursuits she'd seen since he'd arrived. He reached into his back pocket and pulled out his phone before bringing its screen to life. "Yeah. You did." His head angled as his brow furrowed, focus now on the screen in his hand. "That's weird." He blinked several times before shaking his head, like that would cleanse his mind from his sudden questions. "It just... slipped my mind."

"You didn't look at your phone all day?"

"I did. But I guess I just forgot to put your contact in. The security measures I took with my parents." Lines creased across Carter's face, his mouth opening and a sound started, the glimpse of a syllable that ultimately dissolved away. "So it filtered everything out. I was just so caught up with the mammoth." Something happened behind his eyes, a paradox that seemed to tie together knowing and not knowing and not *remembering* despite having an eidetic memory.

Mariana chose to stop it all for now. "It doesn't matter. Something is very wrong. Something is like, I don't know, *breaking* time for this to happen," she said, her hands gesturing for emphasis. "I think we need to find our way out of this as soon as possible. Before this gets worse." This seemed to have worked, the frenetic air gone from her voice but desperation still projecting. The data from yesterday about the earthquake. She'd have to tell him.

"Yeah," he said slowly. "You're right. We should focus."

She took his hands, folding her fingers into his. He looked up, and as he did, everything relaxed, an internal reset that settled the air around him. The pressure of his palms tightened against hers, and he leaned closer, a weight drawing them together. "We do have a problem," she said. "And it's not just a mammoth at Gardner."

She released her grip, causing him to look up inquisitively, though only for a moment. Because before he could react further, she threw her arms around him, pulling Carter to herself as if her hold on him might be the very thing that solved the crisis they faced.

"Hey," he said softly, "we'll figure this out. I know we—"

"Do you remember what happened yesterday?" she asked, her head leaning into his. "Right before the loop ended?"

He pulled back, mouth curved in a surefire grin. "Of course. I cooked. We ate. On a, um, a boat. And then we were back here."

And then we were back here. No mention of when she tried to tell him about the data.

No mention of their kiss.

"Why do you ask?"

"I just," she said before taking a breath, "wanted a sanity check. Given the weirdness of the day."

"I cooked you vegetable Wellington in that massive yacht kitchen. Oh, that reminds me. After we figure out this mammoth stuff, I had this epiphany about what I want to do once we break the loop."

Mariana remained steady and considered her words carefully. "Is it," she said slowly, "a restaurant?"

"Nah, it's better than that," he said, the side of his mouth tilted upward.

Better than that. "Do you," Mariana replayed the conversation on the yacht in her mind as she took a breath, "want to talk about it now?"

"Nah, I'll remember to do it later." He tapped the side of his head. "Photographic memory."

"Eidetic," she said, cheeks and jaw forcing out a smile. Should she tell him? The pockets in his memory. That could mean anything. Details from yesterday, their conversation about cruise ships and a post-loop life, their *kiss*, the fact that those things seemed to vanish from his memory—it opened up so many more questions.

But Mariana's scientific mind regained control. She asked herself a simple question. Would that help anything right now?

No. Moments ago, Carter had arrived panicked and frustrated. Giving him more to worry about would only heighten things.

Besides, another big issue existed, and it had nothing to do with a kiss on the ocean. "You're right. We do have a problem. Did you bring David? Because he can help me run some simulations to show you. It's much harder to do without him."

28

Mariana gave Carter a few moments to sit down and take a breath. She questioned whether a cup of freshly brewed coffee for an already agitated person counted as a point in the sensible host/friend/maybe-more-but-he's-not-remembering column, but given the lack of tea in her pantry, it made the most sense. She did *sometimes* buy a box of Carter's favorite tea during loops, though it often made more sense to simply pick up a freshly brewed cup at a local shop given that pantries, like bank accounts and cholesterol, reset every Thursday at 12:42 p.m.

The coffee maker churned and bubbled before the countertop machine offered a simple chime at the end of its brewing process. She picked up the mug and turned to Carter, who remained still. Tablets sat in stacks in front of him, along with David's mobile unit, though his eyes focused outside the apartment's largest window, where the San Francisco skyline twinkled away, the afternoon having given way to twilight.

He sat quietly, lost enough that not even the smell of a fresh brew caught his attention. "Here," she finally said, breaking his concentration. He looked at her, teeth digging into his bottom lip, before his expression broke and he took the mug.

"Thanks," he said, glancing at the tablets in front of him. "This is really bugging me."

"The coffee or the view?" From behind came a shuffling noise, and Mariana turned to see Maggie's face poking out from underneath the couch.

"I'm stuck."

"You mean *we're stuck*, right?" She thumbed through the test data again. Carter had only seen it once, and they both acknowledged that she had a better brain for analysis once the digging and hacking part was completed. The fact that he *didn't* ask her to run the simulation again or to explain details or to explore geological data, well…

That at least said something about their trust in each other.

"No, not that. I mean, I don't know how to fix an *earthquake* without having them rebuild Hawke."

"Changing the structural integrity of a facility that large is impossible without obtaining the proper permits," David said.

"Thanks, David," Carter said, running his hands through his hair.

"You know what I don't get," Mariana said, trying anything to lighten the mood. "David sure does run a lot of weird tests and simulations for us. But he can't remember from loop to loop, so how does he not object to what we tell him to do?"

"In the end, he's an AI. He'll process what we ask."

"I heard that," David replied.

"Well, it's true, isn't it?"

"I never said it wasn't." David's voice was filled with digital self-amusement, and Mariana wondered if the AI was aware of how Carter hacked David's process inhibitor. "But I did hear it."

"Maybe someday," Carter said as he turned to Mariana, "they'll be a little more, I dunno, a little more—"

"In control of their own destiny?" David asked.

"I was going to say *friendly*."

"You know," Mariana said, "I think he enjoys sparring with you. 'Cause he doesn't really do that to me."

"Lucky me." Carter laughed, possibly the first laugh since they'd come back together. He set the tablet down, then buried his face in his palms. "I don't get it," he finally said, voice muffled by his hands.

"It's the strut that holds the power conduit, and when the system hits a certain charge, it causes some vibration," Mariana said, her voice soft but flat. They'd been over this several times before, and maybe Carter was just fatigued by the whole thing. "But the angle is off just enough for the frequency to—"

"No, not that. I mean..." He clicked his tongue as he adjusted in his seat. "Why didn't I find you earlier? It makes no sense." They'd reset, the wake of panic from earlier no longer trailing him, but in its place grew a gradual pensiveness, Carter's natural curiosity colliding with the fact that they both knew things were off. And they couldn't avoid it anymore. Though, Mariana still chose to leave their kiss out of it.

For now, anyway.

"You're the only person I've talked to in I don't know how many days. And it just didn't come to me? And I didn't check my phone, I didn't call *you*. It was like you disappeared from my memory." He turned to her, black hair falling over his eyes. "I'm sorry. I didn't want you to think I abandoned you."

Mariana sat down next to him, and as he contemplated answers to his own questions, she noticed that David stayed appropriately quiet. Maybe he had politeness instincts programmed into him. Or maybe he only spoke up when he was part of the conversation.

"Well, look, I know you didn't mean to. I know it didn't mean *anything*. Something weird is happening to our loop, and we just have to deal with it." She tried. She tried so hard not to be her plain old pragmatic self, to go into Mariana Mode in the face of all this uncertainty.

But in the end, she gave in. Because for all of the ways knowing Carter Cho had pushed her into unexpected territory, she was still, at her core, the same person that she'd always been.

She was just a little bit of a better version.

"Don't worry about it," she finally said. "What matters is we find a way out before things get worse."

"Yeah," Carter said, locking eyes with her again. "But how?"

Mariana Mode. In a way, it had got her through her academic life, through her gradual journey up the ranks at ReLive, through so many ups and downs. When challenges came, the instinct kicked in, a pragmatism set to internal to-do lists and eyes-on-your-own-work focus. Even when pesky, sometimes difficult emotions burst into her life, she pulled back, into a core of efficiency that would find a way to get to the finish line.

The last time she'd relied on this under such extreme circumstances had nothing to do with time loops. Or learning to cook from Carter, or even focusing on Hawke research. No, the last time she had to forcefully stick to Mariana Mode came in a memory that *shouldn't* have carried the bright and vivid nature of ReLive, though it somehow did.

Because while it wasn't a memory she'd tried to preserve of Shay, it sure was related to her stepsister. And maybe ReLive enhanced *any* memory engrams tied to Shay—or more.

"Mom?" Mariana had asked, standing anxiously in her apartment several months ago. Her mom waved, the call connecting directly to her phone while Mariana talked to her wall screen. Behind her, Maggie chirped and walked in figure eights around Mariana's legs.

"Hi, Mar. Did you need something? We're about to head out to dinner—"

"Is Sam there?" she asked, her voice shaking far more than it should have. Her fingers tightened, nails digging into her palms, and she kept her composure the only way she knew how:

thinking of the steps that needed to happen in the next day, two days, possibly week.

"Are you okay?"

"Yeah." Maggie meowed, as if to challenge her on that fact. Because the truth was that neither of them were okay—Maggie, because three days had passed since Shay was supposed to have picked her up, and Mariana for the same reason, only from a completely different perspective. "No. No, I'm not. Mom," she said, words wanting to burst out of her. She held her composure, reminding her that the purpose of this was to inform, not cause panic. "Shay is missing."

Her mom's eyes darted, seemingly unable to process that information. Shay's father Sam finally walked into view, having missed pieces of the conversation but aware that *something* had created distress between them. "Look, I'm trying not to freak out. She went backpacking. By herself. At Joshua Tree. Said she would be gone two weeks, and you know how technology is when you get in the middle of nowhere. So I hadn't heard from her, but I kind of expected that. Just me and Maggie here, waiting." The cat trilled, and Mariana looked down to meet her bright yellow eyes. "That was it. She was supposed to pick Maggie up on Monday night. And when she didn't show, I got worried but, you know, it's Shay. She makes a choice, and then she *does it*. I thought she would definitely reach out Tuesday, but nothing. And now…" Mariana paused, a conscious applying of brakes at the stream of consciousness that suddenly emerged.

"Now it's Wednesday," said Sam. He pulled out his phone and began tapping on it before pacing out of view.

"What do we do?" her mom asked. Lines crinkled, first around her mouth, then her eyes. Mariana watched as her mom's center of balance seemingly shifted—not a physical loss of control, but a change in demeanor, and Mariana just *knew* that panicked thoughts spiraled through her mother's mind.

She'd seen it before. Not too often, but enough growing

up when situations seemed overwhelming. And Mariana did what she always did: stuffed down her own sense of panic, far below where it could touch her decisions. Instead, she went over everything she'd just researched in the past few hours and gave herself a calm, straightforward presentation.

She *had* to get to Mariana Mode. For her mom, for Shay's dad.

"I'm on it," she said. Sam came back within view, and through the digital signal, both her mom and Shay's dad now locked eyes with her. "Here's the thing. National park jurisdiction belongs to the rangers. So I wanted to talk with you two first. Then I call the police. They'll contact the Joshua Tree rangers." Mariana's lungs filled, a deep, cleansing breath more for the people on the screen than herself. "They'll organize a search and rescue. From what I've read, it's pretty intense. Night and thermal-vision drones, tracking dogs, satellite imaging." She hesitated, wondering if she should mention what Shay had said about spotty signal through Joshua Tree. They'd be able to get *some* GPS data, but how much, how accurate?

Mariana left that part out for now. No need to bring up more questions, not when each passing second ratcheted anxiety through the screen.

"So," Mariana said slowly, "I need you two to stay calm. I'll coordinate this. But I had to let you know first." Her best, forced smile surfaced. "Hey, it's Shay. It's not like it'd be totally out of character for her to, like, go off the grid for an extra few days, right?" She looked back down at Maggie, who'd curled into a ball at her feet, long whiskers poking out among tufts of dark fur.

I can't be late picking her up, otherwise she's gonna love you more than me.

"Right, right. That's our Shay," Sam said through a neutral face.

"You two, go out to dinner. Don't think about this. I'm on it."

Behind her back, Mariana crossed her fingers to herself, a gesture to a universe that hopefully listened every once in a while. Her hand relaxed, and she straightened her posture. "I'm on it."

That night, Mariana's mom and Shay's dad did indeed go out to dinner. And Mariana called the police, kicking off a chain of events that would lead to a search-and-rescue initiative lasting several weeks, all culminating in what the rangers called a *cold case* to her.

And despite weeks eventually becoming months, Shay never came home to pick up Maggie.

But for a few hours, Mariana had put on her bravest face and steadiest voice, because that was what everyone else needed.

That memory wasn't part of her ReLive experience. Instead, it seared into her mind, the way that worst memories often did, a scar in the form of encoded neurological activity, both a reminder of how quickly everything could slip away into nothingness and also how to keep what little she had together.

Keeping it together inside so everything outside wouldn't fall apart. Shay had joked about it so much in terms of academics and work, but every once in a while, it guided her to a steady landing. And here, she did the same thing with Carter over Tuesday and Wednesday. The situations presented so differently on the surface. On the one hand, Shay's disappearance meant a missing person case, search-and-rescue teams, and long discussions with police about Shay's habits and tendencies. On the other, Mariana and Carter were in a time loop with strange fragments of the past being pulled into the now.

Instead of coordinating with police and park rangers before long stretches of *waiting*, here they ran simulations and tests on the structural data of the Hawke Accelerator. And while David's programming seemed primed for verbal sparring with Carter, he offered a kinder, gentler persona to Mariana while helping her learn more about variable identification, try out different algorithmic tools, and simply *discover* more about how Carter did these things.

On the surface, she told Carter it was all to help them move through this faster. But deep down, doubts crept into her mind, little sparks igniting into much bigger fears.

Because cracks appeared in Carter's memory.

Verbalizing that seemed to give it power, and Mariana avoided that. But in the back of her head, she saw it, how his snappy recall stuttered over things that it shouldn't have. And his issue from the first day, how he'd charged headfirst into investigation without even thinking about her?

They didn't bring it up again.

On the final morning, they made their way out to Hawke, though unlike previous loops, they didn't go inside. Instead, they walked far around the facility circumference and over to the edge of the facility's boundaries. They took careful steps through the barbed-wire fencing, entering Gardner Preserve, where the Columbian mammoth still remained, the fourth day of being under examination by scientists and zoologists.

"There it is," Carter said, pointing from their vantage point at the top of the hill. "I guess we just wait. See if something unexpected happens when the loop closes." He pulled the bag off his shoulder, soon followed by an unfurled blanket. "Oh, I didn't tell you what I brought. Some sandwiches, BLT-style but with eggplant bacon. And," he said, handing her a metal canister, a warmth radiating from it, "tortilla soup. Vegetarian, of course. Oh dang," he said and slapped his forehead, "I forgot chips for it." He glanced back at the Hawke facility, a good mile trek through shrubs and weeds. "I suppose I can run back and grab some from the café."

"It's all right. Let's just stay here," Mariana said, settling on the blanket and putting the canister down. "Scientific observations, right?"

"We've got forty-five minutes," Carter said with a huff as he pulled out drinks and napkins. Mariana ate because she was supposed to, because Carter had put in the effort that morning to prepare all this before they set out, because everything would reset anyway. But as she watched the ant-size scientists scanning the prehistoric creature far beneath them, her mind pulled back to their first day of this loop.

Would he simply forget again?

The question lingered, a cloud of tension draped over her as the clock ticked down and their small talk wandered between the preserve, the anomaly ahead of them, even the weather. But none of it seemed to really matter without addressing the larger issue at hand.

Mariana considered it as she took in a spoonful of the still-hot tortilla soup. Six minutes remained in the loop, and somewhere within the facility, things were starting to crack. Here, the mammoth remained and the scientists acted without any concern for their imminent destruction.

The boat. The kiss. That *moment*.

Right then and there, Mariana made a choice.

"Carter," she said quietly, "I wanna tell you something."

"What's that?"

"The last loop." There it was: her pulse quickened, her nerves rippled, her breath paused. She'd forced words out before to protect others, but here, they simply failed to take hold. Her mind knew what to say, *why* she wanted to say them, but they'd melted away before coming to fruition, a *fear* at what his reaction might be.

If it was good, would he forget it again? If it was bad, would that carry through?

Only one way to find out.

"The last loop," she started again, "on the boat. You made me lunch."

"Yeah, seems to be a running theme." He laughed, gesturing to the soup bowls.

"But we did more than just eat. There was a moment." She straightened up and looked at him, a direct-eye contact that locked into him as much as time and space would allow. "We didn't say anything. But we—"

From afar, voices cried out. Mariana turned to see several of the scientists scrambling. More importantly, the mammoth reacted, circling in chaotic stomps as the people nearby backed away.

"What's happening?" Carter stood up and stepped ahead. "Oh. Three minutes left. Things are probably starting to go inside Hawke. The big fella is probably sensing the destruction." He reached down into his bag and pulled out binoculars. "I wish we could record this and carry it into next time."

"Carter," Mariana said. "The last loop—"

"Wait a second. Tell me next time, okay? We gotta watch this."

Which, after a few seconds of consideration, Mariana concluded was true. If they prioritized escaping the loop, they needed all of the relevant data possible. Especially when it involved this new, *different* thing that had crashed into their lives.

"Next time," she said softly.

And though she stood side by side with Carter and her eyes stayed on the Columbian mammoth, her mind drifted, not even paying attention when Hawke imploded and everything went white.

29

Once again, Carter didn't show up.

She gave him space, just enough for any practicalities of the morning to pass by. But with the fact that her messages went unanswered again, Mariana wasn't going to lose any more time to this. She handled her usual duties, having a protein shake while feeding Maggie and then getting dressed.

After that, though? She considered the options in front of her. She could wait for him here. Or she could dash off to his place, see if he was spending the morning there.

Two people in search of each other, but one carrying the unknown variable of a chaotic memory. Mariana thought back to her talks with the Joshua Tree Search and Rescue team, when they described how it was easier to find someone if they remained in the same location, how if Shay was moving—delirious, dehydrated, injured, or all of the above—that dynamic element complicated things. "We hope she stays put," the team leader had said. "Safe, with shelter, away from the elements and wild animals. That way, if we see any signs of her, we won't have to backtrack."

This wasn't Joshua Tree National Park. Freezing nights,

roasting days, rattlesnakes and coyotes—those didn't apply here. Yet, that experience gave Mariana enough sense to channel her panic into a logical plan that split the difference: stay here for several hours while getting a sense of how this loop played out, *then* go to Carter's place if he still hadn't turned up.

Halfway through her vigil, though, she found him.

And an anomaly.

Mariana stared at the screen on her wall, at the words Prehistoric Creature Stomps in Union Square.

Union Square? Not Gardner Preserve?

Something *had* changed. Again.

"…over to Union Square as we see a Columbian mammoth—not a woolly mammoth—seems to have appeared out of nowhere," the reporter said when she turned the volume on.

A crowd gathered around, keeping a safe distance from the mammoth, a security perimeter established around it. The news camera panned across, curious onlookers showing a mix of fear and awe, fingers pointing and mouths moving. One person, though, remained static in the sea of movement, and when he turned his face upward, Mariana caught a clear shot and suddenly understood it all.

Not just who the person was but *why* he stood there.

Suddenly, the anachronism didn't matter. Or it didn't matter as much. "System, rewind the broadcast thirty seconds," she said. The home interface beeped in acknowledgment, and the broadcast jumped back to the wider shot of people gawking at the mammoth.

"System, freeze."

The broadcast image paused, and Mariana walked until she stood mere inches from the glowing panel on the wall. Her weight leaned forward despite her feet staying planted, and the longer she stared at the image, the more the thoughts grounded in her head.

Carter.

His hair swept down over his eyes as he focused on the notebook in his hands, a pen tightly gripped between his fingers. And despite the loop's reset, despite the fact that he looked like the same Carter with his familiar lanky frame, something about him felt off.

"System, begin playback."

He stood still, a near-statue while the crowd gawked around him, his posture much closer to the panicked man who had banged on her door in the last loop than the person who brought a picnic to watch things end and begin again. Maggie must have sensed her sudden tension, as the little cat walked to Mariana's feet before looking up to the screen.

"System, jump to live broadcast." The image changed, an instant flip to a different angle that captured the mammoth, part of the crowd, and the gathering security. Yet Carter remained, furrowed brow peeking out over the notebook, shaking to the rhythm of his hand as he continued taking notes. He closed the book, its bright yellow cover visible even at a distance, and he started to move when the camera cut away to a new angle.

"And now we're speaking to paleontologist Dr. Anna Lee Newitz," the news announcer continued. "Two questions, Doctor. Is this a hoax, and what are the differences between a woolly mammoth and a Columbian mammoth?"

Mariana ignored the bespectacled scientist as they adjusted their brightly colored tie before explaining the scientific possibilities. Her morning involved much more pressing issues: wondering about Carter, reaching out to him, worrying about him. Of course, an anomaly would bring them back together. And then Mariana might finally get some answers, at least if she hurried.

At her feet, Maggie sprinted by, as if she knew what was going to happen. Maggie looked on with a loud meow before

whipping Mariana's ankle with her fluffy tail. "You're right,"
Mariana said, scanning the room for a quick checklist of what
she might need. "I should hurry. After you get a treat."

The mammoth attracted a dense gathering, though it made
its presence felt, even when Mariana couldn't see it beyond the
layers blocking her view. Did the people cluster tighter out of
curiosity, or did the unearthly noises from the mammoth create
a collective unease? From what she could tell, police barricades
created a perimeter, and beyond them stood…well, probably a
mix of zoological professionals and security officers.

The one thing everyone had in common was their focus, a
continuous stare at the anomaly ahead of them. Everyone, that
was, except for Mariana.

She fought through the crowd, sliding past shoulders and
elbows, eyes peeled for either Carter's familiar unkempt hair
peeking out over the crowd or the bright yellow of his notebook between bags and arms. She moved through the gawk-
ers, weaving back and forth to try and cover as much ground
as possible, and as she turned to a sudden roar in noise, she finally saw him.

A cacophony of sound whirled around her, from the excited
chatter behind her to the security guards speaking over projected amplification to the hovering transports overhead. The
current of noise swelled, a disorienting circle that blended into
the wall of voices. She turned, searching for a path through despite the tugs and bumps of humanity.

But as her eyes roamed, an instinct pulled them back, snapping on one specific person at one specific moment.

She blinked, sound seemingly dropping out as her focus tuned
in.

No push or pull of the people around her could loosen her
focus. No sudden clatter could draw her attention. She *saw*
Carter, and she would not lose him again.

The mammoth moved in a circle, seemingly centered on the tall Dewey Monument. That change in angle prompted Carter, and he withdrew from the front of the crowd, his yellow notebook disappearing into the mix. Mariana forced her way through, her normal politeness giving way to an urgency that shoved past those present. But even that wasn't enough to break through the sudden swell of humanity obstructing her, layer upon layer of curious onlookers first surging and then backing away.

And when they'd pulled back in collective movement, the sea of people parted enough for her to see pavement below and space in between. Except Carter was no longer there.

Despite all that effort, she'd lost him. Was she close to where he'd been? Was he still on the move?

Screw politeness, she thought, opting for a direct approach that Shay would have approved of. "Carter?" she called out, loud enough that the person in front of her winced. "Carter?" she yelled again. "I'm here." Other than annoyed looks from those gathered nearby, nothing changed. She stepped through, her knees catching on bags and her wrists brushing past backpacks, and she tried her deepest, loudest yell possible.

"Carter?"

"Over here!"

His voice called, soaring over the din of the crowd and squawk of police chatter. The mammoth moved again, probably just as confused as the people who watched it, and as the crowd reacted, she heard his voice again. "Over here!" Her pace picked up, shoulders angled to drive a wedge through the human density as she stepped.

"Carter!" she yelled, her tone shifting from a search to a siren call. She knew her feet had landed on toes, she knew she'd bumped someone a little too hard, she knew her voice had projected right in someone's ear.

It didn't matter. All those people would reset in a few days anyways, but for right now, she *needed* to find him.

Shoulders slammed into her, bumping her back. Voices yelled at her to watch her step, be more careful, that sort of thing, but politeness wasn't an issue. Not right now. She yelled out his name again, and he yelled back, a call-and-response trick that got his voice getting closer and closer.

The man in front of Mariana turned, phone in his hands, and he stepped out, moving toward the back of the mammoth's audience, and with that, everything parted and a clear path presented itself for them.

Carter appeared in front of her. They stared at each other, a disbelief that their search simply *ended* after all of the looking and yelling and desperation.

Carter moved first, his expression breaking before Mariana suddenly found herself giving into his embrace. The heat of his body pressed against hers; she leaned into it, feeling the rise and fall of his chest as he took each breath. Her arms found their way around him, resting across his shoulder blades, and they remained still, as if the loop or memory or the Hawke explosion or anything else might tear them away this second had both of them relaxed.

"You said you'd call," she said, eyes squeezed shut. "I've been looking for you everywhere."

"Me too. Me too, and I *tried*. It's just, there's something I need to ask you," he said, face buried in her hair. He pulled back, and though she expected to see relief, the lines across his face communicated anything but that. "Your name," he said, wide eyes painted with the desperation that had become all too common in recent days. "What's your name?"

They sat under a tree in a small park, several blocks removed from Union Square, and while the noise of the assembled gawk-ers still carried over the usual din of the city, Mariana found that she'd tuned nearly all of it out. It only poked back through when Carter took pause, turning his face to the gray San Francisco sky. "Something has to be wrong. These things are popping up out of time, my brain isn't remembering things. Crap is messed up." He offered a weary half smile, and she reached over, their fingers intertwining. She squeezed his hand, and the weariness departed, at least for a moment.

"Let's rewind," Mariana said, her scientist brain kicking back in. "The loop started. Then what?"

"I knew I had to get to you. But your name—your *name* escaped me. And your phone number and where you lived. Things that I just *knew*, they were gone. But," he said, "your face. I saw your face." His expression softened, a glisten coming over his eyes. "It was there, and it was clear. Your cat. I knew Maggie. I knew the picnic we had. Tortilla soup. I brought tortilla soup. I knew all of that. But *who* you were...it was gone."

Mariana nodded, pushing down the stew of feelings within herself in an effort to be her best, most scientific self right now. "Did you," she said slowly, "remember to reset the security settings on your phone?" Carter's brow furrowed, a look that Mariana had seen enough to know that his internal criticisms had activated. "It's okay." She squeezed his hand again, though he didn't return the gesture. "Your neurology is clearly going through something. Don't beat yourself up. Then, when you couldn't get to me, what next?"

"I remembered the data notes from the last loop. I can still see it in my head. I knew we had to dig further. A Columbian mammoth at Gardner Preserve."

"And now one at a different location."

"Right, maybe David can run some numbers on the distance, maybe it'll make sense," he said, pulling out the mobile AI unit.

"Well, I figured this has to be related, right? I don't know how, and it's not like we have tests for this sort of thing. So I just went. I observed. I took notes."

"Did you have breakfast?"

Carter offered a familiar shrug, complete with smirk. "Of course. Things are changing, right? Gotta test for consistency."

She wanted to say so much more, about what they'd been through and what was left unspoken at the end of the last loop. But now wasn't the time for that. Not when prehistoric creatures got pulled into Union Square.

"Okay, so fact: The time loop is pulling in things from the past. Bits of your memory are leaving as well. Hypothesis: Well…" She calmed the surging questions in her mind, filtering out the way emotions tugged at her this way and that. What was the cold, objective way to look at this? "Well, I actually have two. One is that your memory issues are related to these anomalies appearing. One is that they're not."

"Which is it?"

"I don't know. I think it could be either. So then, we know that—what's the experiment?"

Carter craned his neck in the direction of Union Square several blocks away. "We figure out what's wrong with me. And why weird things from the past keep popping up. And then we find a way out of this."

"That's not an experiment, Carter," she said with a laugh. "That's, like, a goal. Multiple goals."

"It's good to have goals. We can figure it out from there."

"No more trips out on the ocean?" Mariana asked, the question only a half joke. Could they recreate that? Not rely on a forgotten memory she painted through explanation, but simply put the pieces back together, a recreation with more intention and purpose than the original moment?

Perhaps that was the real experiment.

"Let's save the sightseeing until *after* we fix the world," Carter said, his mouth tilted in his familiar smirk. "And me."

Sightseeing. Not working on the same cruise ship.

Mariana nodded, saying nothing in return.

30

Carter tapped his pen on the notebook page, leaving a series of unintentional dots scattered across an inch. Next to it sat a list of words, the name *Mariana* scrawled across the top rather than the usual shorthand of *M*. Below it, all sorts of details that *should* have been in his head, little bits of habit they'd worked up over continuous cycles of repetition.

Carter handed the notebook over, and Mariana's fingers wrapped around it, the strange weight of sheets of paper in her hand. All this time she'd seen Carter's notebooks, and yet this may have been the first time she'd actually held one.

"Beckett arrives shortly before ten. ReLive meeting starts at eleven. Things like that. I see it all in my memory, like it's right there, it's just happened. I can even see the smudges of lines from the pen." His shoulders bobbed with a quick laugh. "Maggie. I knew that she hid behind the couch. But these?"

Mariana stared at the list, her finger trailing down it. They'd compiled it at a café—one of Carter's picks, of course—and while they awaited some fancy dish that she probably didn't fully appreciate, they'd explored the gaps in his mind, like using the negative space of memory to reconstruct what should have been.

"Patterns," she said, tapping at the list before reading it again. "Which variables are consistent here?"

They leaned over in unison, the list now rotated between them. Mariana's name and address. Half of the bakery items in the Hawke café. Some details from the Gardner Preserve. Historical facts about the Columbian mammoth.

"It's a little bit of everything, isn't it?" Carter said. "Stuff about you. Stuff about Hawke. Stuff about the world."

"So what do you get when you think about me?" she asked, the question coming out like someone playing matchmaker, though she *tried* to be a scientist. "I mean, my address. We know you couldn't find me."

"I know your face. I know your voice. I know about Shay. I know that when you're not sure about something, you cross your fingers behind your back. Or at your side."

"Wait, you noticed that?"

Carter's head tilted, his familiar smirk across his face. They stared at each other while their orders slid in between them, Carter moving the notebook enough to make room. "I see it. As clearly as I see this French dip sandwich." His nail tapped the side of the dish. "Come on, I can't be the first one to notice that."

Mariana thought back to loops ago, when Carter tried explaining how his memory worked, the way he saw images rather than specific words or text or details. And of all those things, he picked up the subtlest of gestures, her own inside joke to herself as someone who found the notion of luck unscientific. Chaos, sure. But not luck.

"Okay. My address. What do you see? The building, the front door?" She unrolled the cloth napkin from the cutlery, then squared it neatly in her lap. "The dog at the front lobby?"

Carter closed his eyes, and he inhaled deeply, though knowing him, such a gesture might have been his usual thing to do when trying a new dish. "I see this," he said, eyes snapping back to open. "A sandwich?"

"No, this." He pointed to the notebook. "The lines of the sheet. The way the ink smudged. My handwriting. I think I'm the only one who can read it. I see that, the words I wrote. Sometimes I can almost feel the pressure of the pen against my fingers. That sort of thing." He turned, a familiar whimsy finally returning to his face. "That's what I see. But what I smell? Right now? I think it's called *priorities.*"

"In case you forgot, you lectured me on sustenance versus eating already."

"Oh, I remember." His eyebrow rose as he dipped the corner of his sandwich in a small cup of brown sauce.

Carter continued eating, and though Mariana's dish awaited her, she let it sit. Instead of taking in the aroma like he'd taught her, her brow furrowed, all of this new information scattered like puzzle pieces on a table, waiting to be locked into place.

What was the variable here? Why would he forget her *name* of all things?

"The loop where we first met," she said, words coming slowly. "When I spilled coffee on you. You said that was when I told you my name. Did you write it down then?"

"No," he said through a bite, "the coffee soaked through my notebook. I couldn't take any more notes."

"Your notebook," she finally said. "Your eidetic memory. I think that's it."

"Get a different colored notebook next time?"

His tone caused a reflexive laugh and smile, the simple way they put each other at ease through the smallest of things. But her mind had already sprinted ahead, ideas forming connections into theories backed by evidence. "You always said writing it down helps you remember it better. That happens for a lot of people, even without a time loop. Tying a physical act to information helps process it. It's part of what we studied on the way to encoding memories for ReLive. When we first got to know each other, did you write down Shay's name and Maggie's name?"

Carter nodded, his pursed lips and focused look giving away the realizations he must have been experiencing. Mariana paused, and she considered taking her first bite from her plate but instead took a sip a water, then dabbed her napkin against her lips. "I don't know why you're losing loop memories. It might be a gradual ebb." Just a short while ago, Carter simply didn't think to call her. And their kiss, that had simply evaporated from his brain.

"It might be a blip. Maybe it was always this way, and you just never noticed before. These are short-term memories. They work differently on a neurological level than your long-term memories, things from your childhood. But I think the one thing that seems consistent here is that your eidetic memory can recall the things you've written down in your notebook. The other stuff?" She shook her head, considering her next words carefully. "It might just be the natural course of things." She didn't think so. Of course she didn't. The fact that Carter forgot her *name*, let alone their kiss, meant they were up against something that pulled like gravity against his mind.

However, she wouldn't say that. They had enough to worry about.

"Well, you've already written these down. We'll just have to wait till the next loop. A test to see if it stays." *Now* she let herself take a bite. Even though she didn't feel hungry, it's what Carter would have wanted.

"We can start off every loop making a list of crap I forgot," he said in between bites. The pages flipped over to a blank, and though he still sat perpendicular to the sheet, he scribbled out in big bold letters *Crap I Forgot*.

Mariana had two hypotheses, the one she explained to Carter about writing things down along with another one that she couldn't quite put into words.

The second wasn't necessarily a separate, divergent question, it just dove a little deeper. Because while evidence seemed to point to the fact that the physical act of writing assisted in Carter's memory retention, none of it pointed to the root cause. Did Carter purposely dance around it too? Mariana hesitated saying anything further, as if verbalizing it might make the worst of it change from speculation to fact.

Because her hypothesis came down to one very specific difference between herself and Carter. Both of them were struck by what Beckett called the CTD wave, an acronym they still hadn't deciphered. Carter had a natural eidetic memory. She did not.

What Mariana did have, though, was a full dose of ReLive, a series of injections and memory-training protocols completed weeks before the loop began. The treatment had been designed to strengthen engrams of specific memories, but she'd gained enough experiential evidence to consider the possibility that it did more. If she was designing a study, she'd also consider how getting struck by the CTD wave might have impacted things.

Not that she had anyone at ReLive to tell about this.

Now at her place, she watched Carter take the delivery at the door, containers of *breakfast for dinner*, per his suggestion. Though she wouldn't say it to him, her hunch centered on the fact that Carter's biology finally couldn't outrun time loops anymore. There were probably technical reasons for this, stuff about how the green beam affected natural brain activity compared to the kind enhanced by ReLive. But for now, all that mattered was that Carter went from a single moment slipping his mind to completely forgetting Mariana's name and address within a short span.

And if their window was closing, what exactly was escaping them? Working together? Collaborating on a way out? Simply *being happy*?

If those were fleeting, then she wouldn't burden him with the truth.

"What do you think scientists are studying with the mam-

moth? Like, DNA tests?" he asked, containers and utensils between their work on the kitchen table, a tablet with footage
from Union Square sitting between her Caribbean French toast
and his, well, several things. His notebook sat open, with a
header of *Anomaly 1*, along with details of the Gardner Preserve from the previous loop.

Did he recall those because the memories stayed vivid in his
mind?

"I'm not sure. I work with the brain, not quantum mechanics." She stretched her arms overhead, leaning back in one of
three chairs surrounding her small kitchen table. By now, the
mammoth still had its share of onlookers, but all reports and
footage showed the crowd dwindling, either out of fatigue or
apathy or heightened security or all of the above. Carter had
suggested the idea of breakfast for dinner loops ago, and Mariana wondered if he'd reverted to this because he'd forgotten that moment or if he just really wanted breakfast food this
evening. She watched a close-up recording of the mammoth,
while Carter served up, nibbling on a piece of what he called
perfectly crisp country potatoes.

She did take his offer to try one. It tasted like…plain potatoes.
Some things she would never understand.

"I don't think your memories and these things are related,
though," she said, taking another bite. "I mean, it's a time loop.
If we're getting pulled back to the start of it every Thursday,
then it seems feasible that something from the past could be
accidentally pulled into it too."

"That's your take?" he asked, his fork splitting into eggs over
easy. Thick yolk spilled out, finding its way over a bed of hash
browns.

"It's reasonable. I don't know if it's accurate, but it's reasonable. I just can't figure out a reason why it would happen *now*.
Like, what changed?" Mariana went quiet, her mind wander-

ing back to the final loop before things started to slide away from them.

Could a single kiss break time this way?

"But if it's getting worse, we've gotta focus on the structural issue. The earthquake simulation, there has to be a way to counter—" she started before something jabbed into her leg. She looked down to find Maggie, paws outstretched on her leg and a dewclaw caught onto the fabric of her pants.

"Well, hello there," Carter said, eyes locked on the little cat. "You've finally come out to see me? It's taken how many loops now? Wow, you weren't kidding when you said your cat was small."

"Those pesky genetic mutations. But that helps her hide behind couches." Maggie ignored her, continuing to stare at Carter with bright eyes. "You have David. I have Maggie. I suppose that's another experiment. Do cats remember through time loops? Because your AI certainly does not."

Maggie's whiskers danced as her nose wiggled, the little cat sniffing the air, and though Maggie never showed too much interest in food, her face remained engaged. Despite the fact that her front legs were planted on Mariana, she was clearly drawn to Carter, perhaps the cat's way of staying comfortable while begging.

"I think," she said slowly, "she wants your egg yolk."

"How about that?" Carter said, dipping the end of his pen in the runny yellow goo. He put it within Maggie's reach, and the cat's eyes went wide as she licked. "Sorry, Mariana. You're surrounded by foodies."

"I guess she's not into protein shakes." As if to emphasize Mariana's point, Maggie pushed off her legs and jumped on Carter's lap, an instantly audible purr upon landing.

"It's all about the pen, huh, Maggie?" he said, dipping it again. As she continued, Carter's eyes went wide. "The pen. That's it."

"What's that?"

"The folder," he said, holding still enough to allow Maggie to finish, but his center of gravity shifted, matching the urgency that gradually took over his face. "The folder in Beckett's archive. Did I tell you about that?"

"I don't think so," Mariana said, her voice keeping a steady pace. "On the boat, you said you'd found something in Beckett's files but you'd get to it later." Her face scrunched at the next thought. "You said you couldn't remember the details. I just forgot to ask," she said, a quiet laugh at the irony.

"I was. I was going to." He sank back into his chair, enough movement that Maggie jumped off, though rather than scurry into her hiding spot, she sat between them, tail whipping back and forth. "I just...forgot."

"I'm sure it's nothing."

"This folder. In Beckett's data," he said, holding up the pen that doubled as Maggie's spoon. "There was a document. Most of it was sealed off, except for the first two pages." Mariana stared at the pen in his hands, the way he gripped it like it was something much more than a simple writing implement. "It had a picture of a pen and a model number. A Bic Classic, model X two zero two eight, one millimeter ball." Carter tapped away at the tablet screen, occasionally pausing to squeeze his eyes shut, as if his thoughts had to catch up with his instincts. The screen flashed, its bright colors tinting his cheeks until he held the device up for Mariana to see. "But why?"

On the screen sat a folder icon, the words *Project Pen* beneath it.

What was so special about a pen in a particle accelerator? She closed her eyes, wishing that she had Carter's eidetic recall, but instead of clear images of notes, everything came back as fragments, details with uneven levels of clarity painted over by anxiety and time.

Except there was one issue, one strange unanswered question they had about mass. At one point, that was one of their mysteries.

"Wait, wait, wait," Mariana said. "What does that model of pen weigh?"

Carter's head tilted, then he looked down at David's mobile unit. "David, what are the specifications of a Bic Classic ballpoint pen, model X two zero two eight?"

"You should know more about ballpoint pens given how much you use them." Carter rolled his eyes at David's jab, though the half smile told Mariana that he probably enjoyed the AI's sass. Maybe not so much outside of the loop, but given his limited options, David's verbal sparring probably kept him on his toes. "Bic Classic ballpoint pen, model X two zero two eight comes in packs of four and eight, or a box of twenty or fifty. Each unit measures eight point one inches with the cap properly on and weighs five point six grams…"

David rattled off more specifications about color, design, and manufacturing date, but the weight measurement caused both Mariana and Carter to sit up and stare at each other.

Because according to Beckett's notes, something weighing five point six grams was tested in the Hawke Accelerator.

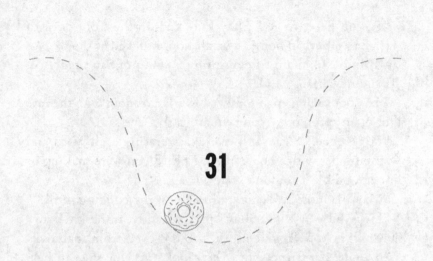

31

On Thursday morning, Mariana and Carter set out on a stealth mission planned over the last two days. Their goal: infiltrate the Hawke Accelerator, steal data from Hawke's chief science officer, and figure out just what Project Pen and that five-point-six-gram measurement were all about.

They stood at the crosswalk, a small group of fellow early-morning pedestrians waiting for traffic to slow down and give them their turn. A cool morning breeze kicked in, tickling Mariana's nose as she considered the *last* time she'd engaged in a stealth mission about ten years ago.

Like today, the method had been infiltration and the outcome was very personal. But in the scheme of things, the stakes were a bit smaller than the untold secrets of Project Pen.

"Okay," Shay had said as they approached the porch, practically vibrating with excitement. "So you're sure you know your mom's password?"

"I mean, if she hasn't updated it in the past decade or so," Mariana said in a whisper. But why was she whispering? It wasn't like her mom knew that they were on a stealth mission. "Knowing her, she probably hasn't. I don't think she ever knew I figured it out."

"Right, here we go." Shay knocked on the front door of Mariana's suburban home, a small house tucked at the base of San Bruno Mountain fifteen minutes south of San Francisco. "Turn on Mariana Mode."

The door swung open to reveal Mariana's mom with the rare sight of an apron on. "You two are early," she said.

"Hi, Renee," Shay said, overexaggerating each word and swamping her with a hug. "Well, I heard you were making us dinner, and I just couldn't wait."

"Mariana must be exaggerating about my cooking skills."

"Hey, did you know Shay's pretty handy in the kitchen?" Shay still held Mariana's mom, though even from that awkward angle, her friend shot over a look. "Maybe she can help you." Shay's arched eyebrow relaxed into understanding, and the two walked inside with Shay going on and on about how she loved being in the kitchen and her dad taught her campfire cooking with things like Dutch ovens. Their voices faded away, the bait taken by Mariana's mom.

"I'm just gonna use the bathroom," Mariana yelled, before sneaking down the hallway. She peered into her childhood bedroom, the furniture largely the same, including the desk which held a line of high-school tennis trophies.

But that wasn't why she'd come. Why *they'd* come. Shay's voice chatted away at full speed and full volume, laughter carrying through the space. It was so natural, Shay's effortless charm and force-of-will personality now at work in the kitchen.

Shay never talked about her mom much, other than that she lived in another state and sent Christmas cards like clockwork, but she could go on for hours about Sam, despite his reserved demeanor. Mild-mannered Sam Freeman, who offered simple yes/no answers to questions and muted smiles as emotions. It was like life had forged father and daughter as polar opposites, and maybe that explained the tightness of their bond.

What it didn't explain, though, was the strange text Mariana received, a message clearly not meant for her. And when she and Shay had arrived at the hypothesis that its intended recipient might just be Sam Freeman, well, an investigation was required.

Mariana picked up the tablet charging on her high-school desk, one of probably only two or three connected devices in the house given her mom's general technophobia. A quick tap unlocked it, and it displayed a synced view with the kitchen's wall screen: the enchilada recipe her mom attempted. "Oh, this will be easy. You've almost got it down," Shay said, her voice clear from the kitchen. "I'd actually cut the oven temperature by like twenty degrees. But turn convection on. It'll cook more evenly." She paused, then turned her volume up for the next part. "I learned that from my dad."

Mariana couldn't hear her mom's exact reaction, but the tone of it gave away enough of their conversation to show that no one suspected anything about her virtual breaking and entering. She tapped through the tablet, the invasion of privacy feeling a little more icky than she would have liked; but on the other hand, she had got an icky message from her mom, who then just acted like it never happened, so…

Then she found it. In clear, black letters against a light blue backdrop, starting with the first message that accidentally got sent to her.

Renee: Thought you should know that waking up next to Sam Freeman is something I could get used to.

Sam: It was wonderful. How did we wait so long?

Renee: We're good parents! There was a line that we couldn't cross!

Sam: I'm nervous for them to find out.

Renee: I think mine will be fine with it. I'm a little scared of Shay, though. :)

Sam: Oh, I am too. That's why she's so great.

Mariana swiped over to the various message folders, sifting through both Sent and Trash, to put together a timeline of what had happened. Based on time stamps and the digital breadcrumbs, her mom had accidentally sent the message to Mariana's device, then deleted it, *then* sent it properly off to Shay's dad. All while not realizing that the deletion only removed it from her own account, not the receiver's.

In this case, the receiver got a far-too-personal look into her mom's love life.

Mariana snapped a photo of the exchange for the record, then closed the messaging app and set it back to sync with the kitchen's recipe. And though some of that same stomach-churning imagery still invaded her mind, reading the whole thing brought a surprising smile to her face. Later, Shay even agreed after reading the photo of their messages. "Aw, that's kind of cute," she'd said. "I'm happy for them. But holy crap, our parents are doing it, and *that* is gross."

That day was the start and end of Mariana's career in espionage, at least until now.

And while those ten minutes of stealth maneuvers, distraction, and hacking came with the low stakes of her mom's system accounts at her childhood home, this current mission with Carter offered something completely different.

They walked side by side as the traffic signal turned to shuffle the foot traffic forward, crossing the street as the Hawke Accelerator loomed in front of them. They had a plan, a very specific plan that required both precision and artistry, all to answer one question that might be the key to *everything*:

What was Project Pen?

★ ★ ★

One hour before the loop ended, the roles now played out opposite to the mission Mariana had undertaken with Shay. Today, Mariana acted as the distraction. To dig into the secrets of Project Pen, Carter needed two high-level security clearances. One came from Beckett, the access password obtained loops ago. The other?

Mariana took an educated guess. She knocked on the door, the small plaque next to it with the name *Samantha Pratt* inscribed on it. Underneath her name was her title, *Chief Science Officer*.

"Hi. I'm with the ReLive group," Mariana said, putting on her best professional voice. "I'm sorry I missed the tour the other day. I wasn't feeling well."

"Oh," Pratt said. She offered a polite smile that showed Mariana's timing was inconvenient. Given that the loop would reset shortly, it wasn't like it mattered. "It happens. What can I do for you?"

Mariana kept one eye on the time, though her onslaught of questions about the accelerator utilized the same strategy Shay had used for Mariana's mom: build trust while stalling. She asked question after question, most of which she already had answers for, and that knowledge allowed her to lead Pratt on for a good ten minutes.

By her estimate, that span marked enough time to earn Pratt's trust. Mariana shifted into the next step. "Oh," she said, intentionally looking at the clock on the wall. "I just realized that I haven't had a single thing to eat today. It's been one of those mornings. Can you show me to the cafeteria?"

Pratt looked at the various screens around her. "I don't know if I should leave. We're actually monitoring an active test cycle right now."

"All the better," Mariana said, trying her warmest smile. "I'd love to hear all about it. I'm fascinated by particle physics. It's so different from the human brain." She nodded toward the hall. "My treat?"

Pratt took one more glance at the screens, then shook her head with a grin. "You win. A snack does sound good."

Mariana turned and stepped into the hallway where Carter had looked busy with a scanner while she baited Pratt out of her office. "Oh," he said, as Pratt came to the doorway. "Can I step in for a second? There's a power conduit in one of your wall panels that's on the fritz. Might be affecting some of your test readings."

"Sure," Pratt said with a wave. "We'll be back soon."

Mariana took one last glance behind her as Carter wheeled his cart in. The door to Pratt's office slid shut, and she moved in step with Hawke's chief science officer. "I'm actually a fan of simple glazed donuts," Mariana said as they moved down the hall.

Shortly after, Mariana had exhausted all of the small talk that came to mind. Carter's food obsession helped, as Pratt seemed to care about baked goods on the same level as Carter, and going off on the merits of glazed donuts provided enough of a distraction that Pratt didn't seem to notice Mariana was slowing her pace considerably as they approached the cafeteria. Her measured study of the bakery display required all of Carter's ramblings about pastries to stretch things out even further, and the timing seemed just right.

Because right when Mariana handed a donut to Pratt, the noise blared out.

"Data breach in Section W-7," a voice said over the loudspeaker. "Security deployed to Section W entrances and exits."

Point to Carter.

Though she lacked Carter's eidetic memory, she knew exactly where W-7 sat on the Hawke facility map: *W* for the science and research wing on the west side of the facility, and 7 for the block of offices where Pratt sat. "Is that bad?" Mariana asked Pratt, her stalling tone built to balance between innocent and curious.

"I'm not sure," Pratt said. She stood still, holding the napkin-wrapped donut as she glanced over at wall screens.

"Is it your test cycle?"

"I hope—" She pulled out her device. "Oh. Oh no."

Mariana didn't need to look at the screen to know what had prompted that response.

"I need to go," Pratt said. "Thank you for the donut."

"I'll catch you at the final ReLive meeting later," Mariana yelled for appearances, though really, that didn't matter. Hawke would have exploded by then. She looked at her own phone, a short message from Carter.

Downloaded the secure database. I got out of Pratt's area. I'm at a terminal on level 4 in the central wing. Meet me there, but be discreet. Security's looking for me.

On my way, she typed in a quick response.

Carter sat huddled, his tablet wired directly into the side of a panel rather than using the typical hardware-free signals that powered data communications. "Hey," he said quickly, though his expression changed as he noticed the cherry scone in her hand. Though the security calls still rang out, they became entangled with the beginning of Hawke's destruction. The occasional shake and pop of the process grew with passing time, enough that the floor jolted as she handed the scone to Carter. It dropped on the floor, crumbs bouncing off, but Carter picked it up without a second thought and chomped into it.

His logic remained sound. They'd both wake up in their beds in a few minutes.

"I like Pratt," he said through the bite. "Guess what her password was?"

Mariana looked above, then down the hall as red security lights flashed. "I don't think we have time for guessing games."

"*Alla griglia*—it's an Italian term for cooking meat. Capitalized and framed by exclamation points, and the number sixty-two at the end. Probably a lucky number. See?" he said, holding up his notebook, the combination of letters and numbers scrawled across in blue ink. "Won't forget next time."

"That's good," Mariana said. "Because either security's gonna get us, or this place is going to blow up."

"Or both." He flipped forward a page, lines and lines of notes running until they ran out of space and crept through the margins. "I'm just going as fast as I can."

"You're getting everything down?" Six minutes left. And though it had been a while since they'd been in Hawke, the mix of rumbles and rattles executed in a familiar order. The only difference was this particular section of the facility, making the reverberation of chaos and the jolt of the structure slightly off from what she'd experienced before.

"No. Just directions of what to look for next time. There's so much information here, and it's very technical and—"

The scone dropped out of Carter's hand as he paused.

"Holy freaking crap," he said, his voice drawing out each syllable. Mariana turned, ears still tuned into the security chatter playing out around them. From beyond, footsteps and voices echoed, their pace picking up as they drew closer and closer.

"What is it?" Mariana asked, now back at the security display on the panel. Section by section changed to red, highlighting their exact route until their specific location on the map began glowing.

"Hold on. I gotta make sure I'm reading this right." The glow across his face shifted, his hands up swiping through the information quickly. "Project Pen is a pen. It's a literal pen." He held up his own ballpoint pen before flicking off the cap with his thumb and scrawling down notes.

"We already guessed that. The Bic pen. What's so special about it?"

"It's not the pen. It's what happened to the pen. This is why Beckett was in DC. This is why his itinerary was classified," Carter said, his eyes still wide and focused on the data flashing before him. "It's Hawke." He paused for a moment, then wrote a sentence just out of view, though she caught the double underline floating beneath it.

Hawke is a time machine.

32

The Hawke Accelerator was a time machine. And Project Pen was its case study.

Despite the destruction and chaos ramping up around them, Mariana knelt down beside Carter, who blurted words out at high speeds while tapping at his tablet screen *and* jotting notes in his notebook. She gave him a pass when he stumbled over some of it, given the cracking windows and blaring security alarms.

First imagined thirtysome years ago, the Hawke Accelerator was the brainchild of physicist Albert Beckett. Collaborating with an international team, Beckett's breakthrough research identified a theory about…well, it wasn't exactly Mariana's specialty. But she understood scientific language enough to get the idea, something about compressing the physical space between atoms to lower the energy required for accelerating an object. What did catch her eye, much more than the pages of mathematical equations, was the theory's name.

Compressive temporal distribution—or CTD.

Beckett's green beam.

The research moved from theoretical to practical, a series of calculations that made enough sense on paper and in simulations to take the next step. Twenty years ago, construction crews broke ground on what would ultimately become the massive facility they now stood in. And while the actual building was completed over several years, the different components of the accelerator itself required development in different stages.

One of the things that had been kept secret for all this time was that Hawke's accelerator actually contained *three* stages, a series of capabilities that built upon each other. The first stage enabled all manners of particle experimentation, the most traditional system with a track length of twenty point six miles that utilized decades of accelerator research dating all the way back to the Proton Synchrotron, the Tevatron at FermiLab, and the Large Hadron Collider. This gave a public face to the science at hand while allowing for secret research to be advanced and funded by international governments.

The second stage of the accelerator was designed specifically for Project Pen. Not that they had a pen in mind when they conceived it, but they needed some small, inanimate, and sturdy object. Beckett's team ultimately decided on a pen for its combination of composite and metal materials, along with the liquid state of the ink. With Project Pen, the team oversaw the activation of the accelerator to send the ballpoint pen back one week in time.

Carter read out bits and pieces of the summary, a combination of techno-babble and practical steps the team took to avoid any grandfather paradoxes. "I'll explain later," he said, the fastest she'd ever seen him talk as he scrolled through the list of folders on the screen. "It's clever. They used robots and cameras to check things and prevent paradoxes."

"What happens if there *is* a paradox?" Mariana asked.

"I dunno," he said with a laugh. A voice crackled through the section's loudspeakers, though the combination of cracking metal and echoed speech made it inscrutable. "I failed out of my degree, remember? But look, here's the end of the experiment." A video floated over the rest of the screen, its time stamp dated seven years ago. The room's corner camera showed Beckett at the control station, arms planted in a tense pose while he remained still. From his left came six more scientists, people of various heights and appearances but all clad in the same white lab coats. And to his right, the door slid open, a small robot rolled in, its mechanical arms holding a tray with a data tablet and a single pen.

"They did it. Seven years ago, they sent the pen back in time," Carter said.

On the video, Beckett knelt down in front of it, first leaning in to examine the pen, then holding it up to show his colleagues, sparking an immediate reaction of arms up, fists pumping, hugs and swirling lab coats. If there had been audio on the recording, Mariana was sure she would have heard yells and cheers as well.

"The accelerator's controls were programmed in advance and operated by robots. Targeted a trip of one week. They all stayed out of the facility during that span, and robots were instructed to pick up the pen and go into storage until the timeline caught up. So, like, the past wouldn't bump into the present," Carter said, the pace of his words picking up. "But it was a beta test for a bigger experiment."

A bigger experiment. Mariana thought back to presentations given to ReLive on Mondays, when one of the scientists said that their current explosion-inducing test was "the first time we've actually run this particular version of the process cycle."

On-screen, Beckett and his crew continued to celebrate while a sidebar of data scrolled by. As Carter explained during the video, the third and final accelerator stage, the largest one with the greatest power draw and most sprawling infrastructure, was designed specifically for the purpose of sending a human back in time.

"We're running out of time," Mariana said.

"Sorry," Carter said. "David processed so much data for me before, but there must have been a security protocol here. I've had to do this all manually, so I'm just skimming as much—"

A loud crash came from above, and down the hall, Mariana saw a cracked ceiling panel tumble to the floor, sparks shooting out. Carter looked over his shoulder at the debris, then shook his head. "I'm just—wait…" His eyebrows furrowed and head tilted at a sharp angle.

"What is it? Did they finish?" Mariana asked, kneeling down to meet Carter's eyes. "Did they ever use that third accelerator stage?"

"Phase two," he said slowly.

Carter squinted as his fingers flew over the tablet. The floor shook, scraps of metal kicking across the floor, drowning out the noise from the security system. "I'm digging," he said. Screens loaded and scrolled, large tables of numbers whipping by, giving way to power diagrams and schematics before going back to data.

"This is new," he said, swiping aside a table of data and tapping on a folder. He pointed to the icon, the words *Phase 2* underneath it.

Mariana blinked, then leaned closer to make sure she'd read that right. "Phase Two? Does that have something to do with the anomalies we've encountered?"

"I don't know. Maybe there's more in here." The folder opened up, though its contents remained blurred out, and the words *Level 5 Security—Requires Multiple Passwords* appeared in a floating box over it. His fingers moved with an effortless instinct, putting in the username and password for Beckett that he'd input over and over.

But at the second slot, he paused, the cursor blinking in anticipation as the seconds counted down to the end of the loop. He blinked several times, then turned to her. "Got any ideas?" he finally asked.

"Does Pratt's not work?" Mariana gave a slight shrug, a reaction that failed to capture the tension growing in her. Despite the collapsing facility, despite the occasional dust and debris shaking from the ceiling and walls, a single name brought more apprehension than physical danger.

"Who?" Carter asked before shaking his head. "Maybe I should try hacking through—"

Before he could finish, she pulled the tablet out of his hands and entered *Samantha Pratt* and the Italian cooking term he'd written down for her moments ago.

The screen flashed green in confirmation, and she avoided Carter's eyes as she handed the device back to him. Down the hall, an explosion blew out the wall, metal and concrete scattering about. The noise brought Carter back to the present, and he started to sift through new folders. Mariana watched over his shoulder, words and names coming to her in pieces too fast to make anything sensible of it.

"Ah," Carter said. "Sixty seconds. I'm gonna take in as much of this as I can."

"There they are," a voice called out from down the hallway. Mariana looked at three silhouettes emerging, one of them with an arm pointed at them. "Stand up! This is a secure area!"

"Phase Two is…well, this is complicated. This is showing months and months of planning." A sudden boom rumbled through, the rattling violent enough for Carter to lose his balance, the pen dropping out of his hands and skittering across the floor. He looked up at the swinging lights overhead, then winced as a crack splintered its way across the large adjacent window. *Kendra Hall.* Who's that?"

"Maybe someone who can help us."

"It's the best lead we got." Carter kept scrolling, the tablet reflection shifting in subtle gradations of black text and blue schematics. "There's so much here. It's a whole *thing*," he said, reaching down for his notebook and pen before checking the time once more. "Look at this, something about a retrieval pro-tocol. I have no idea what that means. Where's David when you need—"

"Don't move!" security called out again, now halfway down the hall to them. Mariana laughed to herself. Whoever those security guards were, they deserved a raise for sticking to their duties as the whole facility collapsed.

"Next time." Carter reached, fingers taking hers and squeez-ing tight. "We're so close. Next time we'll track her down. Her name. Kendra Hall. Remember that name. She's—"

33

Carter's eyes opened.

But then they closed again.

He rolled over, the world still blocked out, and he considered calling in sick today. Not that he necessarily *was* sick—a quick sanity check showed no signs of sniffles or sore throat in the few seconds of being awake. The other thing the check brought him was the sense of simple comfort in being horizontal, wrapped in comfortable sheets knowing that his birthday had passed.

He'd celebrated informally a week ago, his friends pooling together to go for an evening of dim sum–tasting at a place he couldn't normally afford. Yesterday, though, had been a complete communication blackout.

One eye opened just enough to see the phone on his night stand. He reached over and grabbed it. A status notification showed at the top, an octagon icon signaling that any messages or outreach from numbers *not* in his address book would automatically be filtered out.

Including his parents and his brother. Should he deactivate the security level and add them back in?

Nah.

A day or two wouldn't hurt.

He would, however, open his phone and load up his contact list for something completely different. The list scrolled through, dragging behind as his finger pulled downward until he hit a record about halfway down and typed.

Hawke-Technical Staffing Contact

I'm not feeling great, gonna take the day to rest. I'll check my current diagnostics remotely and will be available for consultation if there are any emergencies.

A green check mark appeared, sending the message over to his bosses, colleagues, and everyone else flagged to be copied on scheduling messages.

A little bit of truth existed in that statement. He *wasn't* feeling great, but he wasn't necessarily feeling bad either.

But something felt...off. This morning, that was the only way to put it. Mondays saw a standard routine of fighting off fatigue, dragging himself out from under the covers, and getting going with his day. But the slight headache and a general malaise came out of nowhere, like his body wanted him to break from normalcy and stay still.

So he listened. Not just to his body but his mind too, a weird haziness to his thoughts. He just lay in bed, a true belated birthday gift to himself.

Staying in bed, hiding from anyone that might try to pull him out of this cocoon.

At least for a few hours.

Carter closed his eyes, ignoring the chirping birds outside as he went back to sleep for a few extra hours, then maybe he'd go out for a walk or something, perhaps even a really great lunch.

Simply because he could.

34

This Monday morning, Mariana didn't give Carter much time.
She sent a message right away, knowing that he always started
the loop earlier than her. When he didn't return it, her suspi-
cions activated. Her outreach hit two barriers: the physical wall
of his disappearing memory, and the digital divide created by
the temporary high-security setting that he needed to reset.

Both were tied to his ability to recall the previous loop. Her
faith had been tested over the past several ones, and yet even
as Hawke exploded around them, his memory showed signs
of deterioration. How did Carter not recall Pratt—not just her
password but her name? That information came from the very
same loop, the very same morning.

The morning news showed no anomaly to pursue, no clues
to trace. Whether that meant an anomaly hadn't arrived yet or
one didn't exist in this loop, she wasn't sure. It did, however,
turn her focus to one path of action. Mariana had prepared for
this ever since he'd first showed signs of losing his memory.
Losing might not be the correct term; in many ways, it simply
regressed back to its original state. If the time loop ended, she
figured he wouldn't start experiencing memory loss. But whatever happened during the loop?

Something wiped it away. How much, she wasn't sure, but she approached it the only way she knew how.

With a box of simple glazed donuts.

This was Carter, after all.

She moved, the musty hallway of his apartment building a far cry from the clean upkeep, connected technology, and lobby security of hers. She walked up several flights of stairs, box of donuts with her, then down the hall, past door after door, the architecture likely nearly a century old—and it certainly smelled like it. Without any anomaly hitting the news to chase down, she went straight to his most logical location. Yet when he didn't answer her knock, sitting and waiting remained the only option. But during those quiet hours, she kept pushing forward, trying to dig up any information on the last thing Carter said to her.

Kendra Hall.

What was so important about Kendra Hall that the highest levels of security guarded her history?

That question drove her into a single-minded focus, and while life in a time loop often felt like every second etched definitively into a controlled, even temporal passing, Mariana lost herself, the mystery of Kendra Hall eating away at moments while she waited for Carter.

For most people, little details about their lives existed forever across data networks to a frightening degree. But for this mystery person, all Kendra Hall had online was a name. And the deeper Mariana searched, the less she found. She started with recent records, going back month after month, only to find absolutely nothing.

There might have been a wall in Carter's mind that kept them apart. But the wall of information hiding Kendra Hall's purpose? That proved to be even harder to overcome.

Around two in the afternoon, she finally saw Carter.

His familiar silhouette turned the corner and stepped under

the busted light bulb that kept him in the shadows. She sprung up, like gravity had inverted and pushed her onto her feet. The abrupt movement must have caught his attention, enough to make him pause. She waited several seconds, holding still while telling herself to keep expectations in check. *Nothing means nothing until something happens*, she heard Shay say in her head.

He started again, now walking at a casual pace, footsteps moving without urgency, his eyes tilted downward at his phone. Even then, something seemed different in his gait.

Ever since they'd met, a gnawing pressure drove the two of them. Even in quiet moments, when they managed to find comfort on the ocean, in the kitchen, at Wimbledon, everything always snapped back to the need to escape the loop. It carried in the way they talked, moved, and thought, a life framed around a singular purpose. And with that came an undertow: sometimes panic, sometimes stress, sometimes curiosity, and sometimes grief.

At their best, their moments *meant* more because of the loop. And at their worst, bad news turned into catastrophic levels of despair.

Carter walked with neither. Instead, he moved with a rare relaxed motion, a casual glance at his phone combined with an easy sigh, one that exhaled without the weight of the world behind it.

She knew right away. All it took was one look and she *knew*.

It didn't take the lack of recognition in his eyes as they locked gazes.

That just made it hit harder.

"Can I help you?" he asked. "Oh god, did I accidentally order something? I didn't mean to, but sometimes I push the wrong button when looking at menus and—"

"It's all right," she said, steadying her not–all right voice. Mariana cleared her throat, then glanced down at the donuts. "I have a delivery for someone named Kendra Hall. Donuts."

She cracked the lid, and though hours had passed since they'd came out of the oven, their sugary aroma still came through.

"Glazed donuts," Carter said. "Sometimes, simple is better."

"Do you know her? The order listed this apartment."

Carter shook his head, his hair falling into his eyes. "Nope. Doesn't sound familiar."

"Ah. Maybe she made a typo. I mean, it's too late now. Sorry, Kendra." Mariana said the name with emphasis, but it failed to register with him. He turned back to his phone, one hand shoved in his pocket, though she caught a glance upward at the donut box.

Kendra Hall was simply a name to him. No scientific meaning, no personal significance. "You want one?" she asked.

"A donut?"

"I just," she said, taking a moment, "got the sense that you're someone who appreciates good food."

He leaned in for a closer look at the logo on the side of the box. "Bellisario's. They *are* the best bakery in the city. But," he said, lips twisted in a slight scowl, "it's not for me. Should I pay you for it?"

"You know," Mariana started before hesitation caught her momentum. Moments ago, Carter's relaxed vibe had cracked apart her world. But here, he spoke with a brighter tone, a light in his eyes, the innocence of not having seen the impossible over and over and over again.

Such a light gave her hope.

"Sometimes orders just don't pan out. Why don't you take it?" She raised the box, offering it to him. "I won't tell."

His hands gripped the sides of the box, balancing its weight between them. "You sure?"

She could let go of the box. Her fingers could simply detach, release their grip and leave it with him. Carter, who had given her the gift and curse of awareness in the time loop, now simply existed without anything to tether him to the curse of memory.

Cooking, working, dreaming of a different life—perhaps one where he might confront his parents after all this time.

All of the things they'd done, all of the ways he'd changed, evaporated into the air.

Mariana held herself steady, stifling thoughts of them stealing away on a cruise ship.

For now, all she could do was give him a brief deviation in the form of donuts. And while that wouldn't restore all that he'd lost, her heart beat just a little quicker knowing that she might deliver some joy, as brief as it might be.

"Take it," she said. "I should go."

"Oh, thanks. I can't turn down Bellisario's." By the time she heard him open the box, she'd already turned. She walked, eyes closed and even steps, a steady cadence as she moved toward whatever possible future she might have.

"Hey," Carter called out, stopping her halfway down the hall. She turned, craning her neck over her shoulder.

"You want one?"

He cracked the lid, holding it open at shoulder level. Mariana's eyes darted, first to the open box in his hands, then to the familiar smirk on his face.

She'd seen him like this so many times, a box or bag of something cooked or baked, always with that same expression. Like a reflex, her entire body relaxed at the sight.

"Probably bad for my cholesterol to eat a whole box," he said with a laugh.

She walked back, her pace quicker than before, and while part of that stemmed from the mix of feelings Carter stirred in her, she also realized that she hadn't eaten anything since her breakfast of a protein shake.

Carter would have given her so much grief about that.

"I'm Carter, by the way," he said as she took one of the glazed donuts.

"Mariana," she replied, each syllable struggling to get out.

"Mariana…" His voice trailed off, and for a flash, the glint in his eyes shifted. "Have you delivered stuff here before? Or maybe we have a friend in common?" His lips pursed, a sudden hesitation arriving. "I sound like I'm hitting on you, huh? I'm not. You just *feel* familiar. Never mind," he said and shook his head, "forget I said anything."

"No, you're right." She held the donut, the perfect circle missing a bite-shaped piece, and gauged his reaction. "I've been here before. If you've ordered Bellisario's before? I just didn't put it together until now."

"Oh, right, right." Carter's laugh echoed down the hall, and Mariana resisted the urge to grab him, hold him, find some way to will his memory back into existence.

Instead, she ate the donut.

"Well, maybe I'll see you again someday," he said with a laugh. "I order a lot of takeout. San Francisco has too much to offer, you know?"

This time, it was her turn to remain static as the inside lock whirred. The door slid open, the automatic lights activating from within.

And this time, it was her turn to call him back.

"Hey," she said, with a little more force than necessary.

"Yeah?" He faced her again, the dim lighting around them casting shadows that hid his eyes. "You want another one? I mean, I do have a whole box."

"No. I was just thinking." She'd veered him off his path already. And in a few days, it would snap back to his proper start and finish.

And though the mystery of Kendra Hall awaited, a deeper question demanded attention. At least right now.

"You seem to be the type of guy who knows a lot about food," she said slowly.

Carter's shoulders shrugged, lifting the box up several inches. "Guilty as charged."

"Do you like cooking?" The question formed, the very tip of a much deeper thought, something she hadn't quite yet figured out how to put into words.

Or if it even needed that. Perhaps simply experiencing it would be enough?

"What I mean is, I'm not very good at it, and I'm trying to figure something out. There's, um, a lentil soup recipe I've been struggling with. If you might know how to do it right."

They stood, only the sound of a neighbor coming and going between them. And though Carter's eyes locked with hers for a glimpse, the only glint came from curiosity, not familiarity.

And maybe that was enough.

"Mariana," he said, box still in his hands, "I think we're gonna be pals. Come on in."

35

Second chances. Did this count as one?

Maybe. In the time loop, Shay's definitions didn't necessarily apply, especially given the context of the last time she'd given Mariana grief about it, on a tennis court of all places.

"You're not even calling him back? It took forever to set you two up." Shay's brow creased as she drank from the water bottle. Mariana pretended to ignore her friend's tone, then unzipped her tennis bag to pull out a fresh canister of bright green balls.

"I never asked you to set us up," she said, the familiar rubbery smell of new tennis balls tickling her nose.

"Right, so when you said, 'Who's the guy with good cheekbones in your post-doc program?' you were doing demographic research?"

"I mean, sure, he's hot." Mariana glanced around at the adjacent courts under the early-morning sun, one with a dad trying to teach a young girl how to hit backhands, and the other with two older couples playing doubles. Did they pay any attention to the conversation about Mariana's very boring dating life? Because Shay spoke loudly enough for the wind to carry details over.

"But…"

"But he's—"

"Ah!" Shay clapped her hands, then wagged a finger her way. "There's *always* a *but* with you! Fact. Mariana's standards are, like, beyond the galaxy. Hypothesis. She's afraid of opening up to anyone *besides* her best friend. Experiment. Try going on a second date with Raymond."

"That's not true. I open up to my mom too," Mariana said, pulling her racket out of her bag. She leaned into a hamstring stretch, like the pose might cause the conversation to end.

"Okay, look, I am probably the biggest asshole you know. Right?" Shay asked, now pointing fingers at herself. "So you gave me a second chance at being your friend. And now we're *related* in the eyes of the government! I've been in two semesters with Raymond—I can guarantee he is *less* of an asshole than me. So—" she put her hands on hips, her long dark braids swaying as she spoke "—I think you should go out with him again."

"I really can't. I'm busy." Mariana looked over her shoulder at the old men waiting at the court's fence. "We really should start, otherwise those guys will try to take our court."

"Fine, fine," Shay said, spinning the racket in her hands. "But *one* of these days, you'll need to give a good guy a second chance. A real, honest second chance. Not a *hypothesis*, not an *experiment*," she said, her voice slamming emphasis on each methodological word. "A second chance."

"What does that even mean?" Mariana had asked as she handed her friend a ball.

"Technical definition, *don't give up on someone you like*." Shay bounced the ball several times with her racket before putting it in her skirt's pocket. "Not that hard to do, right?"

Mariana wasn't sure if this technically counted as a second chance with Carter, at least by Shay's standards. Maybe, since they'd started from scratch. And as he walked her through the stages of cooking lentil soup, questions answered themselves. Not the cooking ones—she'd remembered the lessons Carter had given her before, even though she still never put them into practice.

But the important ones. Who was Carter outside of the time loop? Would they even get along? Did they still belong together? *Don't give up on someone you like.*

They started simple, Mariana pulling up the same recipe they'd used loops ago. Carter grabbed his notebook and made a grocery list by hand before tearing it out and leading her to the small market two blocks away. Several hours passed, one meal cooked and eaten, along with a dessert of simple glazed donuts. Time stretched out, a question turning into a discussion into a laugh into a whole evening. But her answer to all those questions arrived right away. It landed in a clear, obvious way, without any need for the walk to pick up groceries or even the shared meal.

Carter had once said that getting her to slow down, even for five minutes, would be life-changing. And here, from the moment she'd stepped inside, his very presence showed her the way. Dinner was simply a bonus.

Because she'd never, ever be as good a cook as Carter.

Now they stood side by side, him washing pots and pans before handing them to her to dry. "I should get going," she said, rubbing a dish towel against the base of a frying pan. "My poor cat is probably wondering where I am."

"You have a cat?" Carter stood back, eyes closed and hand to his temples. "Wait, wait, lemme guess. It's a little dark gray fur ball. Big eyes, fluffy tail. That hides from everyone."

"Pretty close," Mariana said slowly, her reaction hidden from him. She barely managed to push out the next question. "How'd you know?"

"Good guess. I'm not psychic, if you're wondering." He opened his eyes, then rinsed his hands off one more time before shutting the water off. "Photographic memory doesn't count. I mean—"

"Eidetic," they both said. Their laughter filled the space,

Carter's bright chuckle raising his shoulders and bouncing his wavy hair over his eyes. Mariana matched him, though a heaviness weighed her down.

"That's the technical term," she said, handing the now-dry pan over to him, followed by the dish towel.

"See, I'll remember that," he said, tapping the side of his head. "Regardless of what you call it."

For a flash, Mariana considered the possibility of simply existing loop by loop, experiencing different variations of Carter without problems or worries.

Without consequences.

But wasn't that the point? Carter's family history, his frustration at being stuck in his life, all of the things he buried under a facade of a smirk and discussions about pastries: those problems wove into his very essence. Resetting them over and over with only a night here, a lunch there, perhaps even a whirlwind getaway, wouldn't amount to anything.

Marianna straightened, a gesture that Carter missed as he hung the dish towel over the side of the counter. "Kendra Hall," she whispered to herself.

"What was that?"

"Oh," Mariana said. "Kendra Hall. Just wondering if she missed those donuts she ordered."

"Of course she would have." He lifted the lid of the half-empty box and grabbed one more donut before taking a bite and gesturing at it. She shook her head no, to which he grinned. "But hey, her loss, right? If I ever run into her, I'll let her know."

Kendra Hall.

To give Carter any hope of changing for the better, to give *them* a chance, she had to find this mystery woman and finally break out of this loop.

"I gotta feed my cat. Her name is Maggie, by the way."

"It's a fitting name. Totally matches what I pictured. Well, look," he said, gesturing to the door. "This was the weirdest day."

"Sometimes unexpected things happen." Mariana walked close enough to the door that its sensors detected her, sliding it open and bringing in a draft from the outer hall.

"Yeah, I mean, like the freaking dire-wolf skeleton at Lake Merritt this afternoon? How did *that* happen?"

A dire-wolf skeleton? Another anachronism must have happened, and not a Columbian mammoth. She'd been so caught up, first in Kendra Hall and then this semidate with Carter, that she'd missed the afternoon's news about more history-breaking anomalies.

That didn't matter anymore, though. Those anachronisms seemed as consistent as the sun setting and moon rising, and they all somehow tied into Hawke. "Strange times. Maybe the answer really is just *have a donut.*"

She stepped out, though she paused after crossing the threshold. Not because she hesitated to leave Carter; she knew she had to, as much as the ease of the evening felt like a blanket of comfort around her.

No, the interruption in her step came from her fingers feeling her bag for one final check. Because while Carter had been distracted with the dishes, she'd grabbed the mobile David AI unit off his shelf.

She'd need David more than him. And besides, he'd get David back in a few days via a time-loop reset anyways.

The tips of her fingers pushed against the device's familiar shape, and then she turned while he stood at the doorway, that same Carter smirk on his face.

"Look," he said, taking in a deep breath, "I don't usually take baked goods from someone who's barely an acquaintance. Let alone make dinner with them. And have more baked goods. And talk all night."

A smile came to her face, so broad that her cheeks ached. She wanted this for them. As much as they could get. "I hope it was memorable," she said, reaching up to kiss him on the cheek before turning and walking off.

She moved with purpose, and despite the fact that she should have been fatigued, determination powered her movement, and her mind sparked with thoughts and ideas, all sorts of ways to try and discover who Kendra Hall was—and, more important, *where* she was. "Can I see you again?" Carter called out from the hallway.

Mariana turned, though she continued walking away. "I have to go do something for the next few days," she said in a half yell. "It's really important. But after that?" Her feet planted for a second, and she looked at him, letting his image burn into her not-eidetic memory. "I really, really hope so. We could try making a vegetable Wellington."

Carter's head angled. "That sounds difficult. A lot of the juices would make the phyllo soggy."

"Oh," Mariana said, picturing the lunch Carter had prepared on the yacht. All of that experience of cooking loop after loop, not even that remained. "I'm pretty sure you'll figure it out."

36

After getting back from Carter's, Mariana immediately set out to build a bond with David. It felt daunting, given the AI's sass at Carter, and in each previous loop, Carter had made the introduction and explained the time-loop situation.

This time, though, she had to explain both the time loop and *why* she'd stolen him. She'd expected a certain amount of pushback, though in true David fashion, he simply said, "Your story is highly unlikely but not out of the realm of possibility."

And that was that, enough to push into a Tuesday and a Wednesday filled with research about this mysterious Kendra Hall. For the most part, Mariana's initial findings outside of Carter's apartment held up: layer upon layer of searching failed to bring up any recent history, everything seemingly stopping around two years ago.

Having David around to process the public information about all of the Kendra Halls in the world helped narrow it down, leading to a *pretty certain* proclamation of identifying the correct one, though he never gave a percentage to that accuracy.

That offered a starting point, but from there? Kendra seemed like a fairly normal person. Mariana took the days to dig up whatever personal history dotted across records. Public records of various addresses, social posts out with friends around the Bay Area, the occasional mention in archived records, all of it forming the biography of a fairly normal woman in her twenties.

Mariana looked at the stack of data tablets, moving written notes and image captures from place to place to try and find a sensible logic for her complete disappearance. "What do you think, David?"

"I'm not a psychologist, Mariana. I crunch numbers, look at probabilities, and sometimes give directions or look up information."

"Yeah, but can't you have an opinion about why there's nothing recent about her?"

"Because she's in hiding," David said matter-of-factly.

"You're certain?"

"No, it's just an opinion. A death would have brought news about a funeral and public record. If she'd gone missing, there would be news about a search. Going into hiding lines up with the lack of information."

Her social accounts stopped being updated with no notice. Any public activity or tracking vanished. Shay had talked about going off the grid before, one of her extended rants for someone who loved disappearing into the wilderness during a technology-based age, but even she admitted that outside of dying or leaving the country, disappearing from the digital space required actual effort.

"Mariana, my power supply is at twenty percent. You really should charge me."

Problem was that she hadn't stolen David's charging station as well. "Go take a nap, David," she said with a sigh. "I'll need you tomorrow, so I'll try to solve this the old-fashioned way."

"Use that human ingenuity, Mariana," he said, and before she could respond, he beeped to signify deactivation.

Carter could hack David's processing limiter, but couldn't he have done something about the AI's attitude? She shook her head, returning to the task at hand. On the table sat one tablet with a list of things she'd pieced together about Kendra's personal history: where she grew up, where she went to college, how many siblings she had, even her parents' names. All of that came with just a little bit of effort. But as she looked at the list again and again, a pattern began to emerge.

A pattern—but what were the variables?

Mariana opened the list's editing tools and tapped away, assigning a highlight color for different things: red for family, blue for education, yellow for personal, and green for career. She scrolled through the list, minute details getting branded with appropriate colors. An appearance at her cousin's graduation? Red highlight. A mention in a charity 10K run? Yellow highlight. A caption in the local newspaper about students protesting deforestation eight years ago? Blue highlight.

On and on she went, a rhythm to her tapping that painted the list by categorized colors, and when she finished, she scrolled through from bottom to top to confirm her hunch.

In the sea of reds, blues, and yellows, only a handful of green records surfaced. As she sorted through them, some young-adult jobs showed up: internships, barista, customer service.

Yet, *no* mention of Hawke, *despite* her name being so important that Carter made her remember it.

As Mariana stared at the colors in front of her, the pattern emerged in such an obvious way that she bit her lip hard enough to taste blood.

Was this what happened when she didn't have Carter with her to figure things out?

She'd spent days scouring through the records and archives, photos and articles, so much *data* trying to piece together who Kendra was. But none of that mattered; the only thing that *did* matter was the fact that she was important to Beckett and the Hawke team. And while Carter thought they would have another loop together to figure it out, that chance had disappeared, absorbed into his regressed memory.

Mariana let herself go to bed early, Maggie curled up in a ball by her waist. Tomorrow, she'd go to Hawke using everything she'd learned, everything Carter had passed on.

Because information about Kendra Hall existed somewhere within the top-secret archives of the Hawke Accelerator. And if Carter wasn't able to dig it up himself, then she'd have to.

How many times had Mariana walked this path by now?

Like she had the first time, she moved with the ReLive group through the front entrance of the Hawke Accelerator. And from there, she used her well-worn excuse of needing to find a bathroom. She strode forward with precision, a combination of Carter's loops and repetitions based on notes, muscle memory, and visual cues of when to move. Though Carter had said the Columbian mammoth's appearances screwed up the rhythm of sequences, she noticed little on this loop, and maybe a dire-wolf skeleton just wasn't as much of a big deal as a living, breathing prehistoric beast.

She moved with a preternatural grace, no longer bound by the need to put on a convincing performance. Three steps forward, then a pause for five seconds. One step to the left, then a quick dash forward. Twisting sideways to slip between passersby, then a jog forward.

It all brought her where she needed to be, first passing basic security, then plugging David in to grant her access to restricted areas. She didn't even need David reciting itineraries or schedules, with every movement now burned into her memory but fueled by a determination that never existed before.

A group of scientists in lab coats exited a conference room, and Mariana waited two breaths before tracking them, a steady gap of ten feet between. They provided cover for her when the door to the left opened, a man in casual clothing leaving the data center. She paused, pretending to check her phone for several seconds, then as soon as the door began to slide shut, she turned sideways and slipped through.

She walked across the data center's front room with confident steps, strong movements that radiated off a sense of belonging stemming from previous loops when she and Carter had scouted the space. Her pace slowed halfway through, enough to check the time and wait for the exact moment when the next door slid open. A tall woman waited, eyes glued to her data tablet as she passed, and Mariana offered a bright "Oh, hi, Kaitlyn" her way. The woman looked up, a smile on her lips but a blankness to her gaze as she got stuck between politeness and confusion.

"Hey," the woman said, drawing out the word to avoid having to specify a name.

"I'll see you at the thing this afternoon," Mariana called out in a cheerful voice followed by a wave, and the woman offered another smile and nod as the door slid shut. She moved forward, a quick hello to the man typing away at one terminal, then moved to a station in the far corner armed with the only two things she needed: David, and the password they'd recovered from Pratt in previous loops.

She sat down and navigated her way through the data archives until it got to the classified levels.

Mariana's stomach fluttered as she glanced around, arm outstretched with a fake yawn while she took in the scene. Across the way, another person sat with multiple tablets at an interface. At the other corner, two people stood, chatting away.

In fact, any of those people might have illegally been there too. Who knew when they all acted like they belonged?

That perspective provided enough comfort to open the log-in panel, first typing in Beckett's username and password. It flashed and processed, just as she'd seen so many times from Carter's remote infiltration. A second prompt appeared, requiring the additional level of clearance.

Mariana pictured Pratt's expression when the alarms had gone off. Now? Pratt sat in her office, quietly working through her data or messages or whatever she actually did behind closed doors before Mariana had arrived.

She entered Pratt's log-in details, awaiting the secrets of Phase 2 to load.

Kendra Hall was the world's first time traveler. Did that make Carter the second and Mariana the third? A time loop was, Mariana supposed, a form of time travel as well. Not the fun, exciting ways found in stories of visiting the distant past or leaping into the far future, but a mundane, almost hellish landscape of monotony and repetition.

Two hours passed in near silence, people coming and going out of the data center, though security never arrived, sirens never blared, and her access was never locked out. She'd been able to navigate, load, and read all the way to the point where it simply wasn't necessary anymore.

The layers and layers of details behind Kendra's journey still seemed a little unclear, buried behind protocols and procedures designed to safeguard from paradoxes. How were the anomalies from the past connected to this? Nothing offered clarity on that, though what mattered most was an address: a location about two hours north, coordinates centered on a cabin surrounded by a large plot of redwood trees and wildlife that the Hawke foundation had purchased about two years ago. And two other key dates, four months ago, and two months from now.

The how and why of all of that, Mariana didn't have time to figure out. That was the next loop's goal.

For now, she simply enjoyed the remaining sliver of this loop with a cup of coffee from the cafeteria. She eased into an empty seat used for work breaks to admire a half-blocked view of the Gardner Preserve. They had watched the end of the loop from all different locations within Hawke, even outside of it, yet Mariana noticed the odd cadence unfolding from this side of the building. Rather than sudden jolts and loud cracks, noises came more gradually, and most people ignored them. She knew, though, that about a half mile away on the other side of the massive campus, the observation room had already started to tear itself apart.

With two minutes left, suddenly the end of the loop lumbered toward her instead of its usual sprint to the end. And she was all right with that, a quiet moment with a cup of coffee.

Then she heard him.

"Sorry, just gotta get through there."

Carter's voice pierced through the din of footsteps and quiet conversations, beeps and clicks. Was it because she'd gotten used to hearing it as the only voice that mattered? Because for untold days, the rest of the world had become background noise. Even with anomalies redirecting the flow of hours, things still always moved toward their same destination, sometimes merely taking a different path.

Mariana smiled to herself. Kind of like her and Carter.

She turned, her hair whipping across her cheeks with the movement. And as if the motion had caught his attention, he turned to her as well.

Across an entire floor, they locked eyes, a tether of connection despite the comings and goings between them. Even at a distance, she saw his eyes squint, then widen, his lips parting in disbelief.

She stood, their gazes still trained on each other. He mouthed her name; she nodded, chin bobbing with enthusiasm, and when tears welled into her vision, she wondered how she might possibly explain that their seemingly chance encounter in his hall-way was much more than a one-off story.

It carried the weight of time and space for her.

The clock showed just over a minute left. The room rattled, and murmurs started as people realized the warning notifications taking over the status screens. Their paces picked up, now a collective movement toward the exits, but Carter stood still.

He should have been at the observation room. That was his original fix-it assignment, the reason why he got struck by the green beam in the first place. Unless one of the anomalies rolled the dice, randomizing chaos until it somehow got him over on the far side of Hawke this time around.

Did the universe smile upon her? Or did she just get lucky for once?

It didn't matter. Seconds remained, and *that* mattered. "Reverse jinx," she said under her breath before turning her voice up. "Carter!" she yelled above the maddening crowd. She jogged through, dipping and dashing around the oncoming panic until getting face-to-face with him.

What to say? Only moments remained, and she wanted to offer something meaningful and brilliant, a last gasp for them before she dove into wherever the next step took her.

"Sorry, I don't have any donuts this time."

All around them, people started to hurry. Yet, all that mattered was the few seconds that remained, a fragment of time and space for them and only them. She tilted her head up and drew into him.

"Next time, maybe," he said in a soft voice before pulling in until their noses touched.

Her cheeks flushed, and her weight tilted as they kissed. She wasn't sure what went through his eidetic memory at this moment, but a wave of thoughts flooded her, images and sounds and *feelings* from the first time they'd met in the observation room to that quiet time out on the Pacific Ocean. She stayed present, taking in every detail: the barely there scruff on his chin, the weight of his palm on her back, the heat from his body against hers.

For a few seconds, it seemed like the world wouldn't end after all.

37

Mariana started the loop like she always did, feeding Maggie and having a combination breakfast of coffee and a protein shake.

From there, every passing moment became uncharted territory. Not because the news mentioned yet another anomaly, and not even because she lacked Carter by her side. This time, her destination pushed her far north of the Hawke Accelerator. Her car rolled through morning traffic and past the Golden Gate Bridge until San Francisco lay well behind her, the highway winding through the dusty Marin Hills that eventually became a barren two-lane road. Wineries mixed with large patches of empty fields and open space, and Mariana veered beyond, small towns coming and going until giving way to a thin road surrounded by endless redwood trees.

Kendra Hall's location came as coordinates rather than an address, the map eventually getting to a point where no road could reach her. Mariana brought the car to a halt, and on the windshield, tiny droplets appeared, rain clouds above that apparently evaporated over the loop instead of floating down to San Francisco or the rural area east of the Bay Area where the Hawke facility stood. She stepped out, head tilted up as thin

streaks of water fell against the backdrop of redwoods stretching skyward. From behind, another car rolled up and slowed
until she stepped over to the curb, allowing it to pass.

And then she was alone, nothing but the sound of rain dancing between branches and needles. She turned, her back to the
road as she held up the glowing map on her phone.

The coordinates identified a location about three miles into
the forest, probably about an hour of walking through rough
terrain. Mariana reached back into her car for her backpack,
shaking her head at a sudden realization.

She'd forgotten to pack anything to eat.

"I know, I know," she said to the empty breeze. "Guess I really do need you by my side." She dug her boots into the soft
earth, setting out on a late morning hike in the woods that she
would never have chosen to do but that would have been perfect for Carter.

The team at Hawke hadn't just purchased the cabin, they'd
bought the plot of land around it too. At least, that's what Mariana figured. It had to be that, because barbed-wire fence held a
perimeter around it, metal signs warning *Keep Out*. She paused
to examine the wood posts holding up the wire, a rich brown-
orange hue to the wood that showed that they'd been put up
probably within the last year or two. She stepped gingerly between the wire, her backpack weighing down the middle row
for a little more space, though a burr still managed to catch
one sleeve, sticking to the fabric enough to pull a thread. Less
than what had happened at the Gardner Preserve, but at least
Carter wasn't here to see that.

She walked, the cloud cover and light rain eventually giving way to the midday sun, step after step as the line toward
the coordinates gradually shrank on her display.

At first, she didn't see the structure, its wood structure faded by time and obscured by nature. Only after she blinked several times did the small building come into focus, and for all the money and resources of the Hawke team, the mystery cabin looked out of time. Not in the way a mammoth and other anomalies were pulled from history and pasted into the present, but this small home barely still stood, its years, maybe decades of life chipped away.

Mariana stepped on the first board of the porch steps, then over the cracked second board to get to the top plank. Nails hung up a metal sign, an industrial font communicating *Structural Damage—Keep Out*.

Mariana's knuckle rapped against the flat wood door, flecks of broken paint and varnish drifting with the impact. She looked around for further clues about what this place might be, because Kendra definitely couldn't live here. No one should, really, given the drainage pipe hanging from the roof and the smashed windows adjacent to the front door.

No plumbing or electricity. Just shelter from the elements.

She knocked again, this time calling out "Hello?" Her voice echoed into the woods, carrying far beyond her reach and likely evaporating.

She knocked one more time, this time with greater force, except on the final knock, the door moved a little more than it should have.

Not much. It didn't swing back or even crack open, but just enough to show that the hinges and wood weren't exactly reliable.

She pulled her sleeve up over hand and made a fist before pounding the door several times, each time rattling it further. Dust and dirt were jarred from the door's top edge, trickling down with the movement. A spider dashed across the top of the doorframe, pausing long enough as if to check who had disturbed its rest, before disappearing into a crack from the splintering wood.

A crack that, as Mariana just now noticed, housed a red glow. Faint, but definitely radiating, and the light on her phone revealed finer details: a thin composite casing with a black dot in the middle. She angled back and forth to see its hiding place, and she pushed the crack just enough to see carpenter's glue holding a chipped piece of wood over it.

A camera. Hidden but with enough space to get a clear view of anyone that approached the building.

It had to be her.

"Hello?" she said. "I'm looking for Kendra Hall." Several breaths passed, Mariana holding still while tuning into the environment around her. Wind rustled and birds called, though nothing else gave signs of movement, not from the cabin or the space around them. "Kendra?" She banged on the door again, more debris flicking off of the frame. "I just want to talk. I need to know what's happening at Hawke. The Hawke Accelerator."

From inside, noises finally came—soft and muffled, but they projected clear enough for Mariana to know that it wasn't from the surrounding wildlife. And if it came from squirrels nesting in the living room, which was a possibility, there was only one way to find out.

Besides, if something happened to her and she died, she assumed the loop would simply start over for her. That was the one thing she and Carter had never tried. Was it a question of cowardice? Or the fact that given everything they saw and did, it simply never came up?

Maybe it was their unspoken way of showing that they'd never give up on each other.

Standing here, in front of a remote cabin that somehow tied back to the Hawke Accelerator and all the mysteries of its time-travel research, this seemed like an appropriate moment to force a point.

"Hey!" she yelled, more aggression tinting her voice. "Give

me ten minutes. Five minutes. I just need to know something about Hawke." The plank squeaked as she lifted onto her tiptoes, eyes locked onto the camera lodged into the doorframe. "The Hawke Accelerator is going to explode in a few days, and I need to stop it. Somehow."

Another muffled noise came from inside, something like the settling crackles and squeaks of wood bearing weight for the first time in days.

"I can do this, but I need help. I need Kendra Hall."

From behind the door, soft words finally came through. "What do you mean, *explode*?"

A woman's voice. Buried behind layers of wood, but it carried the clear tone of an adult woman.

"Are you Kendra Hall?"

"What do you mean, *explode*?" she repeated.

Mariana considered the question, along with the possibilities of who might actually be behind the door. If it *wasn't* Kendra Hall, who was it? Thoughts popped into her head, the idea that maybe she'd gotten this *all* wrong and something horrible had happened to Kendra and the coordinates related to her name could have been anything from the location of her remains to a random set of numbers.

She adjusted her weight on the plank, feeling its shaky construction pinned down by loose nails as she took a moment. If this wasn't the path to Kendra Hall, then she'd simply have to begin again. At first, the thought made her spirit sink, the notion that nothing mattered except yet another day. But instinct drove her to clench a fist and straighten up, a fury in her now that didn't exist before.

She *would* get Carter back. No matter what.

"It explodes. There's a structural-integrity issue. It causes a chain reaction. There's something about the current test cycle that goes wrong and causes it to explode. At 12:42 p.m. on Thursday."

A sharp inhale quickly became a sigh to reset nerves, a sudden change in what she was willing to do.

"I don't," the woman said, a clear hesitation invading her words, "I don't understand. How do you know this?"

"Please. Are you Kendra Hall? I think she can help."

"Why do you need Kendra Hall?"

Mariana looked around her, in all directions. And she *listened*, focus outstretched for anything that might be something outside of nature. Technology, an observer, anything that might be concerned with the words she was about to say.

Yet nothing came. Just miles and miles of nature.

"Because she's a time traveler."

The thump in Mariana's chest sped along, gaining in intensity as seconds passed without a response.

"And I'm one too," Mariana finally said. "Kind of. It's hard to explain."

From behind the door, a floorboard squeaked, the clear distinct sound of someone moving on the planks of an aged structure. "I'm trying to avoid paradoxes here," the voice said dryly.

"You don't have to worry about that with me. I live in four-day cycles. No one but me remembers anything." A quiet chuckle escaped as her face fell. "You won't even remember me after the explosion. The Hawke explosion caught me in a time loop."

Moments passed without a sound, enough that Mariana wondered if the woman on the other side had given up. And if so, should she just bash the door down?

But right when she considered violence, locks slid open. A strange whirring sound came, a mechanical churn that felt impossible given the dilapidated state of the cabin. The door swung open, revealing a woman in cozy workout pants and slippers, messy auburn hair framing her brown cheeks.

Behind her, the interior of the cabin matched the state of its exterior. But in between the cracked wood and thick cobwebs sat an open hatch, a glowing light beaming upward to illuminate the otherwise dim space.

"I'm Kendra," she said, hand outstretched. "Glad to see another person. It's been a while. You want a coffee or something?"

38

As isolation quarters went, Kendra's turned out to be pretty cushy. Buried underneath the cabin sat a small furnished apartment with all of the necessary amenities: running water, a working stove (which Carter would approve of), full electricity and data connections, and plush furniture, complete with several corgi plushies. Kendra opened the refrigerator to show a healthy stock of fresh vegetables and fruits stealthily delivered by drones every other week. Mariana turned down the apple she offered, though Kendra took one for herself. On the far wall hung a calendar, dates with large red Xs systematically counting down to what looked like two months from now.

"The first time we did this, I only had to prepare for a week. Which was easy. I mean, *Go hide underground for a week to read and relax and nap* is no big deal. This has been a little tougher," she said, grabbing a mug from the counter's coffee maker. She pointed to the apartment's far wall, a floor-to-ceiling screen that showed the video feed from the porch. "That helps with feeling the day/night cycle. But the thing is, I can't even check in with Dr. Beckett or anyone on the team. Any human interaction might cause a paradox, so..." Her mouth twisted in a grimace as she shook her head. "Another two months to go, then I jump back in time and isolate for *another* six months to bring me all the way back to current times. *Then* I get to see people again. Everything's a possible paradox with these scientist types. I have to hide from possibly running into my future self after she jumps. Or anyone working on the project *before* I jump. Or probably even any squirrels climbing trees." A heavy sigh came out, though it arrived with a crooked grin. "They're lucky they pay well. So many rules. Right now, I just have an AI companion. Hey, Bowie?"

The wall screen flashed, the feed of northern Californian nature disappearing, and in its place stood a near-perfect rendering of a tall, thin man with pale skin and floppy blond hair, probably in his fifties. A tight black jacket hung over a black T-shirt and a loosely tied red scarf draped down the middle, and a closer look revealed that his irises were different colors. "Hello there, Kendra," he said, in a London accent that sounded quite familiar.

"He's modeled after an early-century rock star named David Bowie."

"Dr. Beckett is a big fan. He gave me the look circa the 2003 album *Reality*," he said with a laugh before tossing his hair back. "Dr. Beckett liked the irony of that." Bowie turned to Mariana. "Hello there."

"He can see me?" Mariana asked.

"Yes, I can. You're not supposed to be here."

"Bowie, don't alert anyone yet," Kendra said. "There's a reason for this."

Bowie leaned forward, lines forming on his brow. "There's nothing in my protocols about allowing a visitor. And you're not," he said, pointing to Mariana, "on the need-to-know list."

"Wait," Mariana said. She stood up fast enough that a few drops of coffee spilled over the brim, scalding her knuckle. "Your voice. You're the same AI at Hawke. David. The one that greets everyone."

"Not quite. Consider that version one-point-oh. I'm the sleeker, sexier older brother."

"I don't know about that," Kendra said. "But smarter, more powerful for sure. Plus you have a face."

"How powerful an AI are you?" Mariana asked. "I've used the one for guests. And I've worked with the one they give staff. But you," she said, pointing at the image on the wall, "how much more can you do?"

"Now, that is a strange question. What kind of company are you keeping these days, Kendra?"

"I'm still figuring that part out." She took a bite of the apple, then leaned against the wall, eyes bouncing between Mariana and Bowie. "But it sounds like she's here to save the world or something."

Were paradoxes a concern? Kendra abided by a long list of protocols to ensure that she existed within a controlled time-travel experiment, the initial set given to her by Beckett and his team while the rest of it was jotted down by her and Bowie on a work-in-progress list.

Mariana, on the other hand, was just *there*. Again and again. She told the whole story, from the initial run-in with Carter in the observation room to the different ways they tried to reach Beckett to the final data heist and the discovery of Project Pen—with its related Phase 2, which clearly was for Kendra.

"How can you prove this?" Kendra asked.

On the wall screen, a barstool manifested for Bowie, and he sat, leaning forward with chin propped on his hands.

"The US Open. The upset this morning. But I know who won for the rest of the day," she said, reciting match finals with precision.

Bowie lifted an eyebrow. "The morning sessions have finished," he said. "The evening sessions haven't started yet. We'll need to wait until tonight to confirm this."

"Look, I don't have the time to wait." Mariana stood, hands pressed against her temples. She shut her eyes, thinking of that final moment with Carter, the heat of his embrace and the warmth of his lips as everything exploded around them. "If I don't get through to you now, we lose a whole day. That's the thing you don't understand about these resets. I can't carry anything through except my own memory. Everything else starts over." Her eyes widened at the epiphany that suddenly came to her. "You're a time traveler. Did they give you ReLive? To buffer the stability of your memory?"

Kendra gave the same blank stare Carter gave in his apartment's hallway. "What's ReLive?"

"I can answer that," Bowie said. "ReLive is an in-trial memory-preservation treatment. With commercial plans to help the aging population retain their treasured memories."

"I work for ReLive. I'm a neuroscientist."

"In four weeks, a drone will drop off a package with a Re-Live treatment. You're supposed to take it prior to the time jump as a safety net for the core pieces of your mission." Bowie nodded, his smirk at the connection remarkably human for an AI. "That's the current plan, anyway."

Kendra's lips pursed as she met Mariana's gaze. "They only tell me things week by week. Paradoxes and all that."

"Okay," Mariana said, slapping her knees. "New idea. Let's just assume that I am in fact living in a time loop. You'll be able to verify that by the end of the day with the US Open results, right?"

"You might get lucky," Bowie said.

"Fair point. So if I'm just lucky, maybe you'll do this out of the kindness of your heart?"

"I'm an AI, I don't have a heart. Kendra, however," Bowie said and offered a toothy grin, "well, I'm programmed to enjoy her company. But even with that, I can objectively say that she's nice."

"Aw, thanks, Bowie." Kendra pushed out a large grin, batting her eyelashes for emphasis. "If this is your plan to win me over, it's working."

"So," Mariana said, "I'm already here. Let's track the US Open, see if I'm being honest. And in the meantime, can we please figure out how to let the accelerator finish its cycle?"

On the wall screen, Bowie stood up and his stool disappeared. Next to him appeared a green chalkboard that looked straight out of a twentieth-century film. "Done," he said, snapping his fingers. He turned, scribbling on the chalkboard with the same determination as Carter writing in his notebook across the final seconds of a time loop.

Mariana and Kendra exchanged puzzled looks. "Done with what?" Kendra said.

"Done with your solution." He tapped the board for emphasis and stepped away, the board back in view. "How do we fix this? It's simple." He reached over, bits of virtual chalk dust appearing on the screen as he drew sharp lines under the phrase *Time Travel*. "There's only one way to do this. We send Mariana," he said, finger pointing her way, "to the past."

"Well," Kendra said, sinking back into her seat, "you *did* say you were a time traveler."

"Wait a minute," Mariana said, hands up. "To the past? How do I get back?"

"You don't." Bowie tilted his head. "That's the catch."

39

Mariana and Kendra sat, a rapt silence as Bowie broke down his proposal. Based on calculations from his internal AI, he took the structural offset created by the 8.1 earthquake of 2083 and looked at ways to compensate for it. His only conclusion was that no hardware-based solution existed to run a complete cycle of the retrieval program.

"Retrieval?" Mariana asked. From Kendra's blank look, she clearly didn't know about this either.

"Yes," Bowie said. "Retrieval. The test phase that is exceeding power capacity is not for sending a particle back. Or a pen. Or Kendra. She's still scheduled for later. This test is for the retrieval process of pulling an object from the past to the present. Makes sense, when you think about it."

Kendra glanced around at her space: a capsule, no matter how cushy and well-stocked, was still a capsule. "So they can bring people home. Instead of having us wait underground for time to catch up."

"That's correct. They've scheduled a test phase for this at the particle level while you're awaiting your trip. But more importantly," Bowie said, "are you complaining about the quality of my company?"

"Never. You're a great pal," Kendra said with a laugh.

"Wait a minute." Mariana stood, pieces suddenly coming together. "The anomalies from the past. Were they related to this?"

Bowie pulled up a graph with oscillations growing larger and larger as it moved along the timeline, an exponentially increasing sine wave. "Under the assumption that everything you've said is true, I've done some thinking. The destruction of the accelerator during the Hawke retrieval pilot-test cycle caused this disruption," he said, pointing at the first small blip in the graph. "That's your time loop. Going just a little bit back before resetting. But as the ripple energy of the disruption grows stronger over—" he said, a cheeky grin on his face "—*time*, then these bursts get bigger. And some of them are retrieving things from the past. Random things, thanks to the facility's destruction breaking all limiting protocols. Like a Columbian mammoth from around ten thousand years ago."

"This is above my pay grade," Kendra said. "I'm just a technician they bribed to step into the accelerator."

"Don't look at me," Mariana said. "I got the wrong doctorate for this. How can you be sure about all of this?"

"I'm an AI with enough processing power to keep up with every unfolding current event while monitoring Kendra *and* the Hawke team. All while being charming, pleasant company, and looking like David Bowie." The graphs behind Bowie dissolved back into the green chalkboard as he ran a hand through his hair. "Yes, I can pull it off."

The details of the chalkboard became clearer as Mariana approached the wall screen. "You go back twenty years. Augment the design blueprints with a change of two point four degrees in construction strut QL89."

"That's it?"

"Well, then you wait."

Mariana shot a look over at Kendra, though she didn't get anything in return.

"Wait for what?" Mariana asked.

"Wait for twenty years. Then you upload a piece of code into Hawke's system in current times, and flip a power switch as it finishes the test cycle of the retrieval process. The construction fix *should* do it, but these actions also adjust the energy usage by zero point zero two percent to cap it. All of that together should ensure that it bends..." a bar appeared in Bowie's hands, which he bent into a *U* shape "...and doesn't break."

Her calculations with Carter were correct. It all depended on the strut and the earthquake. If only she could reach backward through loops, to shake him and tell him that *yes*, they were correct.

It only needed an AI and twenty years to bring it to fruition.

"And after that?" Mariana asked slowly.

"I calculate a ninety-four point four percent chance that life moves on, the time loop ends. As for you?" Bowie's multicolored eyes locked onto hers before jumping to Kendra and back again. "I'm not sure. Paradoxes aren't exactly a well-researched subject. You might stay in the timeline. You might just disappear."

"Carter," Mariana whispered. Despite the nausea rolling through her gut, she forced herself to stand, to feel the ground beneath her feet. *Just disappear.* What could that possibly mean? What could that possibly *feel* like? "What about Kendra? Will she remember me?"

"Think about this linearly," Bowie said. "If you go back in time twenty years, by the time you enter this four-day period, the other Mariana will have never encountered Carter, never been aware of the loop. Your original path will remain." Kendra shot her a shrug and gestured with her hand sailing over her head. "That means that if this works, if the retrieval test process completes and Hawke does not blow up, Kendra will have never met you. *This* Kendra may exist in a loop in a multiversal offshoot, but that's purely theoretical."

Kendra repeated her over-the-head gesture, then pulled her knees to her chest on the couch.

"Can I wait another loop? I mean, I know we'd have to have this conversation again," Mariana said, hands balled into fists. "But hey, I'll know exactly what to say."

Next to Bowie, the oscillating graph returned. The AI shook his head as he gestured at the graph. "We probably don't want to tempt fate. Things are clearly getting worse."

Point to Bowie on that one.

Mariana stared at Bowie's digital chalkboard, her eyes glued as the enormity of the situation sunk in. Those equations and calculations, she didn't have the training to grasp those.

But the words *Time Travel* written neatly across the top, well…

It didn't take a quantum physicist to understand the sacrifice required.

Kendra's underground apartment didn't offer much in the way of solitude, and even though Bowie removed himself from view and Kendra read quietly in the kitchen, Mariana found the very presence of others distracting. Perhaps this was what happened when so many of the people she met on a day-to-day level became simple inconsequential fodder. The loop filled her life with moving pawns and a lone partner in crime, so the arrival of a mellow time traveler and a know-it-all AI proved an unexplainable shock to the system.

Instead of waiting in the basement space, she stepped up through the hatch into the camouflage of a dilapidated log cabin. She dusted from an old chair a mix of dirt, pollen, and pine needles, all of it collecting on her palm and being stubborn about shaking off. "Come on," she muttered, trying to get her hands clean, though it all stuck enough that sitting on the chair suddenly seemed like a bad idea.

"Just had to get away from us, huh?" Mariana turned to see Kendra's head poking out of the hatch.

"It's a lot to take in," Mariana said, her voice still.

"I don't know," Kendra said with a sigh as she moved up to the surface. "Sounds like you've seen some shit."

A quiet chuckle came out, a response to the joke she heard in her head first before saying it out loud. "Same shit, different loop." Kendra matched her laugh, but Mariana followed with a real question that had been occupying her thoughts over recent minutes. "What's it like? Traveling through time?"

"Two different things. Waiting for time to catch up? That's pretty boring. But the actual act of traveling through time?" she asked. "Like little bits of electricity that tickle you and smash your skull in."

"Getting electrocuted and hit in the face to save the world? I don't know if that sounds worth it."

"So that's why you're doing all this, huh? To break out of the loop. To stop weird stuff from being pulled into the present." Kendra's arms went up, palms out in mock admiration. "To fix things. Way more noble than me."

"You're not doing this to go into the history books?"

"Nah, not even close. They pay extremely well." Mariana chuckled, Kendra's practicality winning out over her own scientific curiosity. "It's not just about problem-solving for you, is it? I saw the way you looked when you talked about this Carter fellow. I don't know if my AI friend got it, but *I* did. I'm guessing he was more than just a lab partner."

Mariana turned, eyes fixated on an empty space on the cabin wall. Flecks of light poked through, beams that managed to escape the layers of wood and shade to find a way into the space.

"There was a moment," Mariana said. "We were out on the ocean. Just us. He cooked us lunch." A grin snuck on her face as she thought about Kendra's stove downstairs. "He loved cooking. *Loves*, that is. He's out there, right now," she said, gesturing beyond them. "That morning, we were going to run some tests, do what we do every day—try to escape the loop. But he wanted to take a break. To see the water. To take *me* to see the water. I'd never been out to sea."

Whether it was the emotion of the moment or her ReLive-enhanced memory engrams, simply talking about that moment brought it all back: the scent of the water, the sound of the waves, the rock of the ocean beneath them. "And the clock ticked down while we sat there. We kissed. We had the water, the air, and each other. That was all that mattered."

That kiss. Even now, she could feel it against her lips. "Then he lost it. It started with that memory. Gone, like it had never happened. Then other memories. Then all of the ones we shared, everything from the loops. But that moment. Those ten or fifteen seconds out on the ocean. Despite being stuck, despite always searching or testing or researching, despite all of the weird *shit* that kept happening…"

Her shoulder tensed, a reaction to the sudden realization of how *unfair* it all was. "For just a sliver of my lifetime, I'd never been happier. So yeah, I'm trying to get out. I'm trying to fix things. But I'm also doing this to give *us* a chance." She turned, now meeting Kendra's gaze. "We deserve more than ten or fifteen seconds of happiness."

The corners of Kendra's lips curled upward, her eyes soft. "Good thing a certain AI's not listening. He'd start crying too."

"I'm surprised he's not chastising you for being upstairs."

"I asked him to give us privacy. Surprised he's complying. But yeah, I'm not supposed to leave the bunker," Kendra said, and though Mariana stared out into the forest, she knew the woman standing next to her offered a warm smile. Her voice dropped to a whisper. "I come up here sometimes, though."

"So they hired someone who breaks the rules to be a time traveler?" Echoes of Shay's voice rang through her mind, variations of the many, many times Shay had gone on and on about breaking rules.

"For what it's worth, they have me write down when I break a rule. To document the psychological impact of all of this so they can update their protocols." Kendra paused. "I'm not going to tell them about you, though."

"Aren't they going to see the footage of me arriving?"

"See, that's the nice thing about Bowie. He's got a mind of his own. When we started, he was the same AI that they gave technicians at Hawke. More or less. Chatty, friendly, just informational. A little personality to spice it up, but very—what's the word…" she took in a breath, eyes turning to the cabin's dirty ceiling "…functional. But after a few weeks, I noticed something about him."

"He had cool hair?"

"That. And he'd developed a sense of humor. He wasn't just laughing at my jokes, he was making his own. Artificial intelligence, huh? So he makes choices now. I ask him what kind of music we'll play for dinner. Or what classic movie to watch. Or what philosophical argument to debate." Mariana raised her eyes at that one, which prompted a knowing nod from Kendra. "I think I'm going to miss him."

"Miss who? Bowie?"

"He's getting shut down at the end of my stay here. I leave this place, they wipe him, then I jump back in time six months and go hide in Bunker B. With a new Bowie. I can't bring his memory core with me. Paradox prevention. Theoretically," Kendra said, "if you go over to wherever Bunker B is, I might be there right now. With this new AI friend. It all messes with your head. At least, that's the plan. A massive explosion at Hawke is a bit of a twist."

"Kendra?" From downstairs, Bowie's voice came through the hatch. "My microphone reactivates whenever you say my name. You realize that, don't you?"

"Stop eavesdropping, Bowie."

"That's part of my job."

"Okay, fine," Kendra shouted toward the open hatch despite what he just said. "Just don't let this feed your ego."

"I am designed without ego, Kendra."

"Could have fooled me. Fine, turn your monitoring back on," she said with a laugh. "You see? He's good company. When you need it. Sometimes I think all of the money in the world isn't worth the isolation." She stepped forward, serious lines now creasing her face, and she pulled the front door slowly open. From above, beams of sunlight broke through the needles and branches, somehow making it through the layers and layers of nature to land a few bits of illumination at their feet. "Do you," Kendra asked slowly, "want to take him with you?"

"What?"

"Bowie. Do you want to take his memory core with you? I mean, I don't know much about how to hook him up into twenty-year-old tech, but I'm sure he does."

"I do," Bowie called. "It's simple. With some 3D printing of conversion interfaces. I'd have limited processing capabilities for the first ten years until the new Stockwell processors are released. My charming personality would remain, though."

"See, he's listening now. So basically, do you want to take *that* with you?"

Mariana stared at the streams of sunlight, the perfect angle to catch them at this time of day. Not that long ago, she and Carter had felt on the cusp of *something* big. And now she stared down two decades in isolation. "Mariana," Bowie said, his voice lower, yet still clearly cutting through the distance. "Twenty years is a long time to isolate. Do you know all your protocols for paradox prevention?"

"Don't assassinate world leaders?"

"Consider Bowie a safeguard of sorts," Kendra said. "To keep you company. And to make sure you don't break time. Because he'd never let you hear the end of it."

40

For nearly every day in the loop, Mariana had woken up to Maggie. Pockets of those days passed without the little cat and her insistent breakfast meowing—if she'd passed out at Carter's or they'd flown off to Wimbledon or something else got in the way. But at least ninety percent of the days in the loop involved a priority of feeding Maggie.

This Thursday was no different. Maggie followed at Mariana's feet, quietly trilling and chirping in anticipation. Mariana knelt down with the small bowl, placing it in the same spot along the wall that she used even before the cat became hers, back when she would simply watch her for a few nights while Shay ventured somewhere in the wilderness.

"This feels the same to you, huh?" she asked. "You won't even know."

Maggie kept eating, the familiar, kinda-gross smell of formulated cat food lingering in the air. Mariana stayed next to her, the cat's animated tail wrapping briefly around her outstretched hand before returning to a happy back-and-forth cadence.

"I guess you really won't. Either this doesn't work and it starts again tomorrow. Or it works and everything is reset without me." As if she understood, Maggie paused long enough to look up. "*Me*-me. The other me would be here still."

But what if the time loop broke and some weird paradoxical *stuff* caused Mariana to *not* be there in any way? She walked over to the kitchen counter to reread the printed sheet Kendra had made for her. So many guidelines and protocols to follow just to avoid the very *chance* of a paradox. But when she pressed Bowie about what might happen in a paradoxical situation, his response continued to be laughter.

In a sort of time-breaking, end-of-everything-we-know sort of scale, that didn't really frighten her. Yet the idea that Maggie might be on her own if everything went wrong?

Well, that wasn't okay.

Mariana typed out a quick message to her neighbor and building manager, a cryptic note about how she might get pulled away suddenly and to please keep an eye on Maggie if there were no logged entry records in the building-security data of her returning in a few days.

"It's too bad Shay can't just pick you up," Mariana called out to the cat.

Maggie looked up, eyes narrowing with a focus and a bright meow seemingly challenging that thought.

What if Shay could? This was *time travel*, after all.

Mariana glanced back at Kendra's sheet, a list of both the protocols suggested by Beckett's team and her own notes on isolation. With time travel, couldn't *anything* be possible? All of their rules had to do with avoiding the detectable past, minimizing any ripples that might rip apart the very fabric of time.

Somehow, somewhere within all of that, though, there had to be a way to do something about Shay.

Mariana had a long history of following directions. She *excelled* at that. And while Carter had pointed out that such a strict way of living missed out on happy culinary accidents, that precision ensured that she would safely travel across time. She walked out of the building elevator, details she'd missed over years of residency suddenly standing out: the way the textures on the ceiling tile were slightly misaligned, the tiny crack in the wallpaper adjacent to the elevator doorframe, the smudge that blurred sunlight through the window.

She looked around, trying to lock in all of the details as images etched into her mind. Would she carry those things with her the way Carter did? Or would they dissolve into the ether of memory, no eidetic mutation or ReLive enhancements to make those details feel as real as this moment?

In her pack, she checked off each item that Bowie prioritized: his memory core, a series of 3D-printed interfaces for historic computer modules when she arrived in the past, and the small comms for her ears, paired to the mobile device to help her get through the next few hours. All of that technology sat tightly nestled in an energy-discharge container to protect it from the rigors of time travel, along with a large wad of appropriately dated paper money purchased at several antique stores across San Francisco, something largely ignored by both the present and the past but honored by banks and collectors. It'd be enough to get situated, then Bowie said to leave the rest to him, whatever that meant.

But if that all failed? Then she had a notebook, simple bound paper with all of the tasks and notes that Bowie offered in an interactive digital checklist, but preserved in the permanence of ink and paper: no power supply, no output interface required, just a fail-safe in case things went really wrong.

She reviewed the list again in her mind while awaiting her morning coffee. The barista handed the drink over, along with a cake donut. Mariana split the baked sweet in half, part of it for her journey to Hawke and part of it to bring across the lobby.

It was too bad that Monday morning dog biscuits weren't on the menu. Buddy Ed deserved that.

As if the dog knew, he perked up from his station, ears up.

Approaching the desk, Mariana held up the smaller half of the plain cake donut until the security guard on duty nodded with approval. She offered it, Buddy Ed taking it gently out of her hand before gobbling it down in three chews and looking up at her with bright eyes and panting tongue.

"You be a good boy, okay, Buddy Ed?" The dog continued panting, and Mariana tried not to humanize the way his wide mouth looked like a grin.

"You all right?" the security guard asked.

"Yeah. Sure." Mariana's lips twisted as she stared the dog in the eye. "Why do you ask?"

"I've just never heard you call him by his full name before." The security guard laughed and reached down to scratch Buddy's head. "Sounds like when children are in trouble."

"No, he's not in trouble. I'm just," Mariana said, planting a kiss on the dog's nose, "feeling a little sentimental today."

"Oh, Ms. Pineda. I saw your message to the building-security staff. You're going to be traveling for a while?"

She stood, a sudden tightness in her legs from the movement, and took in the scene in front of her. All of those little details she'd tried to imprint into her mind moments ago wiped away, the ephemeral nature of plain old memories leaving her only with the here and now.

"Doing something for work," she said. She reached down to pet Buddy one more time for good measure. "But hopefully it'll be like I never left."

41

Would this be the last time Mariana did this?

In the prior loop, she had moved with purpose. This time, despite knowing the end goal, every step carried a weight to it. Like all those other times, she met with the ReLive group and made small talk about the accelerator tour, including apologies for supposedly being ill earlier in the week while in reality, she'd spent the time planning her leap across time. More importantly, security gave her a mobile David unit to use. And like all those other times, she said she needed to use the bathroom before catching back up with them.

She broke free of the group, then checked the time, waiting for 9:42 a.m. like the previous Thursday before setting out.

All of the stops and starts, turns and pauses, those movements returned with a physical ease, though her mind was elsewhere.

Twenty years in the past, to be exact. And the massive space in between, a journey with no way back and no one to ease the isolation other than an AI.

She slipped into the data center, her timing a little off from before, as her greetings and acknowledgments of Kaitlyn and other passing staff members arrived out of sync by several min-

MIKE CHEN

utes. But when she finally sat down at a terminal, it was as available and accessible as in the last loop.

The only difference was that she had Bowie with her. Part of him, at least. The standard units distributed to Hawke guests weren't powerful enough to contain Bowie's full capabilities, but connecting his memory core to the device at least installed Bowie's knowledge of the situation—and the resources he'd prepared yesterday.

She just needed to turn him on to see if it all worked. Because this could go really sideways if it didn't.

The screen flashed, a green check icon appearing to announce that her hacked mobile AI unit successfully connected to the Hawke mainframe. Mariana tapped through various access screens on it to get to the device's folders of support files, an application that Bowie had labeled *DoThisFirst*. She executed it, prompting various status bars and messages. As she waited, she slid the small comm earpiece onto her outer ear, then watched as the upload process inched toward completion. It finished with a blink, and a message popped up, a prompt to execute the uploaded application that Bowie had prepared right before they left Kendra's cabin. She squinted to make sure she'd read the file name properly.

SeeYouSoon.

She tapped the Confirm button, and the screen flashed once before sitting still, Bowie's AI-powered workings all pushing forward under the surface. For all Mariana and Carter had done, digging through Beckett's archives and hacking into records and databases, all it took was finding the project's secret time traveler and her trusty AI to make things move smoothly.

A crackle popped through the earpiece, and soon a familiar voice followed. "I said I'd see you soon, didn't I?"

"Mmm-hmm," she said, soft enough to avoid drawing any attention before walking out of the data center.

"This isn't the real me, of course. Just a fraction of myself hijacking the David AI. Though I must say, David's clothes are a bit uncomfortable."

Bowie meant that metaphorically, of course, unless a visual component of David existed hidden from public use. Mariana shook her head at his cheek: twenty years of this? All those times Carter complained about David, he had no idea what he was missing. "Where to?"

"I see you're not in the mood for small talk."

"I got a lot on my mind." The mobile unit stuck as she pulled, stubbornly refusing to disconnect from the main console until a second, then third tug. It released, and the screen flashed a note that the device had been removed.

"Well, then," Bowie said, "let's cut the pleasantries and send you to the past."

The sheet trembled in front of Mariana's eyes despite the tight grip, pressure between her forefingers and thumbs to hold the piece of paper in place. *Kneel down. Curl in. Close eyes. Strong hold. Deep breath.*

She'd written those steps out, little circles next to each point, as if those tiny blobs of ink would make it easier to both remember and survive.

"I'll be walking you through the steps," Bowie said. "You don't need to keep staring at it. Unless it makes you feel better."

"I think it does."

"Perhaps if I had my full processing power and data core, I'd understand why."

That comment did pull her attention away for a moment to give a quick tap on the electric-discharge container strapped to her abdomen. It remained safely bound, despite the discomfort of holding equipment there. She shook her head and looked around, the dome formation of the chamber echoing sounds in strange ways.

How had security not rushed in and pulled her away? Carter's mere download of a database had triggered alarms, and yet here, Bowie opened and closed doors, activated robots, and initiated protocols, all without causing any stir.

"The power systems were already active from the retrieval test cycle. Two minutes, thirty-eight seconds to finish rerouting it and running a stage-three, one-way jump to March 25, 2074."

"How many robots are you controlling right now?"

"Four, using the same sequence that successfully sent Kendra back one week without any paradoxical human interaction. One to monitor the power threshold. One to reconfigure the accelerator from its retrieval test to a stage-three process capable of sending a human back twenty years. One to ensure safety redundancies are in place." Despite the cool air of the chamber's ventilation system, sweat now dotted her forehead, and she reminded herself to breathe. "And one to watch the door."

Mariana knelt down but extended back, craning her neck to take in the interior of the dim space. From what she understood, the chamber for the first-stage accelerator—the one designed for particles—lay on the other side of the massive door in front of her. At her right stood a metallic cylinder the height of a tennis net, its base connected to a track that led to a spot about ten feet in front of her.

That must have been for the second stage: Project Pen.

And in the center of the space, a flat metal circle about a meter in diameter, two metal rods protruding upwards on one side, ridges molded into them for handgrips.

All for the third stage. So far, that had only involved sending Kendra one week back in time.

Mariana would give it a little bit more of a go.

She hunched over, eyes closed and chin tucked in as her hands gripped the metal rods.

"Your heart rate is accelerating again."

"I'm aware of that," Mariana said, slowing her breath back to a steady in-and-out cadence.

"Accelerated heart rate is going to make you feel worse. Including the possibility of palpitations when you land. And—"

"I don't need to hear what I should be worried about."

"One minute, forty-five seconds." Above her, a systematic series of loud thunks played out, rolling from left to right. Beneath her, a light vibration rippled through the floor grates, the frequency tangible in her knees. She opened her eyes for a mere second, enough to see that whatever activated around her tinted the chamber with green lighting. "Shall I put you at ease?"

"How are you going to do that?"

"Remember, Dr. Beckett modeled me after legendary musician David Bowie. I can sing you a song. Music soothes anxiety due to its rhythm and repetition, particularly when it performs at around sixty beats per minute."

"I know that, I'm a neuroscientist," she said, squeezing her eyes shut.

"Oh. Well, then, pick a song."

"I'm really bad about all things music and—" she started, before a memory tickled her thoughts. That song, the one Carter sang while cooking. "Actually, there's this one, I don't know the title or who did it."

"That narrows it down."

"Someone I knew really liked it. A woman singing about having motion sickness and rolling down windows." Mariana considered where she'd heard it before. "I think it's one of those from like the twenties or so that just lives forever and—"

"'Motion Sickness' by Phoebe Bridgers."

"Um. Maybe? I don't know many singers." Even before Mariana finished the thought, Bowie started, capturing the same melody that Carter sang all those loops ago.

Kendra had described the feeling of time travel as *little bits of electricity that tickle you and smash your skull in* which, in addition to the whole being displaced by twenty years thing, sounded like a terrible thing to experience. Yet, Bowie sang the song in a soothing voice, likely at exactly sixty beats per minute, with an emphasis on a consistent rhythm and repetition.

And it worked, her mind drifting to the cadence of the song and *not* stuck on, well, everything else. Perhaps it came from the resolution that no matter what happened from here, *this* would finally be over.

Mariana shifted her weight on her knees, and her fingers flexed, adjusting her grip, and she paced her breathing to the sound of Bowie's voice.

All around her, the low hum that vibrated the floor roared to life, not with the chaos of Hawke's usual destruction, but the sound of various systems and mechanisms activating, different forms of energy and electricity coursing through them to power up and cool down and contain the very fabric of what shuffled a living, breathing person through time.

"I will stop there and shut down for the time jump," Bowie said in a quiet, even voice. "Good-bye, Mariana. Safe travels across time."

"Thanks, Bowie. Have a good nap."

Fact: Kendra was right. Electricity danced over her skin, tickling her face with needlelike sparkles running up and down, left and right in infinite contact. Every muscle in her body tensed, holding this position while enduring the most impossible of feelings.

Hypothesis: Temporal energy, that green stuff that zapped her before, well, that was encapsulating her into some sort of bubble and safely throwing her back twenty years.

Experiment: If she survived this, she supposed she would know.

While her right hand still gripped the handle, her fingers moved enough to cross them before reverting.

"You're wel—"

The harshest, worst headache of all time hit, like her skull simply imploded despite being completely stable and fine. All around, sound disappeared, a perfect vacuum, and even though her eyes were shut, everything turned to white.

42

The world spun. Or maybe it didn't. Maybe it just felt that way, and it took several seconds for Mariana to realize she was, in fact, in her own body. And while the dizziness felt never-ending, sensations pressing against her body didn't change.

The cold against her cheeks? It wasn't a remnant of the accelerator's energy running through her body, it was nighttime dirt and dew.

The tickle against her forehead? That came from her own hair, a light breeze kicking it across her face.

And her hands, they gripped nothing, knuckles and joints still angled like they held the grips from the launch pad of the Hawke Accelerator.

Mariana struggled to open her eyes, a conscious push to look around and fight for whatever information they might bring. She blinked, then blinked again, trying to will some images into her mind until the reality of the situation finally settled in and grounded her.

She was sideways. In a dirt field. And she hadn't lost her vision or anything like that; her sight was perfectly fine, even though it needed a few minutes to adjust.

Coherent thoughts muddled their way through the sludge of her mind, eventually taking hold into a little bit of clarity. She'd been sent across time and landed here. At which point, she had immediately toppled over onto her left side, everything still poised to hold on the same way she'd started when Bowie counted down. Even her chin remained tucked in, though not out of stiffness or paralysis. She angled her neck, the movement without any of the resistance she'd simply assumed would happen. And as her eyes adjusted, a clarity of focus came in as the tiny bright dots of stars littered across the night sky.

The nausea, though, was real. Kendra somehow missed that part. Her hands felt for solid ground underneath, then pushed her onto her knees. She took in breaths, cold air stinging her lungs, and she debated whether or not to actually stand up right now or just pass out here and hope for the best.

Nausea rolled in again, a crashing sensation that caused her to clutch her stomach with one free hand, though her palm landed on something very different yet no less important.

Bowie's data core.

Strapped to her abdomen in a protected discharge container. Along with a temporary power system, mobile interface with limited capabilities, some 3D-printed interfaces to adapt to computer systems over the next twenty years, and a small earpiece. And money.

Money to get her situated here, now, in the past.

Her free hand planted itself on cold earth, damp soil and broken leaves pressing against her palm. She took several more breaths, the dizziness settling down from spinning into more of a rigorous sway, though the nausea remained.

Think, she told herself. She was just at Hawke's time-jump pad. Bowie controlled the robots and internal configuration to send her back twenty years. She had hardware with her, things she needed to set up to get situated in this new place.

She just needed to go.

But where?

She unbuckled the container from her body, and the very action of doing so knocked her off balance, putting her back onto one knee. She looked down, what little light from the starry sky above disappearing with this shift in focus, and she blinked, trying to get her eyes to adjust. The container came into focus, a near-black rectangle among a field of black, and instinct drove her fingers to snap open the access panel. She felt around until she found the small earpiece. Though her head still swirled, she fumbled her way into getting it in her right ear, along with plugging the mobile David unit into Bowie's memory core to reactivate it.

The palm-sized square glowed, several blue dots lighting up to indicate that it came to life. A red dot began to blink in its center before turning to green and fading out, then her earpiece crackled with a static pop.

"Hello, Mariana. You've arrived?"

"I think so," she said, closing the container and taking a step forward before falling back to one knee again. "What happened?"

"If everything worked out, you're twenty years in the past."

"I'm standing in a big pile of dirt in the middle of the night. Barely standing, that is," she said as she pushed herself up onto her feet.

"Until my proper data core powers up and I connect into a network, I can't verify your time and location."

"Thanks, Bowie," she said, taking several slow, gingerly steps forward. For the first time since she got here, the ground felt solid beneath her feet.

"But, if you've time-jumped correctly, you're in the exact same spot as when you left. Jumping through time, not space."

Mariana blamed the physical intensity of the time jump for the sudden gap in her logic. It was either that or admit to simply missing the obvious. "This is where they're going to build Hawke."

"A little bit colder without the concrete walls, isn't it?"

"Okay. Right," she said, more to herself than to Bowie. Bits and pieces of the plan came back to her, and if she had a light of any kind, she could reference the printed sheet tucked away in the discharge container. Her eyes squeezed shut, trying to picture the sheet as it had sat on her kitchen counter.

"Are you there, Mariana?"

"Trying to recall my to-do list. With the photographic-memory trick," she said.

"Eidetic memory."

Mariana's slow movements came to a pause, the phrase bringing back the echo of Carter's voice through the time-jump fog. "Yeah," she said. "That's the proper term."

"You could just ask me what to do next, you know?"

"Good point. I—"

An overwhelming brightness cut off Mariana's words, a blinding that filled every bit of her vision. She blinked and blinked again, the visual disorientation creating a dissonance in her mind. Could this be a fragment of the time jump? Which was really weird, because the nausea and dizziness had subsided and she was actually able to move.

"Mariana?"

"Hold on, Bowie, I'm just feeling a little weird," she said, squeezing her eyes shut.

"That's not you. That's a security drone. How well can you run?"

43

"Try this trick," Bowie said. "Close your eyes. Then open them very slowly."

Mariana followed Bowie's advice, and from there, the overwhelming brightness became a manageable blinding beam. She turned her head, eyes focused on the ground, weeds and dirt now visible from the ambient illumination.

"Move. You can't get caught."

"Maybe they'll just think I'm a drifter passing through," she said, legs gaining speed, though she still wasn't sure which direction she was headed in.

"It doesn't matter what they think. The impact on the timeline could be catastrophic if security detects you. Go faster."

Steps became a jog, and when her body felt steady enough, she moved to a sprint. Her feet caught a divot in the dirt—or maybe they caught on themselves. Either way, she tumbled forward, a lack of poetry in her movements while she forced herself back on track. The drone above followed, though she'd managed to get ahead of it. Given that the accelerator's grounds were simply a massive patch of bulldozed dirt at this point in the timeline, security was probably more about pests than secrets.

But Bowie was right. She couldn't get caught.

The ambient spotlight provided enough visibility for her to make out the silhouettes in the distance, mostly an endless swatch of trees tilting lightly in the wind. Except when she turned to her left, she saw one very familiar marker.

The biggest tree-covered hill of Gardner Preserve. *You can see the tallest tree in between things. Just keep track of that and that's the waypoint I use,* Carter had said, though in the context of walking during the late, sunny morning.

Here, Mariana ran in disoriented steps to try to evade the drone.

"Bowie," she said, her pace picking up again. "The preserve ahead. I'll lose them there."

"Be cautious. You're dehydrated, and your body's recovering."

"Don't worry," she said. "My friend took me here before." She looked up, and despite her focus spinning, she locked onto the silhouette of the tallest tree, its shape visible thanks to the bright moon above.

It wasn't the exact same view she'd had from before, and not just because Mariana's spot from the first layer of branches on a Douglas fir tree overlooked dirt rather than the Hawke Accelerator. With the sun creeping upward, she could tell her angle was slightly off from before, though such discrepancies didn't really matter much given the combination of cold and tired weighing her down. Simply sitting for an hour had brought a measure of relief, if not sanity, enough that fatigue draped over her, and she leaned against the tree's thick trunk, lost in thoughts.

Then the beeping started.

It came as a short, piercing electronic chime through the earpiece, piquing Mariana's attention. Did time traveling make a body feel extra tired? Or was it just a lack of food combined with the stress of entering into a completely new, completely impossible situation *and* running from security drones?

That seemed more likely.

"Mariana?" Bowie asked. "Did you hear that beep?"

"Yep."

"That means that the power on this mobile unit is half-drained. Should I shift to a low-power state to conserve energy until you resolve your situation?"

"What's that mean?"

"I can provide cursory information but won't be able to process complex queries. Also, I'll be less chatty and won't be able to carry a tune."

Mariana stood up on the thick branch, the arches of her feet planted firmly beneath her. Circulation flowed through her body, a rush of blood after holding tight for too many minutes. She took in the sight ahead of her, a view that she'd seen several times with Carter. And while so much of her immediate surroundings remained from those moments, no superstructure sat in the distance. Instead, the emerging morning sun offered nothing but the trees and hills of the Gardner Preserve, several bulldozers and a crane poking through among the layers of trees. If she'd angled one way or another, she might have been able to see the taped-off areas marking the construction zone and warning people to stay out.

But from this distance and this height, bits and pieces were all she got.

"Where do I even start?"

"You can't stay here. And you'll need to stay out of society as much as possible. I suggest finding a quiet location to get situated without affecting the timeline."

"How do you know it won't affect the timeline?"

"I don't," Bowie said. "But I do have the recorded history we came from as a baseline. When you were in the loop, you said you had no impact on the timeline. Here, everything has ripples outward. So if you're going to stay somewhere, where would it be?"

"Someplace…nice? With good snacks?"

"Anyplace can have good snacks." Good thing Carter wasn't here. Bowie's comment would have unleashed a lecture about equating quality of snacks with quality of venue. Though she did wonder if Bellisario's was open during this era. "You need to keep out of history's way. In a place with power and data access. Without a lot of people."

Mariana considered those variables, lines pointing toward a single convergence. "So a motel. In a rural location. Not the city. For the immediate few days. Then some place more stable. And eventually, look for something I can turn into an off-the-grid home for the long term. Like Kendra's."

"Very good."

"To start, we'll need some place with a lot of vacancy," she continued, mind picking up as things locked into place. "That way, I won't be displacing anyone who would have originally stayed there."

"Exactly. Fortunately, I have a lot of records to help you consider those decisions." Bowie paused, though she couldn't tell if that was his flair for the dramatic or if he was processing something. "I want you to listen very carefully. This is how you have to think now. This is how you have to consider your decisions. Do you understand?"

A loop without consequences. And now, twenty years of infinite consequences.

Mariana sighed at the impossible, unfair nature of *everything*.

"Everything is a potential ripple effect that might lead to a paradox," Bowie said.

Over the horizon, purples started to melt into oranges, a brilliance to the hue announcing the start of a new day. Mariana considered the miracle of that: after how many loops of Monday-through-Thursday, now she was back in the past with so many unknowns ahead of her. "I understand."

"There's a plaza with a bank, a car-charging station, and some restaurants three miles southeast of here. I unfortunately can't load up any reviews for them. But the bank should be able to convert a small amount of your money into digital funds. From there, go to the charging station and buy a prepaid phone. I can connect with that for a live-data interface and find you a place to stay." Mariana grunted an affirmative as she adjusted her balance on the tree branch. She glanced down, the ground some six feet below her. "I'll go in low-power mode and direct you."

Mariana opened the small case in her hands, its firm walls designed to shield technology through the rigors of time travel. But it also held a lot of money—in an antiquated format, sure, but a way to get started, at least until Bowie's advanced AI found its way around modern transactions.

"Okay, then," she said, looking at the rising sun one more time. "Let's get going."

44

Things were going to change.

After a scrambly few days, Bowie helped Mariana find a temporary residence, a small place in an apartment building with multiple vacancies. His research showed records that, historically, the apartment remained empty for seven months, so inserting herself in there for one month provided them with a starting point to get equipment, establish identity records, manipulate digital funds, those types of practicalities.

Also, to upload the stuff necessary to save the timeline.

Mariana watched Bowie's screen, status messages flashing next to passing code. Line upon line scrolled, status bars and other technical ephemera processing, her only option to sit and watch while Bowie hacked into design schematics and construction documents with the advantage of future AI processing power.

Her life, the timeline, possibly the fate of everything would shift once all those status bars on the screen hit one hundred percent. Such a fundamental pivot seemed both simple and daunting at the same time, and a ReLive-enhanced memory of the last time she faced such a crossroads burned in Mariana's mind.

That night, Shay stood at Mariana's side as they paused at the top of the historic home's patio stairs, and while they walked down together, Shay leaned over to whisper. "Look at this shit. If I ever get married, we're going to sign a piece of paper and then disappear onto an island."

"Smile and wave," Mariana said, marching in step like they practiced. "Sister."

"Ha. Governmentally sanctioned siblings," Shay said while they moved down the courtyard path together. "I have no idea what I'm going to say."

"Wait, you didn't prepare a speech?" Mariana asked.

"I *thought* about it, but you know, it was hard. Fuck it, I'll improvise."

"Maybe I'll go first," Mariana said as they approached the large table with photos of their now legally united parents.

The DJ handed them each a microphone, and though Mariana had given plenty of academic presentations at this point, this marked something far more nerve-racking. "It's usually customary for the parents of the bride and groom to give speeches at this time," said Mason, the tall DJ with short-cropped blond hair, black straps of their dress revealing tattooed arms. "But here, we've got the daughters of the happy couple to do the honors." They held a pair of mics out, and while Mariana hesitated for a second to remember her speech outline, Shay grabbed one and stepped right in.

"Hi, everyone. I'm Shay. I'm Sam's daughter. Hey, Dad!" she yelled with a wave, prompting a laugh across the courtyard tables. "Hey, *Mom!*" she said, which prompted a bigger laugh and applause. Shay looked at Mariana, and above her usual toothy grin, Mariana caught the light shifting in her eyes.

Shay had an idea.

"So, you all, this is my legal sister, Mariana. Renee's daughter."

Sprinkles of applause came from the audience, and Mariana braced herself for what was in store. "So here's the thing about

me and Mariana. We've been best friends since freshman year
of college. Roommates. Scientists. Teammates on the UC Davis
tennis team—go, Ags!"

One person shouted, presumably another UC Davis alumni.
"Wooo, that's right! Go, Ags!" More laughter came, Mariana
joining in, marveling at how Shay just knew how to roll with
things.

"We now live, like, a hundred miles apart. Have for a few
years, but you know, we're always with each other in other ways.
Messages. Having dinner across the wall screen. Occasionally on
the court where—" Shay coughed "—sometimes I let her win."

Under the setting sun, smiles beamed from every seat, eyes
locked on Shay in her element. "Mariana is my sister. She's
been my sister ever since we ate ramen together outside of a
broken-down bus on Highway 5. And our parents knew that.
They knew that and they respected that, even though they totally had the hots for each other." Shay pointed at the newly-
wed table with a nod. "Yeah, we saw your messages to each
other. That was gross."

By now, Mariana's mom had her head in her hands, and
Shay's dad clapped with a hearty chuckles. "But that shows you
exactly what kind of people Sam Freeman and Renee Pineda
are. They respect the hell out of love. They didn't want to make
our friendship weird by intruding with their relationship until
everyone was good and ready. Well, we're here now, and Sam
and Renee are going to have the smoothest, best marriage in
the history of the universe. They're in for the long haul because
they're built for this. And I can say that because I'm a theoretical physicist. I do fancy science, so I *know*."

Shay was improvising *this*? Mariana considered just saying
Congrats and walking off at this point. "Look at us," Shay said,
one arm pulling Mariana in. "Legally declared sisters in the
eyes of the government. To sisterhood. And to Sam and Renee,

love-respecters of the highest level. Please raise a glass in toast of the newlyweds."

Mariana did not, in fact, top Shay's speech that night. She managed about two minutes of rambling memories of meeting Sam for the first time, all capped with a standard *Congratulations*, but it ultimately didn't matter. Everything else worked out right, and now she and Shay were sisters.

Outside of time-jumping twenty years into the past, that rite of passage had marked the biggest shift in Mariana's life. Not that their everyday interactions changed, but the context of everything did. For years, Shay had been her chosen family, the person she clung to during the depths of anxiety or the peaks of success. But from that moment onward, their lives became intertwined in different ways, a permanence that started with matching dresses and a little too much champagne.

Built for the long haul.

Here, Mariana's life shifted again. Getting to the past meant the hurdles of time travel, getting oriented, finding sanctuary. But the true milestone came less than twenty-four hours after she'd established a minimalist encampment within a small apartment, once Bowie had access to both a power source and a data stream. His memory core still output through the mobile unit, her earpieces, and his well-clothed self displayed on a book-size portable screen.

One by one, the status bars hit a hundred percent and disappeared.

"The new angle for strut QL89 has been written and saved in the design blueprints. The future is saved. At least for now."

For now. Though this theoretically should correct things, Bowie had a final task at the end of their journey, several safety nets to add into the Hawke power cycle as it finished its process.

But all that would wait. A very, very long time from now.

"That's it?" Mariana said.

"That's it," Bowie said with a laugh. "I'm much more than just a talking box, you know."

"Don't remind me."

"I'll continue to check the status of the construction every week to ensure that the angular alignment remains proper."

Mariana knelt down, going face-to-face with the small device that housed Bowie's voice. "This seems too easy."

"Yes, it was easy." The tone of his voice came with a stare from his different-colored irises, offering equal parts empathy and intensity. Her lips pursed, wondering if there had been any other way to do this simple injection of design data. Because in the end, she'd simply been a taxi driver for Bowie.

Yet maybe that was what mattered—not the actual execution but finding a way to the past safely.

"The hard part?" Bowie asked. "We're going to be stuck together for a while. I'm sorry to say, the real challenge is just beginning."

Point to Bowie because he was right. The hard part came in the form of a complete shift in thinking. That was even more difficult than finding a suitably off-the-grid home, converting money into a reasonably untraceable source, and getting practical things like furniture and solar panels while minimizing timeline risks. Even powering Bowie became a pragmatic choice, the AI fully transferred into a series of CPUs and servers in her home, the mobile unit safely packed up to preserve its integrity until the appropriate time came. After all of the loops she'd experienced with Carter, everything here was executed with a forward momentum, a gradual digging of another clue, another layer of information, another possibility.

This was different. Very different. So different, in fact, that all of the desperation that had previously existed became muted. Instead, everything bound to a new goal of maintaining an absolute status quo. Bowie watched over her every move, calculating any potential risk of interfering with the timeline. And in the first few months, as Mariana learned to focus on stability over progress, she let one very crucial point slip.

"Mariana," Bowie said, in a tone that she'd come to learn was his voice when she'd crossed a specific line. For all his AI capabilities, he didn't realize that she'd pick up on these things.

"Yeah, Bowie?" she asked, staring at her tablet.

"Shay Freeman."

Mariana jolted straight up in her chair, enough that the coffee in her mug nearly spilled out. On the data tablet itself was a picture of Shay making recent headlines as a sixteen-year-old tennis prodigy.

"Oh. Um, what about her?"

"She died. Three months before you time-jumped."

"Yeah." Mariana *almost* argued that a body was never found. "She did."

"I hope you're just looking at old news for nostalgia's sake. And not planning anything further. We have rules to live by."

Shay lit up her screen, the vibrancy of her powerful arms in the middle of a two-handed backhand swing. "You know, Shay would say that she liked to smash through the rules."

"Shay was not trying to prevent the destruction of the Hawke Accelerator. Or break a time loop."

Mariana set the tablet on the small table next to her, then curled up her legs on the couch. She took a long, slow sip of coffee and met Bowie's gaze on the wide wall-mounted monitor. Despite his so-called vision being a combination of sensors, cameras, and microphones placed around the cabin, he knew exactly where to look.

"You have an impossible task ahead of you," he continued. "Let's not make it worse by doing something that will create a paradox."

"How will you know that—"

"I don't, but I do calculate probabilities. And I know that

every single moment leading up to the point you time-jumped is recorded in history. Some of your interactions with the outside world are inevitable. It's my job to make them as benign as possible. But Shay Freeman? She's off-limits." Bowie's mouth turned grimly serious, the usual cheeky half smile completely gone. "Do you understand? There are rules."

Mariana stared at the image on the tablet, Shay's midswing form gradually dimming as the device timed out to a blank screen. "I understand. There are rules," she said firmly.

Though a small part of her refused to believe it.

45

Seventeen years. Six months. And twenty-two days.

Mariana stared at the countdown calendar on the screen. Some days, she turned it off. Some days, she walked past it without even noticing. And some days, she talked it over with Bowie, like asking if something interesting had happened in history on that particular day. Occasionally, she'd watch the news knowing in advance how life unfolded—a surprise election result, a moment of cultural significance, a societal shift playing out in impassioned riots.

Today wasn't like any of those days. Today, she only stared at the large red digits on the screen, eyes fixated on them in a way that urged them to fast-forward.

Survival mode pushed her through that first year, the logistics of finding a place to stay and getting used to the strange rhythm of a day, where the only goal was to arrive at the next one and the next one and every further day. Not in the grind of modern living, where people lived paycheck to paycheck, paying bills and scraping together little blocks of joy on the weekends. No, this was a complete shift in thinking, a gradual understanding of the ripple effects of choice and how to minimize that.

In almost all cases, it boiled down to one thing: staying in isolation at a rural cabin off the grid. There was a reason why Beckett and his team had picked that scenario for Kendra. Bowie calculated the potential impact of doing things like hiring installers for solar panels or determining the best time to go to the nearest town for groceries. That framework of analysis, a risk calculation for every step or choice, took months to integrate into Mariana's instinct.

The second year took that chaos and forced order into it. Building a small farm and learning how to raise crops. Establishing some perimeter security just in case. Actually *decorating* the cabin.

But for three or four months now, Mariana found herself in a plateau, a steady routine that let her simply live day-to-day instead of trying to game a system or build something from the ground up or learn a new skill. She'd done all that, achieving a sustainable life from a food-and-shelter perspective, with Bowie continually tweaking her finances to ensure a safety net with minimal records or red flags.

She simply *was*. Except that didn't account for the fact that she had more than seventeen years remaining until the finish line. And then what? Evaporate into nothingness?

When she got here, she'd thought about Carter. About Shay. About the loop and the anachronisms, about Hawke and the potential for so much greater damage, about theories and concerns and somehow being the one person who might deliver hope through all of it.

Not now. Right now, she simply stared at the numbers in front of her. And what if they were wrong? What if their strategy *didn't* end the loop? What if it repeated these twenty years?

What if it sent her back to the very beginning of the loop *again*?

Mariana swayed, reaching out to steady herself at the thought. Not even good coffee would help this. Her eyes closed, thoughts suddenly incomprehensible other than the fact that everything felt larger and worse than her expectations could have ever projected.

"Bowie?" she finally asked.

The AI appeared on her wall screen, his upper half taking up the view's full span to give a real-world scale of his waist up. "Yes?"

"I…" she started before words caught in her throat. No, not just words.

Everything.

"I…" she said before sinking to her knees, her stare dropping to the floor of the small cabin. She adjusted, now sitting but with knees pulled up to her chin, head tucked in.

"Are you feeling all right? It seems unlikely for you to catch a virus living this remotely, though it is possible to get food poisoning—"

"It's not that. I just…" She angled upward and looked at her only companion over the last few years. "I don't know if I can do this."

Bowie's brow furrowed at the statement. "Define *this*."

"This," she said, a shaking anxiety laced in the word as she gestured around her. "*This*. This life, for how many years?"

"Yes, but there's one point you're missing." His words took on a solemn, gravelly texture despite their curtness. "You have to."

"Do I?" Mariana blurted, a reflex more than anything else. Yet the question sank in, rooting itself in the sudden defiance of her mind. "Do I really?"

"I cannot predict the future, but I can process probabilities. And there's an eighty-four percent chance that the proper completion of a retrieval test cycle will break the loop. Uploading data patches on the final day to limit power usage increases that to ninety-four percent."

"So what?" she asked with an indignation that probably

hadn't existed since a night out with Shay featuring too much alcohol and not enough sleep.

"Mariana," he said, his voice soft, "I'm sensing you are troubled."

"Seventeen years!" The words came out louder than she expected, but she straightened up, buoyed by the surge in her chest. "Seventeen years!" Now they pushed out with force, a blend of desperation and fury. "I can't be alone for seventeen years."

"I will be with you—"

"Yeah? What if you break? It's not like I can bring someone here to fix you."

"I have prepared three layers of redundancy and multiple parallel ongoing diagnostic cycles, including a mobile state that can last for three months without charging. Outside of you shutting me off," he chuckled, though his eyes showed it came from sympathy rather than mockery, "I think you're stuck with me."

"That's not enough."

"I'm going to pretend not to be insulted by that."

Mariana looked all around her, the small cabin with a few potted plants scattered about exercise equipment and a large desk with all of Bowie's equipment. She'd read stories of surviving peril, of course, fictional tales of astronauts getting stranded on alien planets or pirates living on a mystery island, even time travelers visiting hundreds of years ago. All of those offered an uplifting morality, a supposed triumph of the human spirit that powered through the pain and ugliness and overwhelming isolation of it all.

She supposed she was lucky, in a way. Those people didn't have a funny AI that looked like a legendary rock star.

So her truth proved to be stranger than fiction. Which made it *harder* than fiction.

"Look. I like you, Bowie. But it's not enough. This isn't a mission. I'm not military. I never signed up for this. It's a fluke.

It's a complete fluke." Her eyes shut, blacking out the world, and she willed a memory into a full image, Carter's pleading face as he tried to get her to stand in *just one spot*. What would have happened if she'd never done that?

"This is Carter's fault," she said, her voice inching toward a yell with each passing word. "He dragged me into this. If I was stuck in the loop? Like everyone else? I wouldn't know. No one knows. Now I'm just here with an AI to talk to and shitty homegrown vegetables, and I drive into town at weird hours to avoid potential car accidents, and remember when my car got stuck and I had to walk back here because calling a tow truck might create a paradox?"

Her fingers pressed against her temples, breath rippling through her as her chest rose and fell. "Paradoxes. Everything is about paradoxes. Who cares about paradoxes? Maybe creating *paradoxes* is the way to get out of this! Ever think of that?"

"Actually, I have. There is a one point one percent chance that a specific paradox of very lengthy explanation and highly coordinated timing solves the loop, but also a ninety-three percent chance that creates a catastrophic space–time event."

"How do you *know*, though?"

"Mariana, you have a science doctorate, so I am assuming you understand mathematical basics. And in mathematical basics, dividing by zero is very bad."

"Living like *this* is very bad," she yelled, loud enough that her voice probably escaped the cabin. "You're…synthetic. You're not real. Your sense of time is not based on, like, I don't know, just the *holy shit* factor of all of this. *Seventeen* years!"

"I have an internal chronometer that understands the passage of time."

"But does it ever speed up when you're happy? Slow down when you're lost? That moment with Carter—" She stopped, catching herself.

"Which moment with Carter?"

Bowie was her confidant, collaborator, and protector. But also her overseer: he made the rules. And while so much of this was about setting the world *right*, only one thing made her heart surge at just a thought. Wimbledon. Donuts. The ocean. All of those moments when minutes passed in a blink.

Many, many reasons powered Mariana through this, even when she had doubts. But the one she held closest was a simple hope of giving her younger self and Carter a chance. And in her mind, she'd already started plotting ways to make that happen.

Part of that meant *not* letting Bowie know. Just in case he tried to stop any of her machinations for paradox purposes.

"Time is not fair," she finally said, her voice now dry and weak. "It doesn't exist for me as sixty seconds in a minute, sixty minutes in an hour. The good things are so fleeting, so fast. And the wait right now, seventeen years. It's gonna be seventeen years. It'll probably feel like twice that. Like a lifetime. In this cabin."

"With me," Bowie said, his voice now free of snark.

"Yeah," Mariana whispered. "With you."

"You have to do this," Bowie said gently before arching an eyebrow. "But you're allowed to mourn the fact that you have to do this."

Mariana's palms wiped the tears of frustration leaking out the corners. "Do you have a psychology algorithm programmed in there?"

"Yes."

The quick response caught Mariana off guard, so much so that she started laughing. Her shoulders bobbed, hands rubbing her tear-stained cheeks, and she sank backward until she lay flat on the floor's thick rug. "What are we going to do?"

"Pick a fun way to pass the time."

"I don't know. I mean, even in zombie-survival stories, the lone hero has a dog at his side."

Bowie paused long enough that Mariana tilted her neck up just to see if his program had frozen. Instead, she caught him with a hand on his chin, head tilted left. "I think," he said slowly, "I can allow that."

"What?"

"A dog. That seems reasonable. If that's truly what you want. We'll need a plan, of course, to prevent para—"

"Wait, wait." The floor creaked as Mariana sat up. "I got it." Suddenly, all that training, all that discipline, that *new* way of thinking, flooded her very instincts. But instead of treating it as a preventative measure, she now saw all the ways to bend, not break, the rules. "Search the shelters for animals scheduled to be euthanized. I can get one that would otherwise be killed. Right?"

Sitting turned to standing, and Mariana walked, bare feet slapping across the floor as she marched to Bowie. "That won't impact the timeline at all, right? Like, if I adopt it that night, it would not impact anything other than making it easier for the person who would have had to do the euthanasia. Maybe they sleep easier, but that's it."

She met Bowie eye to eye, and though his camera was technically at the top-center of the screen, his eyes tracked like they were real. Whoever programmed his reactions must have researched many, many hours of the real David Bowie's reactions, because Bowie's mix of surprise, amusement, and pride rang completely authentic to the human experience.

"You see?" Bowie said, crossing his arms. "You *are* learning. I'm proud of you. As much as an AI can be."

46

It took another two years for the right circumstance to come up: a young, healthy dog whose time at an underresourced shelter was nearly up. There had been others that Mariana felt were right but Bowie rejected, and while she had the urge to throw money at the shelters and keep the dogs alive, Bowie always reminded her at the risk of tampering with things like that, no matter how much she wanted to help.

Bowie explained the checklist for her: young and healthy, to avoid unnecessary visits to the vet; at a shelter within the same radius as the local suburb where she went grocery shopping; and scheduled for euthanasia on the same day she did her monthly errands, to minimize additional trips.

The stars finally aligned, though, and Mariana knew things simply *felt* right the moment the dog emerged from the kennel: a stout tan pit bull with a big smile and gentle eyes. She knelt down, arms outstretched, and the dog ambled over, his shoulder leaning his entire weight onto her knees.

And that was it. He slept easily on the way back to the cabin, a gentle giant whose patience betrayed the fact that he was only a little over a year old.

The dog walked at a steady pace, staying at her side without tugging back or getting distracted, and Mariana let him relieve himself on a tree before bringing him inside.

"Hello, new friend," Bowie said. The dog seemed unfazed by the AI voice appearing out of nowhere, though once he turned to face the screen, his body stiffened. "Oh, I'm not frightening. I patched in a subroutine to love dogs."

"Thanks, Bowie."

"You still have to clean up after him. My voice and demeanor," he said, leaning down on the screen, "will just connect with him a little easier on a psychological level." As if the dog understood, he took cautious steps forward before sniffing the screen. "Does he have a name yet?"

"I thought we should decide together. Since we're coparenting him," she said with a laugh. "Mom and dad, right?"

"I should also add a nurturing subroutine to my algorithm."

"Oh, you're already good at that. But—" Mariana paused, taking in the sight of the dog as he made himself cozy on the floor "—he reminded me of a dog I used to know. Named Buddy Ed. B.E. for short."

"That seems like a very dog-appropriate name. Buddy Ed it is, then."

From that night, Buddy Ed proved as loyal, as patient, and as hungry as Mariana's old friend at her building's lobby. Day after day, week after week, year upon year, they kept a strict routine of checking the growing vegetables, carefully walking the forest perimeter, then doing a property security check. B.E. would lie quiet and worn-out, a patient snore as Mariana would spend her middays doing a dedicated exercise routine developed by Bowie before settling down. That life, that repeating cycle, it all became so ingrained in the strict balance of her life that the old world disappeared from the forefront of her mind, things like restaurants and bars, even *work* simply losing any importance.

Except tennis. She missed tennis, and though she knew she could never rally against another person again, she still hit a ball over to B.E., who parked himself ready between two tall trees in front of her cabin. They played this game over and over, B.E. often catching the ball off one hop and running it back, repeating it until he tired out and lay down, ball in mouth.

Years passed, history playing out exactly as it should, the timeline clear of any headline-grabbing anomalies.

Bowie theorized that because they existed outside of the loop, no retrieval experiment had been run, and though this still seemed somewhat paradoxical in nature to Mariana, she gave in to the fact that Bowie knew what he was talking about, and she'd stick to neuroscience.

With B.E. at her side, her routine settled in, letting the world evolve so gradually that she barely noticed outside of the fact that she shaved her head every six months or so.

For over a decade, Mariana stuck with the plan. And the advice. Bowie's advice, but also Kendra's from years before—or, technically, about two years from now, depending on the way you looked at it.

Mariana's car rolled over the dirt and needles, weeds and branches, the long drive back from civilization with groceries in the back.

Groceries and, for the first time in eighteen years and some days, one very specific, very outstanding bit of rule-breaking.

Mariana sat on her porch under the cover of night, Buddy Ed following her out despite the clear achiness in his aged hips. The old dog usually groaned when he lay down, circling for several seconds before resting his head on her feet. Soon, only the sounds of night surrounded them. Crickets. Wind. Rustling. So many unknowables, a combination of insects and critters, the types of things preteens would use as fodder for ghost stories at summer camps.

Here, Mariana relished in it, like she and Buddy Ed were the center of the galaxy and everything else slowly revolved around their little claim of space. She looked upward from her porch chair, bright beams littering the moonless sky. B.E. let out a groan, his legs stretching out with the noise. "Good boy," she said, reaching down to pet his scruff. The fact that he'd stayed with her this long, when the average life span of the breed usually clocked in around twelve years, made her wonder at times. With everything she'd seen and done, having faith in anything, even science, seemed illogical, out of reach.

But with him, she'd wondered if the universe gave her a little gift, a loyal companion to ease her through the darkest of tunnels.

It made sense that he sat at her side for this moment, angled on the porch specifically in the blind spot for the security camera built into the ceiling. She'd moved the chair there a few weeks ago, taking her morning coffee on it as the sun rose, just to see if Bowie noticed.

Which he hadn't, of course. Why would he, when she'd settled into a methodical and disciplined routine that had lasted more than a decade, one designed to minimize attention, risk, or any type of complications.

She reached into the final grocery bag, feeling her way past some cans of soup and other nonperishables to get to the smooth hand-size rectangle she'd snuck into her purchases. Its screen lit up, illuminating the groceries within the bag. She put it on her lap as it initialized for the first time, setting it on top of a paper notebook, blue pen clipped to it.

A different form of Project Pen.

The screen flashed, various icons showing an initial data connection to the prepaid device's network. It came with its limitations, at this basic stage only offering rudimentary text-based knowledge and daily information like weather forecasts.

But for her purposes, this was all she needed. Because for years and years, Bowie had instilled a clockwork discipline, an

understanding on how to build a routine and consider movements without any risk to the timeline. When she stepped, she
stepped in a way that wouldn't bump into people, slow them
down, put them off course. When she shopped for necessities,
she always went at late hours, staying in aisles that were free
from crowds and only purchasing items with plenty of stock.

Every action was a calculation, a way to get what she needed
without putting a footprint on this timeline. Even now, as they
moved closer and closer to the world that she'd left, the time
loop she'd escaped, such plans became instinct, a way to scan
and assess wherever she looked, whatever she did.

Now, as her time in isolation hurtled toward its final moments, Mariana told herself that she would give herself—no,
the world—a reward for pushing through the impossible.

And she'd do it in a way that bent—not broke—their rules.

She opened the notebook to the first page and gripped the
pen, fingers pressing deep against it, preparing to document
notes in a way that Bowie would never be able to access. Her
free hand held the fully initialized device, ready to perform rudimentary searches across the vast data networks of the globe.

Ever since she'd plucked Buddy Ed from the brink of death,
an idea had begun to roll in Mariana's mind. It gathered momentum, more in desire than in strategy, a knowing that the
combination of planning and discipline Bowie instilled in her
would simply *find a way* when the time was right.

And that time was now.

With Bowie's ears still picking up and processing noise, she
didn't address the device as *System* to activate a search prompt.
Instead, she clicked an icon of a magnifying glass and typed on
the digital keyboard on the screen.

Shay Freeman.

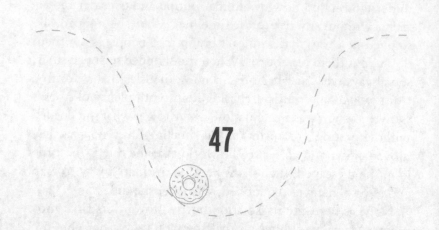

47

The word hung in the air, a clear siren call to another world and another life despite being muttered under breath across a courtyard.

"Motherfucker."

Shay looked down at the bag sitting on another bag stacked on top of the massive mountaineering backpack before sighing, an expression that Mariana hadn't seen in nearly twenty years. Yet, everything about her expression lit up places in Mariana's thoughts and memories like they were just at a tennis tournament, their parents' wedding, hanging out on Shay's couch. Her familiar scowl, twisted pursed lips, and crunched brow that caused her eyes to squint fired through Mariana's brain, unifying the past and present and future into a singular moment.

"Motherfucker," Shay said again, this time in a whisper, and she began checking through her different bags. Something was clearly missing, though Shay's mumbles were too low for Mariana to catch what exactly her friend forgot. "Goddamn it," she finally said with a sigh, then her apartment door slid open.

Maggie's meows came from inside, a distinctive enthusiastic whine that punched nearly as hard as seeing Shay again.

The door shut behind as Shay stepped inside, though her luggage remained in the hall. Urges tugged within Mariana, some telling her to linger and just *watch* and take in her friend's existence again. Others pulled her to break in and sweep Shay up for a hug tight enough to protect her friend from whatever fate awaited her.

But twenty years of discipline activated, a clear understanding of the opportunity presented here. She dashed over to Shay's bags, then placed a thick manila envelope on the top bag. It refused to stay in place, taking several tries before she finally got it in a steady, balanced spot.

"Be good for Mariana, Mag," Shay yelled through the closed door. Mariana dashed down the second-story hallway, the dusk light dim enough that turning the corner provided enough cover as Shay came back out, arms stretched overhead as she let out another sigh before turning. At first, she missed the envelope, her hands fumbling to move all of the bags in a delicate balance. But then her head tilted, and even at this distance, Mariana saw her eyes squint.

"What the hell?" she said to herself. Not loud enough for Mariana's ears to pick up, but the motion of her lips made it very clear. "Paper?"

An entirely different path suddenly presented itself—to Shay, to Mariana, to the *world*. Mariana's pulse quickened, and her fingers crossed as she watched from afar. Shay pulled out the note in the envelope, held it long enough to read, then looked in the envelope again.

Shay glanced up, then over her shoulder. Mariana took the moment to duck fully behind the corner beam that obscured her, then listened. The sound of rustling came through, along with Shay muttering obscenities to herself. Mariana peeked around the corner again once things got quiet.

She saw Shay staring at the envelope, holding it still while doing so, as if the very act of looking at it could reveal its secret origins. "Fuck it," she said, this time loud enough for Mariana to hear, and she knew *exactly* what that meant.

Shay only said that when she'd made a choice.

Mariana exhaled, a full-body relaxation at the moment. Shay would go do something else besides Joshua Tree. She'd follow the letter's advice, access the dummy bank account Mariana had set up, and go *anywhere* else in the world, and then—

Except Shay didn't show any immediate change in plans. Or even demeanor. Instead, she motioned her hand, the door sliding open once more. Maggie meowed from inside again, though Shay shook her head. "No, I'm not back. Just leaving this here. I'll deal with it when I get back."

Maggie trilled again, her floofy silhouette visible. "Okay, *last* pets," she said, kneeling down to stroke the cat's back. "I swear, I got the neediest cat in the world. Okay, gotta go. Joshua Tree awaits. Be good."

Joshua Tree. The very name caused Mariana to sway in place, twenty years of planning and care about to evaporate into desert air. The motion must have caught Shay's attention: she glanced over long enough to see someone in the hall but didn't linger to make out any details. Instead, she went back to tying the smaller bags to the larger backpack.

The timeline. Paradoxes. So many lectures from Bowie about ripple effects, how even making someone late by a few seconds might cause them to be in a car accident or some other life-changing effect. Let alone blatantly and very specifically interrupting them as they stepped forward toward their destiny.

No. Not for Shay. Shay was right—*fuck it.*

If Mariana was going to break time and space, it would be to save her best friend. Though she still gave Bowie a reasonable excuse about doing her regular grocery trip and needing to pick up a part for car repair at the same time. Which *was* true, though Mariana had picked the part up a few months ago specifically for this subterfuge.

Bowie would probably ask why she had disabled all her devices, though. She'd come up with that excuse on the way home.

"Shay!" Mariana called out, an unintended break coming to her voice.

Shay stopped, then looked around, and Mariana wondered just how much her voice sounded like herself. Did twenty years of rough living change that?

She walked over, face hidden behind big sunglasses, her close-cropped hair nothing like what Shay knew as Mariana Pineda. Between that, the whole twenty-years-of-hard-living look, and the fashion sense of a rugged survivalist instead of a professional scientist, Mariana gambled on Shay not putting the pieces together.

She shouldn't, anyway. It wasn't like any of this was logical, even with Shay's training in quantum mechanics.

Shay tracked Mariana as she walked, even steps that bought her time to consider all the different things to say. But when she stood face-to-face with her best friend, her teammate, her stepsister, nothing came out, and the discipline that she'd honed so finely over the decades began to crack. "Don't go to Joshua Tree," she finally blurted out.

"Was that…" She glanced back at the closed door. "Was that envelope from you?"

"Just do anything else. Stay off the grid, and don't go to Joshua Tree. It's really important."

Shay looked her up and down, and Mariana hoped the dim lighting worked to her advantage. "Do I know you? Who are you?"

"I can't tell you, and you wouldn't believe me if I did."

"What are you, some sort of secret agent?" Shay said with a laugh.

"Not quite. I mean, do I *look* like a secret agent?"

"Good call. Point to you."

Bowie's lectures came to mind, but Mariana pushed them all

aside. What would it take to bring Shay to the finish line? "I'm not a secret agent. I wish," she said with a laugh. "I just got stuck doing something really, really strange and important. So can you just trust this complete stranger?"

"That's super cryptic."

"Can I just say it's *weirdo science shit*? 'Cause this is very time-sensitive."

Shay's head tilted at the phrase, her whole posture tightening. She looked Mariana over again, drawing out a long breath. "So let's say you're right," she said slowly. "What do I need to do to avoid whatever *really strange and important* means?"

"Just follow the stuff in the envelope. Leave *right now*. Take the funds. Go to, I don't know, Iceland for a little while. Just go away. Don't leave a trace. Make everyone think you went to Joshua Tree. Don't even check the news or your phone during this time," Mariana said. "Just, like, go commune with nature. And then come back on the date I wrote down."

"Then what?"

"Tell people where you went. Play dumb. Make up a story about how you got stranded without data access and you're sorry if you scared people. And then resume your normal life." Shay's normal life—what could that possibly be after this? Mariana caught herself smiling at the thought. "Don't mention me, of course. There are rules. You stick by the rules, and everything will be fine. Better than fine." The smile grew to a laugh, a gesture born out of the collision of grief and joy. "I know, I *know* you will want to break them. But I am begging you, just this once. Stick to them."

"Iceland." Shay squinted, then looked at the door. "My cat…"

"Your cat will be well-loved during this time. Trust me on that one. I promise you. No one can resist Maggie."

Shay's head angled again, thoughts processing at the semicryptic statements this stranger was making. Mariana took steady breaths, hoping that even though years separated them, she still knew exactly how to harness Shay's one-of-a-kind, calculated impulsivity.

"Huh," she finally said before turning. Without another word, Shay went back into the apartment. Maggie announced herself once again, and Mariana held back from even looking at the cat. Shay returned, envelope in hand, then held it up between them. "This?"

"Read it again. Closely. I'm not asking for much. Just a different place for an extended vacation. All expenses paid. All you have to do is not tell anyone." Mariana found herself nodding, as if that could beg Shay to do it. "That's everything you'll need."

"Good old paper," Shay said, shaking her head. The words came out slow enough to give away the fact that Shay was really thinking about it now.

"That's the thing about paper. It doesn't change." Shay looked up at that, and Mariana locked in, thinking back decades now to the moment they'd stood outside a tiny shop in the rain.

At that moment, she made a choice in what to say, a clear decisive hint at what was actually happening. "It captures who you are right now."

Shay's sudden inhale told Mariana that she should leave before anything went paradoxical. Bowie's playful-but-sharp chastising rang in her head again, an inner shame that drove her back to the discipline that had got her to this very moment.

That would have to be enough. Or at least, all she could do for now. Paradoxes and all of the time-breaking warnings Bowie went on and on about—she'd edged very close to it. Before Shay could say anything further, Mariana turned on her heel and marched away, a flutter in her chest at the new life she might have just created.

48

"Are you ready?"

Bowie awaited a response, lingering in perfect silence as Mariana considered the very essence of his question. Was she?

Twenty years had passed since she'd stepped into the Hawke Accelerator and emerged in the middle of a large roped-off construction zone. Twenty years since she'd seen Kendra Hall and learned what Dr. Beckett and his team were really up to. Twenty years since breaking out of the loop, since saying good-bye to Maggie, since seeing anomalies pulled out of time and land in modern society.

Since kissing Carter as Hawke exploded all around them.

Mariana walked over to the cabin's small window, looking past the tired eyes in the reflection to the small mound about twenty feet away: Buddy Ed's final resting spot sat between a pair of redwood trees that stretched to a seemingly infinite height, the same location where he'd caught countless tennis balls. The dirt still lay fresh, a distinctly different shade of brown compared to its surroundings, only a handful of needles and leaves on top of it.

Three weeks had passed since Buddy Ed simply hadn't woken

up after a long night's sleep. That morning, she knelt as she always did during his senior years, with a few gentle scratches to wake her longtime companion up.

And though he felt warm to the touch, Mariana knew immediately that something was wrong. She rested her hand on Buddy's abdomen, waiting for the rise and fall of deep sleep, but nothing came. "Oh," she said, bending over to cradle the dog on the floor.

For years, Buddy Ed had remained faithful and patient, affectionate despite the occasional flair for chewing on a chair leg. When he hit twelve years old, Mariana knew that breed expectations were out the window, and despite the arthritis and fatigue of old age, he stayed at her feet as much as possible.

"It happened two hours ago. When you were sleeping," Bowie said as she cradled the limp dog.

"Did he suffer?"

"No. I monitor both of your vitals through various environmental sensors. Buddy Ed stopped breathing at 4:18 a.m." Bowie paused, as if putting his virtual hand on her shoulder. "His life just ended."

Mariana took in the sight, the peaceful simplicity of his current state. "Bowie, erase our plan to arrange for his care after I leave," she said with dry words. "That's unnecessary now."

"Done." Bowie remained quiet after that, a good minute or two passing while Mariana held her dog, taking in his smell one more time. She ran her hands over the folds of his ears, the scruff of his muzzle, the whiskers on his left side that poked a little rougher than the ones on his right. "He was a very good boy," Bowie finally said.

Strange how all of that discipline Mariana had built up for years became so critical in controlling her emotions when she encountered Shay. Yet in this moment, in the face of a deep, grievous pain, no tears fought to come out. Emotions stirred in her: the agony of loss fighting the relief at peace, but above all it marked the finality of the days. She found herself whispering things to Buddy Ed, words forming without conscious thought, though in the end one phrase came out, an endless loop as she held him.

"Thank you for staying," she whispered, so many times she lost count, though those four words painted a complete picture of Buddy Ed. He *stayed*, even when his joints hurt and hips ached, well past when his time should have been up.

She had no tears for him. Instead, she found herself smiling at his serene expression, the way it had simply ticked down the clock to zero without any qualm, any fuss.

Mariana wondered if she would be so lucky.

She spent the bulk of that day digging a hole for him between those trees, arms and shoulders burning from the effort needed to go four feet deep. She set his bed down in the space before putting his body on it and tucking him in with his favorite blanket. And right before she started to cover him, she made sure to nestle one tennis ball between his paws.

That was several weeks ago, a final gateway for Mariana's mind to lock onto what she needed to do. Years back, she told Bowie that she wasn't military, that she wasn't on a mission. And yet as she stood in the cabin, pondering Bowie's simple question *Are you ready?* everything felt as much like a mission as possible. She'd trained her own sense of discipline. They'd crafted a plan. They'd built a list of tools and equipment, and she'd mentally prepared, using simulations on Bowie's display, the computer-generated images mirroring what she remembered about the Hawke facility as closely as could be.

And she *remembered*—something that she rooted deep in herself through the process of simply writing down what she knew using a pen and paper.

So was she ready?

"Yeah. I am," she said, looking at the clock. It was 6:04 a.m., about six and a half hours before the Hawke Accelerator would explode. Construction of the facility had gone strictly by design, and Bowie had managed to verify that the strut they'd offset stood exactly as specified. All she needed to do was get inside the building, upload a final patch to limit the power consumption, and flip a few switches, all guided by Bowie. And a little handiwork of her own, a specific plan to replicate what Carter had done all those years ago, a simple series of disabled doors and elevators.

As for Carter? Well, when she asked Bowie a few days ago about voltage limitations in power conduits around the observation room, she'd posed it as a way for her to know what to look for, a comparison against the original catastrophe. But in this case, overloading one of the circuits enough to require a replacement, that would be enough to put Carter at the right place at the right time.

And herself? She wasn't sure. No one could possibly know, and though Bowie ran his own calculations on this quite regularly, in the end she decided it wouldn't matter.

She'd either live or she'd die. Well, not necessarily die, but cease to exist. If she lived? Life would play out unplanned for the first time in far too long.

There was a surprising amount of comfort in either of those options.

As she stared at the fresh soil between two redwood trees, a serenity draped over her nerves, the type of dreamscape that only came with acceptance.

"Very good, Mariana. I'll begin downloading into the mobile unit. We preserved it well over twenty years. It passed all of its diagnostics. I've started the countdown to self-delete and factory-reset all hardware in this cabin."

"It held up well, didn't it? Everything we put together in here."

"This is why every plan requires regular diagnostics and triple redundancy."

"I appreciate your sentimentality, Bowie." She looked over

at the couch, where she'd laid out the final items in almost rit-
ualistic fashion last night: overalls to mimic a technician's uniform, the very same mobile David unit she'd arrived with in
the past, and an earpiece.

"Are you sure you're not forgetting anything?"

Mariana shook her head, but instead of checking equipment
she scanned the space around them one final time. There wasn't
much left at this point: Bowie had suggested a gradual disposal
of items into dumpsters as she drove into town for groceries,
eventually leaving a sparse cabin to minimize evidence of her
existence. But she did leave the plants she'd gradually learned
to keep alive, a handful of succulents with thick round leaves
and a hanging spider plant in a macramé hanger.

And a bowl on the counter, half-filled with fruit from her
final trip into town.

Of course—a snack. Just as Carter would suggest.

"I'm good," Mariana finally said, grabbing the last apple from
the basket on the counter. She took one last look at the mound
between redwood trees, then blew a kiss to Buddy Ed's final
resting spot. "Let's go save time and space."

49

From time to time, Bowie would show Mariana photos of the Hawke Accelerator, particularly during the long years of its initial structural build. Despite the fact that the building and the technology housed inside ruled so much of her life, she never ventured out to see it in person.

Viewing it again with her own eyes, not as an image captured by a camera on a stream or clip, felt strangely enough like coming home. Memories overlapped with real-time images—the people crossing the street, the way the clouds diffused the sun above, the chill wind tickling her ears, all of it triggered an unexpected nostalgia that almost slowed her down. But she stuffed those feelings away, squashing them as she walked toward the Hawke entrance. As if Bowie could read her thoughts, his voice popped into her ear. "It's a bit like a reunion, isn't it?"

"I'm getting those feelings," she said. But it wasn't quite as sentimental: that would have meant wisps of nostalgia coloring memories and heartstrings. In this case, the situation was more like muscle memory. The crosswalk signal flipped, and Mariana set forward from the same spot she had during countless loops, and though she walked earlier than she normally did during the loop, enough of *everything* remained the same. Crosswalks timed on the same frequency, doors opened and closed at the same cadence, security staff greeted visitors with the same phrases.

"Seventeen minutes until sync," Bowie said, triggering a cascade of instincts. She picked up her pace, eyes now focused on all of the same flags and landmarks that she'd used to get through the loop. Bowie started spouting off the list of time markers they'd practiced, but getting through the door and into the facility proved just as easy now as it had years ago, perhaps even more so given that she blended in with staff thanks to technician coveralls. She approached the front desk, but unlike before when she would arrive with ReLive, she had a fake identity gradually built by Bowie over twenty years and the AI whispering the right words in her ear to register and get past security.

She strode forward, then waited for 9:42 a.m. But as she did, a voice caught her ear.

Not the tone or pitch of it but what it said.

"ReLive."

She stepped back by the pillar where she counted down the time and watched as the ReLive group walked in: Curtis, Dean, and others, and there on the very end, her younger self clad in a gray business suit, a bag on her shoulder with Shay's photo in a frame. The younger Mariana moved in muted steps, a heaviness to her gait that seemed to dissolve when a security guard greeted them and informed them that they'd get to tour the guts of the facility today, even meet with Dr. Beckett.

In other loops, after Mariana had become self-aware of their circumstances, this neared the moment when she would break off and speak to Pratt or hack into the Hawke archive. But here, Mariana remembered this feeling, a sliver in time from before she got caught up with time loops, with Carter, with everything. She watched as her younger self moved ahead, and though the bag still hung on her shoulder, she'd tucked it under her arm, fingers gripping the bottom of the bag like she held Shay's hand.

"Mariana," Bowie said. "We're coming up on the time sync."

She turned, looking past the blue digits capturing the time on wide glass panels to catch a glimpse of herself. Lines carved around her eyes and mouth, worn away by time and stress. And the irises, a clarity came with them, a different discipline than how Shay would josh her about work and nothing but work. These stared with purpose, but also resignation.

If she simply disappeared, maybe all of the grief she'd so neatly sewn up over the past twenty years would too.

It was almost 9:42 a.m.

The clock turned, and Mariana snapped to attention, then set out. She moved in an exact replica of how she had before, and even the data center proved simple. She strode past the data analyst named Kaitlyn, offering an identical, smiling hello as she had on one of her final loops. The far terminal and its surrounding stations sat empty, and her legs pumped in a confident march, the same staff lurking absent-mindedly as before.

"Easy, right?" Bowie said. "Don't answer out loud. No need to draw attention to yourself."

If Bowie *could* read thoughts, he would have picked up on Mariana's snark about how the AI simply wanted to hear himself speak right now. Instead, he only recited steps for connecting the mobile unit to the console and applying the data patch to tweak power limitations during the retrieval process.

Mariana watched as the status bar ticked upwards, a process that hung at fifty-four percent for far too long until leaping forward to seventy-eight percent and finally ticking up to a hundred. The screen flashed with confirmation, though she waited for Bowie himself to say it before reacting.

"Good job," he said, prompting a bigger exhale than she would have liked. "Let's get you to the secondary-power control room."

Mariana's teeth dug into her lip.

"One more thing," she said under her breath, pulling up a file titled *Temporal_Corruption_Lessons_Learned* from the memory core. "This. Can you send this to Beckett?"

"Right now?"

"No." A quick glance around the room showed that either no one noticed or no one cared that she was muttering to herself. If they did, they probably just assumed she was using comms. "Right before I leave."

"This file is our daily log," Bowie said.

"It is. I cleaned it up a little bit the other night. All the rules you made me follow."

The document opened on the screen, probably from Bowie trying to prove a point. "Protocols to prevent temporal corruption. You even explain your encounter with Kendra. I do appreciate this last line though. *By the way, I like Bowie. He's a good guy.*"

"I also snuck in some pictures of B.E. And like you said, if this works, Kendra won't remember me." She stared at the bright green text in front of her, twenty years of knowledge and discipline and mistakes put into about five hundred thousand words. "I don't know if I just want someone to have a record that I existed or what. But I figure Beckett would know what to do with it. If nothing else, refine their protocols. But maybe just brighten their day with Buddy Ed. If it makes it through. I mean, there's a chance that it might disappear if *I* disappear, right?"

"Temporal causality is largely theoretical at this point. But if I was a betting man, I'd say that makes it through. However," Bowie said, his tone shifted to color in a hint of parental-esque disappointment, "sending this is temporal corruption in itself."

"Ah, see." Mariana *knew* Bowie would say that, and she came prepared. "If you send it right before we finish, you know Beckett won't open it immediately. He's giving the tour. There's no way it'll corrupt anything. It'll only take up empty space on a server for a few minutes, maybe even a few hours."

"Clever." The display flashed several times, boxes opening and closing, followed by another status bar that quickly filled. "I've taught you well."

Bowie's words came with a rare pride in his tone, and Mariana tried not to let the AI sense how satisfying that felt.

Mariana started to notice the smallest signs of deviation. She walked through the technical wing of the facility, moving past workers dressed like Carter or staff wearing semicasual clothes, the preferred look for scientists and engineers when no presentations or meetings were on the docket. And through all of them, a sense of calm, of normalcy took place.

From what she'd gathered before, the first signs that something went wrong with the accelerator's test cycle started around an hour before the explosion. During those early moments, she'd spent loops observing test engineers moving hurriedly through hallways, technicians being called in from other departments to run checks or diagnostics all across the space. All of this played out quietly, and she'd wondered if part of the issue came down to a toxicity that existed in the culture of work, one that focused too much on projecting a normal sense of calm when an explosion was actually imminent. Each of those separate spikes of anxiety accumulated, hitting higher peaks as the cycle shifted from dangerous internal readings to physical destruction on a continuously grander scale.

None of that scrambling happened now. Instead, the cadence of the Hawke Accelerator followed any normal work day: no matter how exciting the project, people still looked tired and bored, staring too long at their cups of coffee and snacks. They likely didn't notice the gradual disabling of elevators and doors, the series of uploaded hacks firing off in sequence. Bowie had asked what the purpose of this was, and while she said it was simply to avoid running into her younger self, what the AI didn't know was that the pattern mirrored something Carter had done many years ago to funnel a tour group to a very specific location at a very specific time. Between the standard pace of a humdrum workday, Mariana's previous experience, and Bowie's guidance, getting to Hawke's secondary-power control room proved as simple as walking in. From there, they moved through the steps like items on a grocery list, bypassing several security protocols to upload Bowie's safety algorithms limiting energy capacity on the redundant power charge.

Flipping a switch was the only remaining item. Not just in their to-do list but potentially Mariana's *life*.

The moment arrived without ceremony. After the endless loops and the twenty-year wait, they were here and Mariana didn't have the time to savor, fear, or dwell in it too much. The timing required too much precision. Even Bowie moved on without any sentiment in his final actions.

"The message with the archive file has been sent to Dr. Beckett. I'm starting the process of deleting my active state, though Dr. Beckett will have all of my records. This unit will simply be a David interface when I'm done. The oldest one in existence," Bowie said, and though he was a digital construct of a human voice, he still paused and took a breath. "I wonder if anyone will notice. Or perhaps I will disappear as well. A philosophical conundrum, isn't it?"

"You're no longer able to engage with the Hawke mainframe?" Mariana asked, looking at one last screen featuring facility controls.

"I'm just good company for the next few minutes."

Wordless, Mariana tapped through the screen until she got to the status of power conduits by strut QL89. All ran at nominal status, at least until she drove an overload in conduit 22, then returned to the task at hand.

A switch.

The switch. The one that would theoretically end it all. Mariana stared at it, a lever that simply had to go from up to down to physically reroute power into a redundant source, one with a programmed energy cap set to a fraction of a percent lower—a safety net, Bowie had called it, layered mitigations to ensure that the retrieval test cycle completed.

So many thoughts collided in her brain that ultimately it all became an empty, jumbled mess, a question about what she might have possibly left undone. That, more than what might happen to her, weighed heaviest.

As if Bowie read her mind, he offered a final thought. "One last thing, Mariana. I have about sixty seconds before I become inactive. There was a bank account you opened several months ago. Very limited activity on it. But I thought you should know that this morning, a purchase was made. A one-way ticket from Reykjavik, Iceland, to San Francisco, departing in two days."

Bowie rolled out the statement so nonchalantly that it took Mariana several seconds to fully process what it meant.

"Fascinating, isn't it?" he said, a coyness in his voice. "You never told me about that account. Perfect timing for someone to fly home and strategically avoid any—" he let out a quick laugh "—*complications* from our actions today. Anything else you wish to disclose now that we're at the end?"

Of course Bowie would tell her with just enough time for him to experience her reaction, but not enough time for her to respond. Paradoxes and all that.

"The mechanic. Carter. I was stuck in the loop with him. I…" Mariana stopped, unsure of the way to phrase it. After all Bowie's warnings about Shay, she'd vowed to keep her thoughts on Carter even more concealed, an invisible finish line to this whole journey. "I love him. Loved him."

"Interesting. You hid that well. Your stories made him sound like a coworker. I wonder why you kept that from me?"

"Do you remember when I asked about how to disable elevators and lock conference-room doors?" Mariana asked with a grin. "And the voltage limits of power conduits?"

"Yes."

"If you knew I was doing that to influence the future, wouldn't you have stopped me?"

Bowie, so often quick with his reply, paused just long enough that Mariana gave herself a mental cheer for pushing the world's most advanced AI to challenge his thinking for a sliver of time. "A commendable deception. Good-bye, Mariana. The pleasure was mine. Remember to flip the switch at precisely ten minutes left in the test cycle. Files deleted in five. Four. Three. Two."

Bowie's voice stopped, though the earpiece popped with momentary static before nothing.

Mariana looked at the clock as she slowly gripped the switch, a universe of possibilities running through her mind at what the next few seconds might hold. And for a fragment of time, she wondered what might happen if she *didn't* flip the switch, this final fail-safe. But no, curiosity lost out.

She was here to do a job twenty years in the making.

She tugged on the switch.

Except it refused to budge, though Mariana wondered if it might have simply been adrenaline overload. Her fingers gripped the handle, flexing again as they intertwined. She took one more look at the test countdown clock above, seconds slipping away after hitting the ten-minute marker.

Then she pulled, a focused exertion that broke past the mechanism's stubbornness and forced it through. The switch flipped down, first a mechanical clicking before a series of thunks channeled through the air. On one of the displays, one box went from green to orange while the adjacent one highlighted in green.

Mariana let go and stepped back, breath still, waiting for something to happen. Would she fade away? But that didn't make sense from a physiology perspective: bodies couldn't ex-

A QUANTUM LOVE STORY

345

actly fade without weird things happening to bones and organs. Maybe she'd get pulled into another dimension. That seemed much more likely.

Or even another loop?

Whatever happened, Bowie wasn't around to tell her the odds. Instead, she simply waited, every passing second carrying the weight of eternity.

50

Except nothing happened.

Seconds continued ticking away at the test clock. Nine minutes and forty-five seconds left. Then forty-four. Then forty-three.

Fact: The power cap successfully uploaded, and the switch flipped, yet she remained.

Hypothesis: Hopefully the loop broke. Hopefully she'd snuck Shay into a new destiny. Hopefully she gave her younger self and Carter a chance.

But what that meant, she didn't know. She couldn't come up with an experiment. She simply had to wait for the cycle to finish.

Not knowing—what a strange experience, equally terrifying and wonderful.

Instead of panicking, she walked in quiet steps to the secondary-power control window and watched, her view adjacent to the observation room where people came in. She saw the faces: Beckett, Curtis, and the others.

And then herself. Her younger self, photo frame in her hands, lingered, staring at Hawke's hardware. Mariana blinked as she realized something was wrong.

Where was Carter? Why wasn't he nearby?

She'd planned it all out, from funneling the ReLive group the same way that Carter managed during the early loops to overloading a power conduit in the observation room. Not one that would break the Hawke Accelerator, but that would at least flag Carter to come inspect it.

That had happened. That had *all* happened, so why wasn't Carter here now?

Mariana grabbed her mobile interface from her back pocket, its system now reset to default. "Bowie—I mean, David?"

"Welcome to the Hawke Accelerator. My name is David, and I'll be your AI guide to—"

"David, what's the status of power conduit 22 by strut QL89?"

"Checking," David said politely. "That power conduit is running at nominal value."

Then it hit her, one simple thing that she must not have accounted for.

Without a series of catastrophic issues to fix, Carter hadn't lingered to ponder what was happening. Instead, he must have simply replaced the power conduit and moved on to the next task, maybe even headed for the cafeteria.

From there, Carter's path could have been diverted in a million different ways. And the ReLive group, if they hadn't stopped at the observation room, they would have moved ahead to…

The control room.

Of all the times Bowie's probability mechanism could have helped in calculating possibilities, this would have been the most important.

But she didn't have time to dwell on it. Just over nine minutes remained, and *then* what? Would that be the point that everything ended for her, however that happened?

One final mission remained.

"David, locate Carter Cho."

"Let me see…" David said. "Carter Cho is in Hallway A-12, three hundred and eighty-four meters away."

Before David finished his sentence, Mariana's legs were already moving, the slam of her boots against tile echoing down the hallway. Instinct drove her as she ran, the map and all of its different sections burned into her mind with a pure certainty. She hustled, only slowing for a glance at the screens and the accelerator's countdown clock to track her evaporating timeline. Seven minutes. Then six minutes. Then five and four minutes.

She moved around the corner, ducking and dodging past puzzled staff coming out of meetings or walking to lunch or taking a breather, twenty years of discipline giving way to a few fleeting minutes of desperation.

"Carter!"

He stopped in his tracks, his head slowly turning. When she'd seen Shay months ago, the very sight of her best friend had frozen her, short-circuiting two decades of discipline and planning. Here, momentum throttled her forward, and in her most analytical, most *Mariana* way, she scanned the scene in front of her.

Carter, looking puzzled. Standing with his cart of tools, the one she'd seen dozens of times, in his familiar default setup, a tool loadout built for actual work instead of hacking or stealth or anything like that.

And his notebook. It lay open, folded back, pen clearly clipped to it.

That would have to do.

"Let's get some consequences," she said to herself. She sprinted full speed, ignoring his wide eyes and sudden "What the heck?" She snatched the notebook with a single swipe, not even hitting a full stop before turning and running back the other way toward the observation room.

Toward her younger self.

Three minutes on the clock.

What possibilities remained? Either this whole thing, what-ever it was, would end for her. Or it wouldn't. She supposed with Carter on her heels and the younger Mariana at the other side of the hallway door, she would have managed to give them a chance at coming together, at least over the sight of a strange woman running through the hall. What could she do with the remaining time, now less than two minutes?

As she kept running, her pace slowed just enough, a men-tal adjustment as a new idea popped into her head. Legs still churning, she flipped past Carter's notes to an empty page and unclipped the ballpoint pen. Her thumb flicked the cap off and it tumbled to the floor behind her as she approached the control-room door.

She had time for a note. With less than a minute left and a few feet to go, she stopped abruptly, propping the notebook on her knee, and shut her eyes, urging the perfect note out of nothing. What might possibly join Mariana and Carter together, knowing that all of their time, all of their experiences had been erased, sacrificed to give the world a chance to move forward?

Her eyes opened, and she scanned the different screens lin-ing the walls. Most carried the test cycle's countdown clock and various live data to go with it. But halfway down the hall, one screen carried completely different information, something unrelated and unnecessary to particle acceleration but absolutely necessary to the human condition.

The café menu.

She glanced at the clock one more time, and all those long days in the loop, the never-ending stretches of nothing dur-ing the years in the cabin, what she would have given to steal a fraction of those dull, empty moments right now. Her fingers gripped the pen as the seconds whipped by, a precarious balance against her knee as she scribbled down the last best chance she had at connecting two people who would never have given each other the time of day, might never have even passed each other.

From the tint of the screen above, she caught a color change to green and a loud chime indicating the test cycle had completed. She turned to the control-room door and opened her mouth, using whatever strength she had left to call out. "Mari—"

51

Carter ran, but his best pace couldn't keep up with the sprinting woman. Despite the weary—and really, out-of-her-mind—look on her face, she moved swiftly. A glance at his cart showed that none of his tools were disturbed by her manic rush, and actually, it only appeared that she had taken his notebook. Problem was, she sprinted out of view so fast that he couldn't tell.

"Crap," he muttered to himself, turning the corner in shoes not necessarily meant for running at this speed. The screens lining the wall showed the accelerator's test cycle winding down, and he passed windowed rooms of people hunched over at stations, looking at tablets, or otherwise mired in their own business. No one seemed to notice the strange woman running with a paper notebook. He paused at a corner, nearly tripping over himself as he scanned ahead, and he finally caught sight of her.

Kneeling down with his notebook. No, *writing* in his notebook.

And her voice, she called out something. *Mary*, maybe? A name, but he wasn't sure.

A chime came from the screen on the wall, catching Carter's attention. He turned to see a green *Cycle Complete* message on the monitor, then a display of various metrics and statistics that probably meant a lot to people in the rooms all around him. But for him, his job focused on checking power conduits and running hardware diagnostics, not dealing with the actual *purpose* of the accelerator. Other people—smarter people—could worry about that.

He turned back, the door to the observation room still closed at the end of it.

Except the woman was now gone.

Carter moved in a slight jog, the hallway's ventilation blowing a draft that cooled the sweat forming across his forehead. His breath steadied, no longer running at speeds he hadn't attempted regularly since high school, and he squinted to see...

His notebook. On the floor.

As he approached, the control room's door opened, and out stepped a string of people dressed more like salespeople than scientists. Though he didn't recognize most of them, a voice came through that he'd heard enough during facility-wide speeches about milestones or state-of-the-project presentations.

Dr. Beckett moved to the front of the group, arm outstretched as he motioned people down the hall. Out they walked, each person stepping over his notebook without even noticing, and Carter moved swiftly, nodding at the people as they passed.

"Oh, hello," Dr. Beckett said. They locked eyes, and he offered a warm smile which Carter returned, followed by a quick nod. "Excuse us. I'm just giving them a tour."

"Of course," Carter said, waiting for him to finally pass. He turned, already halfway down to pick up his notebook, when he paused at an unexpected sight.

A woman. Another guest, Mariana Pineda from her visitor ID badge, was also kneeling down and already one motion ahead of him. Her fingers gripped the notebook, and in her free hand, she held what appeared to be an old-fashioned photo frame.

They locked eyes, an unexpected second look as they studied each other.

"Hi," Carter said, a sheepish tone to his simple introduction. He snapped back into the moment, voice taking back its normal cadence. "Sorry, that's my notebook. Someone..." He turned, looking all around for the strange woman who came and went. "Someone grabbed it. I think they got confused. But I don't see them anymore. Did you happen to see a woman in technician coverings like mine? Like, did she pass through the control room?"

"Nope. It was just us."

"Huh. It's like she just disappeared on me." Carter angled his head and looked at the writing on the page. "Maybe someone was playing a prank. She took that from my stuff."

"This is yours?" she asked, offering the notebook.

"Yeah." He took it, turning it for them to both see the writing scribbled on it.

"*Glazed donuts at the café,*" she read out loud. The corners of her mouth tilted upward, a brightness to them from reading the sentence. "Funny, it looks like my handwriting."

"Oh. Those donuts are surprisingly tasty." Carter found himself no longer looking for the notebook thief and instead focused on the woman in front of him. "For a corporate café, anyways."

"I don't usually like donuts," she said with a smile. "But glazed, they're simple, you know. Simple is sometimes better." He returned her look, an instinctive nod at her statement. "They're at the Hawke café?"

"Yeah. It's between the different wings." He turned around, gesturing in the general direction at the facility's moderately acceptable café—not the best, of course, but better than a lot of on-site eating at a job, and loads better than his college experience. "I'm Carter, by the way," he said, his ears suddenly burning at the very fact that he introduced himself to this stranger. "I work here. Obviously."

"Mariana." She held out her left hand, her right still holding a photo frame for some reason. He took it, lightly taking in the off-handed gesture as he wrapped his fingers around hers for the briefest of moments. She glanced down at their hands before letting go, but when her eyes met his, he caught her sharp inhale. "I *don't* work here. I'm with the ReLive team. Which," she said and craned her neck, "I seem to have lost. They were going on their lunch break."

"Oh," Carter said, tapping the notebook page. "You know how to get there?"

"No clue. Totally lost. It's my first time on this side of Hawke."

"It's right down this way." Carter motioned forward, the notebook still in hand. "The accelerator wing of Hawke is massive. I'll show you the way out."

EPILOGUE

Kendra opened the cabin door simply because she *could*. She'd done it before, of course. Beckett and his team either didn't notice or were simply too polite to say anything. "How's the weather out there?" Bowie asked.

A different Bowie from the last time she welcomed the outside world, of course. Bowie 2.0 or, as she'd simply started calling him, Two. Not the original that she'd been with during her previous isolation, but a brand-new one who started off with the same quirks yet wound up being different. She thought of her last moment with the first version, leaving the cabin in the redwoods with a simple goodbye as *that* Bowie ran his self-deletion program. Apparently nature versus nurture still applied to AI companions during time-travel experiments, and though Kendra thought of many, many people and places she planned on visiting now that she was legally allowed to step back into the world, she couldn't help but think she'd miss Bowie.

"It's early. Sunrise," she said, the purple hues of the morning cutting through forest cover of pine needles and leaves. Beckett had said she could step outside at 12:01 a.m., or the time when her other self time-jumped. She decided to go to bed, though, and then take in the morning fresh, simply breathing in the air, knowing she'd survived six months of isolation in preparation, then six further months of isolation after she'd time-traveled to the past. For all of her hopping around time, the waiting had brought her to this precise moment when she could be exposed to the world again without fear of paradox, and somehow she got through it no worse for wear. Even Beckett's memory worries didn't seem to be an issue, and Kendra wasn't sure if it was part of the ReLive injection she had taken before stepping into the accelerator at Hawke or if the human body fared a little better than anticipated.

Whatever. They'd poke and prod her over the coming weeks, and even that level of human interaction would be welcome at this stage. But for now, she enjoyed the peace of mind that came with freedom, simply knowing that her every move wouldn't have to be balanced by some concern for time-breaking paradoxes.

Part of her considered the *weirdness* of having lived through the last twelve months while the world only got through six. Sometimes, when she thought about it, she almost grasped everything, though other times it made her head hurt. Something about information accidentally getting propagated forward and how isolation was the only true way to protect against that. Bowie even tried explaining it on a simplified level for her a few times. It turned out that the most technical her mind got was fixing stuff at places like Hawke, not *planning* what those places did.

"Kendra?" Two called out from inside the cabin.

"Yeah, Two?"

"Dr. Beckett is waiting to speak with you."

"Right now?"

"Right now," Two said, his tone far too cheeky for this early in the morning.

Kendra stepped inside and saw the tired face of Dr. Albert

Beckett. He looked like he hadn't slept, and maybe that was the case. She apparently wasn't the only one excited about this day coming. "How is our time traveler?"

"Ready to return to the present."

The next ten minutes passed by, Beckett firing off questions about Kendra's mental acuity, physical condition, and other things that made this seem like a routine health inspection rather than *How are you after isolating and time traveling and then isolating again?*

"No memory issues?" he asked, though his eyes focused off-screen, probably at biometric data forwarded by Bowie.

"Nope. Whatever was in that ReLive stuff must have worked."

"Ah. ReLive. That's good to know." Beckett's head tilted, lines forming across his face and a curious glint in his eye. "I want to ask you about that. I was just discussing some of its long-term efficacy with ReLive's lead scientists." His mouth opened, but it took several seconds for words to come out. "They toured here a few months ago," he finally said. "Good group."

This was the most Kendra had ever heard about ReLive, even when she was tasked with administering the injections and handling the memory-preservation protocol herself. Of all the things to ask her after she got to the project's finish line, did Beckett really want to talk about ReLive scientists?

"By the way," Beckett said, "does the name Mariana Pineda mean anything to you?"

Kendra's lips pursed in thought at the strange question; she considered *why* Beckett would ask such a thing. Everything during this process came down to an extremely meticulous set of rules, checks, and redundancies. Not once had the name Mariana Pineda come up, unless it was some kind of code word or something that she was supposed to remember.

Kendra considered the different ways to answer the question, though she ultimately chose the simplest one.

"Nope."

"Ah," Beckett said, though his face remained inscrutable.

"Should it?"

"No, no. She's just someone who works for ReLive," Beckett said. "I thought you two might have met before." He leaned back in his chair, arms stretched overhead. He glanced off-screen, eyes focused for several seconds before his mouth suddenly turned upward ever so slightly. "My mistake."

★ ★ ★ ★ ★

ACKNOWLEDGMENTS

Writing this book during the latter half of 2022 was a bit strange because it acts as a bit of a bookend with my second novel, *A Beginning at the End*. That particular book, about finding hope after a pandemic shatters it, was written over the span of a decade and released right as COVID-19 started to take over the world in 2020. People refer to that book as *Mike's pandemic book*, and from a fictional perspective, that is true. But in terms of the real emotional processing of these terrible, uncertain years, that's this book.

This novel's origins were actually a pitch for an IP graphic novel that never came to fruition (hints of the IP and characters are actually built into this as a nod to their origins). Which then got turned into a pitch for a time-loop graphic novel that never came to fruition. It sat for a few years, but I returned to it and examined it through the lens of pandemic life. At times, it certainly felt like a time loop. But at other times, it was like a combination of endless waiting and extreme isolation. And one of the few things that got my young daughter through it was technology: in particular, she became friends with another girl who lived five hundred miles away. They got through the darkest days of the pandemic together with weekly play sessions over Zoom, and they still see each other regularly for video games and movies.

With each manuscript, I want to push myself, yet I've always shied away from centering romance in my books: if it's in there, it's very secondary. So in this case, I wanted to try to put that front and center, which fought all of my inherent instincts as a storyteller (and an Asian who grew up without a lot of emotions). I hope it works, and I hope Mariana and Carter have earned that for you.

As for writerly nuts and bolts, there's always a list of people to thank. Wendy Heard and Diana Urban were my sprint partners as we all kept each other in check, in addition to reading my early proposal and discussing logistics of missing person cases. (It's good to know thriller writers for this.) Sierra Godfrey was there for general complaints, which is probably the most important part of the writing process, and Peng Shepherd helped out with character descriptions. That group, along with fellow pandemic parent Meghan Scott Molin, also helped out with title discussions.

This book involved way more semireal-but-mostly-fake science than my other titles, and Annalee Newitz was always there to answer my emails. Annie Zaleski helped brainstorm the musicology aspect about what songs last decades in pop culture—a small nugget in this book, but as a music geek, it's very important to me. And my foodie-wife Mandy, who would totally buy four breakfasts every day if a time loop meant no health consequences, so much of the food bits are things she's taught me, said to me, or made me try. Like Mariana, I honestly still do not care about food.

My agent Eric Smith oversaw this story in all of its different incarnations and ultimately helped bring it to life. And my editor Dina Davis saved me from so many time-loop continuity issues while also helping me understand how to write a love story that's not just a subplot.

I always cast my characters based on real actors as a bit of a writer cheat. In this case, this book features John Cho (particularly from *Cowboy Bebop*), Daniela Pineda, Tawny Newsome, and of course, David Bowie.

Finally, for my daughter and her friend, who found each other during isolation, their friendship remains one of this story's true inspirations. I hope their bond lasts far beyond the shelf life of these printed words.